THE SHEEP LOOK UP

John Brunner

BALLANTINE BOOKS • NEW YORK

Library of Congress Catalog Card Number: 72-79705

SBN 345-23612-2-165

First Printing: November, 1973

Printed in the United States of America

Cover design by Mark Rubin and Irving Freeman,
Plum Studio

BALLANTINE BOOKS, INC.
201 East 50th Street, New York, N.Y. 10022

This angry novel of the future is the logical successor to John Brunner's award-winning story of overpopulation, *Stand on Zanzibar*.

In a brilliant and savage attack on our suicidal complacency in the face of an undeniable truth—that we are killing our planet and all that lives on it with chemicals, drugs, indifference, stupidity and greed—the author leads us from a Europe where the Mediterranean is stagnant and dead to the Rocky Mountain West where the water supply has been flooded with poison gas. In chilling detail he tells of the people who live on earth and their attempts to come to terms with their environment.

> "The world Brunner creates is convincing because the characters within it are real. He defines humanity in terms of individuals . . . using a scrapbook style, pasting together bits and clippings from the next fifty years to give us a wide-angle glimpse of what lies ahead."
>
> *Books of the Day*

Also by
JOHN BRUNNER

THE SQUARES OF THE CITY
THE WHOLE MAN
THE LONG RESULT
DOUBLE, DOUBLE
OUT OF MY MIND
STAND ON ZANZIBAR

Published by Ballantine Books

To
ISOBEL GRACE SAUER (née ROSAMOND)
1887–1970
IN MEMORIAM

CONTENTS

December

January

February

March

PLEASE HELP
KEEP PIER CLEAN
THROW REFUSE OVERSIDE

—Sign pictured in *God's Own Junkyard,*
edited by Peter Blake

DECEMBER

PROSPECTUS

The day shall dawn when never child but may
Go forth upon the sward secure to play.
No cruel wolves shall trespass in their nooks,
Their lore of lions shall come from picture-books.
No aging tree a falling branch shall shed
To strike an unsuspecting infant's head.
From forests shall be tidy copses born
And every desert shall become a lawn.
Lisping their stories with competing zest,
One shall declare, "I come from out the West,
Where Grandpa toiled the fearful sea to take
And pen it tamely to a harmless lake!"
Another shall reply, "My home's the East,
Where, Mama says, dwelt once a savage beast
Whose fangs he oft would bare in horrid rage—
Indeed, I've seen one, safely in a cage!"
Likewise the North, where once was only snow,
The rule of halls and cottages shall know,
The lovely music of a baby's laugh,
The road, the railway and the telegraph,
And eke the South; the oceans round the Pole
Shall be domestic. What a noble goal!
Such dreams unfailingly the brain inspire
And to exploring Englishmen do fire . . .

—"Christmas in the New Rome," 1862

CARNAGE

Hunted?
By wild animals?

In broad daylight on the Santa Monica freeway? Mad! Mad!

It was the archetype of nightmare: trapped, incapable of moving, with monstrous menacing beasts edging closer. Backed up for better than a mile, three lanes trying to cram into an exit meant for two, reeking and stalking and roaring. For the time being, though, he was more afraid of running than of staying where he was.

Bright fangs repeating the gray gleam of the clouds, a cougar.

Claws innocent of any sheath, a jaguar.

Winding up to strike, a cobra.

Hovering, a falcon. Hungry, a barracuda.

However, when his nerve finally broke and he tried running, it wasn't any of these that got him, but a stingray.

SIGNS OF THE TIMES

THIS BEACH NOT SAFE FOR SWIMMING

NOT Drinking Water

UNFIT FOR HUMAN CONSUMPTION

Now Wash Your Hands
(Penalty for noncompliance $50)

FILTERMASK DISPENSER
Use product once only—maximum 1 hour

OXYGEN
25¢

NOT IN OUR STARS The radio said, "You deserve security, Stronghold-style!" Blocking access to the company parking lot on the left of the street was a bus, huge, German, articulated, electric, discharging passengers. Waiting impatiently for it to move on, Philip Mason pricked up his ears. A commercial for a rival corporation?

The unctuous voice went on, backed by non-music from cellos and violas. "You deserve to sleep undisturbed. To go on vacations as long as you can afford, free from worry about the home you've left behind. Don't they say a man's home is his castle—and shouldn't that be true for you?"

No. Not insurance. Some dirty property developer. What the hell was this bus stopped here for, anyhow? It belonged to the City of Los Angeles okay—right color, name painted on the side—but in place of a destination board it just had a stock sign, ON HIRE, and he couldn't see details of its occupants through its grimy windows. But that was hardly surprising since his own windshield was grimy, too. He had been going to hit the horn; instead, he hit the wash-and-wipe stud, and a moment later was glad of the choice he'd made. Now he could discern half a dozen dull-faced kids, three black, two yellow, one white, and the head of a crutch. Oh.

The speech from the radio continued. "What we've done for you is build that castle. Nightly, armed men stand guard at all our gates, the only points of access through our spike-topped walls. Stronghold Estates employ the best-trained staff. Our watchmen are drawn from the police, our sharpshooters are all ex-Marines."

Of whom there's no shortage since they kicked us out of Asia. Ah, the bus signaling a move. Easing forward past its tail and noting from the corner of his eye a placard in its rear window which identified the hiring organization as Earth Community Chest Inc., he flashed his lights at the car next behind, asking permission to cut in front. It was granted, he accelerated—and an instant later had to jam the brakes on again. A cripple was crossing the entrance to the lot, an Asiatic boy in his early teens, most likely Vietnamese, one leg shrunk and doubled up under the hip, his arms widespread to help him keep his balance on a sort of open aluminum cage with numerous straps.

Harold, thank God, isn't *that* bad.

All the armed gate-guards black. A prickling of sweat at the idea he might have run the boy down under the muzzles of their guns. Yellow means honorary black. It is sweet to have companions in adversity. And, thinking of companions— Oh, *shut up!*

"There's never any need to fear for your children," mused the radio. "Daily, armored buses collect them at your door, take them to the school of your choice. Never for a second are they out of sight of responsible, affectionate adults."

The boy completed his hirpling journey to where the sidewalk resumed, and Philip was finally able to ease his car forward. A guard recognized the company sticker on his windshield and hit the lift for the red-and-white pole that closed the lot. Sweating worse than ever, because he was horribly late and even though that wasn't his fault he was perfused with abstract guilt which made him feel vaguely that *everything* today was his fault, from the Baltimore bombings to the communist takeover in Bali, he stared around. Oh, shit. Packed solid. There wasn't one gap he could squeeze into without guidance unless he wasted more precious time in sawing back and forth with inches to spare.

"They will play in air-conditioned recreation halls," the radio promised. "And whatever medical attention they may need is on hand twenty-four hours per day—at low, low contract rates!"

All right for someone earning a hundred thousand a year. For most of us even contract rates are crippling; I should know. Aren't any of those guards going to help me park? Hell, no, all going back to their posts.

Furious, he wound down his window and made violent beckoning gestures. At once the air made him cough and his eyes started to water. He simply wasn't used to these conditions.

"And now a police flash," said the radio.

Maskless, his expression revealing a trace of—what? Surprise? Contempt?—something, anyway, which was a comment on this charley who couldn't even breathe straight air without choking, the nearest guard moved toward him, sighing.

"Rumors that the sun is out at Santa Ynez are without foundation," the radio said. "I'll repeat that." And did, barely audible against the drone of an aircraft invisible over cloud. Philip piled out, clawing a five-dollar bill from his pocket.

"Take care of this thing for me, will you? I'm Mason, Denver area manager. I'm late for a conference with Mr. Chalmers."

He got that much said before he doubled over in another fit of coughing. The acrid air ate at the back of his throat; he could imagine the tissues becoming horny, dense, impermeable. If this job's likely to involve me in frequent trips to LA I'm going to have to buy a filter-mask. And the hell with looking sissy. Saw on the way here it isn't only girls who wear them any more.

The radio mumbled on about extreme congestion affecting all roads northbound.

"Yeah," the guard said, taking the bill and rolling it neatly one-handed into a cylinder, like a joint. "Go right on in. They been expecting you."

He pointed across the lot to where an illuminated sign above a revolving door wished the world a merry Christmas from Angel City Interstate Mutual.

Been expecting? I sure hope that doesn't mean they gave up and went ahead without me!

Feet planted on signs of Libra, Scorpio, Sagittarius, as the revolving door hush-hushed. It turned stiffly; the air-tight seals around it must recently have been renewed. Beyond, a cool marble-walled foyer, also ornamented with zodiacal emblems. Angel City's publicity was geared to the idea of escaping the destiny you'd been born to, and both those who took astrology seriously and those who were sceptical appreciated the semi-poetical quality of the ad copy which resulted.

Here the air was not only purified but delicately perfumed. Waiting on a bench and looking bored, a very pretty light-brown girl in a tight green dress, demurely sleeved, the skirt touching the neat Cuban—correction: Miranda—heels of her black shoes.

But slit to the waist in front. Moreover she was wearing pubic panties, with a tuft of fur at the crotch to suggest hair.

Last night in Vegas. Christ, I must have been out of my mind, knowing I had to sleep well, be in top form for today. But it didn't feel that way at the time. Just . . . Oh, God, I wish I knew. Bravado? Craving for variety? Dennie, I swear I love you, I'm not going to throw my precious job away, won't even look at this girl! Chalmers's floor is three, isn't it? Where's the directory? Oh, behind those filtermask dispensers.

(Yet, intermixed, pride in working for this firm whose progressive image was carried clear through to ensuring that its secretaries wore the trendiest of clothes. That dress wasn't orlon or nylon, either; it was wool.)

However, it was impossible not to look. She rose and greeted him with a broad smile.

"You're Philip Mason!" Her voice a trifle hoarse. Comforting to know that other people were affected by the air in LA. If only the huskiness didn't lend such a sexy quality . . . "We met last time you were here, though probably you wouldn't remember. I'm Bill Chalmers's aide, Felice."

"Yes, I do remember you." The cough conquered, though a faint itchy sensation remained on his eyelids. The statement wasn't mere politeness, either—he did now recall her, but his last visit had been in summer and she'd been wearing a short dress and a different hairstyle.

"Is there somewhere I could wash up?" he added, displaying his palms to prove he meant *wash*. They were almost slimy with the airborne nastiness that had eluded the precipitator on his car. It wasn't designed to cope with California.

"Surely! Just along the hallway to the right. I'll wait for you."

The men's room bore the sign of Aquarius, as the women's did the sign of Virgo. Once when he first joined the company he'd raised a laugh clear around a group of his colleagues by suggesting that in the interests of true equality there should be only one door, marked Gemini. Today he wasn't in a joking mood.

Under the locked door of one of the cubicles: feet. Wary because of the incidence of men's-room muggings these days, he relieved himself with one eye fixed on that door. A faint sucking sound reached his ears, then a chinking. Christ, a syringe being filled! Not an addict with an expensive habit who's sneaked in there for privacy? Should I get out my gas gun?

That way lay paranoia. The shoes were elegantly shined, hardly those of an addict who neglected his appearance. Besides, it was over two years since he'd last been mugged. Things were improving. He moved toward the line of wash-basins, though he took care to select one whose mirror reflected the occupied cubicle.

Not wanting to leave greasy marks on the light fabric of his pants, he felt cautiously in his pocket for a coin to drop in the water-dispenser. Damnation. The dirty thing had been altered since his last visit. He had nickels and quarters, but the sign said only dimes. Wasn't there even one free one? No.

He was on the point of going back to ask Felice for change when the cubicle door swung open. A dark-clad man emerged, shrugging back into a jacket whose right-hand side pocket hung heavy. His features struck a vague chord of memory. Philip relaxed. Neither an addict nor a stranger. Just a diabetic, maybe, or a hepatic. Looking well on it, either way, from his plump cheeks and ruddy complexion. But who . . . ?

"Ah! You must be here for this conference of Chalmers's!" Striding forward, the not-stranger made to extend his hand, then canceled the gesture with a chuckle.

"Sorry, better wash up before shaking with you. Halkin out of San Diego, by the way."

Tactful with it, too. "I'm Mason out of Denver. Ah—you don't have a spare dime, do you?"

"Sure! Be my guest."

"Thank you," Philip muttered, and carefully stoppered the drain hole before letting the water run. He had no idea how much a dime bought you but if it was the same amount that had cost a nickel a year and a half ago it was barely enough to soap and rinse with. He was thirty-two, yet today he felt like a gangling teenager, insecure, confused. His skin itched as though it were dusty. The mirror told him it didn't show, and his swept-back brown hair was still tidy, so that was all right, but Halkin was wearing practical clothes, almost black, whereas he himself had put on his newest and smartest gear—by Colorado standards, much influenced of course by the annual influx of the winter-sports jet set—and it was pale blue because Denise said it matched his eyes, and while it could never be crumpled it was already showing grime at collar and cuffs. Memo to self: next time I come to LA. . .

The water was terrible, not worth the dime. The soap—at least the company kept cakes of it on the basins, instead of demanding another dime for an impregnated tissue—barely lathered between his palms. When he rinsed his face a trickle ran into his mouth and he tasted sea-salt and chlorine.

"You got held up like me, I guess," Halkin said, turning to dry his hands in the hot-air blower. That was free. "What was it—those filthy Trainites occupying Wilshire?"

Washing his face had been a mistake. There were no towels, paper or otherwise. Philip hadn't thought to check beforehand. There's this big thing about cellulose fibers in the water of the Pacific. I read about it and failed to make the connection. His sense of awkward teenageness worse than ever, he had to twist his head into the stream of warm air, meantime wondering: what do they do for toilet paper—round pebbles, Moslem-style?

Keep up the façade at all costs. "No, my delay was on the Santa Monica freeway."

"Oh, yes. I heard traffic was very heavy today. Some rumor about the sun coming out?"

"It wasn't that. Some"—repressing the ridiculous impulse to make sure no one black was in earshot such as Felice or the guards around the parking lot—"crazy spade jumped out of his car in the middle of a jam and tried to run across the other half of the road."

"You don't say. Stoned, was he?"

"I guess he must have been. Oh, thanks"—Halkin courteously holding the door. "Naturally the cars that were still moving in the fast lanes had to brake and swerve and *bang*, must have been forty of them bumped each other. Missed him by a miracle, not that it did him any good. The traffic coming away from the city was doing fifty-sixty at that point, and when he got across the divide he fell in front of a sports car."

"Good lord." This had brought them level with Felice, who was keeping an elevator for them, so they ushered her inside and Halkin hovered his hand over the floor-selection buttons. "Three, isn't it?"

"No, we're not in Bill's office. We're in the conference room on the seventh."

"Was your car damaged?" Halkin went on.

"No, luckily mine wasn't included in the shunt. But we had to sit there for more than half an hour before they got the road clear . . . You said you were held up by Trainites?"

"Yes, on Wilshire." Halkin's professional smile gave way to a scowl. "Lousy dodgers, most of them, I bet! If I'd known I was sweating out my time for their sake . . . ! You did yours, of course?"

"Yes, of course, in Manila."

"My stint was in 'Nam and Laos."

The car was slowing and they all glanced at the lighted numbers. But this wasn't seven, it was five. The doors parted to reveal a woman with a spotty face who said under her breath, "Ah, shit!" And stepped into the car anyway.

"I'll ride up with you and down again," she added more loudly. "You could wait until doomsday in this filthy building."

The windows of the conference room were bright yellow-gray. The proceedings had started without waiting for the last two arrivals; Philip was thankful that he wasn't entering alone. Eight or nine men were present in comfortable chairs with foldaway flaps bearing books, notepads, personal recorders. Facing them across a table shaped like an undernourished boomerang: William Chalmers, vice-president in charge of interstate operations, a black-haired man in his late forties who had developed too much of a paunch to get away with the fashionable figure-hugging gear he was wearing. Standing, interrupted by the intrusion: Thomas Grey, the company's senior actuary, a bald lean man of fifty with such thick spectacles one could imagine their weight accounting for the habitual forward stoop of his shoulders. He looked put out; scratching absently under his left arm, he accorded no more than a curt nod by way of greeting.

Chalmers, however, welcomed the latecomers cordially enough, brushed aside their apologies, waved them to the remaining vacant places—right in the front row, of course. The wall-clock showed two minutes of eleven instead of the scheduled ten-thirty. Trying to ignore it, Philip picked up a folder of papers from his assigned chair and distributed mechanical smiles to those of his colleagues with whom he could claim casual acquaintance.

Casual . . .

Don't think about Laura. Dennie, I love you! I love Josie, I love Harold, I love my family! But if only you hadn't insisted on my—

Oh, shut up. Talk about mountains out of molehills!

But his situation was precarious, after all. Notoriously, he was by nearly seven years the youngest of Angel City's area managers: LA, Bay, SoCal, Oregon, Utah, Arizona, NM, Texas, Colorado. Texas due for subdivision next year, the grapevine said, but as yet it hadn't happened. That meant that his footsteps were being hounded by hordes of skilled, degree-equipped unemployed. He had six salesmen with Ph.D.'s. Running to stay in the same place . . .

"If we can continue?" Grey said. Philip composed himself. The first time he had met the actuary he had assumed him to be a dry extension of his computers, lost in a world where only numbers possessed reality. Since then, however, he had learned that it had been Grey who hit on the notion of adopting astrological symbolism for the firm's promotional material, and thereby endowed Angel City with its unique status as the only major insurance company whose business among clients under thirty was expanding as fast as the proportion of the population they represented. Anyone with that much insight was worth listening to.

"Thank you. I was just explaining why you've come."

Eyes rolling back to the limits of their sockets, mouth ajar, breath hissing in her throat! Useless denying it to myself. No woman ever made me feel more like a man!

Philip touched the inside of his cheek with the tip of his tongue. She had slapped him back-handed and marched out of the motel cabin with blazing eyes because he had offered her money. There was a cut. It had bled for five minutes. It was next to his right upper canine, all his life the sharpest of his teeth.

"It's because," Grey continued, "of the hike in life insurance premiums we're going to impose from January first. Of course we've always predicated our quotations on the assumption that life expectancy in the United States would continue to rise. But during the past three years it has in fact started to go down."

A ROOST FOR CHICKENS

Sharp on nine the Trainites had scattered caltraps in the roadway and created a monumental snarl-up twelve blocks by seven. The fuzz, as usual, was elsewhere—there were always plenty of sympathizers willing to cause a diversion. It was impossible to guess how many allies the movement had; at a rough guess, though, one could say that in New York City, Chicago, Detroit, LA or San Francisco people were apt to cheer, while in the surrounding suburbs or the Midwest people were apt to go fetch guns. In other words, they had least support in the areas which had voted for Prexy.

Next, the stalled cars had their windows opaqued with a cheap commercial compound used for etching glass, and slogans were painted on their doors. Some were long: THIS VEHICLE IS A DANGER TO LIFE AND LIMB. Many were short: IT STINKS! But the commonest of all was the universally known catchphrase: STOP, YOU'RE KILLING ME!

And in every case the inscription was concluded with a rough egg-shape above a saltire—the simplified ideogrammatic version of the invariable Trainite symbol, a skull and crossbones reduced to ☠.

Then, consulting printed data-sheets, many of which were flapping along the gutter hours later in the wind of passing cars, they turned to the nearby store-windows and obscured the goods on offer with similarly appropriate slogans. Unprejudiced, they found something apt for every single store.

It wasn't too hard.

Delighted, kids on the afternoon school shift joined in the job of keeping at bay angry drivers, store-clerks and other meddlers. Some of them weren't smart enough to get lost when the fuzz arrived—by helicopter after frantic radio messages—and made their first trip to Juvenile Hall. But what the hell? They were of an age to realize a conviction was a keen thing to have. Might stop you being drafted. Might save your life.

Most of the drivers, however, had the sense to stay put, fuming behind their blank windshields as they calculated the cost of repairs and repainting. Practically all of them were armed, but not one was stupid enough to pull a gun. It had been tried during a Trainite demonstration in San Francisco last month. A girl had been shot dead. Others, anonymous in whole-head masks and drab mock-homespun clothing, had dragged the killer from his car and used the same violent acid they applied to glass to write MURDERER on his flesh.

In any case, there was little future in rolling down a window to curse the demonstrators. Throats didn't last long in the raw air.

ENTRAINED "It's easy enough to make people understand that cars and guns are inherently dangerous. Statistically, almost everyone in the country now has experience of a relative being shot dead either at home or abroad, while the association between cars and traffic fatalities opens the public mind to the concept of other, subtler threats."

Lead: causes subnormality in children and other disorders. Exceeds 12 mg. per m³. in surface water off California. Probable contributory factor in decline of Roman Empire whose upper class ate food cooked in lead pans and drank wine fermented in lead-lined vats. Common sources are paint, antiknock gas where still in use, and wildfowl from marshes etc. contaminated over generations by lead shot in the water.

"On the other hand it's far harder to make it clear to people that such a superficially innocuous firm as a beauty parlor is dangerous. And I don't mean because some women are allergic to regular cosmetics."

Polychlorinated biphenyls: waste products of the plastics, lubrication and cosmetics industries. Universal distribution at levels similar to DDT, less toxic but having more marked effect on steroid hormones. Found in museum specimens collected as early as 1944. Known to kill birds.

"Similarly it's a short mental step from the notion of killing plants or insects to the notion of killing animals and people. It didn't take the Vietnam disaster to spell that out—it was foreshadowed in everybody's mind."

FARM & GARDEN INC.
Landscaping & Pest Control Experts

Pelican, brown: failed to breed in California where formerly common, 1969 onward, owing to estrogenic effect of DDT on shell secretion. Eggs collapsed when hen birds tried to brood them.

"By contrast, now that we scarcely make use of the substances which used to constitute the bulk of the pharmacopoeia and which were clearly recognizable as poisonous because of their names—arsenic, strychnine, mercury and so on—people seem to assume that any medical drug is good, period. I wasted more of my life than I care to recall going around farms trying to discourage pig and chicken breeders from buying feeds that contained antibiotics, and they simply wouldn't listen. They held that the more of the stuff you scattered around the better. So developing new drugs to replace those wasted in cake for cattle, pap for pigs and pellets for pullets has become like the race between guns and armor!"

Stacy & Schwartz Inc.
IMPORTED GOURMET FOODS

Train, Austin P. (Proudfoot): b. Los Angeles 1938; e. UCLA (B.Sc. 1957), Univ. Coll. London (Ph.D. 1961); m. 1960 Clara Alice née Shoolman, div. 1963, n.c.; a. c/o publishers. Pub: thesis, "Metabolic Degradation of Complex Organophosphates" (Univ. of London Press 1962); "The Great Epidemics" (Potter & Vasarely 1965, rep. as "Death In the Wind," Common Sense Books 1972); "Studies in Refractive Ecology" (P&V 1968, rep. as "The Resistance Movement in Nature," CSB 1972); "Preservatives and Additives in the American Diet" (P&V 1971, rep. as "You Are What You Have To Eat," CSB 1972); "Guide to the Survival of Mankind" (International Information Inc., boards 1972, paper 1973); "A Handbook for 3000 A.D." (III, boards 1973, paper 1975); crt. J. Biol. Sci., J. Ecol., J. Biosph., Intl. Ecol. Rev., Nature, Sci. Am., Proc. Acad. Life Sci., Sat. Rev., New Ykr., New Sci. (London), Envrmt. (London), Paris Match, Der Spiegel (Bonn), Blitz (India), Manchete (Rio) etc.

IT'S A GAS

Leaving behind half his lonely brunch (not that the coffee shop where he'd eaten regularly now for almost a year wasn't crowded with lunchers, but sitting next to the fuzz is prickly), Pete Goddard waited for change to be made for him. Across the street, on the big billboards enclosing the site of Harrigan's Harness and Feed Store—it had kept the name although for years before it was demolished it had sold snowmobiles, motorcycle parts and dude Western gear—which now was scheduled to become forty-two desirable apartments and the Towerhill home of American Express and Colorado Chemical Bank, someone had painted about a dozen black skulls and crossbones.

Well, he was feeling a little that way himself. Last night had been a party: first wedding anniversary. His mouth tasted foul and his head ached and moreover Jeannie had had to get up at the ordinary time because she worked too, at the Bamberley hydroponics plant, and he'd broken his promise to clear away the mess so she wouldn't be faced with it this evening. Besides, that patch on her leg, even if it didn't hurt . . . But they had good doctors at the plant. Had to have.

New, not disposed to like him, the girl cashier dropped his due coins in his palm and turned back to conversation with a friend.

The wall-clock agreed with his watch that he had eight minutes to make the four-minute drive to the station house. Moreover, it was bitterly cold outside, down to around twenty with a strong wind. Fine for the tourists on the slopes of Mount Hawes, not good for the police who measured temperature on a graph of smashed cars, frostbite cases and petty thefts committed by men thrown out of seasonal work.

And women, come to that.

So maybe before going . . . By the door, a large red object with a mirror on the upper part of its front. Installed last fall. Japanese. On a plate at the side: *Mitsuyama Corp., Osaka.* Shaped like a weighing machine. Stand here and insert 25¢. Do not smoke while using. Place mouth and nose to soft black flexible mask. Like an obscene animal's kiss.

Usually he laughed at it because up here in the mountains the air was never so bad you needed to tank up on oxygen to make the next block. On the other hand some people did say it was a hell of a good cure for a hangover . . .

More detail penetrated his mind. Noticing detail was something he prided himself on; when his probationary period was through, he was going to shoot for detective. Having a good wife could spawn ambitiou in any man's mind.

The mirror cut in a curve to fit around the mouthpiece: cracked. Slot for quarters. Below it a line defining the coin-hopper. Around that line, scratches. As though someone had tried to pry the box out with a knife.

Pete thought of bus-drivers murdered for the contents of a change machine.

Turning back to the counter he said, "Miss!"

"What?"

"That oxygen machine of yours—"

"Ah, shit!" the girl said, hitting "No Sale" on the register. "Don't tell me the stinking thing is on the fritz *again!* Here's your quarter back. Go try the drugstore on Tremont—they have three."

THE OPPOSITE OF OVENS White tile, white enamel, stainless steel . . . One spoke here in hushed tones, as though in a church. But that was because of the echoes from the hard walls, hard floor, hard ceiling, not out of respect for what was hidden behind the oblong doors, one above another from ankle-level to the height of a tall man's head, one next to another almost as far as the eye could see. Like an endless series of ovens, except that they weren't to cool, but to chill.

The man walking ahead of her was white, too—coat, pants, surgical mask at present dangling below his chin, tight ugly cap around his hair. Even plastic overshoes also white. Apart from what she had brought in with her, dull brown, there was effectively only one other color in here.

Blood-red.

A man going the other way wheeling a trolley laden with waxed-paper containers (white) labeled (in red) for delivery to the labs attached to this morgue. While he and her companion exchanged helloes, Peg Mankiewicz read some of the directions: 108562 SPLEEN SUSP TYPH CULT, 108563 LIVER VERIFY DEGEN CHGES, 108565 MARSH TEST.

"What's a Marsh test?" she said.

"Presence of arsenic," Dr. Stanway answered, sidling past the trolley and continuing down the long line of corpse closets. He was a pale man, as though his environment had bleached every strong tint out of him; his cheeks had the shade and texture of the organ containers, his visible hair was ash-blond, and his eyes were the dilute blue of shallow water. Peg found him more tolerable than the rest of the morgue staff. He was devoid of emotion—either that, or absolutely homosexual—and never plagued her with the jocular passes most of his colleagues indulged in.

Shit. Maybe I should take a wash in vitriol!

She was beautiful: slim, five-six, with satin skin, huge dark eyes, a mouth juicier than peaches. Especially modern peaches. But she hated it because it meant she was forever being hounded by men collecting pubic scalps. Coming on butch was no help; it was that much more of a challenge to men and started the ki-ki types after her as well. Without make-up, perfume or jewelry, in a deliberately unflattering brown coat and drab shoes, she still felt like a pot of honey surrounded by noisy flies.

Poised to unzip if she so much as smiled.

To distract herself she said, "A murder case?"

"No, that suit someone filed in Orange County. Accused a fruit grower of using an illegal spray." Eyes roaming the numbered doors. "Ah, here we are."

But he didn't open the compartment at once.

"He isn't pretty, you know," he said after a pause. "The car splattered his brains all over everywhere."

Peg buried her hands in the pockets of her coat so that he couldn't see how pale her knuckles were. It might, just conceivably might be a thief who'd stolen his ID. . . .

"Go ahead," she said.

And it wasn't a thief.

The whole right-hand side of the dark head was—well, *soft*. Also the lower eyelid had been torn away and only roughly laid back where it belonged, so the underside of the eyeball was exposed. A graze clotted with blood rasped from the level of the mouth down and out of sight beneath the chin. And the crown was so badly smashed, they'd put a kind of Saran sack around it, to hold it together.

But it was pointless to pretend this wasn't Decimus.

"Well?" Stanway said at length.

"Yes, put him away."

He complied. Turning to lead her to the entrance again, he said, "How did you hear about this? And what makes the guy so important?"

"Oh . . . People call the paper, you know. Like ambulance-drivers. We give them a few bucks for tipping us off."

As though floating ahead of her like a horrible sick-joke balloon on a string: the softened face. She swallowed hard against nausea.

"And he's—I mean he was—one of Austin Train's top men."

Stanway turned his head sharply. "No wonder you're interested, then! Local guy, was he? I heard Trainites were out in force again today."

"No, from Colorado. Runs—ran—a wat near Denver."

They had come to the end of the corridor between the anti-ovens. With the formal politeness due to her sex, which she ordinarily detested but could accept from this man on a host-and-guest basis, Stanway held the door for her to pass through ahead of him and noticed her properly for the first time since her arrival.

"Say! Would you like to—uh . . . ?" A poor communicator, this Stanway, at least where women were concerned. "Would you like to sit down? You're kind of green."

"No thanks!" Over-forcefully. Peg hated to display any sign of weakness for fear it might be interpreted as "feminine." She relented fractionally a second later. Of all the men she knew she suspected this one least of hoping to exploit chinks in her guard.

"You see," she admitted, "I knew him."

"Ah." Satisfied. "A close friend?"

There was another corridor here, floored with soft green resilient composition and wallpapered with drifts of monotonous Muzak. A girl came out of a gilt-lettered door bearing a tray of coffee-cups. Peg scented fragrant steam.

"Yes . . . Have the police sent anyone to check on him?"

"Not yet. I hear they're kind of overloaded. The demonstration, I guess."

"Did they take his belongings from the car?"

"I guess they must have. We didn't even get his ID—just one of those forms they fill out at the scene of the accident." Dealing with Christ knew how many such per day, Stanway displayed no particular interest. "Way I read it, though, they'd be concerned. Must have been stoned to do what he did. And if he was one of Train's top men they're bound to show up soon, aren't they?"

They hadn't yet reached the door to the outside, but Peg hastily put on her filtermask.

It covered so much of her traitorous face.

It was a long walk to where she had left her car: a Hailey, of course, on principle. Her vision was so blurred by the time she reached it—not merely because the air stung her eyes—that she twice tried to put the key in the lock upside-down. When she finally realized, she was so annoyed she broke a nail dragging open the door.

And thrust the finger into her mouth and instead of nibbling away the broken bit, tore it. Her finger bled.

But at least the pain offered an anchor to reality. Calming, she wrapped around the injury a tissue from the glove-compartment and thought about calling in her story. It was a story. It would make the TV news services as well as the paper. Killed on the freeway: Decimus Jones, age thirty, busted twice for pot and once for assault, smeared with an average quantity of the grime a young black nowadays expected to acquire. But suddenly reformed (it says here) by the precepts of Austin Train at twenty-six, mastermind of Trainite operations when they spread to Colorado . . . not that he would have acknowledged the name "Trainite" any more than Austin did. Austin said the proper term was "commie", for "commensalist," meaning that you and your dog, and the flea on the dog's back, and the cow and the horse and the jackrabbit and the gopher and the nematode and the paramecium and the spirochete all sit down to the same table in the end. But that had been just a debating point, when he got sick of people screaming at him that he was a traitor.

Ought to make sure Decimus gets returned to the biosphere right away. Forgot to mention that. Should I go back? Hell, I guess he put it in his will. If they take any notice of a black man's will . . .

Somebody's going to have to tell Austin. It would be terrible if he first learned the news in print or from TV.

Me?

Oh, shit. Yes. I'm the first to latch on. So it has to be me.

Her mind was abruptly a chaos of muddled images, as though three people had taken simultaneous possession of her head. Stanway by chance had asked precisely that question she felt constrained to answer honestly: "A close friend?"

Close? More like only! Why? Because he was black and happily married and not interested any more in the exoticism of white girls? (Who'll tell Zena and the kids?) Partly, maybe. But what mattered was that Decimus Jones, healthy, male and hetero, had treated luscious tempting Peg Mankiewicz . . . as a friend.

It had better be Austin who tells Zena. I *couldn't*. And a merry Christmas to you all.

After that the confusion became total. She could foresee events fanning out from this death as though she were reading a crystal ball. Everyone would automatically echo Stanway: "Jumping out of his car that way he must have been stoned—or maybe crazy!"

Yet she'd known him as a very sane man, and being stoned belonged too far back in his past. So it could never have been of his own volition. So somebody must have slipped him a cap of something fierce. And there was only one motive she could think of for doing that. To discredit him at any cost.

She suddenly realized she had been staring, without seeing, at proof of a Trainite's passage through this parking lot, a skull and crossbones on the door of a car parked slantwise to hers. Her own, naturally, would be unmarked.

Yes. It must have been done to discredit Decimus. Must have. These stereotyped interchangeable plastic people with dollar signs in their eyes couldn't bear to share their half-ruined planet with anyone who climbed out of his ordained grooves. A black JD dropout was meant to die in a street brawl, or better yet in jail partway through a spell of ninety-nine. For him to be loved and looked up to like a doctor or a priest, by white as well as black—that turned their stomachs!

Turned stomach. Oh, Christ. She fumbled in her purse for a pill she should have taken over an hour ago. And forced it down despite its size without water.

Usually, nowadays, one had to.

Finally she decided she was getting maudlin and twisted the key in the dashboard lock. There was steam stored from the trip to get here and the car moved silently and instantly away.

And cleanly. No lead alkyls, hardly any CO, nothing worse than CO_2 and water. Praise be, if Anyone is listening, for those who struggle to save us from the consequences of our own mad cleverness.

At the exit from the lot, if she had been going to the office she would have turned right. Instead she turned left. There were probably not more than a hundred people in the country who could rely on locating Austin Train when they wanted to. If her editor had known that among them was one of his own reporters who had never used the information for professional purposes, he would have come after her with a gun.

THE BLEEDING HEART IS A RUNNING SORE

. . . veteran of campaigns in Indochina and the Philippines today became the latest of many distinguished ex-officers to join the Double-V adoption plan, taking into his family an orphaned girl aged eight with severe scars allegedly due to napalm burns. Commenting on his decision the general said, quote, I was not at war with children, only with those seeking the destruction of our way of life. End quote. Questioned concerning his reaction to the growth of the Double-V scheme prior to leaving the White House for his main engagement of the day, a luncheon organized by former members of his official fan club at which he is slated to deliver a major speech on foreign affairs, Prexy said, quote, I guess if they can't break down the front door they have to sneak around the back. End quote. The Congressional inquiry into alleged bribe-taking by officials of the Federal Land Use Commission . . .

THE ROOT OF THE TROUBLE

"Te-goosey-goosey-galpa—" The rain was pelting down so hard the wipers of the Land Rover could barely cope, and the road was terrible. Despite four-wheel drive they were continually sliding and skidding, and every now and then they met a pothole which made Leonard Ross wince.

"Knock 'er down and scalp 'er—"

Dr. Williams's singing was barely audible above the roar of the engine and the hammering of the rain, but it was just possible to discern that the tune belonged to a nursery rhyme: Goosey Gander.

"Up hers! H' and your ass—"

Another pothole. Leonard reflexively glanced back to see if his equipment was okay, and wished he hadn't. The rear seat was also occupied by the policeman assigned to escort him, who had a repulsive weeping skin condition, and Leonard's stomach was queasy enough anyhow.

"Nobody will *halp* 'er!" concluded Williams triumphantly, and added without drawing a fresh breath, "How long have you been with Globe Relief?"

"Oh . . ." For an instant Leonard didn't realize the question was a question. "About four years now."

"And you've never been to this part of the world before?"

"I'm afraid not."

"Bloody typical!" With a snort. "At least I hope they gave you all the gen?"

Leonard nodded. They had submerged him with masses of data, and his head was still ringing. But this country was so full of paradoxes! To start with, when he'd seen that the name of his contact at Guanagua was Williams, he'd assumed an American. He hadn't been prepared for a manic Briton who wore a Harris tweed jacket in this stinking sub-tropical humidity. Yet it seemed of a piece with a nation whose first capital, for 357 years, had been demoted because the citizens objected to the governor keeping a mistress; whose current capital was so relatively unimportant it had never had a railroad, and the international airlines had given up servicing it . . .

"Every time someone tries to haul this country up by its bootstraps," Williams said, "something goes wrong. Act of God! Though if that's really how He likes to amuse Himself, no wonder the Tupamaros are making so much headway! Not around here, of course, but in the cities. Look at this road! By local standards it's a ruddy highway. It's so damned difficult to get goods to market, most people haven't the currency to buy manufactured goods, even proper tools. But now and then someone whips up enthusiasm for cash crops instead of subsistence crops—cotton, coffee, that sort of thing—and it swings along for a while and then all of a sudden, crash. Their hard work goes for nothing. Like this time. Come and see for yourself."

Unexpectedly he braked the Land Rover at a spot where rocks as high as a man's knee flanked the track. Peering through the rain-smeared windshield, Leonard made out that they had arrived within sight of a shabby village surrounded on two sides by lines of coffee plants, on the others by maize and beans. The layout suggested competent husbandry, but every single plant was wilted.

Jumping out, Williams added, "Bring your gear!"

"Ah—"

"Look, the rain isn't going to stop for bloody weeks, you know, so you might as well get used to it!"

Reluctantly Leonard picked up his field kit and ducked into the downpour. His glasses blurred instantly, but his sight was too bad for him to discard them. Water trickling down his collar, he followed the line Williams had marked across the sodden ground.

"Doesn't matter where you look," Williams said, stopping level with the nearest coffee plant. "You'll find the buggers anywhere."

Compliantly Leonard began to trowel in the mud. He said after a pause, "You're English, aren't you, doctor?"

"Welsh, actually." In a frigid tone.

"Do you mind if I ask what brought you here?"

"A girl, if you really want to know."

"I'm sorry, I didn't mean to—"

"Pry? Of course not. But I'll tell you anyway. She was the daughter of one of the embassy staff in London. Very beautiful. I was twenty-four, she was nineteen. But her people were Catholics from Comayagua, where they're strict, and naturally they didn't want her marrying a Methodist. So they shipped her home. I finished my studies, saving like mad to buy a passage here, thinking that if I could convince them I was serious . . . Hell, I'd have converted if I'd had to!"

Down there close to the scrawny root of the coffee plant: something wriggling. "And what happened?"

"I got here and discovered she was dead."

"*What?*"

"Typhus. It's endemic. And this was 1949."

There seemed to be nothing else anyone could possibly say. Leonard dragged up a clod of dirt and broke it in his hands. Exposed, a frantic creature two inches long, at first glance not unlike an earthworm, but of a bluish-red color, with a slight thickening at one end and a few minute bristles, and writhing with more energy than any earthworm ever had.

"Yet, you know, I've never regretted staying here. There has to be someone on the spot to help these people—it's no use trying to do it all by remote control . . . Ah, you got one of them, did you?" His tone reverted to normal. "Recognize it, by any chance? I can't find a technical name for it in the literature. Of course my reference-books aren't up to much. In Spanish it's *sotojuela*, but around here they say *jigra*."

One-handed, leaving fingermarks of mud, Leonard extracted a test-tube from his kit and dropped the pest into it. He tried to examine it with his folding glass, but the rain splashed down too heavily.

"If I could get a look at it under cover," he muttered.

"There may be a roof in the village that isn't leaking. May be . . . And this is what the buggers do to the plants, see?" Williams pulled a coffee bush casually out of the ground. It offered no resistance. The stem was spongy with bore-holes and the foliage limp and sickly.

"They attack corn and beans as well?" Leonard asked.

"Haven't found anything they won't eat yet!"

In the hole left by the uprooted plant, five or six of them squirming to hide.

"And how long have they been a nuisance?"

"They've always been a nuisance," Williams said. "But

until—oh, about the time they cleared this patch for coffee, you only found them in the forest, living off the underbrush. I didn't see more than half a dozen the first ten years I spent at Guanagua. Then about two and a half years ago, boom!"

Leonard straightened, his legs grateful to be released from stooping. "Well, there's no doubt that this is an emergency, as you claimed. So I'll apply for authorization to use high-strength insecticides, and then when we've—"

"*How* long did you say you'd been with Globe Relief?"

Leonard blinked at him. Suddenly he was unaccountably angry.

"Who do you think this ground belongs to, anyway? We're on the private estate of some high government muckamuck who can bend the law as much as he likes! This area's been sprayed and soaked and *saturated* with insecticides!"

From the direction of the village, walking very slowly, a straggling line of men, women and children had emerged. All were thin, all were ragged and barefoot, and several of the children had the belly-bloat characteristic of pellagra.

"The idiot's made the *jigras* resistant to DDT, heptachlor, dieldrin, pyrethrum, the bloody lot! Think I was such a fool the idea hadn't crossed my mind to check? Those people don't need chemicals, they need *food!*"

DEFICIT

Petronella Page: Hi, world!
Studio audience: Hi!

Page: Well, this time as ever we have for you all kinds of people making news. Among others we're to welcome Big Mama Prescott whose hit "The Man with the Forty-Five" is currently the center of a fierce debate about the proper—or improper—material for pop songs. (*Audience laughter.*) And then we'll be talking to a whole group of the ex-officers who've given so many children from Southeast Asia the best of all Christmas presents, a new home and a new family. But first off let's welcome someone who's been making headlines in a different area. He's a scientist, and you've been hearing about him because—well, because if his calculations are right they bode not too well for the future of this nation. Here he is, Professor Lucas Quarrey of Columbia. (*Applause.*)

Quarrey: Good eve— I mean, hello, everyone.

Page: Lucas, because not as much attention is paid to scientific matters these days as perhaps ought to be, maybe you'd refresh the viewers' memories concerning the subject that put you in the news.

Quarrey: Gladly, and if there's someone watching who hasn't heard about this it'll come as—uh—as much of a surprise as it did to me when I first saw the print-out from the university computers. Asked to guess what's the largest single item imported by the United States, people might nominate lots of things—iron, aluminum, copper, many raw materials we no longer possess in economic quantities.

Page: And they'd be wrong?

Quarrey: Very wrong indeed. And they'd be just as wrong if they were asked to name our largest single export, too.

Page: So what is our largest import?

Quarrey: Ton for ton—oxygen. We produce less than sixty per cent of the amount we consume.

Page: And our biggest export?

Quarrey: Ton for ton again, it's noxious gases.

Page: Ah, now this is where the controversy has arisen, isn't it? A lot of people have been wondering how you can claim to trace—oh, smoke from New Jersey clear across the Atlantic. Particularly since you're not a meteorologist or weather scientist. What is your specialty in fact?

Quarrey: Particle precipitation. I'm currently heading a research project designing more compact and efficient filters.

Page: For what—cars?

Quarrey: Oh yes. And buses, and factories too. But mainly for aircraft cabins. We have a commission from a major airline to try and improve cabin air at high altitude. On the most traveled routes the air is so full of exhaust fumes from other planes, passengers get airsick even on a dead calm day—*especially* on a dead calm day, because it takes longer for the fumes to disperse.

Page: So you had to start by analyzing what you needed to filter out, right?

Quarrey: Precisely. I designed a gadget to be mounted on the wing of a plane and catch the contaminants on little sticky plates—I have one here, I don't know if your viewers can see it clearly . . . Yes? Fine. Well, each unit has fifty of these plates, time-switched to collect samples at various stages of a journey. And by plotting the results on a map I've been able to pin down—like you said—factory-smoke from New Jersey over nearly two thousand miles.

Page: Lots of people argue that can't be done with the accuracy you claim.

Quarrey: I wish the people who say that would take the trouble to find out what my equipment is capable of.

Page: Now this is all very disturbing, isn't it? Most people have the impression that since the passage of the Environment Acts things have taken a turn for the better.

Quarrey: I'm afraid this seems to be—uh—an optical illusion, so to speak. For one thing, the Acts don't have enough teeth. One can apply for all kinds of postponements, exemptions, stays of execution, and of course companies which would have their profits shaved by complying with the new regulations use every possible means to evade them. And the other point is that we aren't being as watchful as we used to be. There was a brief flurry of anxiety a few years ago, and the Environment Acts were introduced, as you said, and ever since then we've been sitting back assuming the situation was being taken care of, although in fact it isn't.

Page: I see. Now what do you say to people who maintain that publicizing these allegations of yours is—well, not in the best interests of this country?

Quarrey: You don't serve your country by sweeping unpleasant facts under the carpet. We're not exactly the most popular nation in the world right now, and my view is that we ought to put a stop right away to anything that's apt to make us even less well liked.

Page: I guess there could be something in that. Well, thanks for coming and talking to us, Lucas. Now, right after this next break for station identification . . .

IN SPITE OF HAVING CHARITY A MAN LIKE SOUNDING BRASS

"I guess the nearest analogy would be with cheese," said Mr. Bamberly. To show he was paying attention Hugh Pettingill gave a nod. He was twenty, dark-haired, brown-eyed, with a permanently bad-tempered set to his face—pouting mouth, narrowed eyes, prematurely creased forehead. That had been stamped on him during the bad years from fourteen to nineteen. Allegedly this was the first of many good years he was currently living through, and he was fair-minded enough to expose himself to the possibility of being convinced.

This had started with an argument concerning his future. During it he had said something to the effect that the rich industrial countries were ruining the planet, and he was determined never to have anything to do with commerce, or technology, or the armed forces for which Mr. Bamberley retained an archaic admiration. Whereupon: this instruction, too firmly phrased to be termed an invitation, to go on a guided tour of the hydroponics plant and find out how constructively technology might be applied.

"I don't see why we shouldn't improve on nature!" Mr. Bamberley had chuckled.

Hugh had kept his counter to himself: "So what has to happen before you realize you haven't?"

Portly, but muscular, Mr. Bamberley strode along the steel walkway that spined the roof of the factory, his arms shooting to left and right as he indicated the various stages through which the hydroponically-grown cassava they started with had to pass before it emerged as the end product, "Nutripon." There was a vaguely yeasty smell under the huge semi-transparent dome, as though a baker's shop had been taken over by oil technicians.

And in some senses that was an apt comparison. The Bamberley fortune had been made in oil, though that was two generations back and neither this Mr. Bamberley —whose Christian name was Jacob but who preferred to be called Jack—nor his younger brother Roland had ever stumped around in the slush below a derrick. The fortune had long ago grown to the point where it was not only self-supporting but capable of fission, like an amoeba. Roland's portion was his own, greedily clung to, and destined to descend to his only son Hector (whom Hugh regarded on the strength of their sole meeting as a cotton-wool-wrapped snob . . . but that couldn't be his fault at fifteen, must be his father's); Jacob had vested his in the Bamberley Trust Corporation twenty years ago, since when it had multiplied cancerously.

Hugh had no idea how many people were involved in cultivating the funds of the Trust, since he had never been to the New York office where its tenders hung out, but he pictured a blurred group of several hundred pruning, manuring, watering. The horticultural images came readily to hand because his adopted father had turned the former family ranch, here in Colorado, into one of the finest botanical gardens in the country. All that had taken on reality in his mind, however, as far as the Trust was concerned, was the central fact that the sum was now so vast, Jacob Bamberley could afford to run this, the world's largest hydroponics factory, as a charitable undertaking. Employing six hundred people, it sold its product at cost and sometimes below, and every last ounce of what was made here was shipped abroad.

Lord Bountiful. Well, it was a better way to use inherited money than the one Roland had chosen, lavishing it all on yourself and your son so that he would never have to face the harsh real world . . .

"Cheese," Mr. Bamberley said again. They were overlooking a number of perfectly round vats in which something that distantly resembled spaghetti was being churned in a clear steaming liquid. A masked man in a sterile coverall was taking samples from the vats with a long ladle.

"You give it some kind of chemical treatment here?" Hugh ventured. He hoped this wasn't going to drag on too long; he'd had diarrhea this morning and his stomach was grumbling again.

"Minor correction," Mr. Bamberley said, eyes twinkling. " 'Chemical' is full of wrong associations. Cassava is tricky to handle, though, because its rind contains some highly poisonous compounds. Still, there's nothing extraordinary about a plant some bits of which are safe to eat and other bits of which are not. Probably you can think of other examples?"

Hugh repressed a sigh. He had never said so outright, being far too conscious of the obligations he owed to Jack (orphaned at fourteen in an urban insurrection, dumped in an adolescents' hostel, picked apparently at random to be added to this plump smiling man's growing family of adopted sons: so far, eight), but there were times when he found his habit of asking this kind of question irritating. It was the mannerism of a poor teacher who had grasped the point about making children find out for themselves but not the technique of making them want to ask suitable questions.

He said tiredly, "Potato tops."

"Very good!" Mr. Bamberley clapped him on the shoulder and turned once more to point at the factory floor.

"Considering the complexity of the treatment which is required before cassava yields an edible product—"

Ah, shit. He's off on another of his lousy lectures.

"—and the unlikelihood of anyone stumbling on it by accident, it's always struck me as one of the clearest proofs of supernal intervention in the affairs of primitive mankind," Mr. Bamberley declaimed. "Here's no comparative triviality like oxalic acid, but the deadliest of poisons, cyanide! Yet for centuries people have relied on cassava as a staple diet, and survived, and indeed flourished! Isn't it marvelous when you think of it like that?"

Maybe. Except I *don't* think of it like that. I picture desperate men struggling on the verge of starvation, trying everything that occurs to them in the faint hope that the next person who samples this strange plant won't drop dead.

"Coffee's another case. Who, without prompting, would have thought of drying the berries, husking them, roasting them, then grinding them and *then* infusing them in water?" Mr. Bamberley's voice was rising toward sermon pitch. All of a sudden, though, it dropped back to a normal level.

"So calling this a 'chemical process' is misleading. What we really do is cook the stuff! But there's one major drawback in relying on cassava as a staple. I may have mentioned . . . ?"

"Shortage of protein," Hugh said, thinking of himself as one of those question-and-answer toys they give children, with little lights which come on when the proper button is pressed.

"Right in one!" Mr. Bamberley beamed. "Which is why I compare our job to making cheese. Here"—flinging open the door to the next section of the plant, a vast twilit room where spidery metal girders supported shielded ultraviolet lamps—"we fortify the protein content of the mix. With absolutely natural substances: yeasts, and fungi with especially high nutritive value. If all goes well we turn as much as eight per cent of the cassava into protein, but even six per cent, the average yield, is a vast improvement."

Walking ahead as he talked toward yet another section where the finished product was draped in huge skeins on drying-racks, like knitting-wool, then chopped into finger-sized lengths.

"And you know something else extraordinary? Cassava's a tropical plant, of course. Yet it grows better here than under so-called 'natural' conditions. Do you know why?"

Hugh shook his head.

"Because we draw so much of our water supply from melted snow. That contains less heavy hydrogen—deuterium. A lot of plants simply can't cope with it."

And now the packing room, where men and women in masks and coveralls tamped measured quantities into cardboard cartons lined with polyethylene, then loaded the cartons on to humming fork-lift trucks. Some of them waved on noticing Mr. Bamberley. He grinned almost from ear to ear as he waved back.

Oh, God. Mine, that is—if any. Not Bamberley's cosy cheery paterfamilias kind, who is certainly tall and handsome and white-skinned behind his long gray beard. I mean, this guy paid for the clothes I'm wearing, the college I attend, the car I drive—even if it is only a sluggish electric. So I'd like to like him. If you can't like the people who are kind to you . . .

And he makes it so difficult! Always this feeling, just when you think you're there, that something isn't right. Like he gives all the time to Earth Community Chest, and supplies this cheap food to Globe Relief, and out of eight adopted sons not one a crippled Vietnamese . . .

Hollow. That's the word. Hollow.

But not to start arguments and rows. Another question. "Where are the cases going that they're filling now?"

"Noshri, I think," Mr. Bamberley said. "The postwar aid program, you know. But I'll make sure."

He shouted to a black woman who was stenciling destination names on empty cartons. She tilted the one she'd just finished so it could be read from the gallery.

"Not to Africa!" Mr. Bamberley sounded surprised. "Then someone must have put in a lot of overtime—I'll find out who and make some commendations. They've already started on the new contract with Globe Relief."

"Which one is that?"

"Oh, for some village in Honduras where the coffee crop failed."

SPACE FOR THIS INSERTION IS DONATED BY THE PUBLISHERS AS A SERVICE TO THE COMMUNITY

Where a child cries—or is too weak to cry . . . Where a mother mourns—for one who will not weep again . . .
Where plague and famine and the scourge of war have proved too much for struggling human beings . . .

WE BRING HOPE

*But we can't do it without your help. Think of us now. Remember us in your will. Give generously to the world's largest relief organization: GLOBE RELIEF.**

**All donations wholly tax-deductible.*

HOUSE TO HOUSE

Gilt-tooled on yard-square panels of green leather—imitation, of course—the zodiacal signs looked down from the walls of the executive lunch-room. The air was full of the chatter of voices and the clink of ice-cubes. Waiting to be attacked when the president of the company joined them (he had promised to show at one sharp) was a table laden with expensive food: hard-boiled eggs, shells intact so that it could be seen they were brown, free-range, rich in carotene; lettuces whose outer leaves had been rasped by slugs; apples and pears wearing their maggot-marks like dueling scars, in this case presumably genuine ones though it had been known for fruit growers to fake them with red-hot wires in areas where insects were no longer found; whole hams, very lean, proud of their immunity from antibiotics and copper sulphate; scrawny chickens; bread as coarse as sandstone, dark as mud and nubbled with wheat grains . . .

"Hmm! Looks as though someone bought out the local branch of Puritan!" a voice said within Chalmers's hearing, and he was pleased. He was moving from House to House, measuring a precise three minutes at each stop. Virgo: no women were present apart from Felice with whom he was having an affair and the two girls serving at the bar. In pursuance of its progressive image Angel City had tried appointing female area managers, but of the first two such one had married and quit and the other had suffered a nervous breakdown. Occasionally he had wondered whether Felice slept with him in the hope of climbing that far up the corporation totem-pole.

The policy, however, had been reviewed.

Libra: "Now me, I'd go straight into scrap-reclamation and sewage-plant construction. They're the growth industries of the eighties. You'll see your investment double in next to no time."
Scorpio: "Rats? No, we have a terrier and a tomcat and keep them hungry. But the ants! I spent two thousand on proofing the kitchen and they still got in. So we fell back on—uh—the old reliable. By the way, if you need any, I have a good discreet source of supply."
Sagittarius: "Yes, up our way we've established a *modus vivendi* with the Syndicate. Their interest in Puritan, of course. Very strong around our base. Anyone tries to put in a false claim gets a dusty answer straight away."

No one at Capricorn.

Aquarius: "No ice, thanks—hey! I said NO ICE! Don't you understand plain English? Doctor's orders. Mustn't touch anything but canned mineral water. I lose more working time thanks to digestive trouble . . ."

PISCES: "Why don't we make acceptance of a life proposal conditional on installing an approved water purifier in the guy's home, like we insist on an approved precipitator in his car? I've sounded out a couple of the big firms, and they show every interest in cooperating."

No one at Aries.

Taurus: "If we're going to expand into the cattle states we *must* have solid documentation on the natural incidence of deformed births in domestic animals. I managed to hold his claim down to a refund of the stud fee, but even that came to five thousand, and he insisted the value of this mare that died in foal was twice as much. I had to drop very heavy hints about the cost of litigation before he accepted the settlement."

Gemini: "I've had a rash of demands lately for insurance against egg-bundle fotus. Can't help wondering whether there may not be something behind the scare. Maybe a leak from a research lab?"

No one at Cancer . . . naturally.

Leo: "Yes, the reason I was delayed—this crazy spade . . ."

Chalmers clucked sympathy when he had heard Philip out, and switched instantly to a less depressing subject. "By the way! Tania and I will be in Colorado over the holiday. Get in some skiing."

"Ah-hah? Where you aiming for—Aspen?"

"Oh, Aspen's full of people who read about it in *Playboy*. No, your own stamping ground. Towerhill!"

"Never! Well, call us up! Maybe you could stop by with us and like have lunch?"

Sweating slightly from the *Playboy* putdown.

The conclusion of Chalmers's meticulously timed peregrination brought him within arm's reach of Grey at five to one.

"The man from Denver," Grey said. "Philip Mason."

"What about him?" Anticipating what was coming, and relieved to be able to offer an impenetrably defensive answer. Chalmers had a stake in that man; the personnel board had split three to two and his own vote had been in favor.

"There's something wrong. Or else he's not himself today."

"Not himself. Saw a man killed right before his eyes this morning." And recounted the story.

Grey pondered a while. Uncomfortable, Chalmers waited. It was disturbing to watch this man think; it made the world seem full of the sound of whizzing wheels.

"Someone will have to keep an eye on him," Grey said at last.

"But he's one of our best men!" Chalmers felt personally aggrieved. "He's nearly doubled the business of the Denver office. He was among the first to get wind of the new developments at Towerhill and put us in on the ground floor, and now we cover three-quarters of the place. Besides, this notion of his of sending out proposal forms for short-term injury insurance with hotel booking confirmations is showing a thousand per cent profit."

"I'm not talking about that," Grey said. "What I want to know is what he was doing driving his own car into Los Angeles this morning. It's a long pull from Denver. I'd have expected him to fly."

The door opened to admit the president of the company, and he moved away to greet him. Scowling at his back, Chalmers wondered—not for the first time—when if ever he would dare call Grey "Mike": short for "Mycroft," elder brother of Sherlock Holmes. It was only an inner echelon of the top staff who used the nickname to his face.

THE MORAL OF THE TWENTIETH CENTURY Last valiant sally of a great department store whose customers had quit the city center, six Santa Clauses marched down the road.

"Ho-ho-ho!" Jingle-jangle.

The sidewalks they passed were crowded. Most of the onlookers were black, and many were children whose eyes reflected unfulfillable dreams. The city's heart was dying before its carcass, and these were the poor, trapped in outworn clothes and rat-ridden tenements. If they wanted to escape, like as not they had to steal a car to travel in because the now compulsory clean exhaust systems were expensive. Last time Peg had come down this way it had been to cover the story of a thriving trade in fake filters, home-built out of sheet steel by an enterprising mechanic.

In spite of the few cars, the air stank. She had taken off her mask, not wanting to be conspicuous—at least, no more than was due to being white. In this district people didn't wear them. They seemed inured to the reek. The chests of the children were shallow, as though to discourage overdeep breathing.

She stared at the Santa Clauses. Behind those once-white beards, now grimed from an excursion in the open, she could not make out their features. She did, though, notice that the second man in the line was only moving his lips, not booming out his "Ho-ho-ho!" His eyes were bulging with the effort of repressing a cough.

Which would be very out of character for Saint Nick.

They broke the line to distribute come-on leaflets, most of which were immediately dropped, and dispersed into a dark alley where notices warned that only "authorized personnel" might enter.

Was one of the six, as she'd been assured, Austin Train?

The idea seemed crazy on the surface. Underneath, maybe it wasn't wholly absurd. She hadn't seen Austin since just after he recovered from his breakdown, but when he vanished from the public eye it had been with the promise that he was going to live as the poor were living, even if it meant risking what they risked. That decision had caused trendy Catholic television spokesmen to mention openly the possibility that the Church might recognize a new category of "secular saints." She'd watched one such program with Decimus and Zena, and they'd laughed aloud.

But if this was the path Austin had chosen, it was different from Decimus's. His principle, at the Colorado wat, was third-world oriented; his community grew its own food, or tried to—crops had a nasty habit of failing because of wind-borne defoliants or industrial contaminants in the rain—and likewise wove its own cloth, while its chief source of income lay in handicrafts. The underlying concept was to dramatize the predicament of the majority of mankind. Often, prior to a meal, there had been little homilies: "You're each getting about twice as much at this table as someone in a Bolivian mountain village gets in a day." And sometimes there were strange unexciting dishes: glutinous African sauces of fine-chopped okra, tasteless cakes of anonymous grain, samples of relief shipments sympathizers had paid for and mailed to the wat.

"This is what we're giving away," Decimus would say. "Not steak or chicken or big fat Idaho potatoes. This is made from"—and it could be algae, or yeast, or grass clippings, or on one occasion, incredibly, sawmill wastes. "See how *you* like it, and think of those who have only such shit to be grateful for!"

But that had been a long time ago.

Around the back of the store she found a half-empty parking lot. There was a door marked *Employees Only*. She found it barred from inside. Nearby, though, was a reeded-glass window. She could make out blurred images if she leaned close to the panes. Inside, red forms changing to white as the Santa Clauses stripped off their suits and padding.

She listened, hoping to discern Austin's voice.

"In a bad way, aren't you, pal? Ah, leave him be! Well, just don't cough on me, I have kids at home and all the time doctor's bills. Don't we all?"

And so on. Some of them went through a door at the back of the room and noise of running water indicated showers. A man in a dark suit appeared and shouted, "Easy with that water! There's a shortage!"

"Shortage hell." Husky, consumptive; the voice might belong to the man who hadn't been able to shout. Louder, he added, "Is it hot?"

"Shit, of course not!" someone called back. "Tepid!"

"In that case give me my pay and I'll go. The doc warned me not to get chilled. So I won't be wasting your precious water, okay?"

"Don't blame me." With a sigh. "I don't make the rules around here."

In the dusk none of the men noticed Peg as they headed toward their cars. Five got into three vehicles. The last traced a line of smoke across the lot—liable to be arrested, him. The sixth man didn't make for a car.

"Austin!" Peg said in a low voice.

He didn't break stride and scarcely looked around. "The girl reporter!" he said. "Finally decided to throw me to the wolves?"

"What?" She fell in beside him, matching step for step the well-remembered paces that were too long for a man of his height, an average five-ten. Making the muscles do penance came naturally when Austin Train was around.

"You mean you're not here on business?" His tone was tinged with sarcasm.

She prevaricated, pointing to her right beyond the lot; it was going to be hard to hear herself speak the news she had brought. "My car's that way. Can I give you a lift? It is a Hailey!"

"Ah. The precepts are being kept, hm? Steam is cleaner than gas! No, thanks. I walk. Have you forgotten?"

She caught his hand and forced him to turn and face her. Looking at him, she found little change revealed by the poor light, apart from his having shaved off the beard he'd worn during his period of notoriety. The high cheekbones were the same, the curiously arched eyebrows, almost semicircular, the thin sour lips . . . Though maybe his sparse brown hair had receded a trifle. It had been nearly three years.

His mouth parodied a smile: a tilt of a few degrees at one corner. Abruptly furious, determined to wipe away his complacency, she burst out, "I came to tell you Decimus is dead!"

And he said, "Yes. I know."

All those hours of searching, without food or rest, aware that every moment increased the likelihood of losing her job—gone to waste? Peg said weakly, "But it only happened this morning . . ."

"I'm sorry." His look of mockery softened. "You loved him, didn't you? Okay, I'll come to your car."

Mechanically she walked on; now, for a change, he matched her strides, though it was perceptibly frustrating to his energetic frame. Nothing more was said until they reached the spot where she had left the little Hailey under the harsh beams of a mercury-vapor light.

"I wonder if I did love him," she said suddenly.

"You were the person who thought she didn't know how, weren't you? But you must have. Coming in search of me like this is proof of it. It can't have been easy."

"No, it wasn't." The finger whose nail she had torn was still tender; she had trouble guiding her key into the lock.

"Funny," Austin said, looking at the car.

"What is?"

"People thinking of steam as being clean. My grandmother lived in a house backing on a railroad. Couldn't hang out laundry for fear of smuts. I grew up thinking of steam as filthy."

"Sermon time?" Peg snapped, reaching to open the passenger door. "And you called Train, come to that!"

"A stale joke," he said, getting in. "Train as in powder train. A very old name. Originally it meant a trap or snare."

"Yes, you told me. I'm sorry. Next time I want to try and get one of these Freon-vapor cars . . . Oh, shit! I'm rambling. Do you—do you mind if I have a cigarette?"

"No."

"You mean yes."

"I mean no. You need a tranquilizer, and tobacco isn't the most dangerous kind." He half turned in the narrow seat. "Peg, you went to a lot of trouble. I do appreciate it."

"Then why do I get a welcome about as warm as someone carrying plague?" Fumbling in her purse. "How did you hear, anyway?"

"He had a meet with me this morning. When he didn't show I made inquiries."

"Shit, I should have guessed."

"But he didn't come just to see me. He has a sister working in LA, you know, and there's some family problem he wanted to sort out."

"No, I don't know. He never told *me* he had a sister!" With a vicious jab at the dashboard lighter.

"They quarreled. Hadn't met for years . . . Peg, I really am sorry! It's—well, it's the nature of your job that makes me react badly. I lived in the spotlight for a long time, you know, and I just couldn't stand it any more once I realized what they were doing to me: using me to prove they cared about the world when in fact they didn't give a fart. After me the deluge! So I generated my smokescreen and disappeared. But if things go on the way they've been going lately . . ."

He spread his hands. They were the first things that had suggested to Peg she might learn to like him, thorny though he was, because they were fractionally overlarge for his body, the sort of hands nature might have reserved for a sculptor or a pianist, and despite being thick-knuckled they were somehow beautiful. "Well, if one reporter knows how to find me, another may, and eventually it may be the fuzz."

"Are you really afraid of being arrested?"

"Do you think I shouldn't be? Don't you know what happened right on Wilshire this morning?"

"Yes, but you don't organize their demonstrations!" The lighter clicked out; her hand shook so much she could barely guide it to the cigarette.

"True. But I wrote their bible and their creed, and if I were put on oath I couldn't deny that I meant every last word."

"I should hope not," she muttered, letting go a ragged puff of gray smoke. The taste, though, wasn't soothing but irritating, because she'd stood on that corner for more than half an hour without her filtermask. After a second unpleasant drag she stubbed it.

"How old are you, Austin?"

"What?"

"How old are you is what I said. I'm twenty-eight and it's a matter of public record. The president of the United States is sixty-six. The chairman of the Supreme Court is sixty-two. My editor is fifty-one. Decimus was thirty last September."

"And he's dead."

"Yes. Christ, what a waste!" Peg stared blankly through the windshield. Approaching with grunts and snorts was one of the eight-ton crane-trucks used to collect automobiles without legal filters. This one had trapped exotic prey; a Fiat and a Karmann-Ghia were clamped on its chain-hung magnet.

"Nearly forty," Austin murmured.

"Aries, aren't you?"

"Yes, provided you're asking as a joke."

"What the hell does that mean?"

"Well, I could say anything. There are over two hundred of me, you know."

"Joke!" She almost slapped him, wrenching around in her seat. "Hell, don't you understand? Decimus is filthily horribly disgustingly *dead!*"

"You mean no one saw it coming in his horoscope?"

"Oh, you're inhuman! Why the hell don't you get out? You hate cars!"

And a fraction of a second later: "No, I didn't mean that! Don't go!"

He hadn't moved. Another pause.

"Any idea who did it?" she said at length.

"You're sure it was—ah—*done?*"

"Must have been! Mustn't it?"

"I guess so." Austin drew his rounded eyebrows together, not looking at her, but she could see sidelong how they formed a child's sketch for a sea gull. (How long before there were kids who didn't know what a gull was?) "Well, I can imagine a lot of people being glad to see him go. Did you check out the police?"

"I was about to when I decided to find you instead. I thought it ought to be you who broke the news to Zena."

"It was. Or rather, I called the wat and made sure she'd hear it first from someone she knew."

"Those poor kids!"

"Better off than some," Austin reminded her. Which was true, it being dogmatic Trainite policy never to bear your own as long as there were orphans to be fostered.

"I guess so . . . " Peg passed a tired hand over her face. "I wish I'd realized I was wasting my time! Now I don't know if the news has made the papers, or the TV, or anything." She rolled the car away from the curb at last. "Where to?" she added.

"Straight ahead about ten blocks. Worried about losing your job, Peg?"

"More thinking why don't I quit right now."

He hesitated. "Maybe it would be a good idea if you stuck with it."

"Why? Because you want someone in the media on your side? Don't give me that. Thanks to Prexy just about everyone is—except the owners."

"I wasn't thinking of that. More that you might give me —well, the occasional warning."

"You are afraid, aren't you?" She halted for a red light. "Okay, if I can. And if the job lasts . . . Who's going to take over from Decimus?"

"I don't know. I'm not in charge of anything."

"Sorry. It's fatally easy to fall into the notion that you are, what with people saying 'Trainite' all the time. I do try and remember to say 'commensalist,' but everyone shortens that to 'commie' and it's generally a quick way to start a fist-fight . . . Does it worry you, having your name taken in vain?"

"What the hell do you think I'm scared of?" He uttered a short harsh laugh. "It gives me goose-bumps!"

"Obviously not because of the wats. Because of demonstrations like this morning's?"

"Them? No! They annoy people, but they do no real harm. Create a lot of publicity, provide a few object lessons for the bastards who are wrecking the planet for commercial gain . . . And they allow the demonstrators to feel they're being constructive. No, the kind of thing I have in mind is this. Suppose someone decides a whole city is offending against the biosphere, and pulls the plug on a nuclear bomb?"

"You think they might? That'd be crazy!"

"Isn't the moral of the twentieth century that we *are* crazy?" Austin sighed. "Worse still, if it did happen, any proof of the insanity of the guy who did it—or guys: the collective bit is becoming more popular, you noticed?—the evidence, anyway, would be burned up. Along with everything else for miles around."

She didn't know what to say to that.

Two blocks further on, he tapped her arm. "Here!"

"What?" Peg stared at her surroundings. This was a desolate, down-at-the-heels area, partly razed for redevelopment, the rest struggling along in a vampiric half-life. A few young blacks were passing a furtive joint in the porchway of a bankrupt store; otherwise no one was visible.

"Oh, don't worry about me," Austin said. "I told you: there are over two hundred of me."

"Yes. I didn't understand."

"People tend not to. But it's literal. You keep seeing references in the underground press. There are at least that many people who decided to call themselves Austin Train after I disappeared—half in California, the rest scattered across the country. I don't know whether to love them or hate them. But I guess they keep the heat off me."

"Sunshades."

"Okay, sunshades. But you shouldn't make remarks like that, Peg. It dates you. When did you last see somebody carrying a parasol?"

He made to get out of the car. Peg checked him.

"What do you call yourself? No one told me."

One foot on the road, Austin chuckled. "Didn't they say you should ask for Fred Smith? Well, thanks for the ride. And by the way!"

"Yes?"

"If anything goes wrong, you can rely on Zena. You know that, don't you? You can always find sanctuary at the wat."

BADMIXTURE Certain types of medication, chiefly tranquilizers, must not be taken by someone who has also recently eaten cheese or chocolate.

RELIEF

All of a sudden it felt like a different world. There was an end to the endless succession of round white-rimmed hopeful eyes in dark faces, to the offering of handleless cups and empty cans and greedy dishes and the pale palms of those who were too apathetic even to collect a spent shell-case by way of a container, because everything they had once owned had been snatched from them and they couldn't believe it was worth investing precious energy in acquiring something else. And there was still a whole heap, at least a kilo, in the carton she'd been distributing from, and more cartons were stacked against the wall behind her, and more yet, incredibly many more, were being unloaded down a slide from the dark overshadowing shape of the ancient VC-10 which had somehow been set down on the improvised landing strip.

Disbelieving, Lucy Ramage brushed back a strand of fair hair from her eyes and turned to examine a segment of the peculiar substance she had been measuring out by the flaring acetylene lamp hung from a pole at the end of the trestle table.

It had a name. A trade name, no doubt properly registered. "Bamberley Nutripon." The bit she had chosen was about as long as her little finger, cream-colored and of the consistency of stale Cheddar cheese. According to the instructions on every carton it was best to boil it because that made more of the starch digestible, or triturate it in water to make a dough, then fry it in small cakes or bake it on an iron griddle.

That, though, was for later: the elaboration, the cuisine bit. What counted right now was that it could be eaten as it was, and for the first time since she came here four mortal months ago she need not feel guilty about enjoying a balanced meal in her comfortable quarters tonight, because everyone who could be found had been given enough to fill the belly. She had seen them come to the table one by one and gape at the vast quantities they were allotted: ex-soldiers shy of an arm or leg; old men with cataracts filming their eyes; mothers with little children who struggled to make their babies mumble the food because they had starved past the point at which they forgot even how to cry.

And one in particular, there in front of me, when her mother tried to rouse and feed her . . .

Oh, *God!* No, there can't be a god. At least none that I want to believe in. I won't accept a god who'd let a mother find her baby dead on her hip when there was food in her hand that might have saved it!

Blackness—of sky, ground, human skins—crowded in on her and built an Africa-wide torture chamber in her head.

A helpful grip enfolded her arm as she felt herself sway and a quiet voice spoke in good English.

"You have been overdoing things, I suspect, Miss Ramage!"

She blinked. It was the nice major, Hippolyte Obou, who had been educated at the Sorbonne and was reputedly no older than her own age of twenty-four. He was extremely handsome, if one discounted the tribal scars striping his cheeks, and had always appeared to maintain a detached view of the war.

Which was more than could be said for General Kaika . . .

But she wasn't here to take sides or criticize. She was here to pick up pieces and patch them together. And although there had been moments when it seemed the job was impossible, everyone had been fed today, food was left over for tomorrow, and another consignment was promised immediately after the new year.

A different world.

"You will come to my office for a pick-you-up," the major said; he didn't make it a question. "Then I will ride you back to your accommodation in my jeep."

"There's no need to—"

But he brushed her words aside, taking her arm again, this time with a touch of gallantry. "Ah, it is little to do for someone who has brought such a Christmas present! This way, please."

"The office," a mere hut of planks and clay, had been one of the many headquarters of the invaders' district commander. Fighting had continued at Noshri a week after the official armistice. Right across one wall was stitched the line of holes left by a salvo of fifty-caliber machine-gun slugs. Opposite, the corresponding line of marks had two gaps in it where the slugs had been stopped before they crossed the little room. Lucy tried not to look in that direction, because she had had to tend the obstacles.

It was terribly hot, even this long after sunset. The air was saturated with moisture. She had thought about going half-naked like the local girls, and come close to that climax. Her formal nurse's uniform had vanished within days of her arrival. Her neat new aprons had been ripped into emergency bandages, then her dresses, her caps, and even the legs of her jeans one desperate day. For weeks now she had gone about in what was left of them, threads dangling above her knees, and shirts lacking so many buttons she had to knot the tails in front. At least, though, they were regularly washed by the girl Maua—not local, some sort of camp-follower—acting as her personal maid. Never having had a servant in her life, she had at first rebelled at being given one, and still was not reconciled to the idea; however, others of the UN team had pointed out that the girl was unskilled and by taking routine tasks off her could free Lucy to make maximum use of her own training.

And all this because a sea had died which she had never seen . . .

At one of the two rickety tables which, apart from chairs, constituted the entire furniture of the office, a tall thin sergeant was adding up figures on a printed form. Major Obou rapped an order at him, and from a battered olive-green ammunition case he dug out a bottle of good French brandy and a tin cup. Handing Lucy two fingers of the liquor, the major raised the bottle to his broad lips.

"Here's how!" he said. "And do sit down!"

She complied. The drink was too strong for her; after half a mouthful she set the cup on her knees and held it with both hands to stop herself trembling from fatigue. She thought of asking for water to dilute it, but decided it wouldn't be fair to involve the sergeant in that much trouble. Drinkable water was hard to find in Noshri. Rain, caught in buckets and tanks, was safe if you added a purifying tablet, but the rivers were sour with defoliants from the campaign of last summer and the invaders had filled most of the wells with carrion as they retreated.

"That should put—if you forgive the remark—a little color in your cheeks," encouraged Major Obou. She forced a smile in reply, and wondered for the latest of many times what sho should make of this handsome dark man who took such pains to salt his English with bookish idioms, right or wrong. Her eyes were very tired from the heat and dust of the day, so she closed them. But that was no help. Behind the lids she saw the sights she had encountered wherever she went in this formerly flourishing town: a crossroads where a mortar shell had exploded squarely on a bus, leaving a shallow pit hemmed with smashed metal; charred roof-beams jutting over the ashes of what had been furniture and possibly people; trees curtailed by the wing of a crashing aircraft, shot down by a patrolling fighter because it was suspected of carrying arms, though she had seen for herself it contained only medical supplies . . .

She touched the base of her left thumbnail. Salvaging what she could from the wreckage, she had cut herself and had to have three stitches in the wound. A nerve had been severed, and there was a patch a quarter-inch on a side where she would never feel anything again.

At least she'd been inoculated against tetanus.

In one corner of the office a back-pack radio suddenly said something in the local language of which even yet Lucy had learned only a few words. Major Obou answered it, and rose.

"Drink up, Miss Ramage. There will be a government plane in one hour and I must be on hand. Before that I shall keep my promise to convey you home."

"There's no need to—"

"But there is." His face was suddenly stern. "I know it makes no sense to lay blame at anybody's door, and the causes of our war were very complex. But the people here have understood one thing, that it was the greed and carelessness of—forgive me—people like you which poisoned the Mediterranean and started the chain of events which led to our neighbors from the north invading us. So long as they were apathetic from hunger they were silent. Now that they have been fed, one fears that they will remember what they have been taught by agitators. I am aware that you come from New Zealand, very far away, with good motives. But a man seething with rage because he lost his home, his wife, his children, would not stop to ask where you come from if he met you in the road."

"Yes." Lucy gave a nod and, nearly choking, gulped down her drink.

"Splendid," the major said, instantly his usual affable self, and ushered her outside. His jeep was waiting near the door. He gestured the driver to get in back with the machinegunner, and took the wheel himself with Lucy at his side. Starting off with a roar, he crossed the boundary of the airstrip at nearly forty and they went bumping down the shell-pocked road to the town with all lights blazing.

"Ah, one day, Miss Ramage," he shouted, "when we have reconstructed the country, I hope I shall have a chance to entertain you more conventionally! Indeed I heard today one may again apply for leave. If you'd care to be shown—uh—more appetizing aspects of my homeland, I'd be delighted. One does not wish strangers to go away thinking this is the country where all the time people shoot each other, hm?"

It dawned on Lucy, belatedly because all that kind of thing seemed to belong in another universe, that he was propositioning her. She felt briefly astonished. At home one simply never came in social contact with black people, and seldom even with Maoris. Then she was annoyed at her own astonishment. She hunted for a polite way to formulate her answer, but before she managed it, when they were crossing what had been the main street of Noshri and was now an avenue of ruins, he braked abruptly.

"Ah, someone else realized it was a Christmas present we have received!"

At the side of the road a parody of a Christmas tree had been erected: branches that must have taken hours to collect because the nearby terrain had been sterilized with herbicides, tied to a pole and lit with three candles. On a strip of white cloth, probably a bandage, someone had written VIVE LA PAIX JOYEUX NOËL.

"Are you Christian, Miss Ramage?"

Lucy was too tired to discuss theological doubts. She gave a nod.

"I also, of course." Obou accelerated around a bend in the direction of the relatively undamaged houses that had been assigned to the overseas aid workers, UN observers, and the most senior of the government officials supervising mopping-up operations. "You know, though, it was a strange thing when I first went to Europe, finding so few people there attend a church. Here it had always been for me and my family the—the *right* thing, the *better* thing. In the provinces, right here for example, it was known the people still made idols, still believed in ghosts and juju. But the educated people you took for granted to be Moslems or Christians. I think, though, it will now be hard for Christians in our country. Knowing it has been the greed of Christian countries which—Ah, look! See already what a change your work has made in this sad place!"

Slowing again, he waved at a group of ten or a dozen people, including a couple of women, who had lit a fire in the open air before what had once been a handsome house and were dancing in a ring, clapping their hands for music. They were all barefoot. Lucy thought one of the women must be drunk; her gaudy wraparound dress had fallen from her bosom and her slack breasts shook as she stamped and swayed.

"Ah, they're good people," Major Obou said. "Simple, perhaps, but good-natured. I'm so glad this damned war is over. And"—with a trace of boldness—"glad that it has brought us friends like you from outside."

He stopped the jeep. They had reached her quarters, one of a cluster of houses originally built by one of the Paris-based companies operating here for its lower-ranking employees. Then they had enjoyed the privacy of dense greenery. Now the shrubs and trees were gone, victims of defoliants, and the ground was newly scarred with shell-holes. When Lucy had arrived the place had stunk of carrion, mostly human. It still stank, but mainly of the exhaust of trucks and planes.

The major handed her down from the jeep with old-world formality. She almost giggled at the spectacle she must present, dirty and ragged. She was a trifle light-headed from the brandy.

"You will remember what I suggested, won't you?" he murmured, squeezing her hand. Then he let it go, saluted, and jumped back in his seat.

The maid Maua prepared a passable meal: canned beans, reconstituted eggs, canned fruit. Meantime Lucy changed her soiled clothes for a toweling robe and rubbed herself over with impregnated cleansing tissues.

Water for washing was almost as scarce as that for drinking. Noises reached her as other occupants of this row of houses returned—Swedish and Czech doctors, a Mexican agronomist and UN officials attached to the Commission on Refugees were her near neighbors. Further along were some Italian nuns. She had never become used to seeing them in shirts and pants but still with their funny coifs on top. What for? To discourage the attention of men?

Which, as she picked at her food, reminded her. Obou had extended an invitation. She didn't feel inclined to accept. Why not—because he was black? She thought not. She hoped not. Because right now she couldn't think of anything like that with real attention? Very likely. The major, after all, was good-looking, well educated, obviously intelligent if he spoke both French and English as well as his mother tongue . . .

Mother!

Her stomach suddenly convulsed. It was the worst thing to remember while eating. Blindly she ran for the latrine at the back of the house, and there wasted the food she had forced down. Maybe, she thought as she knelt retching, it wasn't the memory which nauseated me, but too much brandy. It made no difference.

So many of those children: dead at birth, mercifully because they were deformed! You'd think that after Vietnam . . . But people don't think, most of the time. Riot gases, tear smoke, sleep gas, defoliants, nerve gas, all the armory of chemicals used in modern war, had saturated the tissues of these people as they had the ground. Once she had delivered three malformed babies in succession among a party of refugees who thought they had found safety at last. But along the way they had sustained themselves on leaves and roots.

She stumbled back eventually, not to the room where she had been eating but to the bedroom, and fell into a stuporous slumber.

Thinking, in the dead middle of the night, that the noise she was hearing belonged to nightmare—her dreams were regularly haunted by the fear that fighting might break out anew—she forced herself awake. Found she was awake. The noise was real. Gunfire.

Horrified, she sat up and strained her ears. The room was absolutely dark, the windows curtained. Her instant of panic passed. There were indeed shots to be heard, but there was a random, almost a cheerful quality to the rattling racket, like strings of firecrackers. Also, at the very edge of hearing, she could discern drumming—possibly even singing.

She made to inch her way toward the window, and was immediately distracted by the discovery that her thighs were wet. Christ. Her period had begun. Funnily, since coming to Noshri, she had stopped suffering the advance warning pains she had been accustomed to at home, as though her mind were so taken up with matters of life and death she had no attention to spare for the complaints of her own body.

She found tissues to wipe herself and called for Maua. Waiting for the maid to enter, she went to the window overlooking the town and peered past the curtains. Oh, yes. Bonfires. Wasteful, but excusable. Liquor had been concealed somewhere, no doubt—she'd seen that drunken woman dancing—or possibly made from garbage. And with Christmas so close . . .

Bonfires?

The patterns of light suddenly acquired perspective. The yellow flames were not small and near, but far and huge. In the direction of the airstrip.

A plane burning!

"Maua!" she cried, and ran in search of the flashlight she kept by her bed. Finding it, she hurried to the lean-to room where the girl slept. The pallet there was empty.

"Oh, Christ!" Lucy whispered.

She dashed back to the bedroom, intending to seize clothes, Tampax, the little .22 pistol her father had given her which she'd never used. But a moment later there was a slam from the living-room as the outer door was flung open, and she settled for just the gun. She still had on the toweling robe she had slumped asleep in.

Mouth dry, hands shaking, she switched off the flashlight and crept on silent bare feet to the living room.

"Hands up!" she shouted, switching on the torch again, and was instantly appalled by the way her finger was tightening on the trigger. Across the threshold lay a form which mingled khaki, dark-brown, bright-red. The red was blood. It was Major Obou, sprawled on his belly, his right hand limp beside his automatic, his left shoulder slashed to the bone.

"Major?" she tried to say, and found her voice wasn't there. She saw his good hand, like a colossal spider, scrabbling for the lost gun.

"Major Obou!"

He heard her and rolled his head on the reed matting of the floor. "*Vaut rien,*" he said thickly, and corrected himself. "No good. No more bullet."

"But what's happening?" She put down her own gun and stooped with her flashlight playing on his wound, her mind spinning with thirty different things each as urgent as another: call out her neighbor the Swedish doctor, cleanse the cut, close the outside door, make sure he hadn't been followed by his attacker . . .

He summoned a supreme effort and seized her by the wrist as she made to rise and shut the door.

"Don't go out, miss! Don't go there! All mad, all crazy! Look, my arm! One of my men did that, my own men! See, I caught him take bowl food from widow with baby, and corporal say it third time tonight, so I order with my gun give back, go find more at airstrip for poor others he rob. Right for officer to say, no? Your food not for soldiers, for poor starve devils in town! So he took that axe and hit me, see? Oh, but it hurts!"

"Let me get bandages!" Lucy cried, but he seemed not to hear. Large, staring, his eyes were fixed on nowhere.

He tightened his grip and words poured out frantically, his careful European syntax giving way to the grammar of his own language.

"No, not go! Gone crazy, say! Shout the town is full ghosts, ghosts everywhere, shoot at them, fire guns all time at shadow, anything! Say kill ghosts, kill ghosts, *kill kill ghosts!*"

Outside there were footsteps. Lucy tried again to release her hand so she could close the door, failed, and thought at least of switching off the flashlight so that would not attract a mad prowler. What Obou had said made no sense, but the firing was louder and closer and through the open door she could see that more and still more flames were springing up, as though the town were turning into a volcano.

Footsteps again. Nearer. And her .22 was out of reach and Obou's gun was empty. At first gently, then in growing panic, she fought to make him let go. A new bright light shone in the doorway. The instant before it dazzled her she saw a white man in a white shirt holding a pistol; the instant after, she realized what the torch-beam would show—a white girl in the grip of a black man, her thighs apart and smeared with blood, a case of rape.

She started to shout, "Don't—!"

And was too late. The gun exploded. The bullet spattered her with bits of Obou.

Later someone kept trying to say to her—it was the Swedish doctor, Bertil—"But we didn't know you were here! When the trouble started we saw Maua and she swore you weren't in the house. We went down into the town, and all these madmen came at us with guns and hatchets, screaming that we were evil ghosts, kill the ghosts!"

I heard that before. Listless, Lucy rocked back and forth, eyes shut, right hand mechanically rubbing the spot on her left arm where she had been given some sort of injection, the two rhythms crisscrossing the lilt of Bertil's accent.

"Be glad you didn't see what we saw: the whole town gone insane, looting and burning and killing!"

The person I saw killing was you. You shot a nice man. I was going on leave with him. I liked his smile. He had a round dark face with funny stripes on his cheeks. He's dead. You killed him.

She moaned and fell to the floor.

JANUARY

MARCHING ORDERS

"Go ye and bring the Light
  To savage strands afar.
Take ye the Law of Right
  Where'er the unblest are.

*"Heathens and stubborn Jews,
  Lovers of Juggernaut,
Give them the chance to choose
  That which the Saviour taught.

"Go where the gentle Lord
  Is still as yet unknown,
There where the tribes ignored
  Strive in the dark alone.

"Arm ye to face the foe,
  Carib and cannibal,
Men who must live as low
  As any animal.

*"Cover the naked limb,
  Shoe ye the unshod foot,
Silence the pagan hymn,
  Conquer the godless brute.

"Tell them the news of Love,
  Preach them the Prince of Peace,
Tear down their pagan grove,
  Give them divine release."

—"The Sacred Sower: Being a Collection of Hymns and Devout Songs Adapted to the Use of Missionary Societies", 1887; verses marked * may be omitted if desired.

ABOVE THE SOUND OF SPEED

RM-1808, out of Phoenix for Seattle, had reported acute catting—clear air turbulence—in the vicinity of Salt Lake City. Hearing of this, the navigator of TW-6036, the Montreal-Los Angeles direct SST, punched the keys of his computer and passed a course-correction to the pilot. Then he leaned back to resume his snooze.

They would be super for over a thousand miles yet.

SNOW JOB

Disregarded, the twenty-nine-inch color TV displayed images of today's violence. The camera lingeringly swept the gutters of far-off Noshri, pausing occasionally at corpses. A dog, miraculous survivor of the period last summer when people had paid a hundred local francs for a rat, fifty for a handful of mealies, was seen snuffling the body of a child, and a tall black soldier broke its back with the butt of his carbine.

"Shit! You see what that black mother did to that poor dog?"

"What?"

But the screen had switched to the wreckage of a plane.

This was Towerhill, latest of the prosperous winter-sports resorts of Colorado, and they were in the Apennine Lodge, smartest and most expensive of its accommodations. Brand-new, the place struggled hard to appear old. Skis hung from plastic beams, a simulated log fire burned in a stone hearth. Beyond a double-glazed window taking up most of one wall powerful arc lights played on a magnificent dark-striped snow-slope running nearly to the crest of Mount Hawes. Until last year, although this town was barely fifty miles from Denver, the road had been bad and only a handful of visitors had chanced on it. The increasing tendency for people to take mountain vacations, however, since the sea had become too filthy to be tolerable, could not be ignored. The road now was excellent and the area had exploded. There were three ultramodern ski-lifts and a branch of Puritan Health Supermarkets. There were facilities for skijoring behind snowmobiles and Colorado Chemical Bank planned to double the size of its operation here. One could go skating and curling and American Express had taken up its option on some offices. Next year they promised a ski-jump of Olympic standard.

On the screen a group of men, women and children were shown shivering outside a cluster of improbably-shaped buildings. They were poorly dressed but on average rather good-looking. Meantime police with dogs conducted a search.

Oh. Trainites. What the hell?

After his second drink Bill Chalmers was feeling better. It had been a filthy day: driving to Denver this morning over roads that had been ploughed and sanded but were still slithery; sweating out that awful lunch at the Masons', aware of "an atmosphere" but unable to pin down the cause; breaking it up finally when their son Anton, six, had a row with the Mason kids aged five and four and ran away screaming . . .

But they were back safely, and he liked Towerhill: its air of affluence which was a snook cocked at the prophets of doom, its enclosing mountains, its unbelievably blessedly fresh air. One saw big-city visitors, their first day, going out in filtermasks, not convinced they were okay without them.

The screen showed a map of Central America with an arrow pointing to somewhere, then photographs of two men, both white.

"Tania!"

"Yes, I'd love another," his wife said, and went right on comparing symptoms with the lawyer's wife from Oakland she'd met yesterday. "Now me, I had this funny rash, and a prickly feeling all over . . ."

Christ! Can't anybody talk about anything these days except allergies and neuroses? Once a man could be satisfied to be a breadwinner. Now he has to be a medicine-winner as well. And it never does any good.

"Yes, well!" the lawyer's wife said. "Now I got this hot-and-cold feeling, and sometimes actual dizziness."

Abruptly he realized they were talking about pregnancy, and instead of fuming he found himself shivering. Of course he'd taken out abnormality insurance when Anton was on the way, but despite his position with Angel City it hadn't come cheap, and when Anton had been safely delivered Tom Grey had told him just what odds they had been bucking. Words reheard in memory made him tremble: cystic fibrosis, phenylketonuria, hemophilia, hypothyroidism, mongolism, Tetralogy of Fallot, alexia, dichromatism . . . A list that went on forever, as though it were a miracle anyone at all became a normal adult!

It made one understand why Grey was a bachelor. He himself wouldn't risk a second kid.

The TV went over to sports results. For the first time several people paid it full attention.

"Tania!"

She finally turned. The lawyer's wife escaped to join her husband on the far side of the room.

"Did you have that heart-to-heart with Denise?"

"Oh, God," Tania said, leaning back and crossing her arms. "So that was why you brought us here—to spy on the Masons!"

"It was not!"

"Then what in hell makes it so urgent? You don't have to be back at the office before Monday! And why didn't you ask me in the car instead of snapping my head off every time I spoke?"

All around, their attention caught by voices sharpening toward the pitch of a quarrel, people were turning to look. Hideously embarrassed, Chalmers adopted a conciliatory manner.

"Tania honey, I'm sorry, but it *is* important."

"Obviously! More important than me or Tony! More important than my first chance in years to relax and make some new friends! Look what you've done—chased Sally away!"

He just sat there.

After a moment, however, she relented. Four years ago they had been through the unemployable stage; she knew what it would mean to lose his job.

"Oh, hell . . . Yes, I wormed it out of her. She's a crank. Practically a Trainite."

Chalmers pricked up his ears. "How do you mean?"

"A crank, like I say. Won't let him fly. Says she wants her grandchildren to see the sun. What difference it makes if a plane flies with one seat empty, *I* don't know! But she thinks Phil's in some kind of trouble because she made him drive to LA, only he won't come out and put the blame squarely on her. And she wants desperately to know what the problem is. In fact she brought the matter up. I didn't have to. Because he was awful over Christmas, apparently. What's more he keeps finding excuses not to screw her. Wouldn't have made it even on New Year's, she said, not unless she'd actually *seduced* him—"

The last word was drowned out by a sudden thudding noise from the sky, as though a giant had clapped hands around a mosquito. Everyone winced. An anonymous voice said, "Oh, a filthy sonic boom. Don't you hate them?"

But it should have been over in an instant. It continued: after the initial bang, a growling sound, lower-pitched, but enduring, like stones being rubbed by the current of a fast river or a vigorous tide on a pebbly headland. Poised to renew their conversation, people realized that this wasn't right. The noise grew louder, grinding. They turned and looked at the window.

Tania screamed.

With implacable majesty, to the beating of countless drums, half a million tons of snow and ice were marching on the town of Towerhill.

CHARGE ACCOUNT *Reporter:* General, it's no exaggeration to say the world has been appalled at your decision to arrest and expel the American relief workers from Noshri—

General Kaika: Do you expect us to let them remain when they have poisoned thousands of our people, killed them or, worse still, driven them mad?

Reporter: There's no proof that—

General Kaika: Yes, there is proof. All the people of the town went mad. They attacked our own troops who had freed them from the occupying forces. They were poisoned by the evil food sent under the pretence of relief supplies.

Reporter: But what conceivable motive could—?

General Kaika: Plenty of motive. For one thing, Americans go to any length to prevent an independent country whose government does not have white skin. Colored governments must bow to Washington. Consider China. Consider Vietnam, Cambodia, Laos, Thailand, Ceylon, Indonesia. If ever we have a strong united country of black people in Africa they will no longer be able to tread down their black countrymen.

Reporter: Are you saying there was a deliberate plot to weaken your forces and win the war for the invaders?

General Kaika: I am making investigations to confirm. But it is white men who made the war to start with.

Reporter: There weren't even any white mercenaries with the—

General Kaika: Was it black men who filled the Mediterranean with poison? No, it was destroyed by the filthy wastes from European factories!

Reporter: Well, the Aswan dam—

General Kaika: Yes, yes, the Aswan dam may have tipped the balance finally, but before that the sea was dying. Because so many had to starve on the African coast there began this war. That is why I say the white countries are responsible. It is the typical white habit to ruin what you have and then go to steal from other people.

Reporter: Oh, General, you're stretching the facts a bit!

General Kaika: Is the fact that it is dangerous to swim in the Mediterranean? Is the fact that the fish have died?

Reporter: Well, yes, but—

General Kaika: I have no more to say.

RATS

Jeannie was already home, of course, her Stephenson electric tucked into a corner of the garage. Pete was on the ten-to-six shift today and her job at Bamberley's stopped at five.

Pete Goddard hated his wife going to work. He wanted her at home, looking after a couple of kids. That, though, would have to wait until after his next promotion. These days nobody in his right mind would start a family before he could afford proper medical care for his children. Up here in the mountains it wasn't so bad as in the cities; even so you couldn't be too careful.

As he scraped his boots before treading on the front step, there was a slamming sound in the sky. He glanced up just in time to meet an eyeful of snow shaken off the overhang of the porch. Ah, shit, a sonic boom. Oughtn't to have been that loud! One grew used to one or two a day, but faint, far away, doing no damage beyond maybe startling you into spilling a cup of coffee. Down at the station house Sergeant Chain could look forward to a rash of complaints. As though there were anything the police here could do. As though there were anything anybody could do.

Jeannie was in the kitchen. Not much of a kitchen, equipped with repossessed appliances. But they usually worked. She was busy at the stove: a pretty girl, much lighter than he and a year older, bound to be plump before thirty but what the hell? He liked plenty of meat. Blowing her a kiss, he collected his evening pill, the one for his allergy, and headed for the sink to draw some water.

But she stopped him with a cry. "No, Pete! I found a don't-drink notice when I got home. See, on the table?"

Startled, he turned and spotted the bright red paper printed in bold black letters. The familiar phrases leapt out at him: *fault in the purifying plant—must not be drunk without boiling—rectified as soon as possible . . .*

"Shit!" he exclaimed. "It's getting to be as bad as Denver!"

"Oh, no, honey! Down in the city they get these all the time, like every week, and that's only our second since the summer. Won't a beer do?"

"A beer? Sure it will!"

"In the icebox. And one for me. I got this complicated recipe going." She brandished a clipping from the newspaper.

Grinning, he made to comply—and his hand flew to his hip after his not-present gun as he exclaimed in dismay.

"What?" Jeannie spun around. "Oh, not another rat?"

"Just the biggest I ever saw!" But it was gone now. "I thought I told you to call the exterminator!" he snapped.

"Well, I did! But he said he has so much business we'll have to wait at least another week."

"Yeah, I guess so." Pete sighed. "Everybody I meet . . ." He let the words trail away and opened the icebox. On two shelves, packages with a familiar trade mark: a girl holding an ear of corn between her tits, to make a sort of prick-and-balls pattern of them.

"Hey, you been to Puritan again!"

"Well, I spent my bonus," Jeannie said defensively. "And things there aren't that much more expensive! Besides, they do really taste much better."

"What bonus?"

"Oh, you know! I told you! All us girls in the packing section who worked overtime to get that shipment away before Christmas. Twenty bucks extra from Mr. Bamberley!"

"Oh. Oh, yeah." Taking his beer and hers from the six-pack. What the hell? Twenty bucks today was a spit in the ocean. Though he would rather have put it toward their policy with Angel City, saving against the time when they could afford a baby. All these scare stories about chemicals. Just an excuse to double the prices at Puritan . . .

Reminded of the plant, though: "Say, baby, how's your leg?" That smooth patch of skin, as though part of her thigh had been glazed.

"Oh, they were right first time. It is a fungus. You know we have to wear masks against actino-what's-its-name. I picked up something of the same kind. But the ointment's fixing it."

Pete repressed a shudder. Catching a fungus! Christ, like something out of a horror movie! It had dragged on for more than a month, and even now he kept finding himself obsessively inspecting his own body. He gulped at his beer.

"Say, honey, I meant to tell you," Jeannie said suddenly. "I saw you on TV!"

"What, at the Trainite wat?" He dropped into a chair. "Yes, I noticed the guy with the camera."

"What were you there for?"

"Didn't they explain?"

"I only switched on in time to catch the end of it."

"Ah-hah. Well, we had this call from LA. Remember

the cat who used to run the wat was killed down there before Christmas? Seems he was either crazy or stoned. So they said turn the place over for drugs."

"I thought Trainites didn't hold with them."

"Well, it's true we didn't find anything . . . Weird place, baby! All like fixed up from scrap. Kind of handmade. And the people kind of—*I* don't know. Odd!"

"I saw some of them at Puritan," Jeannie said. "They looked pretty ordinary. And their kids are very well behaved."

Too soon to talk about the best way to raise kids. Some day, though . . .

"They may look harmless," Pete said. "But that's because here there aren't enough to cause real trouble. I mean like apart from painting up these dirty skulls and crossbones. Down in LA, though, they block streets, wreck cars, smash up stores!"

"But Carl says everything they do is meant to wake people up to the danger we're in."

Oh, the hell with Carl! But Pete kept that to himself, knowing how fond Jeannie was of him: her younger brother, nineteen going on twenty, the bright one of their family of five kids who'd dropped out of college after a year complaining of lousy teaching and was currently also working at the Bamberley plant.

"Look, any way they want to live is fine by me," he grunted. "But it's my job to stop anybody wrecking or looting or interfering with the way *other* people want to live."

"Well, Carl's been to the wat several times and according to him— Oh, let's not argue!" Consulting her recipe. "Well, we have to wait ten minutes now, it says. Let's go into the living room and sit down . . ." Her face clouded. "Know something, honey?"

"What?"

"I do wish I had one of those instant cookers. Microwave. Then it wouldn't matter when you came in, dinner could be ready in a moment."

The phone rang.

"Go sit down. I'll get it," she said. He grinned at her and obeyed. But, even before he'd made himself comfortable, she was calling to him in a near-scream.

"Pete! Pete! Get your coat and boots!"

"What? What the hell for?"

"There's been an avalanche! It's buried all those new places the other side of town!"

NO BIGGER THAN A MAN'S HAND

. . . published today as a United Nations Special Report. The alleged rise of intelligence in so-called backward countries is ascribed by the scientists who conducted the three-year investigation to improved diet and sanitation, while the as-yet unconfirmed decline in advancd nations is attributed to intensified pollution. Asked to comment on the report just prior to leaving for Hollywood, where he is tonight slated to open his annual retrospective, Prexy said, quote, Well, if they're so smart why aren't they clever? End quote. At a press conference in Tegucigalpa the disappearance of Leonard Ross, field agent for Globe Relief, and Dr. Isaiah Williams, the British medico who's also unaccounted for, was officially ascribed today to terrorism. Troops are searching the area intensively, but so far have reported no success. Following the shock resignation of the former president of the "Save the Med" Fund, Dottore Giovanni Crespinolo, the Italian government has flatly denied his charge that the vast sums donated by corporations and individuals in forty-eight countries in the hope of saving the doomed landlocked sea have been embezzled. Reports from Rome, however . . .

MEMENTO LAURAE

Never in his life had Philip Mason felt so miserable. He paced endlessly around the apartment, snapping at the children, telling Denise to leave him alone for God's sake, when all the time what he really wanted to say was that he loved them desperately and always would.

Yet the consequences of New Year's Eve . . .

When he felt depressed at the last place, things had been easier to bear: a house, much further from the city center—beyond the river—with its own garden. There he'd been able to hide away and be miserable by himself. But the river fires had been bad last year; more than once he'd been unable to get to work because the bridge was closed, and half the time smoke made it impossible to use the garden or even open the windows.

So they'd moved to this air-conditioned apartment block. Handier for the office. And, of course, for the hospital where Josie's squint was being treated and the short muscles in Harold's leg were being drawn out.

He couldn't explain! Dared not! And now couldn't get out of explaining, either!

But at least he had a few minutes to himself. The kids were asleep, having taken a long time to calm down following their disastrous encounter with Anton Chalmers: pushy, arrogant, greedy, bullying, bad-tempered—but, of course, absolutely healthy. "Survival of the fittest and all that shit" . . . to quote his insufferable father.

And Denise had gone to the Henlowes' apartment on the second floor. That was where you scored in this building. Everyone nowadays seemed to know a means of getting something from somebody. But it was best to stay out on the fringes. It was becoming as bad as what the history books recounted about Prohibition, what with the black gangs fighting on the streets over the right to distribute African khat, and the white gangs blowing up each other's homes for the right to trade in Mexican grass.

So she'd come back in half an hour, having socialized, and show what she'd got, and say, "Darling, don't worry, whatever's the matter it'll come right in the end, let's turn on and relax, hm?"

Dennie, I love you terribly, and if you're sweet and kind to me one more time tonight I shall scream.

Here was the phone. He dialed with shaking fingers, and shortly a woman replied. He said, "Dr. Clayford, please. It's urgent."

"Dr. Clayford will be in his office on Monday as usual," the woman replied.

"This is Philip Mason. Area manager of—"

"Oh, Mr. Mason!" Abruptly cordial. Clayford was one of the physicians Philip sent Angel City's clients to for examination prior to taking out a life policy; it behooved the doctor to be cooperative. "Just a second, I'll see if my husband's free."

"Thank you." Nervous, he fumbled out a cigarette. His smoking had nearly doubled since his trip to LA. He'd been trying to cut it down; instead, here he was getting through two packs a day.

"Yes?" A gruff voice. He started.

"Ah, doctor!" One didn't say "doc" to Clayford, let alone call him by his first name. He was an old-fashioned family GP, who at sixty still affected the dark suits and white shirts that had marked out sober young men with "a great future ahead of them" when he was in college. Talking to him was a little like talking to a minister; one felt a sense of distance, an intangible barrier. But right now it had to be breached.

"Look, I need you advice, and—uh—help."

"Well?"

Philip swallowed hard. "It's like this. Just before Christmas I was called to LA, to the headquarters of my company, and because my wife doesn't like planes—you know, pollution—I drove, and broke the trip in Vegas. And there I—uh—well, I got involved with a girl. Absolutely without meaning to. Time and opportunity, you know!"

"So?"

"So . . . Well, I wasn't certain until days later, but now I don't think there's any doubt. She left me with—uh—gonorrhea."

Stained undershorts floating around him, like mocking bats.

"I see." Clayford not in the least sympathetic. "Well, you should go to the clinic on Market, then. I believe they're open Saturday mornings."

Philip had seen it, in a depressed and depressing area: ashamed of its function, persecuted by the righteous majority, always full of young people pretending rebellious defiance.

"But surely, doctor—"

"Mr. Mason, that's my professional advice, and there's an end of it."

"But my wife!"

"Have you had relations with her since this escapade of yours?"

"Well, on New Year's—" Philip began, head full of all the reasons: can't not, this is *the* day of the year, it's kind of symbolic and we've made a tradition of it since we first met . . .

"Then you'll have to take her with you," Clayford said, and didn't even add a good-night.

The bastard! The filthy stuck-up stiff-necked—!

Oh, what's the use?

He set down the phone, thinking of all the suggestions he'd had ready: a white lie, say about hepatitis which everyone knew to be endemic in California, anything that might require a short course of a suitable antibiotic . . .

My God! All I have is the second commonest infectious disease after measles! It says so in the papers all the time.

Distraction. Anything. Switch on the TV. Maybe the doctor at the clinic will be more helpful and I'll still be able to cover up. If I only had to confess about screwing Laura that'd be okay, Denise wouldn't leave me over that. But telling her she's been given the clap courtesy of a man-hungry stranger . . . !

Transistorized, the sound came on quicker than the picture, and his ears suddenly stung with the sense of what was being said. It was the late news summary. He felt as though the earth had opened and he was falling, miles deep.

"—still coming in about the extent of tonight's avalanche disaster at Towerhill."

The picture jelled. Police cars. Searchlights. Helicopters. Fire trucks. Ambulances. Bulldozers. Snowplows.

"The Apennine Lodge, which stood right here, is totally buried," a voice said in doom-laden tones. A shapeless mass of snow with men digging. "Other nearby lodges and hotels were carried downhill, some for a quarter of a mile. Damage will certainly be in excess of fifteen million and may well run as high as fifty million dollars—"

"Phil, I'm back!" Denise called, having worked her way through the complex locks of the entrance door. "Say, I managed to score from Jed and Beryl, and—"

"There's been an avalanche at Towerhill!" he shouted.

"What?" She advanced into the living-room, a slim girl with delicate bones, a graceful walk, an auburn wig that exactly matched her former mop of curls and completely hid her ringworm scars. Sometimes Philip thought she was the most beautiful woman he had ever seen.

"Oh, lord," she said thinly. On the screen, a body being lifted out of dirty snow. "That's where Bill and Tania are staying!" She sat down automatically on the arm of his chair. He clutched her fingers and spoke through terror, despair, nausea.

"They said fifteen million bucks' worth of damage, maybe fifty. And you know who carries their insurance? We do!"

She looked at him, shocked. "Phil, think of the damage when you get back to the office! You should call up, find out if Bill and Tania are okay, and Anton too. Right now you ought to be worrying about people, not money!"

"I am. You and me."

"Phil—"

"I haven't finished reinsuring that place. I had so much new business to cope with. And not one of my staff has made it through the winter without falling sick. I only had about half the risk reinsured."

Comprehension dawned, and a look of horror.

"I'm through," Philip said. "God, I wish I were dead."

AHEAD OF THE NEWS "Globo Relief? Mr. Thorne, please," said the State Department expert in Central American affairs, and then: "Morning, Gerry—Dirk here. Say, how's your eye? . . . That's good . . . Me? I'm fine. Touch of mono is all. Well, why I'm calling up, I thought you'd like to be among the first to know they found your boy Ross. Washed up on a rock alongside that river that runs through San Pablo . . . No, no sign of the English doctor yet . . . Well, they say his head was battered in. It could have been on the rocks of the river, but they're doing an autopsy to confirm . . . Yes, with luck. Those stinking Tupas have had it all their own way for far too long. We finally have the excuse to hit back. I'll keep you posted."

IT FIGURES The armed guards who patrolled the headquarters of Angel City Interstate Mutual over the dead ten-day period of the holiday were surprised to find one of the corporation's senior executives keeping them company.

But not surprised that the man in question should be

Dr. Thomas Grey. From him they were used to eccentricity.

"Crazy!" people said, and were happy to assume that because he was so devoted to his profession he had never even married he must necessarily be a crank.

In fact, that was extremely unfair to him. He was probably among the most rational men alive.

"To the editor of The Christian Science Monitor: Sir . . .

His typing was, as always, impeccable, the envy of professional secretaries. He sat in the near-silence of the fourth floor, surrounded by the metal carcasses of computers.

"One is dismayed to find a journal with an international reputation echoing the cries of what I have no hesitation in calling scare-mongers—people who apparently would have us revert to the wild state without even the caveman's privilege of wearing furs."

He glanced around to confirm that no malfunction lamps were shining, and took the opportunity to scratch himself. He had a slight but nagging dermatitis due to washing-powder enzymes.

"Admittedly, we alter the order of things by the way we live. But the same can be said of any organism. How many of those who cry out for vast sums to be spent on preserving coral reefs from starfish realize that the reefs are themselves the result of a living species' impact on the ecology of the planet? Grass completely revolutionized the 'balance of nature'; so did the evolution of trees. Every plant, every animal, every fish—one might safely say every humble micro-organism, too—has a discernible influence on the world."

A light winked at him. He broke off, went to change a spool of tape, returned to his chair. Having read once more through the editorial in the *Monitor* which had so offended him—it might, in his view, have been written by that bigot Austin Train himself—he sharpened the next barb of his reply.

"If the extremists had their way, we would sit and mope, resigned to having four out of five children die because the nuts and berries within walking distance had been frosted."

He was only passing time by writing this letter; he did not expect it to do any good. What he was chiefly here for was to add a few more tiny bricks to the monumental structure of a private undertaking he had been engaged on for years. Having begun as a hobby, it had developed into something approaching an obsession, and constituted the main reason why he was still working for Angel City. The company had a lot of spare computer capacity; right now, there was a nationwide glut of it. Accordingly no one objected when he made use of it on evenings and weekends. He had been well paid for most of his working life, and thanks to having simple tastes he was now rich. But hiring the computer capacity he currently needed would wipe out his fortune in a month.

Of course he scrupulously reimbursed the firm for the materials he used, the tape, the paper and the power.

His project stemmed from the fact that, being a very rational man indeed, he could become nearly as angry as a dedicated Trainite when the most spectacular fruit of some promising new human achievement turned out to be a disaster. Computers, he maintained, had made it possible for virtually every advance to be studied beforehand in enough model situations to allow of sober, constructive exploitation. Of course, renting them was expensive—but so was hiring lawyers to defend you if you were charged with infringing the Environment Acts: so was fighting an FDA ban; so was a suit from some injured nobody with a strong pressure-group at his back. And when you added money spent on vain attempts to shut the stable door by such organizations as Earth Community Chest, Globe Relief or the "Save the Med" Fund, the total cost became heartbreaking. What a waste!

When, at thirty-three, he had abandoned his former career as a freelance R&D consultant and decided to train as an actuary, he had vaguely hoped that an insurance company, being concerned with the effects of human shortsightedness, might set up a special department to foster his project and pay for proper staff. That hadn't worked out. It had had to remain effectively a one-man show.

So he was a long, long way from his ultimate goal: nothing less than a world-simulation program.

But he was a patient man, and the shock of such catastrophes as the creation of the Mekong Desert had brought more and more people around to the conclusion he had reached long ago. Whether or not it could be done, it absolutely *must* be done.

Of course, he was in the same predicament as weather forecasters had been before computers, continually overwhelmed by fresh data that required slow, piecemeal processing. But he had already worked out many trial-and-error techniques for automatically updating his program, and in another twenty years . . . He enjoyed good health, and watched his diet carefully.

Besides, he wasn't after perfect accuracy. Something about as precise as weather forecasting would suit admirably. Just so long as it permitted men who were neither reckless nor cowardly to monitor human progress. (He often used the word in conversation. Many of his acquaintances regarded him as old-fashioned because of it.)

"When someone next complains that the use of insecticides has resulted in an orchard-bred pest eating his magnolias, remind him that but for the improved diet made possible when the orchards were cleared of maggots he might not own a garden to plant magnolias in. Verb. sap.

Yours, etc.,
T.M. Grey,
Ph.D., M.Sc."

COME CLEAN *One thing you can tell right away about the owner of a Hailey. He has a healthy respect for other people.*
A Hailey takes up no more of the road than is necessary.
The noise a Hailey makes is only a gentle hum.
And it leaves the air far cleaner than gas-driven cars.
Even if they are filter-tipped.
So the driver of a Hailey can get close enough to other people to see their smiles and hear their murmurs of approval.
What's your car doing for interpersonal relations?

YOU DIG The shovel bit in, carried away another cubic foot or so of snow—and there wasn't anywhere to put it except on top of more snow.

Still, at least he hadn't hit a body when he plunged it in.

Pete Goddard ached. Or rather, what he could feel of himself ached. It had started in his soles when he'd been in the snow for half an hour. Then it had crept up to his ankles. Around the time the pain infected his calves he'd lost contact with his feet. He had to take it for granted they were still inside his boots.

Also his hands were tender and assured of blisters despite his gloves. It was down to twenty with a vicious wind; his eyes were sore and if the tears that leaked from them hadn't been salty he believed they would have frozen on his cheeks.

This was a foretaste of hell. Stark lights, harsh as curses, had been dragged up treacherous snow-mounds, coupled to emergency generators whose complaints at overload filled the air with a noise like grinding teeth. All the time there were shouts: "Here, quick!" And every shout meant another victim, most likely dead, but sometimes with a broken back, broken leg, broken pelvis. The avalanche had operated like a press. It had condensed the buildings closest to Mount Hawes into a state akin to fiberboard: human remains, structural timbers, cars, winter-sports gear, food, liquor, furniture, carpets, more human remains, had been squashed together until they could be crushed no further, and then the whole horrible disgusting mass had been forced downhill to transfer the shock to more distant locations.

Red among the snow here. He burrowed with his fingers for fear his shovel might hurt someone, and discovered a side of beef.

"Hey! Mister policeman!"

A kid's voice. For an instant he was haunted by the fear of standing on a buried child. But the call was from here on the surface, loud to overcome the drone of a helicopter. He glanced up. Facing him, balanced on a broken wall, a light-colored boy of eleven or twelve, wearing dark woolen pants and a parka and offering a tin cup that steamed like a geyser.

"Like some soup?"

Pete's stomach reminded him suddenly that he'd been on the point of eating when he left home. He dropped his shovel.

"Sure would," he agreed. This was no place for a kid—no telling what horrors he might see—but getting food down him was a good idea. It was bound to be a long job. He took the cup and made to sip, but the soup was hotter even than it looked. The kid was carrying a big vacuum-jug behind him on a strap. Must be efficient.

"You found many dead people?" the boy inquired.

"A few," Pete muttered.

"I never saw anybody dead before. Now I've seen maybe a dozen."

His tone was matter-of-fact, but Pete was shocked. After a pause he said, "Uh—I guess your mom knows you're here?"

"Sure, that's her soup. When she heard about the

accident she put on a big pan of it and told us all to wrap up warm and come and help."

Well, okay; you don't tell other people what's good and what's bad for their kids. And it was kind of a constructive action. Pete tried the soup again, found it had cooled quickly in the bitter wind, and swallowed greedily. It was delicious, with big chunks of vegetables in it and strong-scented herbs.

"I was interested to see the dead people," the kid said suddenly. "My father was killed the other day."

Pete blinked at him.

"Not my real father. I called him that because he adopted me. And my two sisters. It was in the papers, and they even put his picture on TV."

"What does your mom use for this soup?" Pete said, thinking to change a ghoulish subject. "It's great."

"I'll tell her you said so. It's like yeast extract, and any vegetables around, and"—the boy gave a strangely adult shrug—"water, boiled up with marjoram and stuff. . . Finished?"

"Not quite."

"I only have this one cup, you see, so after it's been drunk from I have to clean it in the snow to kill the germs and go find someone else." The boy's tone was virtuous. "Did *you* see my dad's picture on TV?"

"Ah . . . " Pete's mind raced. "Well, I don't get to watch it too much, you know. I'm pretty tied up with my job."

"Yeah, sure. Just thought you might have seen him." A hint of unhappiness tinged the words. "I miss him a lot . . . Finished now?"

Pete drained the mug and gave it back. "You tell your mom she makes great soup, okay?" he said, and clapped the boy's shoulder. At the back of his mind he was thinking about Jeannie; she being so much lighter than he, their kids ought to come out just about the same shade as this boy here. If only they were equally bright, equally healthy . . .

"Sure will," the boy said, and added, struck by a

thought, "Say, you need anyone else up here? You're working pretty much on your own, aren't you?"

"Well, we have to spread out because there are so many places to dig," Pete said. He was never at ease talking to children, having had problems when he was a kid himself. His father hadn't died and made the papers, but simply vanished.

"Well, there's lots of us down by the ambulances."

"Us?"

"Sure. We're from the Trainite wat my dad used to run before he died. I'll send someone up to help you—Harry, maybe. He's big. What's your name, so he'll know who to come to?"

"Uh . . . I'm Pete. Pete Goddard."

"I'm Rick Jones. Okay, someone will be along in a minute!"

"Hey!"

But the kid had gone scrambling and leaping down the trenched mounds of snow. Pete reclaimed his shovel, alarmed. Only this morning at the wat he'd had to guard the occupants as they stood out in the cold while detectives searched for drugs. Having a Trainite partner him . . .

The hell with it. What mattered was to pull out any more poor bastards who might be buried under this load of white shit.

It was okay. Harry wasn't one of the people he'd met this morning. He wasn't too much bigger than Pete, but he was fresher. He hardly said more than hello before he started shifting snow, and they concentrated on the job until they uncovered their first victim: dead, blue with cyanosis and cold. Stretcher-bearers came, and a young Air Force officer—they'd turned out the Academy, of course—took particulars of the ID in the man's pocket. He was local. Pete had given him a parking ticket once. One of the stretcher-bearers had a transistor radio, and while it was in earshot it said something about Towerhill being declared a disaster zone.

"First of many," Harry muttered.

"What?"

"I said first of many. You don't think this is the only avalanche they're going to cause with their stinking SST's, do you? The Swiss won't let them overfly the country between October and May—said they'd shoot them down first. So did the Austrians."

Pete handed Harry his shovel. "Let's dig," he sighed.

About ten minutes later it became clear what they'd got into at this spot: a whole collapsed room, if not a building. Uphill, a wall of rough stone had broken the worst impact of the avalanche, but it had shifted on its foundations and twisted into an irregular line of precariously poised fragments. Over that the roof-beams had folded, but not fallen, leaving a small vacant space in which—

"Christ!" Harry said. "Alive!"

Something moved feebly in darkness. White darkness. The snow had burst in through a window, fanned out on the floor.

"Ah-yah-ahh!" The treble cry of a child.

"Look out, you fucking idiot!" Pete roared as Harry made to drop his shovel and dive straight in under the arching timbers. He grabbed his arm.

"What? That's a kid! Get your hands off—!"

"Look, look, *look!*" And Pete pointed to the huge trembling overhang of snow that had broken against the stone wall like a frozen wave. Because of their digging it loured above the space in which the child—children, he realized, hearing a second cry discord with the first—in which the children were trapped.

"Ah . . . Yeah." Harry regained his self-possession and blinked down into the dark hollow. A bed, overset. A lot of snow. "See what you mean. We could bring that whole pile down on us. Got a flashlight?"

"Loaned it to someone. Go get another. And lots of help. See, that beam?" Pete didn't dare so much as touch it. Now it was exposed, the single crucial roof-strut that had spared the children looked like a match, and on the slanted broken roof that it supported lay God knew how many tons of snow and rock.

"Sure! Be back right away!" Turning to run.

"Hang on, kids," Pete called into the cold dark. "We'll get you out soon's we can."

One of the half-seen shapes moved. Stood up. Shedding snow.

Moving snow.

Trying to climb to the light!

"Oh, my God! Harry, HARRY! BE QUICK!"

Crying. And the crying drowned by the noise of weight leaning on a fractured beam. *The* beam, the one that held back the incredible mass of snow. He saw it spray tiny white flakes, like dust, that danced in the glow of the distant emergency lights.

Christ . . . Jeannie, Jeannie, it could be a kid of ours down there—I don't mean *could,* not at fifty bucks a day, but I mean it's a kid, and we could have kids, and . . .

But those thoughts were spin-off, and had nothing to do with him moving. Shovel dropped. The beam yielding. Turning so his shoulders came under it, his numb hands felt for it. The weight, the incredible intolerable unthinkable weight. He looked down and saw his boots had been driven in over ankles in the packed snow.

At least, though, he could still hear the crying.

THE TINIEST TRACE "Did it go okay, Peg?" Mel Torrance called as she wended her way through the maze of desks, glass partitions, file cabinets. The paper was losing money. Most papers were losing money. Even Mel had only a cubbyhole for an office, whose door stood permanently open except when he was taking his pills. He was embarrassed about that for some reason.

Ridiculous. Who do you know who doesn't have to take pills of some kind nowadays? Which reminds me, I'm past due for mine.

"Oh, fine," Peg muttered. She'd been out to cover a sewer explosion. Someone had poured something he shouldn't have down the drain, and it had reacted with something else. Big deal. It happened all the time. Today nobody had even been killed.

"Did Rod get any good pictures?"

"Said he'd have some for you in about two hours."

"He didn't get Polaroids? Shit, of course not—the pol count is up today, isn't it?" Mel sighed. Days you couldn't get Polaroids were starting to outnumber those when you could; it was something in the air that affected the emulsion. "Well, a couple of hours should be okay . . . Message for you, by the way. It's on your desk."

"Later."

But the note said she should contact the city morgue, so she put the call in while rolling paper into her typewriter with her other hand, and after five wrong numbers—about par for the course—the phone said, "Stanway."

"Peg Mankiewicz."

"Oh, yes." Stanway's voice dropped a trifle. "Look, we finally had the definitive lab report on your friend Jones."

"Christ! You mean they've been on at him all this time?" Peg heard her voice ragged. Couldn't they even leave his corpse alone? Weren't they content with hurling insults at his memory? "This self-appointed prophet of a better world who turned out to be just another acid-head." Quote/unquote.

"Well, it's a slow process looking for these very tiny traces of a drug," Stanway said, missing the point. "Paper chromatography work. Long-column separation, even, sometimes."

"All right, what did they find?"

"A hallucinogen in his system. Not LSD or psilocybin or any of the regular ones, but something with a similar molecular structure. I don't really understand the report myself—I'm an anatomist, not a biochemist. But I thought you'd like to know right away."

Like! No, it was the thing in all the world she least wanted to hear. But there it was: evidence.

"Any special reason why they went to all that trouble?"

Stanway hesitated. He said at length, "Well, the fuzz insisted."

"The lousy mothers! They didn't find drugs in his car!"

Not strictly his, but rented. Trainites did their best not to contribute to pollution, and the entire community of sixty-some at the Denver wat owned one vehicle between them, a jeep. Apart from bicycles.

Moreover they didn't hold with drugs, not even pot, though they did tolerate beer and wine.

She slid open a drawer in her desk, where she kept the file she'd compiled about Decimus's death, and reread the list of things that had been found in the car—more or less what you would expect. A traveling-bag with a change of clothes, razor, toothbrush and so on, a folder of papers about chemicals in food, another concerned with the family business which had brought him to LA to see his sister Felice, and a sort of picnic basket. That fitted, too; he'd have brought his own food along, the good wholesome kind the wat community grew themselves.

Stanway coughed in the phone. It started as a polite attention-catching noise; a few seconds, and it developed into a real cough, punctuated with gasps of, "Sorry!" When he recovered, he said, "Was there anything else?"

"No." Absently. "Thanks very much for letting me know."

Having hung up she sat for long minutes staring at nothing. Anger burned in her mind like a sullen flame.

She was convinced—beyond the possibility of argument—Decimus must have been poisoned.

But how? By whom? They'd backtracked on his route, discovered a couple of truck-drivers who'd noticed him asleep in the park outside a diner when they stopped for a snack, then found him awake when they came out again, shaving in the men's room; also a gas station where he'd filled up—and that was that. No one else seemed to have seen or spoken to him on the way.

And his sister, of course, knew nothing useful. She'd refused to be interviewed directly after his death, claiming with good grounds that since she hadn't met her brother in years she hardly knew him, but then the make-up for their December 23rd issue had been half a column short and Peg had dashed off a moralizing Christmassy bit about Decimus which Mel reluctantly approved with only minor changes, and Felice had seen it and called up and thanked her. But they still hadn't met, and it was clear from the way she spoke that she didn't sympathize with her brother's views.

That food. Had it been analyzed? No, of course not. And it was mainly crumbs anyhow. Probably just thrown out...

Sudden decision. She reached for the phone again and this time by a minor miracle got through to Angel City first go. She asked for Felice.

"I'm afraid she's in conference right now. Shall I take a message?"

Peg hesitated. "Yes! Yes, tell her Peg Mankiewicz called. Tell her that her brother was definitely poisoned."

"I'm sorry, I don't quite understand." And a sneeze, hastily apologized for.

"Oh, shit," Peg said wearily. "Never mind."

She found her eyesight was blurred. Tears? No. Watering. And her forehead tight and starting to throb. Hell and damnation, another lousy bout of sinusitis.

She hurried to the water-cooler to wash down her belated pill.

AND IT GOES ON *. . . and Dr. Isaiah Williams, whose body was recovered from a ravine near San Pablo. Inquiries are being hampered by what an Army spokesman termed the obstinate attitude of the local people. "They won't admit they know their left hands from their right," he asserted. Here at home Senator Richard Howell (Rep., Col.) today launched a fierce attack on the quote chlorophyll addicts unquote who, he claims, are hamstringing American business, already staggering under the load of high unemployment and recession, by insisting that our manufacturers comply with regulations ignored by foreign competition. In Southern Italy rioting continues in many small towns formerly dependent on fishing. Meantime, dust storms in the Camargue . . .*

EARTHMOVER "Hi, Fred!"

"Hi!"

Austin Train/Fred Smith continued up the stairs. It was incredibly noisy here—squalling kids, TV sound, radio, a record, someone practicing drums, and ahead on the top floor his neighbors the Blores quarreling again. Their apartment was like a bombed site. Either there would be murder done one day, or the eventual victor would inherit a mere heap of rubble.

Which was full of lessons for today. But the hell with it. He was tired, and the cut on his leg which he'd sustained a couple of days ago had swollen up and begun to throb. It looked as though it might be infected.

Pausing as he thrust his key into his own door, he noticed there was a new graffito on the landing, the Trainite slogan: YOU'RE KILLING ME.

In purple lipstick. Very fashionable.

He glanced around, not really worried as to whether someone had broken in during his absence and robbed him, apart from the inconvenience of having to buy replacements. This belonged to Fred Smith, not Austin Train. The store-closet and icebox were full of commonplace cheap foods (if any food could be called cheap nowadays): canned, frozen, freeze-dried, irradiated, precooked and even predigested. The walls were chipped and needed paint. The windows were mostly okay but one pane was blocked with cardboard. There were fleas the exterminator couldn't kill and rats that scrabbled in the walls and mice who left droppings like a cocked snook and roaches that thrived on insecticide, even the illegal kinds. He wouldn't touch those himself—that would have been carrying his "Fred Smith" role too far—but everyone else in the house knew where to score for DDT and dieldrin and so forth, and it hadn't helped.

He didn't really see his surroundings, though. One could live this way, and he was proving it. It meant something to him to be here. It implied—

Hope? Possibly. Suppose that great heretic St. Francis of Assisi had been put (as he, Austin Train, had been) in front of twenty-eight million viewers on the Petronella Page Show and told to define his reasons for behaving as he did. We are told that "the meek shall inherit the earth." It follows that the meek are chosen of God. I shall try to be meek, not because I want the earth—you can keep it, after the way you've fucked it around it's not worth having—but because I too should like to be chosen of God. QED.

Besides, I like animals better than you bastards.

Of all the vices human beings are capable of, Austin Train detested hypocrisy most. He hadn't realized that until a matter of three years or so ago, following the period of notoriety which had begun a couple of years before with the publication of his *Handbook for 3000 AD*. Prior to that he had enjoyed moderate success; a group of his books had been reissued as matched paperbacks and attracted attention from an increasingly worried public, but it had all been low-key stuff. Suddenly, one might say overnight, he had become a celebrity, in demand for TV interviews, commissioned to write for popular journals, called in as consultant on government committees. And then, equally abruptly, stop.

He had six hundred thousand dollars in the bank and lived in a slum tenement in the heart of a dying city.

Back there—he had come to think of it as another world—lying and fakery were a way of life. Sponsoring the programs on which he appeared as Cassandra: a plastics company, daily pouring half a million gallons of hot and poisoned water into a river that served eleven cities before it reached the ocean. Printing the articles he wrote: a corporation whose paper demanded the felling of half a forest every month. Ruling the country which paraded him as a prime example of the benefits of free speech: madmen who had made a desert and misnamed it peace.

It made him sick.

Literally.

He lay in the hospital for two months, shivering without cease, spat at people who came to wish him well, tore up cables from strangers saying they hoped he'd get better quickly, threw food on the floor because it was poisoned, caught nurses around the neck and lectured them, helplessly pinioned, on egg-bundle fetus, sulphur dioxide, lead alkyls, DDE. Not that they heard much of what he told them. They were screaming too loudly.

When they released him, doped on tranquilizers, he went to live with the people who didn't make a professional habit of omitting to let their left hands know. He settled in the dirtiest back streets of the city he'd been born in. He'd considered alternatives: Barcelona, by the open cesspool of the Mediterranean; the rabbit-warrens of Rome, almost permanently under martial law; Osaka, where they were marketing airlocks to be fitted in place of regular front doors. Still, he wanted to be able to talk to the people around him—so he came home. "I am a man," he had said many times during his moment of fame. "I am as guilty as you, and you are as guilty as me. We can repent together, or we can die together; it must be our joint decision."

He hadn't expected to leave behind, in that world he'd abandoned, such a surprising legacy: the Trainites, who had no formal organization, not even a newspaper, yet now and then manifested themselves—one might almost believe as the result of some telepathic trigger, some upsurge of the collective unconscious—to put a brand on some company or enterprise that was endangering mankind. Obviously, he had not created them. They must have been there, waiting. Mainly they were the former radical students for whom it had become a matter of principle to say, "Yes, I'm a commie!" That habit had followed the Vietnam disaster, when the tons upon thousands of tons of herbicides, defoliants, riot gases, toxic agents, had finally broken the land down into desert. All of a sudden, in a single summer, dead plants, dead animals, dead rivers.

Dead people.

And when he popularized the term "commensalist" a little later, the reference was rapidly transferred. But didn't stick. Instead the news media invented the name "Trainite," and now it was universal.

He was half pleased by the flattery this implied, half frightened for complex reasons of which he had cited one to Peg. He dreamed occasionally of meeting the men who had taken his name in place of their own, and would wake sweating and moaning, because that led to visions of endless millions of identical people, impossible to tell apart.

Anyway, here he was in half the upper floor of a derelict building in downtown LA, formerly offices, converted to dwellings five years ago, never repaired or painted since. The people around him, though, didn't lie except to protect their egos, and he found that tolerable. What he loathed was a deed such as he would no longer term a crime, but a sin. Unto the third and fourth generation, General Motors, you have visited your greed on the children. Unto the twentieth, AEC, you have twisted their limbs and closed their eyes. Unto the last dawn of man you have cursed us, O Father. Our Father. Our Father Which art in Washington, give us this day our daily calcium propionate, sodium diacetate monoglyceride, potassium bromate, calcium phosphate, monobasic chloramine T, aluminium potassium sulphate, sodium benzoate, butylated hydroxyanisole, mono-iso-propyl citrate, axerophthol and calciferol. Include with it a little flour and salt.

Amen.

Something had infected his hair-roots and eyebrows, that made the skin flake away in dry crusty yellow scurf and left little raw patches of exposed flesh. He rubbed in a lotion Mrs. Blore had recommended; she and her husband suffered from the same complaint, and so did the kids on the lower floor. The lotion certainly helped—his scalp wasn't nearly as sore as it had been last week.

Then he ate, absently, not so much food as fuel: tasting of cottonwool or cardboard, the human counterpart of the fertilizers they were continuing to pour on land that daily grew more and more barren, hardened, scoriated, turned to dust. Like his scalp. He was shaping something he sensed to be important. He had given up books, even his favorites: the Bible, the *Bhagavad-Gita*, the *Precepts of Patanjali*, the *I Ching*, the *Popul Vuh*, the *Book of the Dead*...

If I don't know enough now, I shall never know enough. I couldn't stand that.

While he ate, he was thinking. While he worked during the day, he had been thinking. He had a job with the city sanitation department, and garbage was full of morals: sermons in trash-cans, books in running drains.

The others on the gang he worked with thought he was odd, maybe touched in the head. Could be. What had touched him, though, felt—significant. Suddenly, in recent weeks, the conviction had come on him: I matter. I count. I have an insight. I think a thing no one else thinks. I believe with the certainty of faith. I must *must* make others hear and understand.

When it is time.

At night, when he lay down to sleep, he felt that his brain was resonating with the heartbeat of the planet.

SHOWDOWN

"Get me a wig—quickly!"

Startled by the shout, Terry Fenton glanced up from inventorying his equipment: paints, powders, dyes, lacquers—all of the finest quality, of course, Peruvian and Mexican, based on herbal essences and vegetable waxes and flower pigments, not a trace of anything synthetic. Nothing but the best for Terry Fenton. He was at the apex of his profession, senior makeup supervisor for the entire New York studio complex of ABS, far more trendily clad and infinitely better groomed than almost all the stars who nightly fed visual pablum to the admass.

"Pet! Christ, what have you done to your *hair*?"

Forty, but glamorous and rigorously dieted slim, Petronella Page stormed to her usual chair. She was wearing a magnificent pants suit in abstract scarlet and yellow and her face was so flawless Terry would as ever need to add only minor touches. But her hair was streaked with irregular muddy marks.

She ran the Monday and Wednesday late-night talk show, and was popular, and expected to take on Friday as well because the trans-Atlantic commuting compère, the Englishman Adrian Sprague, was verging on a nervous breakdown at long-awaited last and moreover had missed three shows in three months owing to bomb scares aboard the planes he was taking.

"I'll sue the mother!" she said between clenched teeth as the full horror of her appearance clanged back from the merciless mirrors.

"But what *happened?*" Terry snapped his fingers and his current assistant, Marlon, a light-brown boy who adored him, absolutely adored him, and thought Petronella was okay—for a woman, you know—came scurrying into the room. So also, a moment later, did Lola Crown, assistant to Ian Farley the producer, with a pile of briefing documents concerning the night's guests. The show was due on camera in about twenty minutes.

"Thank God you finally made it!" Lola cried. "Ian's been pissing himself!"

"Shut up! Drop dead!" Petronella rasped, and slapped the papers out of Lola's hand as she offered them. "I don't give a fart who we have on the show, not if it's the stinking King of England! I sure as hell am *not* going out looking like this!"

"You won't have to, baby," Terry soothed, inspecting the discolored tresses. Lola, on the point of weeping, went down on hands and knees to reclaim the scattered papers. "Lord, though, why didn't you have it done at Guido's same as usual?"

"This happened at Guido's."

"What?" Terry was horrified. He insisted on everyone he handled having their hair washed, styled, cut at Guido's, because it was the only place in New York where they guaranteed their shampoos were done with imported rainwater. They shipped it specially from Chile.

"Silver nitrate," Petronella sighed. "I contacted Guido at home and blew my stack, and he checked up and called back almost weeping. Seems they've been rainmaking down there—remember I had a rainmaker on the show last year? Guido thinks it reacted with the setting lotion."

Marlon brought a choice of wigs. Terry seized one, and a brush and comb and aerosol of lacquer. He brutally sabotaged Guido's efforts into a tight layer close to the scalp and set about re-creating the same style on the wig.

"Going to take long?" Petronella demanded.

"Couple of minutes," Terry said. He forbore to add that anything Guido's best stylist could do, he could copy, only in a tenth of the time. Everyone knew how good he was.

"Thank God. Lola, you bitch, where are my briefings?"

"Here!" the girl snuffled. Petronella flicked through the pages.

"Oh, yes, I remember. Jacob Bamberley—"

"He likes to be called Jack!" Lola cut in.

"Stuff what he likes. *I* run this show. Terry baby, we got the man who sent all that poisoned shit to Africa. Know what I'm going to make him do? I'm going to make him eat a bowlful of it right at the start of the show, then come back to him at the end so people can see what it's done to him."

Turning to the next briefing, she added thoughtfully, "And I shall definitely call him Jacob."

This was a Globe Relief operation on behalf of Globe Relief. When it became clear that Kaika's accusations weren't just propaganda, it had been a matter of panic stations all around. It was no use stressing the true fact that Globe was the largest aid organization on the planet and invariably the soonest on the scene of a disaster. Simply because it was American-based and American-funded, it was tarred with the Vietnam brush. There was almost certain to be a UN inquiry shortly.

Accordingly State had made it very clear that unless Globe came up promptly with a full defense the organization would have to be thrown to the wolves. Inestimable trouble had already been caused by black militants instantly prepared to believe in chemical genocide.

The obvious steps had naturally been taken. Samples of the Nutripon still in store had been analyzed and given a clean bill. Now suspicion had turned on the yeasts and fungi in the hydroponics plant: could a rogue, akin say to the ergot mold of rye, have infected one batch of the stuff with a natural psychedelic poison? It would have helped if they'd had a sample from Noshri to study, but apparently it had all been consumed or burned during the riots. So it was going to be a slow job.

Casting around for some form of distraction, the directors of Globe had realized that Jacob Bamberley was due in New York for his monthly visit to the headquarters of the Bamberley Trust, and seen a heaven-sent chance to pass the buck one stage further. They pulled a lot of strings extremely hard. The Petronella Page Show had a nightly audience of around thirty million; sometimes on a Monday when people stayed home after the heavy spending of a weekend, it approached forty. To be exposed on it, moveover, meant a lot of spin-off in newspaper and magazine publicity. They wanted that exposure now, today. "Thrice armed is he whose cause is just, but four times he who gets a blow in fust."

Besides, if war is hell, so is peace.

So here he was under the bright studio lights, flanked on one side by Gerry Thorne from Globe, small and tense and with a tic in his left cheek, and on the other by Moses Greenbriar, senior treasurer of the Bamberley Trust, a fat and jolly man who could answer any questions about the financing of the hydroponics plant.

Terry and his wig had worked a miracle. Nonetheless Petronella was still in a foul mood when she took her place. She cheered up slightly as the first commercials were run, because they had wonderful sponsors on this show and inasmuch as she was proud of anything she was proud of these: Puritan Health Supermarkets, Hailey Cars —or rather the agency which imported them from Britain, where they cost too much to be common—and Johnson & Johnson's filtermasks. Even so the smile she bestowed on the audience was forced.

"Hi, world!" And, mindful of their status as a representative cross-section of the species Man, they echoed her.

"Now this time we got for you people who are very much making news, and people we predict will make the news tomorrow. And not only here but half around the world, such as for instance in Africa."

Ah, good. She didn't have to tell Ian Farley more than once about anything. As arranged, the cameras had picked up on Mr. Bamberley, ignoring the men at his left and right, and were closing like the gun-muzzles of a firing squad.

"We've all been shocked and horrified by the outbreak of—well, mass insanity that occurred at Noshri before Christmas. Just as we thought that terrible war was finally over, we've seen the pictures and heard the stories of people literally running amok. We've even heard accusations of"—hushed—"cannibalism among the starving survivors.

"Now it's been charged that poison in relief supplies caused these people to go out of their minds. Specifically, a consignment of Nutripon from the Bamberley hydroponics plant near Denver, Colorado . . ."

Bless you, Ian baby!

Farley had kept one camera practically squinting up Mr. Bamberley's nostrils throughout the intro. Of course that wasn't what stayed on the monitor all the time; the audience and Petronella had been intercut. But Bamberley wasn't to know that. He was visibly afraid to twist around and get a sight of the monitor, in case he *was* on it.

Oh, Ian baby, I don't have to tell you, do I?

"Jacob! You don't mind if I call you Jacob?" With a dazzling smile.

"Well, people usually—"

"I'm sure they do. No one with such a reputation for good works could be other than on the best of terms with everyone." The voice syrupy, the tiniest fraction too far in the direction of sentimentality. "So now, Jacob, this stuff Nutripon that's been called in question—what exactly does it consist of?"

"Well, it's cassava, processed in a way not unlike making cheese—"

"Cassava. I see." Time to let the smile make way for a slight frown. "Now I'm no expert on this"—though the briefings had been thorough as always and she was a quick study—"but I seem to remember cassava is kind of a dangerous plant to meddle with. Eye disease, isn't that right?"

"Well, I guess you must be referring to cassava amblyopia, which is—"

"An eye condition?" She noticed, though the admass didn't because the camera wasn't on the guy, that Gerry Thorne reflexively touched one of his own eyes at that. Right; he'd had conjunctivitis recently. And now here he was pulling out a pair of shades against the brilliant lights. Splendid. He looked positively sinister in them. Prompt to his unspoken cue, Ian pulled back his camera.

"Yes, but you see Nutripon is fortified—"

"Just a second!" The word was on the teleprompter, but she hadn't needed the reminder; it was too full of possibilities. "I hadn't quite covered my point. Isn't there cyanide in cassava?"

"In the raw rind, yes, but not after it's been processed!" Mr. Bamberley was sweating. Petronella looked forward to the moment when he would begin to squirm. His companions had reached it already.

"You claim your treatment makes it quite safe?"

"Oh, yes!"

"Are the details of the treatment a trade secret, or can anybody hear them?"

"Goodness, not in the least secret! Though I'm afraid if you want the technical details you'd have to—"

"Yes, we appreciate that you're not a hydroponics expert. You do grow the stuff hydroponically, right?"

"Quite correct, we do."

"That means you grow it artificially, in sand or cellulite, in controlled conditions with a solution of nutrient chemicals. That's what 'hydroponics' means, isn't it?" Barb after barb stabbing into the audience's ears, fresh from their exposure to the Puritan commercial with its emphasis on food grown in the open air, in natural soil.

"Yes. Uh—yes!" Mr. Bamberley was becoming confused. Beside him Greenbriar, the fat man, was signaling with his eyebrows: *Call on me, I can cope!*

Ho no, baby. *Ho* no! We aren't here to help Globe Relief justify itself to all those blacks who already believe your charley outfit has been genociding their African cousins. No more are we here to help you elude the stockholders in the Bamberley Trust who resent seeing what might have been profit in their pockets squandered on ungrateful bastards overseas. No, baby! That ain't what we're here for at all!

Like to know what we are here for? Then stick around.

She smiled again, sweetly. "There are no doubt reasons for growing your cassava in this way. Does it have anything to do with reducing the amount of cyanide in it?"

"No, no, no! The most important reason is that we need something that's widely acceptable in those areas where famine is likeliest to strike, and cassava is—"

"Yes, you ship everything you make abroad, don't you?" Petronella inserted, with the precision of a surgeon's scalpel. The breath he was taking to launch into the next segment of his prepared exposition had to be diverted to a different purpose.

"Well, yes, everything we make does go for aid projects."

"And this is a non-profit operation?" Petronella said, knowing the official answer. "You are, after all, one of the richest men in the world; according to its last annual report the Bamberley Trust disposes of assets in excess of half a billion dollars. Don't you take any profit on your relief contracts?"

"Definitely not! At most we aim to cover our costs. The hydroponics plant is absolutely *not* required to make a profit."

"Why not?"

The phrase stuck there, as though a thrown knife had found a lodging in mid-air. Mr. Bamberley blinked.

"I beg your pardon?"

"I asked why not. All your other business interests have to, or you get rid of them. During the past year, for instance, you disposed of a chain of supermarkets in Tennessee, which hadn't shown a profit in two years, and shed all your airline holdings. Well?"

"Uh—well!" Mr. Bamberley did exactly what she had hoped he would, and Thorne and Greenbriar had been praying he would *not* do: tugged a handkerchief from his pocket and wiped his face. It was very hot under the lights—designedly so. "Well, I regard this as a . . . Well, a charitable undertaking, you see. A practical way of helping people with my—uh—my good fortune."

"Not the only expression of your charitable impulses, I gather," Petronella murmured.

"No, of course not. I believe—I mean, I'm a Christian and all Christians should believe—that we're the children of the Lord, made in His image, and no man is an island, heh-heh!" Terribly embarrassed, like so many professing a religion when faced with admitting the fact before anonymous millions. But sincere. Oh, *painfully* sincere.

"Yes, I'm told you've surrounded yourself with boys who've been orphaned. Eight of them right now."

"Ah, you mean my adopted sons. Well, yes. It's one thing, isn't it, to send aid to some faraway country? And something else again to bring deserving cases into your own home." Blinking on every word, flicker-flicker.

In the goldfish bowl Ian making fierce gestures: don't lean on the queer bit too hard. But the hell with him.

The Bible Belt goes to bed early, this may be the last chance to catch them.

"We've talked a lot about adoption on this show recently—because of the success of the Double-V scheme, of course. Are you a patron of Double-V?"

"Ah . . . As a matter of fact, no, because there are after all a great many orphans right here in this country. Worse still, children abandoned by their parents!"

"Yes, that is an alarming problem, isn't it? We had a social worker on the show last month who mentioned just that point, in connection with these gangs of black kids who have taken to terrorizing city centers. She said thousands of them have suffered just as badly as the Asian children who are being adopted in. But none of your—ah—sons are black, are they?"

Dead silence. Just long enough to let the point fester. And then resuming in a let's-get-on-with-it tone, "Well, I guess that's by the way, Jacob. Your private life is your concern and presumably a white Protestant is entitled to prefer white Protestant boys." Fester, fester! "So let's get back to the main line of the discussion."

That was one of her favorite words. Sharp-tongued guests on the show sometimes managed to sneak in the more accurate term, "interrogation," but tonight she was in top form, and even though Thorne was pale and shaking and Greenbriar almost bouncing up and down with fury, neither had contrived to interrupt her. Maybe she wouldn't sue Guido after all. Blessings in disguise, and all that shit.

"So anyhow: what have you to say to the charge that the food you sent to Noshri was poisoned?"

"As God is my witness, Nutripon is wholesome and delicious!" Mr. Bamberley sat up very straight and jutted his jaw forward as though trying to look like Winston Churchill.

"I'm glad to hear it. But have you yourself been to Noshri to investigate, or any of your associates?" Naturally not; Kaika had booted the American relief workers out of the country and broken off diplomatic relations.

"Ah . . ." Mr. Bamberley was trembling now, enough for the cameras to pick it up. "It simply hasn't been possible—but our quality controls are of the highest standard, we test the product at every stage of manufacture!"

"So the consignment in question must have been poisoned after it left the factory?"

"I'm not admitting it was poisoned at all!"

Got him. He'd actually used the word. And it was clear how dreadful an effect that had had on Thorne and Greenbriar. The admass would have seen, too; Ian had pulled back his cameras. The man being pilloried between two thieves. Everyone but *everyone* knew about those two—mansion homes, luxury cars, private planes . . .

"Never mind! *We'd*"—identifying emphasis, you out there for whom I speak—"like to conduct a small experiment of our own, which won't of course be scientifically rigorous but may indicate *something* . . . " Camera 1 pulled in on her and she spoke confidingly to it.

"This afternoon we sent one of our staff to Kennedy International Airport, where a consignment of this processed cassava was being loaded on a chartered aircraft. We bought a carton of it." Not *case*. Overtones of breakfast cereal. "We paid the price on the loading manifest, which was eighty-three dollars—oh, don't worry that we deprived anybody! We substituted food of equivalent value, such as powdered milk and dried egg and bags of flour, and put that into the shipment to replace what we'd taken.

"Then we brought the stuff back here, and followed the instructions on the packet precisely, and—well, here's the result. Lola?"

Recovered from her pre-show fit of sniveling, Lola came smiling on to the stage carrying a tray on which reposed a large bowl, steaming slightly, a spoon and fork, and a cruet. A glass of water was already in front of Mr. Bamberley.

"Jacob, a random sample of your relief supplies. May we see you eat it?"

"Well, yes!" Running a finger around his collar—but what else could he say? "I did have . . ."

"Yes?"

He had been going to add: a very rich dinner. But one couldn't admit that, not when the subject was the feeding of starving millions. (And all across the country one could almost hear people saying, "Eighty-three dollars? For that muck?") He compromised. "I did have dinner before I came to the studio, so I may not have much of an appetite, but I'll be glad to prove that this is safe to eat!"

Thorne and Greenbriar looked frightened—the latter especially, wishing he hadn't fed his employer so well. Suppose he were taken ill, not because of the Nutripon but because of that dish of eggplants in oil, or the lobster! Seafood was such a gamble nowadays, even with an FDA certificate . . .

"That's a good boy, Jacob!" Petronella approved ironically. "Well, world, here's a sight to remember: one of this rich country's richest men eating a sample of the diet we ship to poverty-stricken, famine-ridden lands overseas. Later on, at the end of the show, we'll call Jacob back and ask how he liked his unexpected snack."

Under the table, out of camera view, she couldn't resist the temptation to rub her hands.

But . . .

"What the hell?" She spoke very softly to the mike in the right-hand wing of her throne-like chair, the one which was reserved for outright emergencies. Ian was signaling frantically from the goldfish bowl, and suddenly his voice rang out from the speaker under its window.

"Ladies and gentlemen, I'm afraid we shall have to discontinue the show. Please proceed calmly to the exits. We've been warned that there is a bomb in the building. We're sure this is a hoax, but—"

They screamed.

Panicked.

Fought like maddened animals, charging the doors. One of the doors broke off its hinges and a girl was cut across the face by its fall and the rest pushed her out of the way and she tripped and they walked on her, stamped on her, broke her ribs and her nose and crushed her left hand into blue pulp.

But they got out, which was all they cared about.

"The bomb is for you, Mr. Bamberley," Ian Farley said as he, Petronella, others of the staff took their backstage route to the street.

"What?" He was whiter than his own Nutripon: pasty, like raw dough.

"Yes. Someone called up and said he was black and a cousin of the people you've been poisoning in Africa, and he was going to take revenge on their behalf."

FEBRUARY

IN PRAISE OF BIOCIDE

Than fund he ther fisceras: and weltoghte fugeleras,
The makede hym mickel welcom: as maistre of londes.
Craft was in hir kilyng: with hem the cyning
Than hyede hym to hontyng: hartis and brockis.
Fowlis and faunis: fain had the fled hym,
Sauf that his sotil shaft: strock hem on ronyng.
Ol that war on lyve: overcam he of bestis.
Togh it ben to tel: talye of targetis.
For that
Ferce fukkis: felte smerte,
Dove and dawe: darte to herte,
Faible falwe: fel aperte,
Deth draggede: divers sterte.
Wantede the water: welvers ne froggis,
Scars war to se: sluggis ne snakis.
Than cam the croude: to cyninges hal again.
Ful war the festers: fourten daies fed the.
So fal the Saxon: so be hir sloghter,
So befal foemen: wold frighten hys relme . . .

—"The Chronicle of That Great Progress Made by our Lord the King through his Eastern Lands This Summer Past," 938 (text corrupt, a late copy by a post-Conquest scribe).

THIS HURTS ME MORE

Yesterday Phelan Murphy had stood by, sick at heart, while the government man argued about the cattle with Dr. Advowson. It was very cold; it was the coldest and longest winter in ten years. The pastures were in terrible condition. Some were still under snow from the November falls, and those which were snow-free were naturally overgrazed. To keep his stock alive he had had to buy bales of hay and dump them around the fields. It had been expensive, because the land had been in a poor state last summer, too. Some said—it had even been in *The Independent*—that it had to do with smoke from the factories near Shannon Airport.

But the government man had said he didn't know anything about that.

Now, today, he was back, with soldiers. The market at Balpenny was not to be held. They had brought big signs saying LIMISTÉAR CORAINTÍN and set them up on the roadside. More cows had died in the night, bellies bloated, blood leaking from their mouths and nostrils, frozen smears of blood under their tails. Before the children were allowed to go to school they had to dip their rubber boots in pans of milky disinfectant. The same had been sprayed on the tires of the bus.

The soldiers took spades and picks and dug holes in the frozen ground, and brought bags of quicklime. Cows too weak to try and move away allowed the humane killer to be put to their heads: thud. Again, a minute later: thud. And again.

Bridie had wept most of the night, and the children—not knowing why—had copied her.

"Damned fools!" Dr. Advowson kept repeating and repeating under his breath, chewing his pipe at Phelan's side. "I did my best to stop them, but—oh, the damned *idiots!*"

"There'll be compensation," the government man said, listing on a long printed form the details of the animals that were being killed.

Then the soldiers dragged the carcasses to the pits.

THE CONTINUING DEBATE

. . . left for Honduras this morning. Questioned concerning his decision just prior to his annual birthday banquet and family reunion at which he is slated to deliver a major speech on overseas aid, Prexy

said, quote, Those Tupas got to understand that if you bite the hand that feeds you, you're apt to get a mouthful of fist. End quote. Pressure for a UN inquiry into the Noshri tragedy continues to grow. Trainites and black militant groups are threatening to attack planes carrying further relief consignments if this is not done immediately, according to various anonymous letters and phone calls received recently at our studios. Hopes are high that the matter may however be settled without such an inquiry. In Paris this morning famed scientist Dr. Louis-Marie Duval, who has been examining a group of the survivors . . .

FIRE WHEN READY

"No, Peg, it won't do," Mel Torrance said, and exploded into a sneeze.

She looked at him with hurt in her eyes: knowing it showed, hating herself for letting it show, unable to prevent it. He held out to her the draft of the story she'd given him; when she made no move to accept it he let it go, and it sideslipped over the desk edge, settling to the floor like a tired untidy bird.

"I'm sick of your obsession with this lousy bastard Jones! He's been dead since December. It's been proved he was stoned when he died. I am *not* about to give houseroom to your crazy fantasies about him being poisoned!"

"But—"

He rushed on. "Listen, will you? Now Jones was a Trainite, right? And these Trainites are getting to be a filthy nuisance! They block traffic, they foul up business, they commit sabotage, they've even gone as far as murder—"

"Nonsense!"

"That man in San Francisco last fall?"

"He'd shot a girl, an unarmed girl!" Peg was trembling from head to foot.

"He died of his acid burns, didn't he? Are you saying these mothers have the right to take the law into their own hands? Are they vigilantes? Are they a lynch-mob?"

"I—"

"Yes, yes, *yes!*" Mel stormed. "Every last bunch of Trainites is a potential lynch-mob! I don't give a fart what they claim their motives are—I judge by results, and what I see is that they wreck, they destroy, and when it comes to the crunch, they kill."

"The killers are the people who are ruining the world to line their pockets, poisoning us, burying us under garbage!"

"Are you a Trainite, Peg?"

Drawing back, she passed her hand over her face. "I —I guess I sympathize," she said at length. "I mean in LA you have to. Beaches fouled with oil and sewage, air so bad you can't go out without a mask, the water at your sink reeking of chlorine . . ." Her forehead was pounding again; her sinus trouble was dragging endlessly on.

"Sure, there's some truth in all that. Like up at our place in Sherman Oaks we lost half the flowers in our garden last summer—bad wind from somewhere, had defoliants in it so we couldn't even make compost out of what was left. Sure, things aren't exactly like paradise. But that's no reason for making them like hell, is it? That's what these Trainites are doing. They don't offer something better than what we already have, or if they did I'd sign on like a shot and so would just about everybody. But they simply spoil it and leave rubble in its place."

He sneezed again, cursed and grabbed an inhaler from the corner of his desk. Peg said, feeling helpless, "You don't understand what they're trying to do. If you'd known Decimus you might—"

"I've heard all I ever want to hear about your Decimus," Mel snapped. "Last chance, Peg. Get down off this hobbyhorse of yours, start doing the same kind of good work you used to, or quit."

"I quit."

"Good. Goodbye. I'll make sure the accounts department issues your month's salary in lieu of notice. Now take that litter off my floor and pack your gear. I'm busy."

Outside, rising from a chair, a pretty colored girl who said, "Ah, you must be Peg Mankiewicz. I'm Felice Jones — Why, what's wrong?"

"I've been fired," Peg said bitterly.

"No, you haven't!" A shout from Mel's office. "I heard that! You resigned!"

THE NATURAL LOOK *Did you ever study the small print on a cosmetics package?*

Ever try to pronounce the jaw-breaking words? Ever find you were below your best at a party—or on a date with a very special man—because you were wondering what all those complicated chemicals might be?

You can always pronounce what we put in MAYA PURA.

Try it right now. Say "natural." Say "flower petals." Say "herbal essence."

See?

Yes, of course. And because you see, other people will notice.

POSSESSION IS NINE POINTS *"Retro me, Sathanas!"* the priest roared: haggard, unshaven, his cassock filthy with mud and dried blood. He held up his crucifix before the advancing jeep. Behind him the people of the village stood their ground, fearful but determined, many armed with ancient guns and the rest with whatever came to hand—axes, machetes, knives.

From the jeep two men got down on opposite sides. One was called Irving S. Hannigan; he'd come from Washington to investigate the death of Leonard Ross.

He wasn't enjoying the assignment. It was like trying to catch a handful of smoke, because everyone you talked to who might know anything helpful seemed to lose touch with reality without warning and go off rambling about angels and the Queen of Heaven.

The other was Major José Concepción Madariaga de Crizo García, youngest son of one of the country's largest landowners, raised from the cradle to command instant obedience from the rabble.

"Make way, you old fool!" he rasped. "Hurry up!"

The priest stood his ground, fixing him with wild bloodshot eyes. Sensing something he hadn't expected, the major glanced at the American for advice. This Hannigan was apparently some kind of detective, or spy, or government agent at any rate, and might have the "common touch" inaccessible to an officer and an aristocrat.

"These people don't look like a Tupa resistance group to me," Hannigan murmured. "Try telling them we've brought food."

That was as might be, the major thought. The problem with Tupamaros was that they always looked like just anybody—a valet, a cook, a clerk in a store—until the crunch came. However, the idea was a sound one; the rabble were always much concerned with their bellies.

He said in a soothing tone, "Father, we have come to help your people. The government has sent us with food and medicine."

"We have had this kind of help before," the priest rumbled. He looked and sounded as though he had been without proper sleep for a month. "But do you bring holy water from the Vatican?"

"What?"

"Do you bring sacred relics that will frighten devils?"

The major shook his head, bewildered.

"They're agents of the devil themselves!" shouted a burly man who had been standing at the back of the crowd with a shotgun. Now he battered his way to the front, taking station beside the priest.

"The town is full of wicked spirits!" he cried. "Men, women, even children are possessed! We've seen the demons walk through walls, enter our homes, even trespass in the church!"

"True!" the priest said, and clutched his crucifix very tightly.

"Ah, they're out of their minds," the major muttered. "Or pretending to be! Let's see how they like a volley over their heads!"

Hannigan scowled. "If they are crazy, it won't do any good. If they aren't, we'll learn more by playing along with them. Try again."

Sighing, but aware of who was in charge, the major turned back to the priest, who suddenly spat in the dirt at his feet.

"We want nothing to do with you," he said. "Or your foreign masters. Go to the bishop, if he can spare a moment from his mistresses. Go to the cardinal, if he isn't too busy stuffing his belly. Tell them our poor hamlet of San Pablo is infested with devils. Bring us the kind of help that will exorcise them. Meantime we know our duty. We shall fast and pray."

"Aye!" chorused the villagers.

"Yes, but while you're fasting," Hannigan cut in in fair Spanish, "your children are likely to starve, aren't they?"

"Better to starve and go to heaven than live possessed by imps of Satan," rasped the burly man. "Holy water from Rome, that's what we need! Use your airplanes to bring us that!"

"You could bless the food we've brought," Hannigan insisted. "Sprinkle it with water from your church font—"

"We're accursed!" the priest burst out. "Holy water here has no effect! It's the time of the coming of Antichrist!"

A gun went off. Hannigan and the major dropped reflexively on their bellies. Over their heads the soldiers in the jeeps returned a withering fire, and the priest and his congregation fell like wheat before the scythe.

Obviously they must have been Tupas after all.

THE OFFER OF RESISTANCE

It was the third time Philip Mason had come to the cheerless waiting room of the Market Street clinic, decorated solely with warning posters. But it was the first time he'd found the place so empty. Before, he'd found it crowded with youngsters. Today only one other patient was present, and instead of being teenaged or in his twenties, he was in his late thirties, well-dressed, growing comfortably plump, and in general assignable to Philip's own social bracket.

Before Philip could take refuge as usual behind some shabby back issue of *Scientific American* or *The National Geographic*, the stranger had caught his eye and grinned at him. He was dark-haired, brown-eyed, clean-shaven, in general unremarkable bar two things: his obvious atypical prosperity and a small round scar on the back of his left hand. A bullet mark?

"Morning!" he said in precisely that matter-of-fact tone Philip would have liked to be able to command but couldn't. The whole world was leaning on him. Denise was permanently hurt by his behavior. The Towerhill avalanche was still spawning so many claims he hadn't dared punch for the total for over a week. And . . .

Oh, that mother Clayford! But it was a Pyrrhic victory to know he was going to lose his fees for insurance examinations.

He dived into the shelter of a magazine he'd already read.

In a little while they called his number and he went for the regular humiliating treatment—massage with a sterile-gloved finger up his anus, a drip of prostatic secretion smeared on a slide. Things had been better the past few days and then this morning they'd been worse again, and Dennie—

Stop, stop. He was in the office of Dr. McNeil, and the doctor was youthful, casual, unprejudiced. Philip liked this man a few years his junior, who kept a silly doll of a Highland bagpiper on the corner of his desk. He'd come here the first time almost incapable of talking, and McNeil had drawn him out in minutes, making him feel —just so long as he was in the office—that this really was a complaint anyone might suffer from, not to be ashamed of, easily put right. Though not, of course, under any circumstances to be neglected.

"How are you getting on?" McNeil said, taking the folder Philip had brought with him and extracting the morning's test report to add to the file of Mason Philip A. #605-193.

Philip told him.

"I see." McNeil plucked his lower lip. "Well, I guess that's not too surprising. The strain of G you have"—he always said "G," not gonorrhea—"seems to be resistant."

"Oh my God. You mean I'm not cured?"

"No, not yet. Says this report." McNeil shut the file with a slap, memorializing another stage in the development of the disaster. "Still, there's definitely no indication of syph, which is a comfort—sometimes those spirochetes can be right buggers. Say! Don't look as if the world's about to end!"

He chuckled, leaning back in his chair. "I'm afraid your problem's getting commoner and commoner. You're not a health-food addict, are you?"

"Uh . . . Not seriously," Philip muttered. "Though we buy from Puritan pretty often." Wondering what on earth this had to do with VD.

"Thought not. You might have got off lighter if you had been. You see, what happens is, you pick up some sub-clinical infection—I don't mean only social diseases, but anything from a whitlow to a sore throat—and at the same time you're getting traces of antibiotic in your diet: what's left in the chicken particularly, but also pork and even steak that you've been eating. And there's just enough of the stuff to select for the resistant strains among the millions of organisms in your body, and when we come along and try to tackle them they thumb their noses at us. Are you with me?"

Philip gave a distracted nod, his mind on Denise and the kids.

"Still, not to worry," McNeil resumed, opening the file again. "We're ahead of the game so far, still got two or three tricks up our sleeves."

"My wife," Philip whispered.

"Judging by this, though," McNeil said, not seeming to have heard, "we'd better do a bit of sifting first. Look, can you come back tomorrow? I'd like to check out your cultures. There's a risk we might have to go over to injections. But we'll get the better of the blighters, never fear."

At which point he appeared to recall being interrupted.

"Oh, yes, your wife. She—uh—still doesn't know?"

"No," Philip confessed miserably. "I made sure she took the penicillin, of course, but I said it was hepatitis I'd caught. She did want to know why I hadn't got medicine for the kids as well, but I managed to evade that. Now, though, Josie—my daughter—she was sick in the night, and . . ."

"And, to be blunt, you don't have a hope in hell of keeping the truth from her," McNeil said briskly. "I did warn you it would cause—ah—rifts in the lute. Look, why don't we cut our losses? I'll send the diagnosis and lab reports to your own doctor, and—"

"Clayford," Philip said raggedly.

"Hell." McNeil bit his lip. "I was forgetting. Yes, that toffy-nosed devil. A good God-fearing type, isn't he? Won't touch a VD case, as though he were a parson refusing to visit someone in jail for witchcraft!" He shuddered elaborately.

"Well, in that case . . . It's probably unethical, but I don't regard it as wrong to save people embarrassment. If you like, I'll take on you and your wife as private patients. I only do this clinic part-time, you know. Sort of on principle. Conditioning, I suppose. I trained in England."

Philip nodded. He had noticed many English turns of phrase in McNeil's speech, though his accent was purely American. "What brought you here, then?"

"Not the shortcomings of their state health service, as most people instantly assume." McNeil chuckled. "Hell, it may be a mess, but half the doctors I've met over here—Clayford, for one—get offended if people fall ill out of office hours. Try refusing house calls in Britain and you get struck off the medical register . . . No, my mother was born right here, and when my father died she decided to retire to her home town. So when I passed twenty-six I came to join her."

Why—? Oh, of course. The draft limit.

McNeil slapped the desk and rose. "Think it over. I'd make it as easy on your wife as possible, of course. But I'm afraid I must insist on your bringing the matter into the open. Good afternoon."

"Bad news," a voice said at Philip's elbow as he descended the stairs. The clinic was over a store selling sports equipment and kinky leather goods.

"What?" Philip glanced around. The speaker was the man who'd been in the waiting room.

"I said bad news. I could read it in the stoop of your shoulders."

"It's none of your fucking business," Philip snapped.

"Well put. I'm feeling pretty low myself. Come and have a drink."

"Ah, go to hell!"

"I'm there," the stranger said, suddenly serious. "Aren't you? Shit, I'm thirty-seven and I never caught a dose before, thought it was something you could laugh off nowadays, like a head cold." He had one, by the sound of him; his n's were more like d's, as though he were holding his nose. "Turns out the stinking bug's resistant. So far it's been four months."

"Four months!" Philip was appalled, envisaging how endless such a sentence would be for himself.

"Now they're giving me six million units a day of some new miracle drug. In the ass. It hurts like fire, but at least it's started to cure me. What about that drink?"

Philip hesitated.

"Name's Alan Prosser," the stranger said. "Prosser Enterprises. Plumbing equipment, sewage pipes, garbage-disposal systems, that kind of shit."

"Christ." Philip blinked at him. "We had your stuff put in at our last place. I remember. But I never met you." He frowned. "Someone called—"

"Bud Burkhardt?"

"Yes! Your partner?"

"Ex-partner." With a scowl. "The mother walked out on me. Went to Towerhill, manage the new branch of Puritan . . . Did you say 'our' last place?"

"Yes."

"So you're married, hm? Then maybe I shouldn't talk about my troubles!"

"You not?"

"Was." Prosser's face suddenly grew strained and lined, as though ten years had passed between words. He raised his left hand to display the palm. There was a round mark on it to match the scar on the back, like a brand.

"What happened?" Philip said uncertainly.

"Shot. The same slug that left this mark on me. We'd wandered into the fringes of a Trainite demonstration, and some trigger-happy National Guardsman . . . Oh, shit, it's ancient history. And luckily Belle couldn't have kids. What about that drink?"

"Yes. Okay. Only one, though. It's supposed to be—uh—bad for the condition."

"Ah, shit. Not having it is far worse for the mind."

THE INDISPENSABLE ASSISTANTS

Grade-A MEXICAN HONEYBEES $165.95/gallon! Grade-A EUROPEAN BEES only $220/gallon! Best quality IRISH EARTHWORMS $67.50/quart! GUARANTEED live on delivery! Plant Fertility Corp., San Clemente, Calif. (Licensed by California State Board of Agriculture.)

BROKENMINDED

After the terrible collective madness of Christmastide in Noshri, Lucy Ramage somehow managed to keep going for a while alongside those members of the original Globe Relief and UN teams who hadn't been deported. It was as though the work of the preceding four months had been wiped out like chalk writing by a wet cloth. Indeed, things were worse than before. When she first arrived, people used to come out willingly from wherever they had found shelter—tumbledown shacks, smashed cars, wrecked buses, holes in the ground—and asked for food and first aid. Now they skulked and shied away, remained in hiding and stared at the world with mad distrustful faces, eyes wide and white-rimmed. To persuade someone to take food, you first had to swallow a mouthful yourself; to bandage a wound was often possible, but they wouldn't allow you to apply ointment or administer oral drugs. They were all agreed on what had happened to them: they were victims of a terrifying magic.

Some, it seemed, had been driven totally insane. For the rest of their lives they would limp around moaning, or break into causeless tears, or scream until their throats were raw at the sight of a harmless insect.

There were insects in Noshri again now. During the war they had completely disappeared.

Directly after the worst time, Lucy had been interrogated by hostile government officials concerning the nature of the madness. Fretting to get back to the miserable people who needed her help, she condensed what she had to report into the briefest possible version and delivered it in dry emotionless tones.

"Characteristic symptoms? They included violent perspiration, facial tics, occasional spasms of the long muscles in the thighs and calves, and extremely marked pupillary dilation. Vomiting? That was reported in only a minority of cases. But everyone suffered acid diarrhea and occasionally the stools were mixed with fresh blood.

"How long to take effect? Typically, about one to three hours after the onset of the sweating and pupillary dilation, a sensation of floating ensued, and one saw the victims staring at their hands and feet unable to believe they any longer belonged to them. This stage was rapidly succeeded by one of hysterical terror, with visual and auditory hallucinations, and in the great majority of cases total loss of self-control. Outbursts of wild rage, often leading to random wrecking of the immediate surroundings and particularly to arson, and later to assault on anybody and anything that moved—especially crying children, who were frequently kicked and beaten to death by their own parents because their noise proved intolerable—lasted six to thirty-six hours. Most sufferers did not sleep for the longer period. If no other target offered itself their own bodies took the brunt and they gashed or battered themselves. I also saw many run to the river and jump in, crying they were dying of thirst. This probably connects with the extreme dehydration the diarrhea entailed.

"The content of the hallucinations? Remarkably uniform. Voices came first, especially those of parents, senior relatives, and—in the case of ex-soldiers—officers and NCO's. Since the majority of these were dead the conviction that ghosts were walking followed logically. Many of those killed were mistaken for evil spirits. Because personal appearance is radically changed by the condition (e.g., the huge staring eyes, the awkward walk due to muscular cramps) close relatives often did not recognize one another and ran screaming even from a wife or husband.

"After-effects? Melancholia, acute hypnophobia—that's fear of going to sleep because of the high incidence of nightmares—anxiety, unaccountable fits of violence . . . A man was murdered the other day for no better reason than that he let his shadow fall on someone else's foot.

"Treatment? Well, we've had some success with doctoring the water supply—you know we're still selling drinking water from carts, and dumping half a pound of tranquilizers into every barrel seems to have helped, a little. But the tranquilizers are running short, so . . ."

Shrug.

She, too, was afraid to sleep. She dreamed always of the little bloody bits of human flesh that had spattered her. Either she doped herself with amphetamines, or—when they ceased to have any effect and her eyelids began to sting—she took enough barbiturates to drive her into coma, insulated against dreams. While she was awake she hardly ate, but wandered around coaxing people from hiding, washing gangrened wounds, helping to rig improvised shelters. At first the black soldiers now cleaning up the town were hostile; when they saw how meekly she worked, and how hard, they grew used to her and more than once when she found herself falling down with fatigue strong anonymous black arms carried her bodily home. Often the man was surprised at being called major when he was a mere private.

She learned about the charge that the relief food contained a hallucinogen from Bertil, who believed the suggestion that it had been infected with ergot or something like it; he said that had been responsible for outbreaks of medieval dancing mania. She was told about it again by the army officers investigating the calamity, who believed there had been poison deliberately added.

She herself had no views on the matter.

Reporters naturally came in swarms. Although the news value of the war had more or less died with the armistice, General Kaika was anxious that the whole world should see the extent of the continuing disaster, so he put government planes at the disposal of journalists and TV camera teams. He even relaxed his embargo on Americans for the sake of a team from ABS's Paris office, provided they were led by a Frenchman. When they heard about Lucy they sensed an angle: beautiful blonde caught up in a night of horror. No one apparently knew exactly where she was, so they set off in search of her.

They came on her burrowing in the ruins of a house. She had uncovered a body the soldiers had overlooked, that of a child about ten years old. She was disinterring it with a pocket-knife.

When she realized the interviewer was an American she bared her teeth and attacked him. He had to have eight stitches in a gash that ran from his collarbone to his sternum.

They flew her, under sedation, to England, to a country mental hospital, where she awoke to discover green lawns, the first flowers of spring peering out under the overcast sky, cows grazing in a field the other side of a pleasant valley, and steel bars across an unopenable window.

EAT IT IN GOOD HEALTH *Special this week at your Puritan Health Supermarket!*

Okinawa squash, reg. $0.89 $0.75!
Penguin eggs (low on DDT, PCB), reg. $6.35 doz. $6.05!
Pacific potatoes (unwashed), reg. $0.89 lb. $0.69!
Butter from sunny New Zealand, reg. $1.35 qrt. $1.15!
YOU TOO CAN AFFORD GOOD HEALTH AT PURITAN!

THE STRONG CAME FORTH

His haunted dreams had finally faded and Pete Goddard was sleeping okay again. His first wakening after the collapse, though, had been appalling: terror, paralysis, pain.

Except that he wasn't paralyzed. They had merely put his legs into traction, cased the whole lower part of his trunk in tight plastic wraps, *stretched* him with weights hung from ceiling-mounted pulleys. As soon as he was alert enough to understand, they explained what they were doing to him, and why, and he very nearly couldn't believe the why.

They said that all by himself he had held up three-quarters of a ton.

Oh, it wasn't any kind of a record. The physiotherapist who attended him daily had mentioned a woman, hysterical with fear for the life of her child, who had lifted a car weighing a ton and a half; also a professional strongman who had demonstrated a lift of two full tons, slung from a harness around his waist. It had something to do with the engineering properties of the femur. She showed him diagrams that he fought to comprehend.

But it was strange how the nurses seemed to be frightened of him, and kept asking whether he had trained as a weight-lifter. Well, he had, though not for over a year, not since he met Jeannie. He said wearily he had kept in shape.

Obviously one couldn't do this kind of thing and not be very badly damaged. All the musculature of his shoulders had suffered subcutaneous hemorrhage, so that he wore a colossal bruise a foot wide, and even supporting the weight of his own arm now tired him within seconds. The cartilaginous discs separating his vertebrae had been crushed when his spine locked into the single solid column that enabled him to stand the weight. All the synovial membranes in his leg joints had been overloaded, so that his knees and ankles had also locked rigid, and the arches of both his feet had collapsed. He had briefly become a pillar of bone, and he didn't remember. He had known only one thing during that terrible time: he couldn't do anything any more except stand straight.

For the first few days he lay there in the hospital he was frightened as much of having to pay for what was being done to him as he was of not being able to walk again. He was doped to kill the pain, of course, and that made his mind fuzzy too, so when they allowed Jeannie to see him he couldn't explain what was troubling him and finally he broke down crying from frustration and they thought it was pain and doped him with a double dose.

But, a day or two after—he wasn't keeping track of time right then—they let him have other visitors, and it all came clear. There were reporters, and photographers, and a man from California, the uncle of the two children he'd saved. Harry had crawled under the beam and brought them back with him, but he'd held up the roof.

Their parents were dead. So their uncle, a successful bee importer, was going to adopt them, and pay for this hospitalization—the best of everything, he said, up to fifty thousand bucks. He insisted he could easily afford it; he'd got right in on the ground floor when the bees of California became extinct in the sixties, and now he ran a million-dollar undertaking.

He also remarked, sounding puzzled, that he'd tried to get Harry to accept a reward, too, but the guy wouldn't take a cent. Said something about ghouls. Some kind of Trainite prejudice.

Then a week or two later a senator called Howard or Howell or something brought him an illuminated scroll, a citation for courage, signed by Prexy himself. They framed it and hung it facing his bed.

"Hi, honey."

"Hi, doll."

They brushed lips. Jeannie had come in as usual, regular as clockwork. But there was something odd about her appearance. Lying surrounded by the papers and books he used to pass the time—his arms were moving freely thanks to the physiotherapist's massage and he could turn pages fine—he took a second look. Her left hand was bandaged.

"You cut yourself, baby?" he demanded.

"Uh . . ." She made to hide it, changed her mind. "No, I got bitten."

"Bitten! What by—a dog?"

"No, a rat. I reached in the cupboard for a bag of flour . . . I keep calling the exterminator, but he can't come. Got too many calls—hey, what you doing?" Pete had seized the bell-push by his bed.

"Calling the nurse! You put that dressing on yourself?"

"Well—yes."

"You have it attended to properly! You know what rats carry? Sometimes plague! Or it might go septic."

The nurse came, prompt because of his benefactor's money, and led Jeannie protesting away. While she was gone he lay there fuming, thinking: Rats? So many rats the exterminator can't cope? Hell!

And it was just as well he inisted. Jeannie had a subclinical fever due to septicemia. When they found out she'd kissed him, they gave him a prophylactic injection as well.

Trying to lighten the mood when she came back with her hand neatly wrapped in white, he said, "Say, baby, good news. Tomorrow they're going to let me try and walk!"

"Honey, that's really great!" Her eyes shone. But mainly with tears. "Is it . . . ?"

"Is it going to be the same?"

She nodded.

"They think it will be. But not for a pretty long time. I'll have to wear a brace for my back, to start with anyway."

"How long?"

He hesitated, then repeated the physiotherapist's estimate. "Two years."

"Oh, *Pete!*"

"But everything else is okay!" He brought out the worst terror, the most fearful fear. "There's nothing wrong with . . . I mean, I'm still a *man.*"

Thank God. Thank God. He'd prayed, really prayed, when that point occurred to him. And one of the doctors, whom he was going to remember every time he prayed again, had told him well, as far as can be judged that ought to be okay, as soon as you've got the strength back in your arms try it for yourself. I'll send you some deep-dirt books in case they help.

Jeannie clutched his hand and began to cry.

Eventually she was able to ask about the future. Obviously a cripple couldn't go back on the force. Could he?

He shook his head. He could do that now without a twinge of pain. They'd been wonderful, the care they'd taken.

"No. But I got the offer of a job already. Man called by this morning who'd heard I can't get back in the police. Friend of one of the doctors, cat called Prosser. Says to let him know as soon as I'm fit and he'll give me a desk job I can handle."

"Back in Towerhill, you mean?"

"No, here in Denver. Of course we'd have to move house, but he said the pay would be good . . . Ah, don't worry, baby. Everything's going to be all right."

MY FINGERS ARE GREEN AND SOMETIMES DROP OFF

Dear Sir: Thank you for your letter of 18th and enclosures. The sample of dirt contains an exceptionally high proportion of lead and mercury, trace quantities of molybdenum and selenium, and a small amount of salts of silver. There is no detectable cadmium. The water sample is contaminated with lead, arsenic, selenium and compounds of sodium and potassium, particularly sodium nitrite. We suspect that the garden of the house you have bought is sited on infill derived from mine tailings, and suggest you raise the matter with the former owners. You do not mention whether you have children, but if you do we would draw your attention to the dangers they face from lead and sodium nitrite in such quantities. Early settlement of your account would be appreciated.

Yours faithfully.

THE REARING OF THE UGLY HEAD

Having dropped Harold, Josie and the Henlowes' boy at their play-school—social behavior should be encouraged at an early age and the hell with the risk of infection that caused parents like Bill and Tania Chalmers (RIP, victims along with Anton of the Towerhill avalanche) to keep their kids at home as late as was legal: what a nasty personality poor Anton had developed!—Denise Mason continued to Dr. Clayford's office.

The room was a perfect frame for his personality. He sat at a mahogany desk, an antique, with a gilt-tooled leather top, in a leather armchair with a swivel base. He was gruff, bluff and tough. He was proud of belonging to what, in a rare moment of jocularity, Denise had once heard him term "the sulfa generation." She had been on his list for years, since long before her marriage, even though she didn't much like him because he was distant and difficult to talk to. All the same there was something reassuring in his old-fashioned manner.

He reminded her more than a little of her father.

For the first time ever he didn't stand up as she entered, merely waved her to the chair facing him. Puzzled, she sat down.

"Well, what's the trouble?"

"Well—uh . . ." Absurbly, she felt herself flushing bright scarlet. "Well, I've been pretty run down lately. But now I've developed—well, a discharge. And irritation."

"Vaginal, you mean? Oh, that's the gonorrhea your husband gave you."

"*What?*"

"I told him to go to the clinic on Market. They specialize in that sort of thing. He didn't tell you?"

She could only shake her head wordlessly. So many things had suddenly become clear.

"Typical," Clayford said with contempt. "Absolutely typical. These products of the so-called permissive generation. Dishonest. Greedy, lazy, self-indulgent, ready at the drop of a hat to tell any lie that will protect them from the consequences of their actions. They're the cause of all the troubles in the world today!"

He leaned suddenly across his desk, shaking a pen at her.

"You should see what I have to see, daily in my practice. Children from good homes, subnormal from lead poisoning! Blind from congenital syphilis, too! Choking with asthma! Bone cancer, leukemia, God knows what!" He was beginning to spray little drops of spittle from his thin lips.

Denise stared at him as though seeing him for the first time.

"You've been treating Philip for a social disease?" she said at last.

"Of course not. I told him where he could get treatment, for you as well as himself. *I'm* not going to help him cover up his tracks. It's that kind of refusal to admit responsibility that's put the world in the mess it's in!"

"He asked you for help, and you refused?"

"I told you," Clayford grunted. "I recommended him to the proper clinic."

Suddenly she couldn't see him any longer. There were stinging tears in her eyes. She stood up in a single jerk that snapped her spine straight like a bowstring when the arrow is released.

"You bastard," she said. "You smug pompous devil. You liar. You filthy dishonest old man. You put the poison in the world, you and your generation. You crippled my children. You made sure they'd never eat clean food, drink pure water, breathe sweet air. And when someone comes to you for help you turn your back."

Suddenly she was crying and hurling things—a big glass inkwell, full of lovely pitch-black ink, a huge beautiful mess all over his white shirt. A book, a tray of papers. Anything.

"Philip isn't—what you called him! He's not, he's not! He's my husband, and I love him!"

She spun around. There was a tall glass-fronted cabinet full of medical texts. She caught at one of the doors, that stood ajar, and leaned her full weight on it, and toppled it in a crashing smashing marvelous miracle of noise.

And marched out.

It was all insured by Angel City, anyway.

DISGRACE

"O Lord!" Mr. Bamberley said, head bowed at the head of his fine long table of seasoned oak, "enter our hearts, we pray, and as this food nourishes our bodies so may our souls be nourished by Thy word, amen."

Amen, said a ragged chorus, cut short by the rattle of porcelain and silver. The silent black girl who worked as the Bamberleys' maid—her name was Christy and she was fat—offered Hugh a basket of rolls and breadsticks. He took a roll. There was as usual too much vinegar on the salad. It made his tongue curl.

He was home for the weekend from college, and this was the ritual of Sunday lunch after church. Apparently servants, in Mr. Bamberley's cosmos, didn't have to be allowed time off for worship, although both Christy and Ethel, the cook, were devout. They could be heard singing gospel songs in the kitchen most of the day.

But Sunday mornings they worked like slaves from six A.M. to get this family meal ready.

Opposite her husband, plump, with a smile on her face as fixed as a wax doll's, sat Mrs. Bamberley—Maud. She was ten years younger than her husband and twenty points lower on the IQ scale. She thought he was wonderful and sometimes gave talks to local women's groups about how wonderful he was. Also she judged flower-arranging competitions and was regularly interviewed by the local press and TV when some vet with a bad conscience joined the Double-V adoption scheme. She was, by courtesy of her husband, a great adopter herself, and when they asked needling questions about race and religion she was prompt with the proper replies: a child of a different color from the rest of the family feels so pitifully self-conscious, and surely all parents want their children to be brought up in their own faith?

Behind her chair, from a wall covered in a very expensive velvet-flock paper, a portrait of her grandfather looked down. He had been an Episcopalian bishop, but the picture showed him in the costume of a New England gentleman keeping up the Old English custom of riding to hounds: red coat, brown boots, distinguished with a white dog-collar and black silk front.

Hugh referred to him as being dressed to kill.

The salad was replaced—though Hugh had sampled only a mouthful of his—by a dish of cold fish with mayonnaise. He didn't even touch this course. He was suddenly afraid of it because it had come from the sea.

It was the first time he had been here since the disastrous interview Mr. Bamberley had given on the Petronella Page show, and the consequent closing down of the hydroponics plant. Everyone had been prepared to believe, as soon as that expert in Paris had published his verdict about the victims, that there was indeed poison in the Nutripon. He'd arrived—home—on Friday evening. So far there hadn't been a single reference to this event.

Petronella Page was notoriously merciless with any kind of fake. Hugh had been interested to learn that she agreed with his opinion: Mr. Bamberley was a phony on the grand scale.

Correspondingly, behind Mr. Bamberley's own chair, another portrait looked down, of his grandfather. It showed him—a burly man with his legs planted a yard apart, fists on his hips—committing rape. At least that was Hugh's description. People who didn't know the story might be content to recognize the oil gusher in the background.

The fish was replaced by platters of roast meat, dishes of baked and boiled potatoes, carrots, cabbage, peas. Also there were sauce-boats of gravy and imported English horseradish cream. Silent as ever, Christy brought a pitcher of beer of a brand Hugh didn't like, a weekly treat for the older boys, and another of lemonade for Maud and "the kids."

So far nothing of any consequence had been said.

The remainder of the company at table consisted of Mr. Bamberley's adopted sons, with omissions. Cyril, who as well as being the oldest was also the longest-established, was in Manila. He'd graduated with distinction from West Point and was now personal aide, at twenty-four, to one of the generals setting up what Prexy kept terming "the Pacific bastion"—in other words, a white alliance including Australia, New Zealand and what few Latin American countries were still right-wing dictatorships, designed to contain the pro-Chinese, neo-Marxist tidal wave surging around the planet.

Hugh had met Cyril only once, just after his own recruitment to the family, and taken an instant loathing to him. But at the time he'd been too overwhelmed with his new prospects to say anything.

The second omission was Jared. Jared, who was twenty-one, was in jail. One didn't speak of him in Mr. Bamberley's presence. He'd been convicted of helping to organize a pro-Tupamaro movement among the Chicanos of New Mexico. Hugh hadn't met him; he was serving a five-year term.

But he thought he'd probably like him a lot.

And Noel, five, was in bed with a fever, but the rest were here. Down at Maud's end there sat Ronald, who was sixteen and rather dull; Cornelius, dutiful and bright but the victim of occasional fits since his twelfth birthday—not epilepsy, something to do with enzymes that fouled up the interchange of energy between one nerve-cell and the next, kept under control by a special diet; then Norman, eight, with the facial tic, and Claude, ten, with the bad teeth that sometimes cracked edge to edge and fell out of his mouth. A fairly typical family in its way, despite having been assembled from so many different sources: those in their teens physically healthy, those younger, not. Hugh had a girl-friend in college with a younger brother who vomited back anything cooked in corn-oil.

And still those mothers won't admit how they've fucked up the world.

"Hugh," Mr. Bamberley said, "did you speak?"

He hadn't meant to. But he recalled the echo of his

words. Not looking to his right, he reached for his beer.

"I'm sorry, Jack. Did you ask me a question?"

"Yes, I did!" Mr. Bamberley laid down his knife and fork next to massive slices of beef partly sectioned. "It was my distinct impression that you—ah—murmured a word I disapprove of."

Hugh drained his glass and leaned back with a sigh. "So what if I did?"

Mr. Bamberley slowly turned pink all the way to his receding hairline. "What reason had you for employing such a word?"

"The reason's all around you," Hugh snapped, and made a gesture that embraced the luxuriously furnished dining-room, the food piled on the table, the maid waiting in the corner like a store-window dummy.

"Explain further!" Mr. Bamberley was about to choke with the effort of controlling his fury.

"Okay, I will!" Suddenly Hugh could stand the pressure no longer. He leapt to his feet, his chair crashing over backwards. "Here you sit, stuffing your fat paunch with food from all over the stinking world, when you've poisoned thousands of poor black buggers in Africa—haven't you? Are you out sharing their suffering, helping them pick up the bits? The hell you are! You're fighting tooth and nail the one thing that might help to get to the bottom of the disaster, screaming that a UN inquiry would 'serve no useful purpose'—I saw that quote in the papers! Here you are at your beautiful table, gobbling and guzzling and saying *graoe* for Chrissake, as though you expect God to thank you for all the people you've killed and driven out of their minds!"

Mr. Bamberley extended toward the door a shaking hand from which his napkin depended like a crumpled flag.

"Leave this room!" he roared. "Leave this *house!* And don't come back until you're willing to apologize!"

"Exactly what I'd have expected you to say," Hugh said in a dead voice. He felt suddenly very grown-up indeed, very mature, almost old. "Right square in the tradition: you kick people in the balls and expect them to do the apologizing. Because of you and people like you we sit here in the richest country in the world surrounded by sick kids—"

"You have a foul mouth and a foul mind!"

"You trying to tell me you adopted Norman because of his tic? Don't give me that shit. I heard from Maud: you found out when the papers had been signed. Look at Claude's teeth, like punk from a rotten stump! Look at Corny envying us because we can eat regular food! You—"

But the tension overcame Corny at that point. It was always stress that brought on his attacks. He collapsed into his plate, face down, shattering it and spattering his special mush all over everywhere. As Maud and Christy rushed to attend him, Hugh delivered his parting shot.

"You and your ancestors treated the world like a fucking great toilet bowl. You shat in it and boasted about the mess you'd made. And now it's full and overflowing, and you're fat and happy and black kids are going crazy to keep you rich. *Goodbye!*"

He slammed the door as hard as he could when storming out, hoping the crash might shake down the portrait of Jacob Holmes Bamberley I.

But the nail was too solidly imbedded in the wall.

NOT MAKING HEADLINES

. . . guilty of using brominated vegetable oil, an illegal emulsifying agent. Despite defense submissions that no harm had been proved to anyone who ate the food in question, the company was fined one hundred dollars. Now the weather. SO_2, *ozone and lead alkyl counts all remain high . . .*

A CALL TO ALMS

Outside the gray stone house that Michael Advowson called home, on the gray road, a green official car was standing, the dirty rain smearing its smart paint. He ignored it. He ignored, equally, the man in the fawn raincoat who rose to meet him in the hallway—or would have done so, but that the stranger blocked the door to his surgery, and Advowson was carrying a bleeding child in his arms, crying at the top of her lungs.

"Get out of my *way!*" he snapped, and shouldered the man bodily aside.

"But, doctor, this is—" The voice of his housekeeper, Mrs. Byrne.

"I know Mr. Clark! He was here last month! There, there, darling, it'll stop hurting soon. You be calm!" Laying the little girl on his examination couch. At once the white disposable cover turned bright red around her foot.

"Come inside and make yourself useful or get the hell out," he added to the man in the raincoat. "Better make yourself useful. Wash your hands, quick!" Meantime he was seizing from the cabinets around the room bandages, powders, a syringe, scissors to cut away the shoe and sock.

Taking an uncertain step into the room, Clark said, "What—ah—what happened?"

"Glass. Use that soap, the dark red one. It's antiseptic."

"I don't quite—"

"I said glass!" Michael soothed the little girl with a pat on the cheek. She was so terrified she had wet herself, but that could be cleaned up in a moment. Continuing as he drove the needle of the syringe through the rubber seal of a phial: "She was playing up by the Donovan farm, where for years they used to dump rubbish. She trod on a broken bottle, and . . ."

With sudden perfectly-controlled strength he grasped the child's leg and held it still by force while he sank the needle home. Almost at once her eyelids closed.

"And she's likely to lose her great toe. Blood-poisoning too, unless we're quick. Is that your car outside, a government car?"

"Well—yes."

"Then maybe we shan't have to wait on an ambulance. My own car is in to be mended. Now come and help me. Do as I tell you, that's all."

Clark came: too young to be a father, perhaps, and live day and night with fear of what might happen to his or any child. The great toe had been wholly severed. Michael gave it to him to hold while he staunched the blood.

He was valiant, and at least managed to set the toe on a table before running from the room, and in a moment was heard vomiting on the lawn.

Yet he came back, which also was valiant, and held the toe while Michael secured it with rough rapid stitches —all according to principles enunciated in a medical journal from China (make sure you maintain the blood supply at all costs until there's time to match the nerves and muscles)—and then an ambulance arrived and Michael didn't need to requisition the government car after all.

"When a child can't even play safely in a field . . ." Michael said. He had called Clark into the sitting-room and the offer of a tot had been approved. Two fingers for each of them. It was sometimes necessary to give the healers medicine too. "*Slainte!*"

"*Slainte!*"

"Now, what was it you came for?" Michael inquired, dropping into his favorite chair. "Did they send you to apologize for that scandal at Murphy's farm?"

The government man had the grace to look uncomfortable. "No. But I was told that you were right all along."

"Kind of them to admit it!" Michael snorted. "I'm not even a vet, just a boy raised on a farm, but I recognize dicoumarin poisoning from spoiled hay when I see it. But you didn't believe me, did you? No more did they—probably never heard of dicoumarin! Oh, they're such fools, they make me see red. You know if they'd had their way I might not have saved young Eileen's toe?"

Clark blinked at him. He found this aggressive redhead with the green eyes too close together curiously disturbing.

"It's a fact. I learned the right way of it out of a Chinese medical journal, that they tried to stop me subscribing to because it would mean giving the Chinese Western currency!" Scowling, he drained his glass.

"Well, I wouldn't know about that," the other said, reaching to the inside pocket of his smart blue suit, likely English. "I was told to give you this." He proffered an envelope bearing a green wax official seal.

"Ah, perhaps they sent the apology in writing!" Michael grunted, tearing it open. A long pause. Eventually he looked up with a bitter smile.

"Well, that'll teach me not to try and beat the government. Even if you win they find a way of doing you down. Did you know I spent five years as a medical officer in the army? No? Well, I did. So now they're recalling me from the reserve to go with a UN team to investigate the matter of this poisoned food at Noshri. Well, I suppose it's one means of putting me out of the way!"

He threw the letter angrily to the floor.

"But who's going to tend the next child like Eileen Murphy?"

MARCH

LONG MULTIPLICATION

Behold! th' industrious *Hind,* who daily walks
His narrow fields, and with a miser's care
(Tho' with a nobler motive, for to spare
Foul waste, and weeds) inspects the sep'rate stalks,

Who roots out all that are infect with blight
(For plants, like men, fall ill) and, mouthing ire,
Sets the sere stalks upon a smoky fire,
Then chooses from the seed that grew aright

Such as will, after golden harvest-time,
Repeat their kind, but bettered, sweet and sound,
Their chaff stript off by thrashers as of yore:
Him do I sing, as worthy of my rime,
Him whose devotion to the pregnant ground
Makes two ears grow where one ear grew before.

—"The Agricultural Muse," 1710

A GIFT OF INSECTS

This high up there was still a lot of snow. Peg drove cautiously along the steep and winding road. She had seen scarcely any other cars for several miles. Still, there was always the chance of encountering some idiot who believed he had the road to himself.

Idiot . . .

Am I one?

She hadn't intended to utter the rhetorical question aloud; however, Felice—shivering because the driver's window was open despite being wrappod to the ears in fur, and real fur at that, Peg suspected, though she'd not been so impolite as to ask outright—said wryly, "I've been wondering the same about myself. But I should have taken over from Bill Chalmers when he was killed, and finding that bastard Halkin slotted in over my head . . ."

Peg gave a nod. She knew exactly how Felice felt. She herself was sorry to have lost her job, but underlying her decision had been a fierce pride which was still sustaining her.

"I wasn't thinking about that," she said. "I mean, here we are, going to arrive after dark, without even having phoned ahead . . ."

"You can phone the wat?" Felice sounded surprised.

"Sure. They even have a listed number, just the one for the whole fifty-sixty of them." In the name of Jones. Perhaps that was why she hadn't called ahead. She was trying not to think too much about Decimus being dead, even though his sister was right here in the car with her, even though they were retracing his last journey the opposite way.

As though at the end of the trip I expect to find him alive and well.

"Somehow I didn't think of them as having a phone at all," Felice said.

Well, that was natural, knowing their distrust of modern technology. Moreover, they didn't have too much truck with the outside world. And the outside world disapproved of them, which was a reason. A brief moment of approbation had followed the Towerhill avalanche, when even the governor had commended their rescue work. But that was over.

It being so late, she'd suggested to Felice when they came to the turning signposted for Towerhill that they spend the night there. Since the avalanche it was no secret that the tourists had vanished, phfft. There would be plenty of vacant rooms. No one but ghouls now cared to make for the town.

But Felice had said she preferred not to be a ghoul.

Suddenly, at the very edge of her headlight beams, Peg spotted another car drawn up by the roadside: a little Stephenson electric not meant for long distances, with only a hundred-mile range between rechargings. A young man was inspecting its works. Hearing the soft cat-hiss of the Hailey, he turned and waved.

"Think I should stop?" she muttered to Felice. Normally the idea wouldn't have occurred to her; she'd have carried straight on, and the hell with whether the guy was found frozen in the morning. But since reaching the thousand-foot line, 'way back, she'd been able to drive with the ventilator off and the window down, and crisp fresh mountain air had made her lightheaded. Even the cold was refreshing; she hadn't been this cold in years, living in LA where the only chance of staving off her sinusitis lay in wearing a filtermask and changing the air-purifier on the car every thousand miles and spending as much time as possible indoors.

Apparently Felice had been affected the same way. Instead of uttering sensible warnings about being mugged and left in the snow while thieves drove off in the car, she said, "Oh, he looks pretty harmless. And I wouldn't like to be stuck here in this cold."

So Peg pulled up alongside him.

"Say, are you going to the Trainite wat?" he demanded, leaning to her window and brushing back lank hair.

"Yes."

"Me too. Only my car quit on me—the stinking charge-level gauge stuck at high. Can I ride in with you?"

Peg gave a doubtful glance at the tiny back seat of the Hailey, a mere shelf intended to save a couple with a kid from having to change to a bigger car. It was already almost covered with Felice's traveling-bag and a big canister with a label in bold red and black saying LIVE WITH CARE.

"I just have the one small bag," the young man pleaded.

"Oh . . . Okay."

"Great, thanks!"

So she got out—the Hailey had only two doors—and watched him closely and noted that he locked the electric car. Then it was presumably his own; she'd half imagined it might be stolen. She relaxed and held the door for him as he returned, carrying an airline-size bag.

"You'll have to move that canister," she said. "Mind, it's heavy."

He complied. "What is it?" he asked as he read the label.

"Gallon of imported worms," Felice told him. "Thought it would make a useful present for the wat."

"Yeah, good idea." He settled himself awkwardly, his long legs folded almost double. "By the way, I'm Hugh, Hugh Pettingill."

The name sounded as though it ought to mean something. It declined to.

"I'm Peg. This is Felice." She slammed the door and drove off.

"You live at the wat?"

"No. You?"

"Thinking maybe I ought to." In the windshield, by the faint glow of the instruments, she caught a glimpse of his face set in a frown, like a Pepper's ghost against the black road and white-grey soiled snow-banks. "I just been drifting around the past few weeks. Trying to figure things out."

Me too.

Peg thought of the long hours she'd wasted in her apartment, staring at the TV as though it were some kind of crystal ball and would suggest a right course of action, until that unexpected phone-call from Felice, who wanted to meet her for dinner, wanted to talk about the way she had regarded her late brother, wanted to find out if she'd been wrong in quarreling with him when he committed himself to Trainite ideals.

She said she'd been wondering ever since the day she was told that life expectancy in the United States was going down.

The calmly spoken statement had shaken Peg to the core; the dinner had lasted past midnight, conversation turning to argument and back again, until eventually this plan had come from it: to visit the Denver wat, talk to Decimus's widow Zena, forget the official view of Trainites ("their founder went crazy and his chief disciple died stoned!") and try to make up their own minds for a change.

Peg had fallen in with the proposal with a sense of fatalism. The prospect of seeing the wat again, Zena and Rick and the other kids, without Decimus—that frightened her. But it had to be done, she recognized that. After all the world hadn't ended with that one man's death.

Not quite.

She grew aware that the boy in the back—youth, young man, whatever—was talking as though he'd spoken to no one for days and desperately needed the chance to disburden his mind.

"I mean, I couldn't go on taking things from him after that, could I? I mean could I?"

She fished back into memory, and abruptly recognized the name. Pettingill. Click. One of Jacob Bamberley's adopted sons vanishing from college. But apparently Felice had been listening with more attention, because she said now, "Seen any of this food of his, this stuff they claimed was poisoned and killed all those people at Noshri?"

"Seen, sure, but not on his table." There was venom in Hugh's tone. "Oh no. Prime beef for him! Smug self-important do-gooding bastard. Expects you to lick his boots for every favor he does, whether you asked for it or not. Wants to be surrounded by billions of people all saying, 'Yes, Mr. Bamberley! No, Mr. Bamberley! Anything you say, Mr. Bamberley!' Makes me sick to my stomach."

He fished inside his heavy parka and produced something in a limp plastic envelope. "Say, I got some khat. Either of you want a chaw?"

"Sure," Felice said, reaching back. Peg repressed a shudder. Putting something in your mouth that had been soaked in a stranger's saliva . . . Even if they did say the stuff contained a natural bactericide and the risk of infection was less than from kissing.

She didn't go too much for the kissing bit, either.

She said in a harsh voice, "Better make the most of it. Those must be the lights of the wat, across the valley there. And you know how they feel about drugs."

"Peg, baby! Oh, Peg, how wonderful! And this must be Felice, yes?" Tall, very dark, with a stately presence Peg had always envied because it might have helped to put down pestiferous men, Zena embraced her and hurried them all away from the cold, into the curious abstract cave that was her home: marvelously warm from only a few light-bulbs because it was so efficiently insulated, full of a delicious aroma of beans and herbs.

"How's Rick? How are the girls?"

"Oh, they're fine. Just gone to bed a minute ago. I won't disturb them right now, but they'll be so pleased to see you in the morning. Felice dear, I'm so glad to meet you at last—Decimus talked about you a lot, you know, and he was always so sorry you'd fallen out." And kissed her too.

Meantime Hugh waited by the door with a look on his face that struck Peg as somehow *hungry*. As though there were no place on earth he could go and find a welcome this effusive. She did her best to make amends by presenting him to other members of the wat community as they appeared: burly Harry Molton, bearded Paul Prince and his pretty wife Sue, Ralph Henderson who had gone bald since she last met him, and half a dozen more who were new. Yes, of course they'd offer hospitality. It was part of the thing. They made it literal and brought bread and salt.

Later, showing her to a bed that was going spare tonight, Zena mentioned how badly they were being plagued with people who claimed to be Trainites and weren't: wanted to wreck and burn and kill and went away in a week or two when they didn't find any support here for their violent plans.

A STRAW TO A DROWNING MAN

. . . positively identified as Uruguayan. Following this disclosure the Honduran government called on one million dollars of standby credit which will be applied to the purchase of arms and other urgently-needed supplies, and appealed to Washington for assistance in combating the Tupamaro threat. The Pentagon announced an hour ago that the aircraft carrier Wounded Knee *has been diverted from routine patrols in the Atlantic and is already flying survey missions over the rebel-held area. Commenting just prior to leaving for a vacation in Honolulu, Prexy said, quote, They can pull just so many feathers out of the eagle's tail before it pecks. End quote. Contacted at his West Virginia home, the president of the Audubon Society, Dr. Ike Mostyn, stated that the last reported sighting of a nesting pair of bald-headed eagles three years ago had proved to be a hoax. New York: Professor Lucas Quarrey of Columbia University, under attack for his allegedly anti-American statements recently in the press and on TV, said at a press conference this morning that his contract to research into improved airplane ventilators had been terminated with-*

out warning. Asked whether political motivations underlay the decision, the professor said . . .

RIPOSTE About forty miles out of Medano, almost exactly due west of the border between California and Baja California, the boat hove to, drifting very slowly on the vast circulation of the Pacific.

Even this far from shore, the night stank. The sea moved lazily, its embryo waves aborted before cresting by the layer of oily residues surrounding the hull, impermeable as sheet plastic: a mixture of detergents, sewage, industrial chemicals and the microscopic cellulose fibers due to toilet paper and newsprint. There was no sound of fish breaking surface. There were no fish.

The boat's skipper was blind in one eye and had been so from birth. He was the illegitimate son of a woman who had gone to California to pick grapes and inhaled something they sprayed on the vines to kill insects, and died. Befriended by a helpful priest, he had survived and gone to school and won a government scholarship. Now he knew about physics and chemistry and meteorology and combustion and the action of poisons.

He was also a Tupa, but that went without saying.

The calendar said there should be a full moon tonight. Perhaps there was. One couldn't see it; one almost never could—or the sun, either. On the afterdeck twenty-four big balloons were laid out like the empty skins of fish, slightly glistening as a flashlight played across them. There were cylinders of compressed hydrogen. And twenty-four precisely calculated payloads. Carrying them, the balloons could be relied on to rise to about two hundred meters and float shorewards at nine or ten kilometers an hour. They would cross the coast above or near the city of San Diego.

Roger Halkin was exhausted. Strain, like that of the past few days, always aggravated his diabetes. Still, everything was ready for the morning now; all the fragile stuff had been packed, all the records and books, and the house was littered with full cardboard cartons waiting for the moving men.

"Brandy, darling?" asked his wife Belinda.

"I guess I could risk a small one," he muttered. "I surely need it."

He didn't look or sound like a man who had just been promoted vice-president of his company. There were good reasons. As he'd said with gallows humor to Belinda, he was going to vice-preside over a wake. Today had brought bad news, worse than anyone had expected. Except, presumably, for Tom Grey; that cold fish with his almost symbiotic comprehension of computed trends would have known or at least suspected long ago.

It had never been a secret that Angel City had been hit hard by the Towerhill affair, but the load, one assumed, must have been spread—they regularly reinsured as far afield as Lloyd's of London—and in any event there was a clear case for a claim against the airline whose SST had triggered the avalanche.

Only this morning he'd heard that the airline was going to fight, maintaining that it hadn't been the boom which caused the disaster, but an earthquake; they'd started occurring around Denver in 1962 and were now common. And the suit might take a year and cost a million. So when he stepped into Bill Chalmers's shoes his first task would be to shed half the section he was supposed to be in charge of, Angel City's out-of-state operations.

"If I could get my hands on that stinking idiot from Denver, that Philip Mason," he said between clenched teeth, "I'd tear him limb from limb. And I'm not the only one. I—"

He was interrupted by a cry from the back of the house where their boy Teddy was supposed to be asleep. He was eight, and among the lucky ones; he had nothing worse than occasional asthma. Ever since news of their impending move to LA broke, it had been touch and go whether he'd collapse with another bout, but so far they'd escaped that.

"Dad! Mom! Hey, look—there's fireworks!"

"Christ, isn't that kid asleep yet?" Halkin jumped to his feet. "I'll give him fireworks!"

"Rodge, don't be angry with him!" Belinda cried, and came running after him.

And the kid wasn't in his bed, or even in his room. He was out on the back patio, staring at the sky. Over the city there was nothing to be seen except the usual yellowish reflection of its lights on the low haze that had blotted out the stars since last October.

"Now you come right back indoors!" Belinda snapped, diving past her husband and sweeping the boy off his feet. "How often do I have to tell you? You *never* go outside without your mask!"

"But I saw fireworks!" the boy howled. "Right from my window! I wanna watch the rest of the show!"

"I don't see any fireworks," Halkin muttered, gazing around. "Maybe you dreamed it. Let's get back inside." Already the night air was making his eyelids tingle. He could foresee another stint of watching by Teddy's bed with the oxygen mask poised, and that was the last thing he wanted right now. Tomorrow he'd have to have all his wits about him.

"Right up there!" Teddy shouted, and began to gasp and wheeze and choke as well as cry.

They looked up automatically. Yes, overhead! Something very bright, a flower of flame!

And, on the slant roof of the house, a crash, and a wave of fire that splashed, and soaked their clothes, and clung to their skins, and killed them screaming. It was very good napalm, the best American brand, made by Bamberley Oil.

THE PRECAUTIONARY MEASURE

Twice in the past week a man had followed him home. It was the same one who, for the first time about ten days ago, had shown up at the garbage terminal of the SCRR where the wagons were loaded for disposal inland. He was there ostensibly because he was curious about this notion of reclaiming desert by using metal-free and plastic-free household refuse to impregnate the dusty ground with humus, but he'd shown more interest in the men themselves than in the job they were doing.

If he wasn't a policeman, he was probably a reporter. He tried to reach Peg Mankiewicz, but at the office of her former paper all they could tell him was that she had quit the city. Before the third time could arrive, therefore, Austin Train left his rent for the balance of the month where the landlord would find it first and took a bus north to San Francisco. There was plenty of garbage there too.

And there was something going on inside his head he didn't want screwed up by a glare of renewed publicity.

PICK YOURSELF UP AND START OVER

Weary, Philip Mason let himself into the apartment and hung up his coat and filter-mask. As soon as she heard the door Denise appeared to kiss him hello, and instead of making it a casual embrace threw her arms tight around him and drove her tongue violently into his mouth.

"How can you bear to after what I've done to you?" he muttered when their lips finally separated.

"You silly fool!" She sounded as though she was crying, but her face was against his cheek where he couldn't see it.

"But it's definite now. I've been fired, and they're selling the office complete to some other company—"

"Idiot! I married you because I love you, not to put a

ball and chain on you, and I married *you* and not your job! 'In sickness, in health'—and all that shit."

"I don't deserve you," he said. "I swear I don't . . . Say!" Struck by a sudden thought. "Did you remember to call Douglas?" They had taken to calling Dr. McNeil by his first name.

Her face clouded. "Yes."

"What did he say?"

"Improving, but still not fixed. Another month. Still, that's better news than we've had before . . ." She took his arm. "Come in the living-room, honey. Alan's here, and I was just fixing him a drink."

"Alan Prosser? What does he want?"

"To talk to you, he said. Come on."

"Where are the kids? Aren't they here?"

"No, down with the Henlowes. It's Lydia's birthday. They'll be back in about an hour."

And after greetings Alan leaned back in the big chair he'd been allotted and accepted the drink Denise poured. "You lucky devil," he said to Philip.

"Am I?" Philip said sourly, dropping into his own chair.

"Sure! Having a beautiful wife"—Denise was within arm's reach so he patted her bottom and provoked a wan smile—"a beautiful home that's properly looked after . . . Christ, my place is a shambles!"

"Don't you have—well, a housekeeper or something?" Denise asked. She had only met Alan a couple of times, and on neither occasion had he talked much about himself.

"I tried that." Alan looked lugubrious. "Got me one of those girls from Dominica."

"Oh, the island where they cut down all those trees?" Philip said, more to make polite chitchat than because he was interested.

"That's the one. Now dust storms blow off it all the time, reach as far away as Trinidad, so I was told. Sounds like hell. But anyway, this chick: she didn't work out. Pretty, sure, and likable enough, but—well, I practically had to show her how to use the can, you dig? So when she had to go home, nurse her mother who'd taken sick, I wasn't sorry . . . Still, I guess you aren't thinking so much about your luck as your troubles right now. You are in trouble, aren't you?"

"Did Denise tell you or did you guess?"

"Neither. I just have good financial contacts coast to coast. And the rumors about Angel City are so loud now you can't ignore them. I had stock in your firm—like insurance companies, they cut the meat close to the bone—but I shed my holding weeks ago. Are they going bankrupt, or are they just going to sell their out-of-state operations and retrench on California?"

"Sell off the fringes, of course." But Philip was looking at Alan with new respect. The company had sweated blood to conceal the fact that their total loss was in a fair way to breaking them, and their shares had fallen by only twenty or thirty per cent instead of the probable ninety. "Which includes me," he continued. "I've been given the copper handshake and the business here is being traded as a going concern to a New York company who'll put their own people in. So as of now I'm unemployed."

"No, you're not."

"What?"

"Got any money? Or can you raise some?"

"Ah . . . I don't think I'm with you."

"Plain English, isn't it?" Alan waved his glass in the air. "Do you have any money? A life policy you can borrow against? Second mortgage? Bank loan? Savings?"

"Well, we've never touched what Dennie's father left her— Say! What's all this about?"

"I'm telling you you're not out of work. Not unless you insist. Remember I told you my partner quit me, Bud Burkhardt that you said you'd met?"

"Sure. What about him?"

"Well, I think he was a damned fool to start with,

taking that post at Puritan, so I wasn't sorry to be shut of him—"

"He's with Puritan now?" Denise interrupted. "The man we met when we had the plumbing done over at our last home?"

"That's right." Alan nodded. "He's managing their Towerhill branch."

"Oh, I see what you mean," she said, and bit her lip. "The place is—well, not quite a ghost town now, but . . ." A wave of her elegantly manicured hand.

"I didn't mean that," Alan said. "The profits Puritan take on everything they sell—hell, he's probably already made twice what he could have made if he'd stayed with me. But the Trainites are gunning for Puritan. Didn't you know?"

"No, I didn't!" Philip sat forward in his chair. "I got some Puritan stock. Always understood it was rock-solid. They do say it's a Syndicate company, don't they?"

"Well, it is. But the Trainites are a force to be reckoned with now, and quite pigheaded enough to take on anybody. Besides, what the hell could the Syndicate do against them?"

"So tell me the rest of it!" Philip said impatiently. "I'm far enough down on my luck not to want to lose what I have left."

"Well, I got a lot of Trainites working for me, you know—it's the kind of job they approve of, like providing clean water and getting sewage where it can be useful, and all that stuff. Me, I don't hold with their alarmist ideas, but they're conscientious, reliable, turn up for work on time . . ." His glass was empty; when he tilted it against his mouth Denise rose to refill it. "Thanks. Well, most of the ones work for me come from this wat over by Towerhill, and I heard the other day they're involved in this countrywide project, buying stuff at Puritan and analyzing it."

"Can they?" Denise said.

"I guess so. They're not ignorant, you know—half of

them are college dropouts, but they learned plenty before they quit formal study, and apparently every wat has at least one chemist who keeps a check on their food, makes sure it's safe."

"That sounds sensible," Philip approved. "Especially for the sake of the children."

"Oh, don't think I'm putting down all their ideas. Thanks"—as Denise handed his glass back. "Just the extremist ones. Must admit, if I had kids, I'd like routine food analysis for them."

"So would we!" Denise said forcefully. "Only we made inquiries—and the cost!"

"You don't have to tell *me*." Alan scowled terribly. "You know I bought that house when Belle and I got married, and sold it off when she—uh—when she got shot." Absently curling his fingers around to touch the scar on his palm. "Well, the other day I got this letter from the guy who bought it, saying he's had the dirt in the garden analyzed and it's full of poison because it was laid out on a heap of old mine tailings, and he's going to sue me."

"That's not fair," Denise exclaimed.

"I guess I might have done the same if . . . But the hell!" Gulping at his fresh drink. "The lawyers tell me it's caveat emptor stuff, so it's no skin off my nose. But when I think what could have become of *my* kids . . . !" He shuddered.

"You were talking about your ex-partner," Philip ventured. The prospect of becoming not just unemployed but unemployable, like so many thousands of others, had been haunting him; that tempting half-promise of Alan's was intriguing, and he wanted to hear more.

"Ah, yes! I was going to say, you know I'm having hell's own job since he quit, coping with the business on my own. I'm not a salesman! I'm the practical type. It's my boast that I never hired anyone to do anything I couldn't do myself. I started off laying pipe and digging drains, and I can still drive some of those lazy bastards on my payroll into the ground. But—well, my head's ringing with projects I don't have time for! Come to that, one day I'd like to get married again, and I can't find time to go look for a girl!"

"Yes, you should remarry," Denise said. "You'd make a good husband."

Alan pulled a face. "Sure, a great husband! Home at midnight, out again at seven . . . Hell, that's not the point. The point *is*"—and his new drink emptied at the second swig—"Phil, I need help. I need someone who understands the administrative side of a business. If you want to buy in, ten thousand bucks' worth, even five, I'd like you for my new partner. I've got my eye on something I know I can't handle on my own."

He hunched forward and continued before Philip could speak.

"You think of what's going on all over the country—all over the world, come to that. You've been to LA recently, for example. How's the water?"

"Makes you want to puke," Philip said.

"Did you go down to the beach?"

"Who'd want to?"

"Exactly. Who'd want to? Masochists with a yen for pharyngitis and bowel upsets! Who goes swimming any more except in a private pool? It isn't safe. Hell, I know girls who won't wash their faces except with bottled water, in case it runs into their mouths."

Philip glanced at Denise, who gave a firm nod. "I use it for the kids," she said. "To be on the safe side."

"Well, then, look at this—shit, I thought I brought my bag in with me!" Alan stared around him.

"Under your chair," Denise said, pointing.

"Ah, thanks." He drew out a black portfolio and from it produced a pack of brightly-colored brochures.

"There, that's the latest of Mitsuyama's gadgets. A home water-purifier. Rechargable cartridge system. Cheap—I figure a hundred sixty bucks installed. Cartridges five bucks, last the average family a month, sell 'em in packs of six, lots of repeat business. Recondition them by boiling in a solution that costs fifteen cents a gallon—though naturally you don't tell the clients that. Hell, given the right promotion we could have 'em in every home in Denver inside the year, go on and cover the state!"

"A hundred sixty bucks?" Philip frowned, turning the shiny bright pages of the brochure. "Doesn't sound like it leaves much margin for profit, what with labor costs."

"Hell, I could install one of those things in thirty minutes from the moment I came in the front door!"

"Ah. You're after the city franchise." Philip felt his heart suddenly hammering on his ribs. Alan was right; something like this did have immense commercial potential.

"I'll take the state franchise if I can," Alan grunted. "And what's more I think I have it sewn up. My ex-partner Bud—well, I persuaded him he owes me a favor, and he's not so stupid he's forgetting that he may need a favor himself one of these days. He has good contacts at Colorado Chemical. I've been to see them, they like the idea, and if I can convince them I can handle the volume of business they'll back me to a bid five per cent higher than anyone else."

He sat back with a satisfied grin.

"Well, I don't know they'd approve of me," Philip said after a pause. "I mean, Angel City aren't going to give me the best references in the world, are they?"

"Oh, shit on Angel City!" Alan waved his hand airily. "I explained my publicity gimmick to them, and they like it so much I could hire Fidel Castro for all they'd care."

"What is it?"

"Remember that black cat who made like a hero because of the Towerhill thing? The policeman—what's his name? Oh, yes: Peter Goddard."

"But isn't he paralyzed?" Denise demanded.

"Right now, he's on the mend. Walking already, like from one side of the room to the other. Well, more hobbling, I guess. So naturally they won't take him back on the force. But I was down at the hospital a while back, talking to a doctor I know, and I met the uncle of those kids he saved. Stinking rich bastard, rolling in it! Bee importer. And he was going on about this poor bastard who can't go back to his old job, and getting his hospital care paid for but you can't like have permanent pensioners on your roster for the one favor, and I thought Christ, a hero *and* a black man, what more do you want? And now this comes up, and bang, inspiration! We shame those fat white cats—like you and me for example—into buying our filters, and we get everyone else trailing right along." Alan rubbed his hands gleefully.

"*Oh*, yes! Doesn't it all go click-click into pretty patterns?"

LAB REPORT

SUMMARY: In the presence of Dr. Michael Advowson, the observer appointed by the UN, samples were taken from the batch of "Bamberley Nutripon" allegedly reclaimed from the collapsed cellar in Noshri. These were not from a sealed container and therefore the possibility of later contamination cannot be excluded. Portions were triturated in a variety of solvents and the solution in each case was assayed by standard paper chromatography techniques (Hansen's Analytical Paper Type III). Traces were found in all samples of the same complex alkaloid as had previously been isolated from the urine and blood-serum of human beings from Noshri, resembling certain hydrolyzed derivatives of ergot. Administration of this substance to laboratory animals engendered muscular spasms, aberrant behavior, irrational panic and bloodstained stools. It appears in the highest degree probable that this substance was the causative agent of the Noshri disaster; however, it has not been possible to determine at what point it was introduced into the foodstuff.

—Paris, at the *Institut Pasteur:*
L.-M. DUVAL (*D. Méd., D.Chim.*)

THE MARVELS OF MODERN CIVILIZATION The small neat secretary, a girl in the smartest of advanced fashionable styles including a skirt slit up to the waist to display at her crotch a tuft of shiny steel wool attached to her panties, listened to the ultramodern intercom on her highly-polished desk. The sound was directionalized, of course. It was cool and quiet in here because instead of windows there were cosmoramic projections, latest of late devices to prevent the intrusion of untasteful exterior reality. Nearby the chimneys reeked a twenty-four-hour day yet the view was of clean white clouds, blue sky, yellow sun not so bright that it dazzled. Superior to the natural article, yes.

Also birds flew or perched between two layers of glass on real branches in air-conditioned environment. It was not ordinary to see birds. Very yes.

"Mr. Hideki Katsamura," the girl said. Mr. Hideki Katsamura rose from the plastic seat, faultless imitation of natural fur without risk of disease or perhaps pejorative associations owing to demise of so many regretted species. Solid family man, well-established, excellent command of English, correctly clad with sober fabric. Unflighty. Not excessively anxious to please and bowing to secretaries as some.

The wait had been long but one understood: the pressure of urgent business.

Very modern, the girl opened the door to Dr. Hirasaku's office by pushing a hidden button.

Later, when Dr. Hirasaku and his co-directors had clearly given instructions for the visit to America allotting the franchises for new water-purifier, also many lists of competing products to be explained inferior and amounts of bids recorded so far and further details to be studied with care, Mr. Katsamura went home to new house in suburb of Osaka where the honey-carts called promptly and the center of the street received replenishment of other household waters in landscaped rivulets arched at one-block intervals with highly artistic ancient Chinese-pattern bridges, typical of supermodern pedestrian-precinct city planning must not be jammed uptight with cars. All excellent. All nylon.

RAVELED SLEEVE The flight they put Michael Advowson on from Paris to New York was routed via London. Subsonic; he insisted. A minor but regular feature of his practice at home had been dressing the scalds of people who had been startled by a sonic boom when picking up the kettle from the fire.

The plane was scheduled to depart Orly at 2129. It was ninety minutes late. There was a bomb scare and they had to search the baggage.

He was in first class, since he wasn't paying the fare himself. When he came aboard he was the only passenger ahead of the dividing curtain. First class kept getting smaller and smaller, harder and harder to fill, and the airlines were always pleased when some large international organization, or a major corporation, lashed out with the higher rate by way of compensating somebody for sending him or her to a place they didn't want to go.

But then there weren't many people in second class, either. People didn't fly the Atlantic any more if they could help it, except from bravado. Even if your plane wasn't sabotaged or hijacked, it was certain to be behind schedule.

Not that there was much to be said for ocean travel either, since the sinking of the *Paolo Rizzi* last summer and the drowning of thirteen hundred passengers in a sea made foul by a hundred and eighty thousand tons of oil from the tanker she'd collided with.

Moral, definitely: stay home.

When they shut off the appalling Muzak, he tried to doze, and nearly made it, but was awoken by the order to fasten his seat belt for the landing at London, which effectively put paid to his chances of sleeping for the moment.

Here, two new passengers took the seats across the aisle from him. In the nearer there was a pretty blonde girl with a drawn, sad expression, and in the window seat a dark-haired man some years her senior who was snoring almost before the plane took off again.

In the vast dim insulated cabin, feeling like Jonah in the belly of the great fish, Michael sat railing against fate.

Why me? Why pick *me* from the quiet fields of Ireland and pitch me into the horrible battlegrounds of the world?

Oh, intellectually he knew very well the reasons for his being selected. Irishmen had often been the mainstay of a UN peace-keeping force; as ex-MO, still on the reserve, who had recently come to the attention of a wide public because he had kicked up a noisy fuss over the slaughtering of cattle which were not in fact suffering an infectious disease . . . Everywhere there had been the gantlets of reporters to run, incompetently aided by minor officials of WHO and/or the Commission on Refugees. He detested public life, which was why he had opted for a quiet country practice instead of the posts he could have had his pick of in major city hospitals, advancing to consultant rank before forty, but condemned to involvement in hospital politics, subservient to committees of civil servants—*no thanks*, he had said, very firmly.

But this he hadn't been able to turn down.

Now when he closed his eyes he saw that poor child Eileen who had nearly lost her toe, multiplied over and over and turned black. He'd never before understood, in the guts where it counts, the misery a modern war could cause.

They had shown him the state people still were in at Noshri, victims of mindless terror, dazed, incapable of concentrating on the simplest tasks, often unable to work out how to feed themselves. Then they had flown him back to Paris, to meet the handful of other victims being cared for in good hospital conditions because Professor Duval was studying them. He had taken with him, in a portfolio chained to his wrist, a sample of Nutripon which, during his stay at Noshri, had been discovered in a cellar—a hole in the ground, really—half-filling a shell-case, a hoard perhaps put away by someone who did not believe there would be more food tomorrow, and who had gone insane or died before returning to eat the rest of what he had been given. He had taken part in the examination of it, watched the analysis, supervised the administration of minute doses to laboratory rats and monkeys . . . There could be no doubt any longer; the food was poisoned. But it remained to be determined how, when, where.

So now to New York, to the UN. When he had never been further from Ireland before than on visits to relatives in Glasgow, Liverpool and London. Often, during the army service which entitled him to his rank of captain and the uniform he was currently compelled to wear since he was traveling on official business, he'd talked to people who had served with peace-keeping forces, sensed the vague pride they felt at being recruited to a cause that had as yet barely been invented, that larger and wealthier countries seemed to despise.

He had tried to encourage that pride in himself. He hadn't had much success.

"What's the uniform?"

An unexpected question from the girl across the aisle as the plane settled to its cruising altitude.

"Ah . . . Irish Army, miss."

"Do they approve of foreign soldiers invading America?" There was a hard bright sneer on her face, a hard bright edge of sarcasm on her voice.

He sighed, and turned his jacket—hanging from a hook at the side of his seat—to display the green-and-white UN brassard on its arm. The world-map symbol was becoming better known as the people of the planet became more frightened of themselves.

"Are you going to the UN, then?"

"Yes."

"Me too. What for?"

"I'm testifying before the inquiry into the Noshri disaster."

"So am I."

He blinked at her in surprise.

"You don't believe me?" Her tone was mocking. "Then you don't know who I am. I'm Lucy Ramage. I'm a nurse. I was working at Noshri. *I* saw what those devils did." The words had an eerie quality in the thrumming twilit cylinder of the plane. "I'm going to tell the world about it, too. You know they locked me up to try and stop me? Said I was crazy and dumped me in a mental home. Well, maybe it's true. What I went through would drive anybody insane. This is the guy who got me out, snoring beside me. Without him I'd still be behind bars. Señor Arriegas, that's his name, but he lets me call him Fernando. He's from the Uruguayan Embassy in London."

The mention of her name had struck a chord in Michael's memory; he'd heard about this girl from one of the doctors at Noshri, a big Swede called Bertil or something. But the reference to Uruguay altered the whole perspective. What in the world could have interested the Tupamaros in a nurse from—wasn't it New Zealand?—who had been working in Africa? Purely because they didn't want to miss another chance to foment anti-American feeling? They were, everyone knew, embittered; when they seized power in the midst of the chaos their sabotage and Robin Hood-style attacks had created, the United States had kicked Uruguay out of the OAS, like Cuba, and then attempted to banish them from the UN as well. Thanks to a brilliant *coup* by the Secretary-General, who whistled up the support not only of both communist blocs but of all but a handful of the nominally neutralist nations, the motion had been overwhelmingly defeated.

So, fuming, Washington had had to choose between expelling the entire UN from its soil—a move that had a lot of backing, of course—and permitting these avowed Marxist-Maoists to enter the States. The compromise had been to let them in, but only on UN passports, not those of their own country. A fiction, and everyone knew it, but at least it had saved the rest of the world from ganging up on America.

Lucy had gone on while he was reviewing all this. He heard her say, "You know, back home in New Zealand I never thought much about politics. I never voted. If I had, I suppose I might have been a Liberal. I only went to work for Globe Relief because it was a chance to travel, see the world before I got married and settled down. It's a good place for kids, New Zealand. I mean I have three nieces and a nephew and they're all okay. But then I saw all those horrors at Noshri and I realized. What they say about the Americans isn't just propaganda, it's all true. Have you been to Noshri?"

"Yes." Michael's voice felt like gravel in his throat. It was becoming clearer by the minute that this girl was mentally disoriented, to put it kindly. She had all the signs: wandering gaze, high-pitched nonstop talking, irrelevance of affect, the lot. How to break off this unwished-for conversation without being downright insulting? Which would certainly lead to a big fuss.

"Yes, I saw in Noshri what the imperialists are doing," Lucy went on, staring straight ahead now. "The rich countries have ruined what they own, so they're out to steal from the people who have a little left. They want the copper, the zinc, the tin, the oil. And of course there's the timber, which is getting scarce." She sounded as though she was reciting a memorized list. Probably was. "Now they've thought of a new way to get it—drive everybody crazy so they can't set up a strong stable independent government. It nearly worked at Noshri, would have done but for General Kaika, so now they're trying it in Honduras."

Michael started. He knew, of course, that there had been some sort of rebellion there, and that the government had called on American aid, but this was the first he'd heard of this particular accusation.

"Ah, you don't want to talk about it, do you?" the girl said. "Your mind's made up and you don't want to be confused with any more facts!" She crowed with laughter and turned her back, curling up on her seat, knees doubled up and her hands interlocked around them.

The plane droned on through the black sky, above the clouds masking the Atlantic. It suddenly occurred to Michael that he ought to look at the moon. He hadn't seen it all the time he was in Paris, nor the stars.

He slid up the blind of his window and peered out. There was no moon visible. When he consulted his diary he discovered that it had set, a tiny sliver, at exactly the time the plane had taken off from London.

Turn right and go home. (He realized he was in his home time zone.)

Wish I could.

APRIL

HERO FIDDLING

Hey, man with the big muscles!
  Yes, you!
Steam-powered, gas-powered, electrically-powered,
You with the big concrete and cement footprints!
Globe-girdler, continent-tamer, putting the planet
    through hoops,
  You I hail!
Packer and preserver of food in incorruptible cans,
Blocker-out of winter-blast with bricks and mortar,
Wheeled, shod, tracked with rails of shining iron,
Multiplier of goods and chattels, chewer-up of forests,
Furrow-maker across the unpopulous plains,
Flier higher than eagles, swimmer swifter than sharks,
Trafficker in the world's wealth, miracle-worker,
  I salute you, I sing your praises . . .

—"Song of the States Unborn," 1924

A VICTIM OF THE FIRST WORLD WAR

"I've done *my* best," Gerry Thorne said, sounding aggrieved, and well he might be. Both he and Moses Greenbriar had been doing nicely out of the aid shipments from the Bamberley hydroponics plant—half a cent per person fed had added up to a considerable sum over the years. Moreover, several of the left and center group in Congress, small though that might nowadays be, had been advocating purchase of Nutripon by organizations like Earth Community Chest to maintain the welfare allotments in major cities where right-wing mayors were axing their welfare budgets on grounds of economy. There had been fairly widespread starvation during the past winter.

"I can't work miracles," he added.

Well . . . maybe only conjuring tricks. Like this second home in the Virgins, splendid with its high stone-and-timber walls and this verandah on which you could pretty often sit right outdoors, provided the wind was from the south, not from the fetid puddle of the Gulf of Mexico or the colossal revolving sewer of the Sargasso. Never mind that the venom of the Trainites had reached this far and there was a fading line of skull-and-crossbones symbols facing the sea. Nobody really begrudged such luxury to a man who'd made his money in a Good Cause. He might have gone to work for DuPont.

The most remarkable thing of all was that you could still swim from here; although the Canary Current did sometimes sweep the ordure of Europe this far over, the Antilles Current came from the relatively cleanly coast of underdeveloped South America. This morning's Coast Guard bulletin had said the water was okay, so Elly Greenbriar and Nancy Thorne were proving it.

"But where the hell did the stuff come from? The drug, the whatever!" Thorne's question was rhetorical; the UN inquiry had been set up to determine exactly that.

"Well, it wasn't the factory," Greenbriar said, and took another sip of his gin. "We asked the Federal Narcotics Bureau for one of their top forensic chemists, and he tested fifty random samples from the warehouse. All clean. We're set to give his report to the inquiry next week, but it won't be much help."

"I guess not. We've got everybody against us now, from the stinking isolationists who 'don't see why we should give away our precious food to ungrateful bastards,' clear to the ungrateful bastards themselves. Anyway, a denial never catches up with a rumor. Did you hear about the raid on San Diego, for example? Some crazy Mex-Tup kid—say, you heard that one? Petronella Page used it on her show the other night. Mex-Tup kid! I thought it was kind of neat."

"What do you mean, raid?" grunted Greenbriar. "Raids, plural. Three so far, according to my cousin Sophie."

"How many?"

"Three. Sophie's lived out there for twenty years, but when she called me the other day she said she's thinking of moving back east. After the first raid they had another —they don't think it was the same gang, because the payload was thermite instead of napalm—and then there was a third that burned out a block of black tenements."

"Bastards," Thorne said. "Burning people in their homes, hell!" His eyes were following a ship that had emerged into blurred view from the haze to the north: new and smart, one of the latest deep-trawling fish factories designed to bring up squid from the relatively safe bottom water. Surface fish nowadays were either so rare as to be prohibitively expensive, like cod and herring, or hopelessly high in dangerous substances such as organic mercury. But so far squid were generally okay.

"Is that the second or third we've seen today?" Greenbriar asked.

"Third. Must be a good season for fishing . . . I imagine you told your cousin she ought to move?"

"Oh, I've been telling her since the LA quake of '71, but of course she'd have taken such a loss on her home . . . Still, I guess she's finally made up her mind."

"Speaking of losses," Thorne murmured, "did you have stock in Angel City?"

Greenbriar gave a rueful smile.

"Me too. And they went through the floor. I switched into Puritan, but I lost a packet even so."

"You take my advice," Greenbriar said, "you switch right back *out* of Puritan."

"Why in the world? They're a Syndicate operation, aren't they? Which makes them just about the solidest stock in the market."

"Oh, sure, anything the Syndicate is backing turns to gold. But"—Greenbriar dropped his voice—"I hear gossip. Maybe only scuttlebutt, of course. Even so . . ."

"Such as what?"

"The Trainites are after them."

"Impossible!" Thorne jolted upright in his chair. "But the Trainites are on their side, always have been!"

"Then why are they conducting massive analyses of Puritan products?"

"Who says they are? Or even if they are, what does it signify? You know how paranoid they are about what they eat."

"Paranoid enough to enlist Lucas Quarrey of Columbia?"

Thorne stared.

"It's a fact," Greenbriar said. "I know someone who knows him; in fact he's done some minor contract work for the Trust now and then. Apparently he was discreetly approached the other day and asked if he would coordinate this project the Trainites' own chemists have already launched."

Thorne rounded his mouth into an O. "That's a change of gear for them, isn't it? But what can they hope to gain by attacking the only company that devotes itself exclusively to pure foods? Let alone bucking the Syndicate, of course."

"My guess is that they want to try and drive their prices down. Maybe collect data on as many slip-ups as possible—in an operation that size, some stuff must leak through now and then which isn't as good as the advertising claims—and use these as a pistol to hold to the company's head."

Thorne rubbed his chin. "Yes, that fits. I remember an article by Train in which he was very scathing about people profiteering from public concern about diet. Who's behind this, though—it couldn't be Train himself, could it?"

"Hardly. Train's dead. Killed himself. I had it on very

good authority. Never really recovered from his breakdown, you know. But I guess it could be one of these people who took over his name." Greenbriar cocked his head and sniffed loudly. "Hey, spring must be really here!"

"What?" Bewildered, both at the irrelevance and also because here in the Virgins there was always luxuriant vegetation the year around.

Greenbriar chuckled. "Try a noseful. Violets!"

Thorne complied: hmff, hmff! "You're right," he said in surprise. "But if it's that strong it's not likely to be flowers, is it?"

"I guess not. Hmm! Very odd! Which way's the wind now? Oh yes, it's still off the water." He stared down toward the beach where Elly and Nancy were splashing about in the shallows, obviously on their way back to the house.

Well, the world was full of mysteries. Thorne shrugged. "Looks as though they're coming in for lunch," he said. "I'll just go tell—"

He was interrupted by a scream.

Both he and Greenbriar leapt from their chairs. Down there in the water Nancy was thrashing wildly about, and Elly, who had wandered some distance from her, had spun around to rush and help her.

"Quick!" Thorne snapped, dumped his glass on the handiest table and ran down the steps to the shore. He continued straight into the water as Elly tried to raise Nancy to her feet.

The stink of violets was incredibly strong.

"Look—out!" Nancy choked, and with one arm around Elly's shoulders pointed to an object just barely showing above the water. Shapeless, encrusted, it could have been mistaken for a rock. But something yellowish was dispersing from it through a narrow crack in its end.

Thorne stared at his wife in horror. Her eyes were swelling, puffing out almost literally as he watched, turning the whole upper part of her face into a hideous bloated mass. Also her lips were dotted with pustules, her shoulders, her breasts.

"Moses! Phone a doctor!" he screamed. "Helicopter ambulance service!"

The fat man turned and stumbled back indoors, and in the same moment Nancy doubled over, vomiting, then slumped in a faint.

Helped by one of their local manservants who appeared in answer to Greenbriar's frantic shouting, Thorne and Elly carried her awkwardly into the house, laid her down on a couch, sent the cook for clean water, soothing ointment, the first-aid kit.

"They're sending the ambulance right away, with a doctor," Greenbriar panted, hurrying back from the phone. "But what can have happened to her? A jellyfish?"

"Damn it, no!" But of course he hadn't been down on the beach, seen the drum, or barrel, or whatever, half-sunk in the sand. "Did they say what we should do in the meantime?" Thorne demanded.

"I—" Greenbriar put his hand to his mouth in absurdly childlike fashion. "I didn't ask."

"Idiot!" Thorne was beside himself with panic. "Get right back and—"

But Greenbriar was already on his way.

"What the hell *can* it be?" Elly moaned.

"Lewisite," the doctor said when he'd finished administering emergency oxygen. Not only the doctor, but a nurse and a sergeant of police had turned up in the helicopter.

"What's that?" Thorne asked, bewildered.

"A poison gas."

"*What?*"

"Yes, the smell of violets is unmistakable. I've seen two or three cases like this—not here, in Florida where I used to live. It's an arsenical compound they invented in the First World War. Didn't get around to using it, so they dumped it in the ocean. What happened in

Florida was that they'd dropped a batch into the Hatteras Canyon, and one of these new deep-trawling fishing boats hauled a lot of it up. They had no idea what they'd got—after sixty years they were all crusted with barnacles and things, of course—so they cracked one of the drums open, thinking it might be valuable. When they found it was dangerous, they just pitched the lot overside again, but by then they were in shallow water and some of the drums smashed on the bottom rocks. A hell of a lot washed up on shore."

"I never heard about that," Thorne whispered.

"Would you expect to? It would have ruined the winter vacation trade—not that there's much left of it anyway. I got out because I wanted clean beaches for my kids, not because Florida was so healthy I didn't have enough patients!" With an ironical chuckle he turned to examine Nancy again; the oxygen had had its effect and she was breathing easier.

"I guess we can move her now," he said. "Don't worry too much. There may not be permanent scars. Though of course if she inhaled or swallowed the stuff . . . Well, we'll see."

"This time," Thorne said as though he hadn't been listening, "the news is going to get around. I'll see to that."

DON'T TOUCH . . . *alleging, quote, intelligence with a proscribed country. End quote. It's claimed that he attempted to obtain air-pollution data from Cuban sources. Protesting the arrest, some two hundred students from Columbia were joined by approximately a thousand Trainites in a demonstration which the police dispersed with tear smoke. Eighty-eight hospitalizations were reported, but no deaths. Asked to comment just prior to his departure for Hollywood where he will again preside at the Oscar ceremonies, Prexy said, quote, If that's the guy who claims we're running short of oxygen, tell him I don't find any difficulty in breathing. End quote. Heavy fighting again today in Guanagua province as Honduran government forces supported by American air cover . . .*

REHEARSAL

Exactly what Hugh Pettingill had expected to find at the wat, he couldn't have said. After only a short while, though, he was certain it wasn't there. Day in, day out, he drifted through it and around it, watching the snows melt and spring come hesitantly to the surrounding high valleys. He didn't click. He didn't fit in. He felt excluded. And despite not being sure whether he wanted to fit in or not, he resented being denied the choice.

Physically, the environment was comfortable: shabby, pieced together from scrap, but practical and in many respects attractive. What jarred on him, though, was the way in which everyone at the wat took it for granted that this was a rehearsal: not for the aftermath of an all-over war, just a dry run for the ordinary life of the twenty-first century. He couldn't see it. For him it was more like escapism, running to hide from the real world.

Granted, they had some things going for them: the food, for example, though plain was delicious, better even than what he'd had at the Bamberleys', and he ate voraciously of the savory soups, the home-baked bread, the vegetables and salads grown under glass. That interested him, a little. He hadn't watched things grow before, except some pot seeds he'd planted at college, and for a while he joined in with some of the routine spring tasks out of doors. When he had to distribute the gallon of worms Felice had brought, though, he found the job so distasteful—tipping all those anonymous wrigglers out in doses of ten or a dozen and watching them dive among what was going to become food that he might eat—he moved on to other things. There was a handicrafts shop, and he helped in the making of some rough stools and tables, because last year for the first time ever more Americans had taken vacations inland than by the sea, and the idea was to run a restaurant for tourists during the coming summer, get some wholesome natural-grown food down them in the hope of showing them what they were missing. But turning out one stool exactly like another grew monotonous. He moved on again.

All the time, though: this feeling that the world was *bound* to go to hell! Okay, so it's true these mothers have turned prairies into dustbowls and used the sea for a giant sewer and laid concrete where there used to be forests. So stop them! Don't just let them walk over you, crush you face-down into the dirt!

Crush them first!

That strange cold Peg: she must, he concluded, be queer, because she didn't—not only not with him, not with anybody. (Not even with Felice whom he'd naturally assumed to be her girl, who did, though also not with him. Shit!) Yet she seemed somehow happy.

Found something here. What? Resignation? Could a former crusading reporter and campaigner for Women's Lib be satisfied with such a drab existence?

Well, the fact stood. Even though Felice had left after a week or so, uttering some kind of weird apology to everyone and saying she'd had a fantastic vacation—hell, *vacation*, in a place where work literally never stopped! —Peg had stayed, and seemed content, inasmuch as you could figure out what she was thinking behind that lovely but stone-cold face . . .

If he'd been asked before he came here, "Are you a Trainite?", Hugh would have answered that he was without hesitation, on the strength of having taken part in Trainite demonstrations at college. Recruiters for the big corporations came around all the time nowadays, not just in spring and summer, because the number of students taking up science and engineering had fallen by around 60 per cent and those taking business management by 30 per cent and those who couldn't get into something constructive like agriculture or forestry (which generally meant emigrating, of course) preferred to drop out. So these frantic recruiters were a nuisance and now and then one of them gave particular offense and it was necessary to dump him in a dirty river or strip him and paint the skull and crossbones on his belly.

The people here, though, weren't in the least like the Trainites he'd known outside. And obviously this was more what Austin Train himself had had in mind. This cat Jones had been a personal friend of Train's, and he'd had the guy to stay several times before he vanished. (He wasn't dead; Hugh had learned that much for certain. Nobody, though, would admit to knowing where he was.)

He struggled and struggled to make sense of what was going on around him, and bits of it fitted fine. Only whenever he thought he had the pattern straight in his head, something turned up which completely screwed him.

The simple life bit, the natural foods—so far, so good. Also the clothing woven from natural fibers which would rot: cotton, linen, wool. Fine. The composting of vegetable peelings and such, the sorting and cleaning of the inescapable cans, the return of plastics to the nearest reclamation company, which called for a once-monthly trip by the communal jeep. Great. But if it was the simple life they were after, how come they used electricity? It was all very well to say it was clean power and could be generated from waterfalls and tides. The fact stood: it hadn't been. And their insistence that tomorrow it would have to be and (here it came again, the same dirty argument) they were rehearsing for tomorrow, devising a viable life-style by trial and error—that didn't convince him. Sixty-some people in this wat, and this the largest out of only about four or five hundred in the whole of the States and Canada: how many of the human race were going to learn about this life-style before the crunch came? Every day in the news some fresh warning signl

Of course it was as well they did have electricity, or

his car would still be stranded where Peg and Felice had found him. Instead they'd brought the batteries in and recharged them, and now it was here and any time he wanted to get the hell out, he could. He was becoming daily more tempted. The whole scene here struck him as play-acting.

They listened to radio news a lot and talked a lot about things he was sure they didn't properly understand, like the Honduras war and the starvation in Europe since the Med stagnated. And didn't give. Somehow. Even the kids. There was this Rick in particular that made his skin crawl, Zena's adopted son (and formerly Decimus's; the cat being dead you'd think they might stop talking about him, but they never seemed to, especially Rick who claimed that when he grew up he was going to find the person who'd poisoned his dad. Christ!)—this Rick, anyway, kept hanging around him all day maybe because other people were busy, and asking crazy questions he couldn't answer, like why isn't the sun always square overhead when it's noon on the clock and if you can't tell me what book do I look in for the answer, huh? He wanted to be an astronomer when he grew up, he said. Fat chance. They were closing down observatories all over.

What the hell did all this have to do with being a Trainite? Out there those stinking bastards raping and murdering and poisoning . . . Christ. Where's a pistol? Where's a bomb?

He tried to read Austin Train's works. They had a complete set. It was dull.

The only person he met during his stay at the wat whom he took to was an outsider, laid off from the Bamberley hydroponics plant: a light-colored cat about his own age, named Carl Travers. He had a vague feeling he might have seen the guy before, but he wasn't sure.

Carl looked in pretty frequently, and talked friendly,

but didn't show any inclination to stay—wouldn't have come so often but for being out of work. He had good khat, which right now Hugh didn't dig too well because it intensified his feeling of having too much energy all pent up inside and no way to let it out, and also pot. So now and then they went out together for a smoke. It had to be out. The Trainites didn't approve.

"You got family?" Hugh said one day when they were pretty high, parked in Carl's second-hand Ford on a curving mountain road watching the sun sink red toward the haze along the coast.

"Like brothers and sisters," Carl said.

"Older, younger?"

"Younger except Jeannie. I don't see her too often. She married into the fuzz. This cat who got made like a hero in the avalanche."

"Ah-hah?"

Time passed. Impossible to tell how long. It was the high.

"You?"

"No." Don't count the Bamberley gang as family. Never mentioned that bunch of creeps to Carl.

"That why you're at the wat?"

"Hell, *I* don't know why I'm at the wat."

"You don't like it?"

"Nope. You live with your folks?"

"Shit, no. Furnished room, other side of town from them. Self-supporting, me. Working man. I mean, I was."

More silence. To roll another joint.

"Thinking of moving away. Wait till hell freezes over before they reopen the plant. Never liked the work anyhow."

"Where to?"

"Maybe Berkeley."

"Ah, shit, California you don't see the sun one year's end to the next! Whole state stinks!"

"Maybe so, but they gon' have that big quake one day soon, and I'd kinda like to be on hand and laugh . . . Got friends in Berkeley, though. Was in college a year."

"Me too."

"Dropped out?"

"Dropped out."

More silence. To burn up the joint.

"Make the scene together?"

"Yeah."

"Man, I'm *high*. Want to screw?"

"Yeah."

BEFORE WE ARE SO RUDELY INTERRUPTED

"I have an appointment with Mr. Bamberley," Michael said, and glanced at the wall clock. "I see I'm a few minutes early, though."

"Oh, you must be Captain Advowson!" the girl at the reception desk said brightly—but not very clearly; there was something in her mouth and her voice was hoarse. On the corner of her desk, an open package of throat pastilles. They scented the vicinity strongly with menthol. "Do sit down and I'll tell Mr. Bamberley you're here. Would you like me to take your filtermask?"

"Thank you." He undid the strap and gave it to her, and she added it to a rack where there were already eight or ten dangling.

Moving to a chair on the other side of this spacious ante-room, he glanced back at her, and she noticed and smiled, thinking it was because she was pretty. In fact it was because she reminded him of the nurse from Noshri—the same shade of fair hair, the same general cast of features. Though much plumper and lacking the dark undereye pouches that marred Lucy Ramage's good looks.

He'd seen her twice again since their meeting on the plane, once in the flesh at the UN building and once late at night on TV, on a talk show run by a woman called Petronella Page. She'd sat dead still, impervious to even the most subtly vicious verbal jabs, and recited a low-voiced account of incredible suffering which the commère had tried to interrupt, and tried again, and each time failed. Cold as falling snow, settling ultimately into a dead weight of horror, huge, massive, stifling, the words followed one another until when they turned the cameras on the audience they weren't quite quick enough to avoid the sight of a girl in the second row fainting and falling from her chair.

When she started on accusations of deliberate genocide they brought the next commercials in early.

Who the hell *had* poisoned that relief food? Someone out to discredit Western aid programs must have got at the affected consignment, opened the cartons, sprayed the contents, resealed them. Even though Duval insisted that this was inconsistent with the uniform distribution of the drug throughout the interior of the pieces he'd examined . . .

How much longer was that damned inquiry going to drag on? He wanted more than anything to go home, but he was under orders to remain until the distinguished international jurists now sifting the evidence issued their final report. If he survived that long.

Gingerly he touched a bruise at the corner of his jaw. About a week ago he'd been to a party, six blocks from his hotel, and he'd been incautious enough to walk home after midnight. Someone had jumped him with a blackjack. Luckily the bruise was the worst effect.

Also he'd developed conjunctivitis two days after his arrival, and as a result was still wearing a piratical black patch over his left eye. Then he'd been warned to get rid of his beard, because the police didn't like them, and a minor shaving cut—on the side opposite his bruise—had become infected, and he'd been assured it was because he'd been stupid enough to shave with regular tap-water. No one he'd met at the UN used anything but an electric shaver, and in fact the drugstore clerk from whom he'd bought his razor and shaving cream had looked puzzled and tried to insist on his buying a bactericidal after-shave lotion as well. But he'd thought the man was just trying to squeeze out a drop of extra profit.

Now the cut had festered into a miniature boil, with an ugly white head on it. It was protected by a bandaid, but sooner or later he feared it would have to be lanced.

Incredible. But he'd been told repeatedly that every stranger to New York suffered the same way. The natives, of course, were resistant, but anyone from more than say a hundred miles distant lacked the immunities the residents had acquired.

And even the residents weren't too happy. . . At one of the many parties around the diplomatic circuit which he'd been obliged to attend he'd met a girl in her middle twenties, pretty with dark hair and a good figure, very drunk although the party had only been under way for an hour. She was looking for an ear to bend, and out of politeness—or perhaps boredom—Michael lent her his. She was working at the UN as a secretary, because, she said, she'd wanted to do something to improve the world. And found it simply wasn't possible. She claimed that she'd hoped to marry a man she knew from college, who turned her down when he learned she wanted to work for those stinking commie-front bastards; that he was so far from unique that she'd lost friend after friend until now her only social life was on this level, these endless formal cocktail parties where people of a dozen different nationalities misunderstood one another at the tops of their voices.

"But we're all stuck on this same ball of mud, aren't we?" He heard her voice again in memory, nearly breaking into a sob. "And the only people who seem to care are the wrong ones, I mean the ones you're not supposed to be friends with. I met this Uruguayan the other day, Fernando Arri—something, I forget. But did you hear what happened to him?"

Michael shook his head.

"He was going home to the place where all the Uruguayans live—they're not allowed off Manhattan, you know, and they have to live in this block near the UN

Plaza—and it was raining, and four men who'd been pretending to shelter under an awning jumped him. Kicked him in the balls and knocked out four of his teeth."

"Good lord," Michael said. "Did the police—?"

"Police!" A hard brittle laugh, like a scream. "They were the police! They found the sole-marks of a police boot on his face!"

At which point she sobered, almost like magic, because it was time for the party to break up, and said, "Thank you for listening to my drunken babbling. Unless I get someone to take me seriously now and then I think it must really all be a dream. Can I buy you dinner? You deserve it."

And, when he hesitated, she added, "I know a marvelous restaurant where they still have real food."

Which was the bait he couldn't resist. Everything he'd eaten here tasted to him of plastic and chewed paper.

Over the meal—which was good, despite his astonished discovery that what he thought of as everyday basics at home, such as ham and herring, appeared here in the "gourmet" section of the menu and were charged extra—she talked calmly and reasonably of fearful things. About her elder sister who had borne two children in New York, and they were both sub-normal: not moronic, just slow, the older beginning to read at last after his ninth birthday; about flowers she had tried to grow in a window-box at her apartment, that wilted and dropped their leaves after a week; about the cost of hospitalization insurance; about the panhandler she had found wheezing against a wall, begging a quarter for oxygen; about the rain that melted stockings and panty-hose into holes. Michael had experienced New York rain. It had ruined one of his uniforms. But at least he was able to revert to mufti now.

And then, when he escorted her home—by taxi, of course—she said on the threshold, "I'd like to ask you up and make love. But it'll have to be next time. I have another week to go before it's safe."

He'd thought: rhythm method? But she'd disabused him.

The commonest disease after measles . . .

"Captain Advowson!"

He rose and went through the door smilingly held for him.

Bamberley's office was like every other room he had been in since arriving here: armored against exterior reality. Windows that must not be opened. Air processed and scented. Pictures, originals, expensive but bad. Much modern gadgetry. A built-in bar with its door ajar. And not one book.

How long, Michael wondered, before he went mad for lack of an Atlantic breeze blowing across the butter-yellow miles of flowering furze?

Mr. Bamberley, affably extending his hand, was not alone. With him was the thin man Gerry Thorne whom Michael had met at the UN inquiry which he'd attended on behalf of Globe Relief, and Moses Greenbriar, the trust's senior treasurer. Thorne appeared distracted. Dutifully Michael shook hands, refused a cigar, accepted a drop of Irish whiskey from a full bottle probably specially obtained in his honor.

"Well, now!" The preliminaries over, Mr. Bamberley didn't seem quite in control of the situation, and looked beseechingly at Greenbriar, who coughed discreetly. Which was a mistake, because a second later he coughed for real, and wheezed, and had to stifle it with a tissue and sniff some kind of a cure from a white plastic tube. Michael waited. Eventually he recovered and apologized.

"Well, captain, I imagine you can guess why we've asked you to spare us a little of your valuable time. We're in an impossible position. Our Colorado plant is shut down, as you know, the staff has had to be laid off—"

"And starving people are being deprived of what could make the difference between life and death!" Mr. Bamberley burst out.

"I'm sorry to have to say this," Michael sighed. "But at Noshri I saw people who would literally be better off dead."

There was an awkward pause.

"Perhaps," Greenbriar said at length. "But the fact stands: Bamberley relief foods have saved thousands, one might even say millions, of lives on previous occasions, and the sabotaging of one consignment must not be allowed to put a full stop to our work. And if these damned Tupas manage to make their accusations stick, regardless of what the official inquiry reports, that's what will happen."

"You have heard what they're saying, have you?" Mr. Bamberley said. "Lies, of course—damnable lies! They'll stick at nothing to malign this country."

Outside the UN building itself, this was the first time Michael had heard reference here to the charge that relief food sent to Honduras had been poisoned the same way as that in Noshri. The Uruguayans had made a formal deposition to the inquiry and demanded that a neutral team of doctors be sent to investigate, but no action had been taken. He'd watched for comment on TV or in the few surviving New York newspapers, expecting at least an indignant rebuttal, but to his amazement the matter was being ignored. He'd been told at home, a year or so ago, by someone returned from visiting an American cousin, that the news media were complying with the president's celebrated dictum, "If the papers know what's good for them they'll print what's good for America!" He hadn't believed it. He was still trying not to. But it was getting harder by the day.

"According to what I learned at the inquiry," he ventured, "the Nutripon sent to Honduras was manufactured and dispatched at just about the same time as the African supplies—"

"Yes, and no doubt the Tupas' next step," Greenbriar broke in, "will be to fake up some poisoned Nutripon and claim it was found at San Pablo! But if this were true, why did we hear nothing about it until last month? Why haven't Honduran government doctors reported mass psychosis similar to that at Noshri? Why did the forensic people give the stored Nutripon a clean bill of health, although our stocks went right back to the end of the Christmas-New Year holiday and must have been the very next batch off the production line?"

"Well, of course that's what the inquiry's trying to find out," Michael said. "But one assumes that either someone got at your vats and deliberately added the drug—and you insist that's impossible—or some natural ergot-like fungus contaminated your regular yeasts."

"That seems to be the only acceptable explanation," Mr. Bamberley said with a shrug. "And it's not something we can be blamed for. We can only take steps to prevent a recurrence, and of course offer compensation for what it's worth."

"And in pursuit of that goal," Greenbriar said, "we're having the air-purifying system of the plant redesigned by a firm specializing in germ-free operation theaters. I think you'll concede they must work to pretty demanding standards?"

"One would hope so," Michael said dryly. "But standards are only as good as the people who comply with them. I once saw a small boy given gangrene in a modern hospital because a surgeon who should have known better lifted a dressing to inspect an incision without putting on a mask. He breathed resistant staph all over the wound. The boy died."

There was another pause, this time a very uncomfortable one. During it, Michael decided he didn't much like Moses Greenbriar. He had already concluded he didn't like Gerry Thorne.

Why not? He was getting a glimmering of the reason. It had something to do with the fact that these incredibly rich people had grown fat on charitable undertakings. For Michael—raised as a Catholic, although no longer a believer—the image they evoked was that of the Borgia popes.

"Naturally we'd go to any length to avoid that kind of oversight," Greenbriar said at last. "But the main point is this, captain. Clearly, before we can put the plant back into operation, we shall need to have our new arrangements approved by some disinterested party. We can hardly ask for a UN team, as such—as you know, any hint of 'UN meddling' in the domestic affairs of this country provokes a tremendous outcry. On the other hand there's a great traditional sympathy, one might almost say a great love, for Ireland, so it occurred to us that we should invite you to—"

He got that far, when there was a sudden vast *thump*, as though the building had been kicked by a passing giant a thousand feet tall, and the not-supposed-to-be-opened windows fell in big brilliant splinters and the ceiling slammed down on them and the stomach-turning street air of New York came rolling in.

Minutes before, a car painted with a skull and crossbones had been illegally parked in front of the building, on 42nd Street. The driver—masked, of course, like everyone on the sidewalks—jumped out and ran toward a nearby drugstore. A patrolman across the street noticed, and thought little of it; Trainites were forever drawing skull-and-crossbones signs on cars, and not everyone could spare the time or money to clean them off straight away. Besides, if the guy had run into a drugstore he was likely in need of urgent medicine.

So he just made a mental note to tell him off when he came back.

Only he didn't come back. He continued out the other door of the drugstore and doubled into the bowels of Grand Central Station, and was well out of reach when the fuse in the back of the car reached what they later estimated to be over fifty sticks of dynamite.

BLEST ARE THE PURE IN BOWEL

It turned out that Doug McNeil had actually been to Japan. Denise was gossiping in his office after he'd treated Josie for a minor bout of worms—probably picked up off a dog, and how could you stop a kid fondling a puppy or a kitten?—and he happened to mention that he'd attended a medical conference in Tokyo.

So naturally when the question came up of how to entertain this Mr. Hideki Katsamura who was in the States letting the franchises for the new water-purifier, they consulted him. Katsamura was making a grand tour, starting in California—where the franchise was obviously going to Roland Bamberley and thank goodness he'd confined himself to bidding for a single state because no one else stood a chance—and continuing via Texas and the Atlantic seaboard to New York and New England, and finally doubling back to Chicago and Denver. Afraid of being outdone because a big Chicago-based corporation was bidding for exclusive rights covering six states, Alan had instantly let his reflexes be triggered: the Denver Hilton, a restaurant in Larimer Square, the best nightclub in town, where can I get a girl because of geishas—?

But Doug said hold it just a moment: not the Hilton but the Brown Palace, and the old part at that provided they've fixed the earthquake damage. These Japanese are nuts about other countries' traditions. And don't take him to a restaurant, either; lots of Japanese are envious of the freedom with which Europeans and Americans invite guests into their own homes, instead of entertaining them in restaurants which is Japanese SOP.

Plainly, though, Alan couldn't invite the guy for dinner in his small bachelor pad, and at first it looked as though Philip couldn't either because Denise went straight into a tizzy. She'd never minded being hostess to Philip's superiors from Angel City, but a Japanese was a different matter. She kept talking about not knowing how to make tempura or sukiyaki.

"Come off it!" Doug chided her. "If you went to Tokyo would you want to be greeted with hamburgers and French fries? I admit you probably would, because even when I was there four years ago they'd had to give up most of their traditional dishes like raw fish. I tried some that was supposed to be okay, and it tasted great, but I went down with dysentery the next day—did I have cramps! But anyway that's not the point. You fix steaks, with lots of fried onions, and maybe start with some New Zealand clam chowder, which is pretty much like the New England stuff and a sight safer, and get lots of salad from Puritan, and . . ."

"It's going to cost the earth!" Denise worried, making up her shopping list.

"It's on the firm," Alan said. "Just get the stuff!"

So of course because he'd been such a help they invited Doug, and his pretty English wife Angela, and inevitably, his mother, a spry, bright-eyed woman of sixty-five called Millicent by everybody including her son and daughter-in-law with whom she appeared to have a marvelous relationship. And Alan, of course, and the man from Colorado Chemical who was sponsoring the Prosser Enterprises bid, Sandy Bollinger with his wife Mabel, and to make up the even number because Katsamura was traveling alone without a secretary Alan's right-hand woman, Dorothy Black, thirty-five, plain, single, but a good talker with a fund of jokes.

All planes of course were always late, but they hadn't expected Katsamura's to be quite so far behind schedule. When Philip, tired by an hour's waiting at the airport, made inquiries, he learned that among the baggage being loaded at Chicago O'Hare had been a case marked with a skull and crossbones, which naturally they opened. When it proved to contain nothing but a printed data sheet repeating Professor Quarrey's findings on high-altitude exhaust residues they concluded it must be meant to distract attention from something else, maybe a bomb. So they searched everything and everybody and instead of arriving at 1650 Mr. Katsamura landed at 1912.

During the wait Alan had said, "By the way, how are you?"

"Doug says another week at most."

"Isn't it hell, sweating out the time? This is my longest stretch without since I was sixteen."

At least it was a relief to be able to talk casually about it. With it so common, it was absurd to pretend it didn't exist.

The flight number went up on the arrivals board and they headed for the barrier, looking. Philip was vaguely expecting someone small and yellow with horn-rimmed glasses and a habit of continual stooping, half-formed bows. But there wasn't anyone like that. There was only a man of about forty, wearing a black coat, roughly as tall as himself, slightly sallow and with the skin around his eyes drawn tight on the bone.

"Mr. Katsamura?" Alan said, offering his hand.

"Yes, sir!" said Mr. Katsamura, who had learned a great deal very quickly during his so far two and a half weeks in the States, chiefly concerning proper social conduct and right use of jargon—correction, *slang*. He shook, smiled, was introduced to Philip too, and apologized for making them wait yet one moment longer.

It was face-losing. But utterly unavoidable. Had been also on the plane. Troublesome and problematic. Moreover, of excessive long-standing: since the first day of the tour! Medicine bought in Texas was used up and had not cured the distressing malfunction. It would be constructive to investigate a doctor here.

Behind him the door swung to which was marked MEN.

Nervous in a gown bought specially for the occasion and a brand-new wig, Denise served cocktails and appetizers when they brought him on from the hotel where he'd dumped his bags—and made further use of excellent American apparatus. Her nervousness faded within minutes. He talked freely and fluently with everyone: to Doug about their respective reactions to the foreignness of each other's countries; to Sandy Bollinger about the impact of the European depression on international finance; to Denise about the ailments of children because his own were continually suffering minor allergies, fevers, similar disorders. Behind his back Millicent caught Philip's eye and ringed her thumb and forefinger: okay! Philip grinned back, thinking what a stroke of luck it had been to meet Doug.

And Katsamura faded to the bathroom again.

"Something's wrong with that guy," Alan said in a low tone. "He went at the airport too, and the hotel."

"*Turismo?*" offered Angela McNeil.

"But he's been in the country over two weeks," Mabel Bollinger objected. "Even in Brazil I never had it longer than three or four days."

"Well, we have a doctor right here," Dorothy Black said practically.

Doug bit his lip. "I'll see if I can help," he said, but sounded doubtful. "Phil, do you keep any specifics for diarrhea? Chlorhydroxyquinoline, say?"

"Well—uh—no. I generally use khat, and we could hardly offer him that. I mean it's not legal. Honey, you got anything for the kids?"

"Not right now," Denise said. "I used up the last lot. Meant to get some more but in all this rush I forgot."

"Khat, did you say?" Dorothy inquired. "What does that have to do with it?"

"Entrains constipation as a side effect," Doug answered. And snapped his fingers. "Side effect! Yes, I think I have something in my bag."

"If it's not impolite of me," he murmured a minute later, "you do know I'm a doctor, don't you?"

Katsamura flushed sallow rose.

"Swallow two of these—not with tap-water, I got you some bottled water from the kitchen. Here. Tomorrow I'll arrange for Phil Mason to deliver you something better, but this will help for a few hours." Slipping a little white packet into the other's hand.

Alone again, Katsamura reflected that this was most sound, most sensible, calculated to reduce the risk of later and worse embarrassments. It was known there were substantial funds behind the Prosser bid, if not as great as those at Chicago. This had led to acceptance of the dinner invitation in a private home and other unstrictly protocolic gestures.

He decided suddenly: I will recommend the Colorado franchise go to these people. I should like it to go to them. Most uncommercial. Antibusinesslike. Not allow personal bias to interfere with better judgment. Even so.

How long for the tablets to work? It was to be hoped another two minutes would not spoil the dinner. Hastily he lifted the toilet lid again.

THE TRIAL RUNS *Latro, California:* "Terrible diarrhea, Doctor, and I feel so weak!"/"Take these pills and come back in three days if you're not better."

Parkington, Texas: "Terrible diarrhea. . . ."/"Take these pills . . ."

Hainesport, Louisiana: "Terrible . . ." "Take . . ."

Baker Bay, Florida . . .

Washington, DC. . . .

Philadelphia, Pennsylvania . . .

New York, New York . . .

Boston, Massachuetts . . .

Chicago, Illinois: "Doctor, I know it's Sunday, but the kid's in such a terrible state—you've got to help me!"/

"Give him some junior aspirin and bring him to my office tomorrow. Goodbye."

EVERYWHERE, USA: a sudden upswing in orders for very small coffins, the right size to take a baby dead from acute infantile enteritis.

MAY

GRAB WHILE THE GRABBING'S GOOD

When I came here there was nothing to be seen
But the forest drear and the prairie green.
Coyotes howled in the vale below
With the deer and the bear and the buffalo,
  To my whack-fol-the-day, whack-fol-the-do,
  Whack-fol-the-day-fol-the-didy-o!

So I took my axe and I cut the trees
And I made me a shack for to lie at ease,
With the walls of log and the roof of sod
And I gave my thanks at night to God,
  To my whack . . .

And I took my gun and my powder-horn
And I killed the varmints that stole my corn.
With meat and bread I had a good life,
So I looked for a woman who would be my wife,
  To my whack . . .

When he was a boy I taught my son
To use the plow and the hoe and the gun.
The fields spread out as the trees came down—
There was room at last for a little town,
  To my whack . . .

There's a church of clapboard with a steeple,
And Sunday morning it's full of people.
There's a bank, a saloon and a general store
And a hundred houses weren't there before,
  To my whack . . .

And now that I'm old and prepared to go
There are cattle instead of the buffalo.
They'll carry my coffin to my grave
Down roads they say they're going to pave,
To my whack . . .

So I'm happy to know I made my mark
On the land which once was drear and dark,
And I'm happy to know my funeral prayer
Will be heard in the land that was stark and bare,
To my whack . . .

—"Boelker's Camp Fire Songster," 1873

BLANKET

"Where are they?" Gerry Thorne kept muttering all through Nancy's funeral in the small Pennsylvania town where she had been born and her parents still resided. "Where are the mothers? It's a fucking conspiracy!"

Everyone understood he was overwrought; however, this language did not seem fitting while the substitute minister droned through the service. (The regular minister had enteritis.) So they pretended not to hear.

It was not the guests he meant. There were a great many of those, some of them important and/or famous. Jacob Bamberley had flown east specially to attend, with Maud but without the children. (They had enteritis.) Minor officials from the embassies or UN delegations of countries which had been helped by Globe Relief were likewise in the chapel. Moses Greenbriar had intended to come but he and Elly were unwell. (Enteritis.) Old friends of the family who were prominent in the community, such as the mayor, and the principal of the school Nancy had attended (free today because it was closed through enteritis), were also on hand. But he didn't mean them.

"Christ, not even one reporter!" he muttered. "Let

alone a TV team. And I kicked ABS in the ass over and over!"

He was wrong. There was one reporter. A girl had been sent by a local weekly with a circulation of nearly twenty thousand.

There was a slightly embarrassing incident just before the cremation, when a lady trying to slip away to the toilets fell in the aisle and—well, they did their collective best to ignore that, too. But eventually the coffin was consigned to the flames and they emerged under the yellow-gray sky.

Gerry had been against cremation at first, because of the smoke. He'd changed his mind when he saw how she was scarred.

The sun showed as a bright diffuse blur today; the weather had been exceptionally fine all week. Casting no shadow, face as white as paper, the muscles of his jaw standing out, Thorne kept on saying, "Where are the bastards? I'll murder them for this!"

"There is an epidemic, you know," said Mr. Cowper, his father-in-law, who was very much one to maintain the proprieties and had been shuddering under his black suit throughout the service. "I'm told it's very bad in New York."

His wife, who had also annoyed him by snuffling at his side loud enough to be heard by everyone in the chapel, not from grief but a head cold, excused herself for a moment. Usual trouble.

"Epidemic, hell!" Thorne snapped. "It's official pressure! They don't like the stink I've been kicking up!"

That was true enough, not just a boast. He had taken a savage pride in exploiting his status as a senior executive of Globe Relief to publicize Nancy's death and the cause of it. In consequence resorts all down the Atlantic coast, and throughout the Caribbean, and as far into the ocean as Bermuda, were suffering tens of thousands of canceled bookings. Officials insisted that the quantity of Lewisite dumped in 1919 could not possibly affect so vast an area, and it was mere chance that trawling had brought up two separate batches, and in any case weathering rendered the stuff harmless in a day or two. It made no difference. Thorne had publicized at least one other death from the gas, previously concealed—he had traced relatives of eight other victims, but someone was leaning on them and they wouldn't talk—and that was good enough for the public, having been lied to once before. This year we take our vacation somewhere else. Where is there where Americans aren't likely to be stoned by a howling mob? Spain, Greece? No, got to be out of range of the stench from the Med.

Looks like we might as well stay home.

The substitute minister, Reverend Horace Kirk, came to join them. "A very touching ceremony, Reverend," said Mr. Cowper.

"Thank you."

"I'll sue the bastards, then," Thorne said suddenly. "If that's the way they want it!"

Mr. Cowper touched his arm solicitously. "Gerry, you're overwrought. Come home with us and try to relax."

"No, I'm going straight to my lawyers. If it takes every cent I have I'll get back at the mothers who dumped that gas!"

"One understands how affected you've been by this tragedy," Mr. Bamberley said, matching Mr. Cowper's soothing tone. "But surely you must realize—"

"Jack!"

To everyone's astonishment, the interruption came from Maud, who was stuffing into her sleeve the handkerchief she had soaked with tears during the service.

"Gerry's right!" she exclaimed. "It's disgraceful! It's disgusting! I don't care how long ago they say they threw that stuff in the sea—it belongs to the government, and it's killing people, and the government is responsible!"

"Now, Maud dear—"

"Jack, it's all right for you! The worst thing that ever goes wrong for you is when some bug eats your precious what-you-call-ium thingumbobii! *You* don't spend every hour of every day wondering which of the boys is going to fall sick next! That's all I ever do, from one year's end to the next—if it isn't fits it's fever, if it isn't nausea it's diarrhea! How long can we go on like this? It's like living in hell!"

She broke off, choked with sobs, and leaned blindly on the minister for support, which he awkwardly provided, while her husband stared at her as though he had never seen her before.

Mr. Kirk coughed gently, which was a mistake. It was invariably a mistake nowadays, apparently, even in a small town, and Mr. Cowper had to take over Maud from him. But he recovered without losing his aplomb, and said, "Well, Mr. Thorne, though I'm not fully acquainted with the details of your sad loss—"

"Aren't you?" Thorne broke in. "That's not my fault! I got it on TV, I put it in the papers and magazines!"

"As I was about to say . . ." Frigidly; we are still in the presence of a death and it's not seemly to shout. "I do feel you'd be ill-advised to sue an organ of the government. The chance of securing compensation is bound to be small, and—"

"The hell with compensation!" Thorne blasted. "What I want is justice! You can't tell me that when they dumped that gas they didn't know people would want to fish the ocean, bathe in it, build houses fronting on the beach! You can't tell me the bastards didn't know what they were doing—they just relied on not being around when the trouble started! So I'm going to make trouble! Before I'm through I'll have those stinking generals fishing it up with their bare hands!"

He spun on his heel and headed at a run toward his car.

After a long pause Mr. Kirk said uncertainly, "I think it may rain, don't you? Perhaps we should make a move."

"Ah—yes," Mr. Cowper agreed. "One wouldn't want to be caught in a shower, would one?"

THUS FAR: NO FATHER Later, when they were alone, Mr. Bamberley snapped at Maud, "Well, what would you have me do with the boys—lock 'em up like Roland does with Hector, so he wouldn't know what dirt looks like if he saw it?"

THE ILL WIND Like most modern high-priced apartment blocks, the building where the Masons lived was protected by a sliding steel portcullis, bullet-proof glass, and a man with a gun on duty night and day. Doug McNeil presented his ID to the suspicious black who sat in the gas-proof booth today. It was a Saturday, which probably accounted for his not having seen this guard before. What with the soaring cost of living, especially food, a lot of people moonlighted jobs like this for evenings or weekends only.

"You making a house call on a Saturday?" the guard said, disbelieving.

"Why not?" Doug snapped. "There's a sick kid up there!"

"Well, hell," the guard said, shaking his heavy head with its fringe of grizzled beard. He opened the grille. Doug was halfway to the elevators when the man called after him.

"Say, doc!"

He glanced around.

"Doc, do you take—uh—colored patients?"

"Sure, why not?"

"Well, doc . . ." Emerging shyly from his booth, as though afraid of being reprimanded. He was much older than he had looked at first sight, Doug realized; well preserved, but probably in his upper sixties. "It's my wife. Nothing you can like put a finger on, if you see what I mean, but all the time she gets these like fits of weakness, so if it don't cost too much . . . ?"

Ending on a rising, hopeful note.

Doug tried not to sigh. Without seeing the woman he could make his diagnosis: poor food leading to sub-clinical malnutrition, poor water leading to recurrent minor bowel upsets, general debility and the rest. But he said, "Well, I'm in the phone book. Douglas McNeil."

"Thanks, sir! Thanks a million!"

He was still upset by the encounter when he entered the Masons' apartment. Denise was so eager to greet him, she had all the locks open ready, the door on a mere security chain, and didn't bar it as she rushed him inside.

"Doug, thank God you're here! I've had to change Harold's bed twice since I called you!"

Resignedly he followed her, and it was what he'd expected. Three minutes, and he'd written out a prescription the duplicate of—how many?—maybe ninety in the past week. Washing his hands, he recited the usual advice concerning diet and not worrying about minor stomach cramps.

At which point Philip showed up demanding the verdict.

"Not serious," Doug said, throwing his towel at a hook.

"Not serious! Doug, they've had to close schools all over the city, and every kid in this building seems to have it, and most of the adults, and—"

"And babies sometimes don't recover," Doug snapped. "I know!"

He caught himself. "Sorry," he added, passing a tired hand over his eyes. "This is my sixth call today for the same thing, you know. I'm worn out."

"Yes, of course." Philip looked apologetic. "It's just that when it's your own kids . . ."

"Yours aren't babies any more," Doug pointed out. "They should be fine in another few days."

"Yes, but . . . Oh, I'm being stupid. Say, can you spare the time for a drink? There are some people here you might like to meet."

"I guess I need it," Doug said wryly, and followed him.

In the living-room: a plump, pretty, light-colored girl, perched shyly on the edge of a chair, and next to her a man several shades darker who sat with the characteristic stiffness that Doug instantly assigned to a back-brace. His face was vaguely familiar, and the moment Philip made the introductions he remembered where he'd seen it.

"Mr. Goddard! Very glad to meet you, very glad indeed!" And to Denise as she handed him his regular vodka rickey, "Oh, thanks."

"Are your children okay, Mrs. Mason?" the girl asked.

"Doug says they will be in a few days."

"What is it, this—this epidemic?" Pete inquired. "I had a touch of it myself last week. Which made for—uh—problems." A self-conscious grin. "I don't get around too fast right now, you see."

Doug smiled, but it was forced. Dropping into an armchair, he said, "Oh . . . Basically it's an abnormal strain of *E. coli.* A bug that ordinarily lives in the bowel quite happily. But the strains vary from place to place, and some get altered by exposure to antibiotics and so forth, and that's why you get diarrhea. It's the same really as *turismo,* or as they call it in England 'Delhi belly.' You always adjust to the new strain, though. Sooner or later."

"But don't babies . . .?" That was Jeannie, hesitant.

"Well, yes, they are vulnerable. They get dehydrated, you see, and of course their food squirts through the system so fast they—well, you get the picture."

Pete nodded. "But why is there so much of it right now? It's all over the country, according to the news this morning."

"Somebody told me it was being spread deliberately," Jeannie ventured.

"Oh, really!" Doug snorted and sipped his drink. "You don't have to invent enemy agents to explain it, for heaven's sake! I'm no public health expert, but I imagine it's a simple vicious circle process. You know we're at the limit of our water resources, don't you?"

"No need to tell me," Denise sighed. "We have a don't-drink notice in force right now. Matter of fact, I suspect that's why the kids caught this bug. They're so proud of being able to go to the sink and help themselves to a glass of water . . . Sorry, go on."

"Well, figure it yourself. With eight or ten million people—"

"Eight or ten *million*?" Philip burst out.

"So they say, and we can't have hit the peak yet. Well, obviously, with that many people flushing the pan ten, fifteen, twenty times a day, we're using far more water than usual, and at least half this country is supplied with water that's already been used."

He spread his hands. "So there you are. Vicious circle. It'll probably drag on all summer."

"Christ almighty," Philip said.

"What are you worrying about?" Doug said sourly. "You and Alan got your water-purifier franchise, didn't you?"

Philip scowled. "That's a sick joke if ever I heard one. Still, I guess you're right—look on the bright side. And it's nice to be one of the few who have a bright side to look on . . . By the way, Pete!"

"Yes?"

"Didn't Alan say he was going to recommend you to Doug?"

"You're a friend of Alan's too?" Doug put in.

"Sure." Pete nodded. "Going to work for him."

"Oh, he's been just great!" Jeannie exclaimed. "Found us an apartment, and everything. That's why we came to Denver today, to look it over, and it's fine."

"Not like having a house," Pete said. "But." He contrived a sketch for a shrug despite his back-brace.

Jeannie frowned at him. After a moment she added, "One thing I didn't ask, though. Mrs. Mason—"

"Denise, please!"

"Uh—sure, Denise. Do you have much trouble with rats?"

"No, why?"

"They're bad right now in Towerhill. I been bitten myself. And the other day . . ." Her voice trailed away.

"What?" Philip prompted.

"They killed a baby," Pete grunted. "Just chewed it to death."

There was a pause. At length Doug drained his glass and rose. "Well, I don't know of any plague of rats in Denver," he said. "But I guess you may have a little trouble with fleas and lice. Around half the houses I go to on my rounds have them now. Resistant, of course."

"Even to the—uh—strong ones?" Philip said, using the common euphemism for "banned."

"Oh, especially those," Doug said, smiling without humor. "These are the survivors. They've taken the worst we could offer and come back jeering. The only thing they care about now is a direct hit with a brick, and I'm not too sure about that . . . Well, thanks for the drink. I'd better be on my way."

He was amused to notice, as he took his leave, that all of them were trying not to scratch themselves.

But he didn't find it so funny when a psychosomatic itch overtook him too in the elevator going down.

SIDE EFFECTS *. . . officially attributed to the debilitating effects of enteritis among troops newly arrived from this country. This marks the greatest single territorial gain for the Tupamaros since the uprising began. No comment on the battle was available from the president this morning owing to his indisposition. The epidemic continues to gather momentum in all states except Alaska and Hawaii, and many major* *corporations are working with a skeleton staff. Public services have been heavily hit, especially garbagemen and sewage workers. Bus and subway schedules in New York have been cut back, on certain routes to as few as one per hour, while the chief of police in New Orleans has forecast an unprecedented crime-wave owing to the sickness of more than half his men. Trainite demonstrations this morning . . .*

OVERCAST

"These potatoes look as limp as I feel," said Peg, attempting a joke as she set down the bucket of compost she'd brought to hoe in among the sickly plants. It was her first day back at work after her recent bout of enteritis, and she was still weak and a trifle lightheaded, but she couldn't stand any more sitting around.

"Yes, I guess what they mainly need is some sun," Zena said absently. Rolling up her sleeves, she frowned at the high faint gray cloud that masked the entire sky.

Peg heard the words and experienced a sudden moment of enlightenment: a sort of rapid astral projection. She seemed, for a flash, to be looking down at herself, not only seeing herself in space but in time also.

It was over, and she was staring at the by now familiar mountains that surrounded the wat, and the curious irregular roofs of the buildings which themselves were like mountains, dome next to pyramid next to cube. One of the community's architects had studied in England under Albarn.

"Peg, honey, you all right?" Zena demanded.

"Oh, sure," Peg insisted. She had swayed a little without realizing.

"Well, don't you overdo it, hear? Take as much rest as you need."

"Yes, of course," Peg muttered, and picked up her hoe and began to do as she'd been shown: make a little pit next to each of the sickly plants, scoop in an ounce of compost, cover it over. Later they'd water the fertilizer in.

Before she had finished the first hole, however, she heard a sharp exclamation from Zena and glanced around to discover—with a tremor of nausea—that she was holding up something thin and wriggly.

"Hey, look at this!" she cried.

Peg complied, reluctantly, and after a moment could think of nothing better to say than, "It's an odd color for a worm. Aren't they usually pink?" This thing was a livid color, somewhat bluish, as though it were engorged with venous blood.

"Yes," Zena muttered. "I wonder if it's been affected by some sort of poison, same as the potatoes, or if . . ." One-handed, she used her hoe to expose the roots of the nearest plant.

"Well, there's our answer," she said grimly. The tubers, which by now should have been a fair size, were only an inch or two in diameter and riddled with holes. And each hole was surrounded by a patch of blackish rot.

"If that's what's ruining this whole field . . ." Zena turned slowly, surveying the acreage they'd put down to potatoes last fall. "We been taking it for granted it was—well, something in the rain, or the ground. It usually is."

Yes. It usually is.

And then, staring at the wriggling thing, Peg was struck by a horrible suspicion.

"Zena! That— Oh, no. They were a different color."

"What?"

"That gallon of worms Felice brought. I thought for a moment . . ." Peg shook her head. "But we looked at them in the store, and they were pink."

"And they came from Plant Fertility," Zena said. "We've had their insects before. Got our bees from them, in fact." There were a dozen hives around the wat. "So . . . Well, we sure as hell don't have enough garlic juice to treat an area this size. So I guess all we can do is call the State Agriculture Board and find out if there's something we can plant between the rows to attract the little buggers. Come on, let's go back inside. No future in this."

"Zena!" Peg said abruptly.

"Yes?"

"I think I'm going to move on." How to explain that fit of insight a moment ago? She'd viewed herself as it were in the role of a passenger on the stream of time. She'd been content for weeks to let the wat insulate her, because life here was so undemanding and harmonious. Meanwhile, though, Out There, bad things were happening. Like the bad thing which had drawn her here. Like death and destruction. Like poison in the rain which killed your crops.

"I was expecting that," Zena said. "It isn't your kind of life, is it? You need competition, and we don't have it here."

"No, not exactly." Peg hunted for the right words, leaning on her hoe. "More—more making a mark. More wanting to do *one* thing to change the course of the world, instead of preparing to survive while the world does its worst."

"That was why you became a reporter, I guess."

"I guess so." Peg pulled a face. She was more relaxed here, more able to reveal her feelings in her expression or with her body. The wat made its own herb wines, to traditional European recipes, and sold them not only to summer tourists but by mail, and the other night there had been a party to try out an especially successful brew. She'd danced for hours and felt great—just before she went down with enteritis. And no man had plagued her to get in the sack with him, except that poor disorganized boy Hugh whom you couldn't really count as a man yet, and perhaps because of that she'd recently found herself wondering whether she might not try it again and enjoy it this time. On the few previous occasions she'd been as locked up as a bank vault.

That was the point at which young Rick turned up, and they showed him the wriggling insect and he took authoritative charge of it, promising to compare it with all the pictures of pests he could find in the library. On impulse, she added, "Rick, I'm thinking of moving on."

"Go back to work on a paper?" he asked absently, examining the insect with concentration.

"I don't know. Maybe."

"Ah-hah. Come back and see us often, won't you?" He folded a handkerchief carefully around the creature and made off. A moment before going out of sight, he called back, "And see if you can find out how my dad was poisoned, please!"

It was like being doused in ice water. She stood frozen for long seconds before she was able to say, "*I* didn't tell him Decimus was poisoned, Zena!"

"Of course not."

"Though . . ." She had to swallow. "Though I'm certain he must have been."

"I think so, too," Zena said. "But we all are."

That snapped together in Peg's mind with lack of sunlight and rain that didn't nourish plants but killed them, and all of a sudden she let fall her hoe and was crying with her face in her palms. Part of her was standing back in amazement and thinking: Peg Mankiewicz crying? It can't be true!

But it was a catharsis and a cleansing.

"I can't stand it!" she said after a while, feeling Zena's arm comforting around her shoulders. She blinked her tears away and looked at the dying potatoes: stock selected on the assumption that every plant would be doused with artificial fertilizers, systemic insecticides, plastic leaf-sprays to minimize water loss, and the hell with how they tasted so long as they looked good and weighed heavy. Cast back on the resources of nature, they wilted because the resources had been stolen.

"What kind of future do we have, Zena? A few thousand of us living underground in air-conditioned caves, fed from hydroponics plants like Bamberley's? While the rest of our descendants grub around on the poisoned surface, their kids sickly and crippled, worse off than Bushmen after centuries of proud civilization?"

She felt Zena wince. The younger of her adopted daughters suffered from allergies, and half the time went around wheezing and choking and gasping.

"We've got to make them listen!" Peg declared. "Isn't that the message of all Austin's books? You can't blame the people who can't hear the warnings; you *have* to blame the ones who can, and who ignore them. I have one talent, and that's for stringing words together. Austin's vanished, Decimus is dead, but someone's got to go on shouting!"

On the point of striding away, she checked. "Give the kids my love," she said. And added, to her own surprise, in a husky whisper, "And remember I love you too, won't you?"

FROM THE BOWELS OF THE EARTH

Duplicate at home the famous SPA WATERS OF THE WORLD!

Laugh at that "Don't-Drink" notice! We supply the salts from every major spa in packet form—VICHY! PERRIER! FONTELLA! APOLLINARIS! MALVERN! ALL $9.95/oz!

Gallon cans of PURE water: $1.50!

SYPHOON BRAND and other famous makes of MIXER IN STOCK!

Guard the health of your family! DON'T TAKE RISKS WITH WATER!

THE DOG DAYS

Christ! Flies!

Austin Train stopped dead in his tracks, listening to the buzz of wings around the heaped-up garbage. There hadn't been a clearance here in five weeks. The epidemic meant the removal gangs were working at under half strength, and there had been an order from high up that the prosperous areas should get the benefit before the poor ones.

"Hell, they chuck their trash straight out the window anyway," someone had said.

And it looked as though he'd been right. Every can in sight along the narrow alley, which angled back between two buildings four and five stories high, was overflowing, and huge sodden cartons bulged and leaked beside them and on top of that mess was yet one more layer which certainly must have been tossed from windows. The lot stank.

But there were flies. Incredible. Last summer down in LA he hadn't seen one, that he could remember.

His back ached and his feet were sore and that condition on his scalp had killed off most of his hair and the whole of his head itched abominably, but all of a sudden he was cheerful, and he was whistling when he forced the nose of his trolley under the first of the cans to be wheeled to the truck waiting on the main street.

"Hey! Hey, mister!"

A cry from overhead. A small swarthy boy peering from a window on the third floor, most likely a Chicano kid. He waved.

"Wait a minute! Please don't go 'way!"

The kid vanished. Now what was all that about? He shrugged and went on trying to load up the can. It was tricky with so much loose muck in the way. In the end he had to use his boots to expose its base.

A door to the alley swung open and here was the kid, in a torn shirt and faded jeans, a grimy bandage wrapped around his right arm. His eyes were swollen as though from long weeping.

"Mister, would you take away my dog, please? He—he died."

Oh.

Austin sighed and brushed his hands on the side of his pants. "He upstairs? Too heavy to carry down with your bad arm?"

"No, he's right around the corner in the alley. Not allowed to keep him in the apartment," the boy said, and snuffled a little. "I wanted to take him and—well, bury him properly. But mom said not."

"Your mom's quite right," Austin approved. Right here in the dense-packed city center you didn't bury carcasses, though the odd dog or cat rotting in the ground wouldn't be half the health hazard of this uncleared garbage. "Okay, let's see him."

He followed the kid around the angle of the alley, and there was a kind of kennel nailed together out of scrap wood and plastic. The dog's muzzle protruded over the lip of the entrance. Austin hunkered down to look at the body, and whistled.

"Say! He was a handsome beast, wasn't he?"

The kid sighed. "Yeah. I called him Rey. Mom said that was 'king' in Spanish. He was half German shepherd and half chow . . . Only he got in this fight, see? And where he was bitten it went all kind of rotten." He pointed.

Austin saw, on the side of the dog's neck, an infected wound. Must have hurt like hell.

"We did everything we could for him. Didn't help. It hurt so much he even bit me." Waving the bandaged arm. "Last night he was howling and howling, you could hear him even with the windows shut. So in the end Mom had to take sleeping pills, and said to give him one as well. Wish I hadn't! But the neighbors were kinda angry for the noise . . ." An empty shrug.

Austin nodded, estimating the weight of the beast. Not under seventy pounds, maybe eighty. A load. How could a family this poor feed that big an extra mouth? Well, better drag him out. He reached for purchase, and his hand brushed something dangling from the underside of the kennel's roof. What the—?

Oh no!

He unhooked the thing from its nail and drew it out. A fly-killing strip. Spanish brand name. No country of origin, of course.

"Where did you get this?" he demanded.

"Mom bought a box. Flies got so bad when the garbagemen stopped coming. And they were crawling all over Rey's sores, so I put that up."

"Your mom got more of these in the apartment?"

"Why, sure. In the kitchen, the bedroom, all over. They work fine."

"You go straight up and tell her she must take them down. They're dangerous."

"Well . . ." Biting his lip. "Well, okay, I'll tell her you said so. When she wakes up."

"What?"

"She ain't up yet. Heard her snoring when I got up. And she hates for me to disturb her."

Austin clenched his fists. "What kind of sleeping pills does she take—barbiturates, aren't they?"

"*I* don't know!" There was fear and astonishment in the boy's eyes. "Just pills, I guess!"

Stupid to have asked. He knew already that they had to be. "Here, take me up to your apartment, quick!"

"Smith!" A roar from the gang-boss, storming up the alley. "What the hell are you playing at? Hey, where do you think you're going?"

Austin waved the fly-strip under his nose. "There's a woman sick upstairs! Taken barbiturates in a room with the windows shut and one of these hanging up! Know what they put in these stinking things? Dichlorvos! It's a cholinesterase antagonist! Mix that with barbiturates and—"

"What's all this crazy doubletalk about?" the gang-boss snapped.

"It's about what killed that dog! Come on, hurry!"

They saved her life. But of course reporters wanted to talk to this unexpectedly well-informed garbage-man, so he had to move on again before they got the chance.

A PLAN TO MAP THE PLANET

As yet they had undertaken only makeshift repairs to the façade of the Bamberley Trust building. The broken windows had been covered, of course—you couldn't let street air leak in—but the store at ground level had been boarded up. Shortage of labor, Tom Grey deduced.

"Looks like it's been hit by an earthquake!" said his cab-driver cheerfully.

"Well, not really," Grey contradicted. "An earthquake produces a highly characteristic type of damage, readily distinguishable from the effect of a bomb." But he was extremely late for his appointment with Moses Greenbriar, so he was disinclined to pursue the point.

Besides, out here on the street it was most depressing. Garbage was piled high by the curb and against the walls of the buildings. Moreover, the air was unbelievably clammy, from air-conditioning systems no doubt—and people at bus-stops were coughing and wiping their streaming eyes because of the fumes. On the way from the airport he'd seen a fight break out at one stop, between two men in working overalls who—astonishingly—were belaboring each other with umbrellas.

His cab-driver had volunteered the information that this bus-route had been particularly hard hit by the enteritis outbreak, and those people might have been waiting in the open for more than an hour, which was bad for the temper. He'd asked about the umbrellas, and the man had chuckled.

"Ah, that's New York rain!" he said with a sort of perverse pride. "Got one myself, wouldn't be without it!" He pointed at the shelf under the dash. "You know, I'm going to quit this job next month. Sick of them Trainites! Saw the skull and crossbones they painted on this cab?" Grey had not; doubtless it was on the other side from the one where he'd entered. "Had enough, me. Gon' put my savings into a dry-cleaning business. Coining it in that line. Five minutes in the rain, umbrella or no umbrella, and if you don't go to the cleaners right away you need a new suit."

Many street-lights had broken down and not yet been repaired. National Guardsmen, masked and helmeted but armed only with pistols, were controlling traffic. It had been in the news: the mayor had reserved all policemen who were well enough for duty to cope with essential jobs like night crime patrols.

There had been huge State Health Authority posters at the airport, warning all out-of-town arrivals to purchase a recognized brand of prophylactic stomach tablets, and under no circumstances to drink unpurified water.

"I never had so many drunks to take home in my life," the cab-driver had said. "Like they took this warning not to risk the water as orders to fill up on hard liquor."

"I don't drink," Tom Grey had said.

He was a little nervous, because he set so much store by his world-simulation program now. Since the financial setbacks suffered by Angel City, first with the Towerhill avalanche, and now because of the enteritis epidemic—they had had enormous success in persuading their youngest clients to take out life insurance policies on their babies at birth, and over ten thousand had so far generated claims—they'd been compelled to find every possible means of improving the situation, even down to renting their computers at cut price to evening and weekend users. Grey therefore needed an alternative sponsor.

Having reviewed every major corporation, he'd decided that Bamberley Trust met all his requirements. It had plenty of capital; it had spare computer capacity, since it was primarily an investment firm and used computers solely for market analysis; and it was desperately in need of something to boost its public image. The UN inquiry into the Noshri disaster had not been able to prove how the dangerous drug was introduced into Nutripon, and the lack of a firm exoneration had allowed suspicion to continue.

He'd forwarded a fully detailed prospectus of his project, with appendices describing sample applications of the completed program. Obviously he had made it persuasive, for they had now invited him to New York to discuss the document.

And, within five minutes of entering Greenbriar's office, he knew—to employ a metaphor that was especially apt on Bamberley territory—he'd struck oil first time.

Of course, with New York in this mess you'd expect people to appreciate the potential advantages.

BURNING YOUR BRIDGES BEFORE YOU COME TO THEM

Chairman: My apologies for the repeated postponements of this meeting, ladies and gentlemen, but—ah—as you know it's been due to the fact that fate wasn't obliging enough to make our various indispositions coincide. For the record, I'm Edward Penwarren, and I'm the President's special representative in this matter. I believe you all know Mr. Bamberley, but I guess I should draw attention to the presence of Captain Advowson—sorry, Major Advowson, special delegate from the UN observation team that went to Noshri. Congratulations on your promotion, by the way, major; I believe it's recent. Yes, senator?

Sen. Howell (Rep., Col.): I want to go on record as objecting very strongly to the presence of this foreigner. I've repeatedly stressed both in public and private that this is a purely internal affair and the UN has no business meddling—

Advowson: Senator, I have been trying to get the hell out of your country for the past month. It stinks, and I mean that literally. I've never been so sick in my life.

I've never had so many sore throats or so much diarrhea. And I've never before been blown up in a bomb outrage.

Chairman: Gentlemen, if you please—

Howell: Isn't that proof enough that everything this man says and does is prejudiced?

Advowson: Prejudice be damned. Based on the experiences of my first and I devoutly hope only visit to—

Chairman: Order! Major, may I remind you that you are here by invitation? And as for you, senator, I must stress that the president personally approved the composition of this committee as best suited to the requirements of the situation. Thank you. Now the proximate reason for this meeting is a report which has not yet been publicly announced, but which I'm afraid will almost certainly be delivered to UN delegates within the next few days, because a copy of it is unaccounted for. I won't go into the background; the matter is *sub judice*. But what it is, this report, it's a confidential US Medical Corps report on the condition of certain of the survivors from the—uh—the village of San Pablo. I'm sorry, major; did you say something?

Advowson: Only "ah-hah!"

Howell: If that's your idea of a constructive contribution to these proceedings—

Advowson: It's just that I've been hearing rumors about—

Chairman: Order! Order! Thank you. Yes, as I was saying, this report. It—ah—it tends to the conclusion that the survivors from San Pablo do display many of the same symptoms as were reported from Noshri. Now I must stress something at once. It's been a long time since Dr. Duval in Paris analyzed the Nutripon from Noshri. It is our firm belief that what has happened is this. The Tupas have had a similar substance prepared, to give identical effects, and have deliberately administered it to hapless civilians to discredit the US intervention in Honduras. What was that, major?

Advowson: Never mind. Go on.

Chairman: Supporting this asumption I'd adduce the following point. If—I say if—Nutripon were again at the root of the trouble, the symptoms would have been noticed long ago, back in January maybe at the time when the search was going on for Dr. Williams and Leonard Ross. Yet the first mention of recognizable mental disturbance, according to the Medical Corps investigation, was not until March, and was so—uh—so unremarkable in the circumstances, what with the necessity of interrogating suspected Tupas and so forth, that . . . Well, the point is that a very small proportion of the persons detained for interrogation showed any mental abnormality, and it was not until the beginning of April that any symptoms were recognized which were sufficiently serious to lead to close psychiatric examination and eventual—uh—serum analysis and so forth. I'm not an expert on this, I'm afraid, just quoting the report. Yes, Mr. Bamberley?

Bamberley: San Pablo was the first place we were asked to send Nutripon to, I think. Globe Relief asked us before Christmas and we got some off, thanks to my workers putting in a lot of overtime. I never heard that Globe's people out there noticed anything in the way of bad effects.

Chairman: Well, I'm afraid it wouldn't follow. Their local agent was Mr. Ross, wasn't it? And he died. Yes, major?

Advowson: Could I ask Mr. Bamberley how many people the contract was for? I mean, how many people was he supposed to feed for how long?

Bamberley: I believe I have those data . . . Yes, here. A hundred adults and eighty children, initially for two days in order to get some kind of relief out on the ground straight away.

Advowson: Well, even at a couple of pounds apiece that doesn't sound like much!

Bamberley: We were closing down for the holiday, remember. It was what we had left from the previous contract, you see—just, like you say, a couple of hundred pounds or so for the worst-hit village. And we sent much greater quantities directly after New Year's, tons and tons of it, and there was no complaint about that lot!

Advowson: If I might ask you something, Mr. Chairman? How many survivors have displayed this mental derangement?

Chairman: Only about a dozen or fifteen including children.

Advowson: Is that because only a dozen or fifteen of the villagers are being held for Tupamaro sympathies, or is it because all the rest have been killed?

Howell: Tupa sympathies! Hell, every damn thing he says comes right out of their own lying propaganda! Mr. Chairman, I demand his removal from the committee!

Chairman: Senator, kindly do not presume to give me orders! I welcome that question, although I don't approve the way it was phrased, because that's exactly the sort of question we're going to have to answer in the UN. Major, I'm afraid the report doesn't specify, but thank you for drawing my attention to the point and I'll try and find out. Now Mr. Bamberley knows the point I'm going to raise next, I believe.

Bamberley: Yes. We seem to have no alternative. We have a great deal of Nutripon still in store, which was prepared before the new filtration system was installed at our plant. It's been suggested that we should have it destroyed with maximum publicity, have its destruction testified to by an unimpeachable witness—the Major here, if he's willing, and a scientist of international reputation as well, Lucas Quarrey for example—

Howell: That anti-American bastard! You must be crazy!

Chairman: Senator, you miss the point. The new installation at the factory must be approved by someone whom no one can conceivably call a—a lackey of the imperialists or whatever the phrase is. Professor Quarrey is not noted for his reluctance to speak his mind, as you correctly observe. His opinion will carry that much more weight abroad. Now, if I may continue—

Howell: I haven't finished. Jack, that stockpile must be worth money. How much?

Bamberley: About half a million dollars. And modifications to the plant have cost as much again.

Chairman: Naturally there will be compensation.

Howell: Whose pocket is it going to come out of? The taxpayer's, as usual?

Chairman: Senator, we shall have to think of it as the premium on an insurance policy. Don't you realize what a desperate situation this country is in right now? We've got to get that plant back in operation, *and* wipe out the prejudice against Nutripon, before the fall, because we're almost certainly going to have to distribute the stuff here at home. Over the past few weeks thirty-five million people have been sick for a week or longer. Factories, farms, all kinds of public services have been shut down or cut back. And according to HEW we're going into a second cycle of the epidemic because we've run out of water, we're having to re-release it before it's been completely sterilized. All the don't-drink warnings in the world won't stop people here and there from catching the bug a second time. And you know what it did in Honduras, don't you?

Advowson: Probably not. I doubt that he reads Uruguayan press releases, and you've kept the matter under wraps.

Chairman: Shut up, major. Sorry. In a sense you're right, much as it galls me to admit it. Publicity wouldn't have been very good for morale, would it?

Howell: What the hell are you talking about?

Advowson: The Tenth Counter-Insurgency Corps, I imagine.

Chairman: Damn it, yes of course. Senator, they didn't just fight a rearguard action and withdraw owing to their debilitated condition, which was the story we released to the media. There's been nothing like it since the First World War. They ran away. They were sick. They had fever over a hundred degrees and most of them were delirious. I guess that's an excuse. But it meant that the entire equipment of the Corps was captured intact by the Tupas. As a result Tegucigalpa is having to be supplied by air, and we may have to pull the government out any day now. And of course practically every big-city ghetto is alive with pro-Tupa black militants, and you can imagine what will happen if we can't clear the name of Nutripon before we have to start issuing it as relief allotments. Not content with poisoning innocent Honduran peasants and African blacks, we're starting genocide operations against black Americans too! That'll be the line, and we've got to prevent it at all costs.

THE UNDERGROUND MOVEMENT

Lem Walbridge had built up his holdings from the five hundred acres his father had left, until now he had over three thousand, all under vegetables: potatoes, beans, salads, beets, plus some corn and sunflowers—for oil—and a few gourmet delicacies like zucchini and scorzonera. The man from the State Board of Agriculture knew him well.

"Never seen anything like it!" Lem said for the tenth time, jumping down from his jeep at the edge of a field of sickly-looking beets. He pulled one up at random and displayed it, alive with horrible writhing worms. "Have you?"

The other nodded. "Yeah. Few days ago. Right the other side of those hills."

"But what the hell are these things? Christ, if this goes on I'll be ruined! I'm only going to get half my usual crop to market as it is, and unless I stop these stinking buggers . . . !" He hurled the rotten beet away with a snort of fury.

"Buy any earthworms this year?"

Lem blinked. "Well, sure! You have to. Like for soil conditioning."

"Put any down around here?"

"I guess maybe sixty, seventy quarts, same as usual. But I got a license, they were all approved."

"You get 'em from Plant Fertility in San Clemente?"

"Sure! Always do! They've been in the business longer'n anyone else. Best quality. And bees, too."

"Yeah, I was afraid of that. Their stuff goes all over the country, doesn't it? Clear to New England!"

"What in hell does that have to do with it?"

"It's beginning to look as though it has everything to do with it."

BY THE DEAD SEA

The wind was bad today. Hugh's filtermask was used up, all clogged, and he didn't have the seventy-five cents for another from a roadside dispenser, and anyway the quality of those things was lousy, didn't even last the hour claimed for them.

Lousy . . .

Absently he scratched his crotch. He'd more or less got used to lice by now, of course; there just didn't seem to be any way of avoiding them. For every evil under the sun there is a remedy or there's none. If there is one try and find it, if there isn't never mind it.

There must be a hell of a lot of evils in the world nowadays that there weren't any remedies for. Anyway: what sun? He hadn't seen the sun in fucking weeks.

It was hot, though. Leaning on the wall overlooking the Pacific, he wondered what this beach had been like when he was a kid. Scattered with pretty girls, maybe. Strong young men showing off their muscles to impress. Now . . .

The water looked more like oil. It was dark gray and barely moved to the breeze. Along the edge of the sand was a rough demarcation line composed of garbage, mainly plastic. Big signs read: THIS BEACH UNSAFE FOR SWIMMING.

Must have been posted last year. This year you wouldn't have needed to put up signs. One whiff of the stench, and *yecch.*

Still, it was great to be out and about again. It had been bad since he hit California. The runs. Everybody had them, but *everybody.* Back in Berkeley, along Telegraph, he'd seen them lying and whimpering, the seats of their jeans stained brown, no one to turn to for help. There had been a free clinic, but it treated VD as well, and the governor had said it encouraged promiscuity and had it closed.

Well, at least you didn't die of the runs, not over about six months of age. Carl had found a part-time job for a couple of weeks after their arrival, nailing together cheap coffins for babies; the cash had been useful.

Though sometimes the runs made you feel you'd *like* to die.

Where in hell was Carl, anyway? The air was hot and harsh, so he'd gone to a soft-drink stand for some Cokes. Taking his time. Bastard. Probably picked someone up.

They were shacking with a girl named Kitty, who'd spread half a dozen mattresses on her floor and didn't really mind who shared them, how many or what sex. She and Carl had been lucky and escaped the runs, and what they brought in, by working, panhandling and hustling, kept the others fed. When Hugh got over the aftereffects, he promised himself, he was going to get a decent job. Garbage clearance, maybe. Beach cleaning. Something constructive, anyhow.

Still no sign of Carl returning. But, drifting toward him, a wind-blown newspaper, almost intact and too heavy for the breeze to move it more than a few inches at each gust. He trod on it and picked it up. Ah, great! A copy of *Tupamaro USA!*

Leaning back against the wall, he shook it around to the front page and at once a name leapt out at him: Bamberley. Not Jacob, Roland. Something about Japanese water-purifiers. Hugh glanced over his shoulder at the befouled ocean and laughed.

But other things of more interest. Trainites in Washington rigged a catapult, Roman-style, bombarded the White House with paper sacks of fleas—hey, crazy, wish I'd been in on that. And a piece about Puritan, saying their food isn't really any better, costs more because of all their advertising . . .

"Hugh!"

He looked up and here came Carl, and Carl wasn't alone. For an instant he was transfixed by jealousy. He'd never imagined he might drift into this kind of scene. But it had happened, and Carl was a good cat, and . . . Well, at least Kitty being around allowed him to keep his—uh—hand in.

"Hey, you should meet this guy!" Carl said, beaming

as he handed over the straw-stuck Coke bottle he'd brought. "Hugh Pettingill, Austin Train!"

Austin Train?

Hugh was so shaken he dropped the paper and nearly let go of the Coke as well, but recovered and took the hand proffered by the thick-set stranger in shabby red shirt and faded blue pants, who grinned and exposed a row of teeth browned by khat.

"Carl says you met at the Denver wat."

"Ah . . . Yeah, we did."

"What do you think of them up there?"

"Full of gas," Carl chimed in. "Right, Hugh baby?"

It didn't seem right to put down a bunch of Trainites to Train himself, but after a moment Hugh nodded. It was true, and what was the good of pretending it wasn't?

"Damned right," Train said. "All gab and contemplation. No action. Now down here in Cal the scene isn't the same. You're shacking in Berkeley, right? So you seen Telegraph."

Hugh nodded again. From end to end, and down most of the cross streets, it was marked with the relics of Trainite demonstrations. Skulls and crossbones stared from every vacant wall.

Like the one on this guy's chest. Not a tattoo but a decal, exposed when he reached up to scratch among the coarse hair inside his shirt.

"Now Carl says you quit the wat because you wanted action," Train pursued, moving to perch on the sea wall at Hugh's side. Overhead there was a loud droning noise, and they all glanced up, but the plane wasn't visible through the haze.

"Well, something's got to be done," Hugh muttered. "And demonstrations aren't enough. They haven't stopped the world getting deeper in shit every day."

"Too damned true," the heavy-set man nodded. For the first time Hugh noticed that there was a bulge—not muscle—under the sleeve of his shirt, and without thinking he touched it. The man withdrew with a grimace.

"Easy there! It's still tender."

"What happened?" He had recognized the softness: an absorbent cotton pad and a bandage.

"Got burned." With a shrug. "Making up some napalm out of Vaseline and stuff. Thought we'd take a leaf out of the Tupas' book. You heard they caught that Mexican who staged the raids on San Diego, by the way?"

Hugh felt a stir of excitement. This was the kind of talk he'd been yearning for: practical talk, with a definite end in view. He said, "Yeah. Some stinking fishery patrol, wasn't it?"

"Right. Claimed he was fishing in illegal waters. Found these balloons all laid out on the foredeck, ready to go."

"But like I was just saying to Austin," Carl cut in, "we're right here in the same country with the mothers. We don't have to strike at random from a distance. We can pick out and identify guilty individuals, right?"

"Only we don't," Train snapped. "I mean, like this cat Bamberley."

"Shit, he's got as much trouble as he deserves," Hugh said with a shrug. "They closed his hydroponics factory, and—"

"Not Jacob! Roland!" Train pointed with his toe at the paper Hugh had dropped. "Going to make a fucking fortune out of these Mitsuyama filters, isn't he? When back before he and his breed got to work on the world, when you felt thirsty you helped yourself at the nearest creek!"

"Right," Hugh agreed. "Now they've used the creeks for sewers, and what happens? Millions of people lie around groaning with the runs."

"That's it," Train approved. "We got to stop them. Hell, d'you hear this one? Some pest got at the crops in Idaho—worm of some kind—so they're demanding to be allowed to turn loose all the old poisons, like DDT!"

"Shit, no!" Hugh said, and felt his cheeks pale.

"It's a fact. Aren't there better ways of handling the problem? Sure there are. Like in China they don't have trouble with flies. You see a fly, you swat it, and pretty soon—no more flies."

"I like the trick they use in Cuba," Carl said. "To keep pests off the sugar cane. Plant something between the rows that the bugs make for first, cut it down and turn it into compost."

"Right! Right! 'Stead of which, over here, they shit in the water until it's dangerous to drink, then make a fucking fortune out of selling us gadgets to purify it again. Why can't they be made to strain out their own shit?"

"Know what I'd like to do?" Carl exclaimed. "Like to soak those mothers right in their own shit until they turn *brown!*"

"We're all in this together now," Train said somberly. "Black, white, red, yellow, we all been screwed up until we got to stick together or go under."

"Sure, but you know these bastards! Darker you are, more they screw you! Like the atom-bomb. Did they drop it on the Germans? Shit, no—Germans are white same as them. So they dropped it on the little yellow man. And then when they found there were *black* men who were standing up on their hind legs and talking back, they joined forces with the yellow ones because they were kind of pale and pretty damned near as good at messing up the environment. Truth or lies?"

"Trying to make me ashamed of being white, baby?" Hugh snapped.

"Shit, of course not." Carl put his arm around Hugh's waist. "But did they send that poisoned food to a white country, baby? Hell, no—they sent it to Africa, and when they found it worked they gave it to the Indians in Honduras, got the excuse they were after to march in with their guns and bombs and napalm and all that shit."

There was a long pause full of confirmatory nods.

At length Train stirred, feeling in his pocket for a pen. "Well, right now I got to split—this chica I'm shacked with promised to fix a meal tonight. I get the impression we talk the same language, though, and I'm working on a kind of plan you might like. Let me leave you a number where you can reach me."

Hugh dived for the abandoned newspaper and tore a strip off its margin for Train to write on.

JUNE

A VIEW STILL EXTREMELY WIDELY ADHERED TO

There's an 'eathen bint out in Malacca
  With an 'orrible 'eathenish name.
As for black, they don't come any blacker—
  But she answered to "Jill" just the same!
Well, a man 'oo's abroad can get lonely,
  Missin' friends an' relations an' such.
She wasn't "me sweet one-an'-only"—
  But there's others as done just as much!

I'm not blushin' or makin' excuses,
  An' I don't think she'd want that, because
When she stopped blubbin' over 'er bruises
  The long an' the short of it was
That I'd bust up 'er 'orrible idol
  An' I'd taught 'er respect for a gun—
Yus, I broke 'er to saddle an' bridle
  An' I left 'er an Englishman's son!

—"Lays of the Long Haul," 1905

STEAM ENGINE TIME Although the sun showed only as a bright patch on pale gray, it was a sunny day in the life of Philip Mason. Against all the odds everything was turning out okay. Talk about blessings in disguise!

They had their franchise. They had the first consignment of a thousand units. Their first spot commercial on the local TV stations—featuring Pete Goddard, who'd done an excellent job considering he had no training as an actor—had brought six hundred inquiries by Monday morning's mail.

Pausing in the task of sorting the inquiries into serious

and frivolous—most of the latter abusive, of course, from anonymous Trainites—he glanced at the clothing store catty-corner from Prosser Enterprises. A man in overalls was scrubbing off a slogan which had been painted on its main window over the weekend; it now read ROTTING IS NATU. The accompanying skull and crossbones had gone.

They were having a man-made fiber week. Trainites objected to orlon, nylon, dacron, anything that didn't come from a plant or an animal.

Hah! They don't mind if a sheep catches cold, he thought cynically, so long as they don't—and speaking of colds . . . He dabbed his watering eyes with a tissue and soaked it with a thorough blast from his nose.

The door of his office opened. It was Alan.

"Hey!" Philip exclaimed. "I thought you had to stay home today. Dorothy said you—"

Alan grimaced. "Yeah, I have the runs again okay. But I heard the good news and decided I couldn't miss out." He stared at the heap of correspondence on Philip's desk.

"Christ, there really are six hundred!"

"And five," Philip said with a smirk.

"I'd never have believed it." Shaking his head, Alan dropped into a chair. "Well, I guess Doug was right, hm?"

"About the enteritis being on our side? I thought that was in kind of bad taste."

"Don't let that stop you getting the point," Alan said. "Know what I like about my job, Phil? They talk all the time about the businessman, the entrepreneur, being an 'enemy of mankind' and all that shit, and it *is* shit! I mean, if anyone has a reason to hate society and want to screw it up, it ought to be me, right?" He held up his bullet-scarred hand. "But I don't. I got my chance to grow fat —least, it looks like that's what's happening—and do I have to be ashamed of how I do it? I do not. Here I am offering a product people really want, really need, and into the bargain creating jobs for people who'd otherwise be on relief. True or false?"

"Well, sure," Philip said, blinking. Especially the point about new jobs. Unemployment throughout the nation was at an all-time high this summer, and on this side of Denver it was particularly bad and would remain so until they finished the modifications to the hydroponics plant and hired back their former six hundred workers.

That too was naturally redounding to the benefit of Prosser Enterprises. Anyone with an ounce of wit could be taught to fit these purifiers in an hour.

"Well, then!" Alan said gruffly, and swiveled his chair to face the window overlooking the street. "Say, there's another bunch of kids. City's alive with them today. Where they all coming from?"

Across the street a group of about eight or ten youngsters—more boys than girls—had paused to jeer at the man washing the slogan off the clothing store.

"Yes, I saw a whole lot of them getting off a bus at the Trailways terminal," Philip agreed. "Must have been—oh—nearly thirty. They asked me the way to the Towerhill road."

"Looks like this lot is heading the same way," Alan muttered. "Wonder what the big attraction is."

"You could run over and ask them."

"Thanks, I don't care that much. Say, by the way: how come you're sorting these letters yourself? What became of that girl we hired for you?"

Philip sighed. "Called in to apologize. Sore throat. She could barely talk on the phone."

"Ah, hell. Remind me, will you? Top priority on filters for the homes of our staff. See if we can cut the sickness rate a bit, hm? Charity begins at home and all that shit." He leafed curiously through a few of the letters. "How many of these are genuine orders and how many are junk?"

"I guess we're running ten to one in favor of genuine ones."

"That's great. That's terrific!"

The door opened again and Dorothy entered, a sheaf of pages from a memo pad in one hand, a handkerchief in the other with which she was wiping her nose. "More inquiries all the time," she said. "Another thirty this morning already."

"This is fantastic!" Alan said, taking the papers from her. From outside there came a rumble of heavy traffic, and Dorothy exclaimed.

"What in the world are those things?"

They glanced up. Pausing at the corner before making a left toward Towerhill, a string of big olive-drab Army trucks, each trailing something on fat deep-cleated tires from which protruded a snub and deadly-looking muzzle. But not guns.

"Hell, I saw those on TV!" Alan said. "They're the new things they're trying out in Honduras—they're battle-lasers!"

"Christ, I guess they must be!" Philip jumped up and went to the window for a closer look. "But why are they bringing them up here? Maneuvers or something?"

"I didn't hear they were planning any," Alan said. "But of course nowadays you don't. Say! Do you think all these kids coming into town might have got wind of maneuvers and decided to screw them up?"

"Well, it's the kind of damn-fool thing they might do," Philip agreed.

"Right. In which case they deserve what's coming to them." Absently Alan rubbed the back of his scarred hand. "Wicked-looking, aren't they? Wouldn't care to be in the way when they let loose. And speaking of letting loose—excuse me!"

He rushed from the room.

IF IT MOVES, SHOOT IT *. . . that the Army is using defoliants in Honduras to create free-fire zones. This charge has been strongly denied by the Pentagon. Asked to comment just prior to leaving for Hawaii, where he will convalesce for the next two or three weeks, Prexy said, quote, Well, if you can't see them you can't shoot them. End quote. Support has been growing for a bill which Senator Richard Howell will introduce at the earliest opportunity, forbidding the issue of a passport to any male between sixteen and sixty not in possession of a valid discharge certificate or medical exemption. Welcoming the proposal, a Pentagon spokesman today admitted that of the last class called for the draft more than one in three failed to report. Your steaks are going to cost you more. This warning was today issued by the Department of Agriculture. The price of animal fodder has quote taken off like a rocket unquote, following the mysterious . . .*

A PLACE TO STAND "A lady and a gentleman to see you, Miss Mankiewicz," said the hotel reception-clerk. He was Puerto Rican and adhered to the old-fashioned formalities. "I don't know if you're expecting them?"

"Who are they?" Peg said. She sounded nervous, knew it, and wasn't surprised. During the previous few weeks she had initiated a very tricky venture, and she was sure that for the past ten days at least someone had been following her. It wasn't beyond the bounds of possibility that she had broken one of the increasingly complex disloyalty laws. The situation was beginning to resemble that in Britain during the eighteenth century: any new law involving a harsher punishment for a vaguer crime was certain of passage through Congress and instant presidential approval.

Granted, Canada wasn't yet a proscribed country. But at this rate it wouldn't be long . . .

"A Mr. Lopez," the clerk said. "And a Miss Ramage. Uh—Ra-*maige*?"

Peg's heart seemed to stop in mid-beat. When she recovered she said, "Tell them I'll be right down."

"They say they'd prefer to come up."

"Whatever they want."

When she put down the phone her hand was trembling. She'd pulled all kinds of strings recently, but she hadn't expected one of them to draw Lucy Ramage to her. Incredible!

Hastily she gathered up some soiled clothing scattered on her bed and thrust it out of sight. The ashtrays needed emptying, and . . . Well, it was a ropy hotel anyhow. But she couldn't afford a better one. Thirty bucks a day was her limit.

She'd come to New York because she had a project on her mind. As she'd told Zena, she had only one talent, and right now the logical use to put it to seemed to be muckraking. So she'd asked herself a key question: what was the most important muck? (Actually she had phrased it, subconsciously, in terms of what Decimus had hated most. But it came to the same in the end.)

It almost answered itself: "Do unto others . . ."

Very well, the starting point would be that claim of Professor Quarrey's, which had been in the news at the beginning of the year, that the country's greatest export was noxious gas. And who would like to stir up the fuss again? Obviously, the Canadians, cramped into a narrow band to the north of their more powerful neighbors, growing daily angrier about the dirt that drifted to them on the wind, spoiling crops, causing chest diseases and soiling laundry hung out to dry. So she'd called the magazine *Hemisphere* in Toronto, and the editor had immediately offered ten thousand dollars for three articles.

Very conscious that all calls out of the country were apt to be monitored, she'd put the proposition to him in highly general terms: the risk of the Baltic going the same way as the Mediterranean, the danger of further dust-bowls like the Mekong Desert, the effects of bringing about climatic change. That was back in the news—the Russians had revived their plan to reverse the Yenisei and Ob. Moreover, there was the Danube problem, worse than the Rhine had ever been, and Welsh nationalists were sabotaging pipelines meant to carry "their" water into England, and the border war in West Pakistan had been dragging on so long most people seemed to have forgotten that it concerned a river.

And so on.

Almost as soon as she started digging, though, she thought she might never be able to stop. It was out of the question to cover the entire planet. Her pledged total of twelve thousand words would be exhausted by North American material alone.

Among her most useful contacts was Felice, née Jones. Having spent more than two months after her return from the wat in hunting for a new job, she had finally resigned herself to being unemployable and married some guy she'd known for years. He had an unexciting but safe job and she was now able to devote much of her time to acting as Peg's unpaid West Coast correspondent. Despite her former dismissal of her brother's ideals, she was obviously very worried now. What seemed to have revised her opinions was the fact that her new husband was going to insist on children.

Among the questions she had drawn Peg's attention to . . .

Why had there been a sharp fall in the value of shares in Plant Fertility? In the spring there had been such a demand for their bees and earthworms, they'd been booming; they'd even initiated a market survey to determine if they should add ants and ladybugs. (Felice said there was a Texas firm which had cornered the market in ichneumon wasps, but Peg hadn't got around to finding what they were wanted for.) There had been no official comment about the company's decline, but undoubtedly someone on the inside was selling his stock in huge quantities.

Was there a connection between Plant Fertility's problems and the fact that potatoes were up a dime a pound over spring prices and still rising?

And could animal feed really have been so severely affected as to account for the rise of meat prices from exorbitant to prohibitive? (It had been years since cattle could be grazed on open land anywhere in the country.) Or was there—as rumor claimed—a wave of contagious abortion decimating the herds, which no antibiotic would touch?

Peg thought: likely both.

Another question. Was it true that Angel City had decided to give up life insurance and realize the value of their out-of-state property because the decline in life expectancy was so sharp it threatened to cut through the profit line?

Similarly: Stephenson Electric Transport was the only car maker in the States whose product met with complete approval from the Trainites. They had been due for a colossal takeover bid from Ford. The negotiations were hanging fire; was that really due to a threat from Chrysler that they'd have them hit with an injunction under the Environment Acts for generating excessive ozone? (Which would leave the pure-exhaust field wide open for foreign companies: Hailey, Peugeot who had just unwrapped their first steamer, and the Japanese Freon-vapor cars.)

Was it true that the Trainites had turned sour on Puritan and dug up some kind of dirt about their operations?

She didn't know. And she was becoming daily more frightened at her inability to find out.

Of course, there were good reasons why companies in trouble with the Trainites should fight tooth and nail to keep their dirty secrets from the public. The government couldn't go on forever bailing out mismanaged giant corporations, even though it was their own supporters, people who ranted against "UN meddling" and "creeping socialism," who yelled the loudest for Federal aid when they got into a mess. With an eye to her next series of articles, she'd compiled a list of companies which were state-owned in all but name and would go broke overnight if the government ever called in its loans. So far it included a chemical company caught by the ban on "strong" insecticides; an oil company ruined by public revulsion against defoliants; a pharmaceutical company that had nearly become a subsidiary of Maya Pura, the enormously successful Mexican producers of herbal remedies and cosmetics (to be bought out by Dagoes! Oh, the shame!); six major computer manufacturers who had glutted the market for their costly products; and, inevitably, several airlines.

And every day senators and Congressmen who in public were inclined to turn purple at the mere mention of state control wheeled and dealed behind the scenes to secure for their home states the fattest government-financed contracts they could nab, or pleaded that if such-and-such a firm which had been run into the ground by its incompetent directors wasn't helped, the unemployment index would rise another point.

It was as though the entire country had been turned into a pork-barrel, with two hundred million people squabbling over the contents. Talk about taking in each other's laundry—this was more like termites, each eating its predecessor's excrement!

On top of which, in some sense at least, the most crucial point of all was not what had happened but what people were afraid might happen. Consider the calamitous drop in air passengers, down 60 per cent in ten years. Consider that one man, Gerry Thorne of Globe Relief, had ruined the summer tourist trade from Maine to Trinidad, just by securing publicity for the death of his wife.

One man with a bomb could break an airline. One man

with a cause could break ten thousand hotel proprietors. One man with enough leverage . . .

Or one woman. Peg was after leverage of her own. That was why she wanted to talk to Lucy Ramage.

At which point there came a knock at her door. She checked the spyhole before opening; it was a favorite mugger's trick in New York hotels to hang around the desk until someone was invited up to a room, then club the visitor in the elevator and come calling in his place.

But she recognized Lucy Ramage from seeing her on TV.

She admitted her and her companion, a swarthy man with recently healed cuts on his face, lacking teeth from both top and bottom jaws. She took their filtermasks, asked if they'd like a drink—both refused—and got down to business right away, sensing they were impatient.

"I'm glad I finally managed to reach you," she said. "It's been a hassle. Like plodding through a swamp."

"It must have seemed harder than it really was," the man said with a faint smile. "I apologize. The delay was on our side. We work under—ah—difficulties here, and we wanted to investigate your credentials before reacting."

A blinding light broke on Peg. "Your name isn't Lopez! It's—" She snapped her fingers in frustration. "You're the Uruguayan who got beaten up and claimed it was by off-duty policemen!"

"Fernando Arriegas," the man said, nodding.

"Are you—are you recovered?" Peg felt herself flushing, as though from shame for her country.

"I was lucky." Arriegas curled his lip. "They destroyed only one of my testicles. I am told I may still hope to be a father—if it is ever safe again to bring a child into this sick world. However, let us not talk about me. You have been trying to contact Lucy. Trying very hard."

Peg nodded.

"Why?" Lucy said, leaning forward. She was wearing a

plastic coat despite the warmth of the weather, and her hands were in its deep pockets out of sight. But there was nothing particularly surprising in that; plastic was the best armor against New York rain. Rubber just rotted.

"I—well." Peg cleared her throat; she was dreadfully catarrhal at the moment. "I'm working on a series of articles for *Hemisphere*, in Toronto. The general theme is what the rich countries are doing to the poor ones even without intending to harm them, and of course the tragedy at Noshri . . ." She spread her hands.

"Not to mention the tragedy in Honduras," Arriegas murmured. He glanced at Lucy, and from the big pockets of her coat she handed him a transparent bag full of objects like soft macaroni.

"You recognize?" he asked, showing it to Peg.

"Is that Nutripon?"

"Yes, of course. What is more, it is Nutripon from San Pablo, a sample of the supplies that drove its people mad and caused them to kill an Englishman and an American, believing them to be devils. For which involuntary crime some ten or twelve thousand Hondurans have now been killed." His voice was as flat as a machine's. "We recaptured—that is to say, the Honduran Tupas did, but their cause is our cause—recaptured San Pablo and went over it with a fine-toothed comb. Part of the original delivery of this food was found in the ruins of the church, where apparently the people took it in the hope of exorcising the evil from it. They must have been dreadfully hungry. We have sent some for analysis in Havana, but the rest we have reserved for other important applications, such as insuring that any American who writes about the *tragedy*"—he leaned on the word with heavy irony—"should know what he or she is talking about."

Peg felt her jaw drop. She forced out, "You mean you want *me* to eat some?"

"Exactly. Most of your brainwashed reporters have repeated the lie that our accusations are untrue. We wish at least one to be able to say the contrary."

He tore a strip of cellulose tape from the bag with a tiny crying noise. "Here! It says on the carton it can be eaten raw—and you need not worry about it being stale. The carton we took this from was completely intact when we found it."

"Hurry up!" snapped Lucy. Peg glanced at her, and suddenly realized that those big pockets were big enough to conceal a gun. They had concealed ono. It was in Lucy's hand now, and the muzzle seemed as wide as a subway tunnel.

It was silenced.

"You're insane!" Peg whispered. "They must know you're here—they'll catch you in minutes if you use that thing!"

"But we shan't have to," Arriegas said with a thin sneer. "You are not so stupid as to resist. We have studied this poison very carefully. We know that this much"—hefting the bag—"produces the effect of a little trip on acid, no more. Or perhaps I should better say STP, because I'm afraid the trip has not been known to be a good one. Maybe you'll be the lucky first, if your conscience is clear."

"And you'd rather live until tomorrow than die now," Lucy said. "Besides, you won't die. I've eaten more than that. Much more."

"Wh-when?" Peg stammered, unable to tear her fascinated gaze from the bag.

"I found some in a ruined house," Lucy said. "Next to the body of a child. I don't know if it was a boy or a girl, it was so crushed. And I suddenly realized I had to share this thing. It was like a vision. Like licking the sores of a leper. I thought I'd stopped believing in God. Maybe I have. Maybe I did it because now I only believe in Satan."

She leaned forward with sudden fearful earnestness.

"Look, take some and eat it—*please!* Because you've *got* to! We'll make you eat it if we must, but it would be so much better if you realized what you have to understand! You've got to see, feel, *grasp* what was done to those poor helpless people—coming to my table where I was doling out the relief supplies, thinking they were being given wholesome nourishment after so long without any food but a few poisoned leaves and roots. You can't write about it, you can't even *talk* about it, unless you know what a horrible loathsome disgusting trick was played on them!"

Almost as though they were acting of their own accord, Peg's fingers took hold of a piece of the food. A sense of doom engulfed her. She looked beseechingly at Arriegas, but could read no mercy in his stone-chill eyes.

"Lucy is right," he said. "Think to yourself: I am so weak from hunger I can barely stand. Think: they have sent help for me, tonight for the first time in months I will sleep soundly with my belly full, and tomorrow there will be more to eat, and the day after. This living hell has come to an end at last. Think about that while you eat. Then later perhaps you will comprehend the magnitude of this cruelty."

But why me? It's not my fault! I'm on their side!

And realized in the same instant as the thought was formulated that it was wrong. It had been shaped, over and over, more times than could conceivably be counted, by millions of others before her . . . and what impact had it had on the world? Had she not spent these past weeks in continual horror at the misjudgment, the incompetence, the outright lunacy of mankind?

These two must be crazy. No doubt about it. But it was even crazier to think that the world as it stood could be called "sane."

Perhaps if she ate just one or two bits, enough to satisfy them . . . Convulsively Peg thrust the piece she held between her lips and started to chew. But her mouth was so dry, her teeth merely balled it into a lump she couldn't swallow.

"Try harder," Arriegas said clinically. "I assure you not to worry. Here is only two ounces, what I myself have eaten. Those who went mad at Noshri ate more than half a kilo."

"Give her water," Lucy said. Cautiously, so as not to block her aim, Arriegas reached for a pitcher and glass that stood on the bedside table. Peg obediently gulped a mouthful, and the food went down.

"More."

She took more.

"More!"

She took more. Was it illusion, or was something happening to her already? She felt giddy, careless of the consequences of what she was doing. The food tasted pretty good, savory on the tongue, and her saliva was back so she could get it down very fast. She took half a dozen bits and thrust them all in together.

And the room seemed to rock from side to side, in rhythm with the chomping of her jaw.

"I—" she said in surprise, and they looked at her with eyes like laser-beams.

"I think I'm going to faint," she said after a pause. She reached for the table to set down the water-glass, and missed. It dropped on the carpet and didn't break, but lashed out a crystalline tongue, the last of its contents. She made to stand up.

"Stay where you are!" Lucy ordered, jerking the gun. "Fernando, grab hold of her. We'll have to force the rest down her throat."

Peg tried to say that wouldn't be any use, but the world tilted and she slid to meet the ground. With a distant corner of her mind she assured herself that this wasn't due to a drug in the food. This stemmed from pure terror.

There was a vast rushing noise in her ears.

But her eyes were open, and she could see everything with a weirdly distorted perspective, as though she were a wide-angle lens with very sharp curvature at the sides. What she saw was the door slamming open and someone —a man—striding in. He was horribly out of proportion, his legs as thin as matches, his torso grotesquely bulging toward a head the size of a pumpkin. She didn't want to look at anyone so ugly. She shut her eyes. In the same instant there were two plopping noises and a heavy weight slumped across her legs. Infuriated, she thrust at it with her hands, trying to push it away.

Wet?

She forced her eyes open again and saw this time through a swimming blur like a wind-blown veil. Bright red surrounded by pale gold. Yes, of course. The back of a head. Lucy Ramage's head. With a hole clear through. A shot perfectly targeted. She had dropped sideways across Peg's thighs. Also there was Arriegas, doubled up and spewing pink froth and red trickles. It was on her now, on her clothes. Less gold, more red. All the time more red. It flooded out to the limits of her already hazy vision. There was darkness.

THE GO SIGNAL "Well, honey, how does it grab you?" Jeannie said proudly as she helped Pete into the living-room. He wouldn't be able to drive himself for a long time, of course, so she had to take him to and from work. But he was getting very clever with his crutches, and this apartment was on the entrance floor, so there weren't too many steps, which he did find hard.

It had been filthy, because it had stood vacant for months—few people wanted ground-floor apartments, they being the easiest for burglars—and as they'd been warned it had been full of fleas. But the exterminator said they were in the best families nowadays, heh-heh!, and they were dealt with, and there was new paint everywhere and today Jeannie must have worked like fury because she had new curtains up and new slipcovers on the old furniture.

"Looks great, baby. Just great." And blew her a kiss.

"Like a beer?"

"I could use one."

"Sit down, I'll bring it." And off to the kitchen. It was still equipped with their old stuff from Towerhill, except they'd had to get a new icebox; the old one had died and the only firm in Denver still making repairs had a two-month waiting list. Through the door she called, "How was your first day at work?"

"Pretty good. Matter of fact I don't hardly feel tired."

"What does a stock supervisor do?"

"Kind of like a dispatcher, I guess. Make sure we record everything we send out for installation, keep a check on what's used and what comes back. Easy bread."

Coming back, she found he wasn't in his chair but heading for the other door.

"Where you going?"

"Bathroom. Back in a minute."

And, returning, took the beer. In a glass, yet. Moving up the scale!

"I got news for you," Jeannie said. "Did you hear they're going to open up the plant again? All the modifications are done, and as soon as they—"

"Baby, you're not going back to the plant."

"Well, not straight away, honey, of course not. I mean until you can drive again, and like that. But here in Denver it's . . . " A vague gesture. "Paying so much rent, and all."

"No," Pete said again, and fished with two fingers in the breast pocket of his shirt. The little plastic dispenser of contraceptive pills. New, untouched. The monthly cycle began today.

"And you can forget about these, too," he said.

"Pete!"

"Cool it, baby. You know what they're going to pay me."

She gave a hesitant nod.

"Add on what I get for these TV commercials, then."

Another nod.

"Well, isn't that enough to raise a kid on?"

She didn't say anything.

"Ah, hell, baby, come on!" he exclaimed. "Now while we got the chance, now's the time! Shit, you know how they're going to lay out the next commercial I make? In the middle like Santa Claus surrounded by kids, telling the mothers all over the state that this here big hero who saved those kids' lives wants them to buy water-filters and save their kids from bellyache!" His tone was abruptly bitter, and just as abruptly reverted to normal.

"Well, it's a good thing to be selling if you have to sell something for a living. I talked to Doc McNeil and he said so. Said it could have helped a lot of babies that died of that enteritis."

"Yes, honey," Jeannie said. "But suppose—ours . . . "

"Baby, I said I talked to Doc McNeil. That's one of the things I talked about. And he says shoot. He says . . . "

"What?" She leaned forward on her chair.

"He says if I like fall down stairs, or do something else bad to myself, there may not—uh—be another chance."

There was a long cold silence. At length Jeannie set her glass aside.

"I get you, honey," she whispered. "Sorry, I never thought of that. What about right now?"

"Yeah, and right here. Doc says it's better if I lie on my back on a hard floor."

RIGHT ABOUT NOW *A DC-10 coming in to land at Tegucigalpa was hit by Tupamaro tracer and crashed on the control tower, which confirmed the decision to pull out. The previous record for the duration of a don't-drink notice was broken in New Orleans (that's a long river and a lot of people use it). The Bamberleys' family doctor called to treat the latest of Cornelius's fits—which was going to earn him a good old-fashioned beating when he recovered, because he knew he was forbidden to eat candy. The enteritis epidemic was declared officially over for the fourth time. And they completed the autopsy on Dr. Stanway, con-*

ducted at his own morgue: verdict, the extremely common one of degenerative nephritis.

He was, admittedly, only thirty-one. But he had after all spent his whole life in Los Angeles and Orange County.

Not surprising.

COMPANIONS IN ADVERSITY

"Delighted to meet you, Mr. Thorne," Professor Quarrey said. His clothes hung loose on him, as though he had lost ten pounds in the past few weeks. "Do sit down. Would you like some sherry?"

An aptly academic drink. Thorne smiled and took the nearest chair as the professor's wife—looking even more exhausted than her husband, with large dark rings under her eyes—filled glasses and offered a dish of nuts. She had a plaster on her nape; the shape of the lump underneath suggested a boil.

"Here's to a fellow-sufferer," Quarrey said. Thorne gave a humorless laugh and drank.

"Congratulations on your acquittal, by the way," he said. "I confess I was expecting you to be pilloried."

"There was some—ah—horse-trading behind the scenes," Quarrey said. "You're aware that they plan to resume production at Bamberley Hydroponics?"

"Yes, I saw Moses Greenbriar recently and he told me."

"Well, they want someone who can't be accused of being a government yes-man to approve their new filtration system. As you know, that's my field, and I was approached, very discreetly, and asked whether I'd cooperate in exchange for a dismissal of that ridiculous charge." A sigh. "It may not have been very courageous of me, but I said yes."

"But they haven't stopped persecuting us!" his wife chimed in, joining her husband on the shabby davenport facing Thorne. "I'm sure our telephone is being tapped."

"And they definitely open my mail," Quarrey grunted.

"Which I wouldn't mind if they had the courtesy to screen out the abusive letters . . . You get any of those? I imagine you do."

Thorne nodded.

"There's our prize exhibit," Quarrey said, pointing to the wall behind his guest. "I had it framed to remind me just how important it is to keep trying."

Thorne twisted around. In a smart new frame, a sheet torn from a cheap yellow memo block. He read the semi-literate capitals that almost covered it: "TO MISTER COMMIE ASS LICKING QUAREY YOU SAY ONE MORE WORD AGANST AMRICA WELL HANG YOU BY YOUR PRICK ON A FAGPOLE GET OUT OR WELL BURN DOWN YOUR HOME AND YOUR NIGGERFUCKING WIFE TOO OUHT TO HAVE A GUN STUFF UP HER CUNT NOW YOU NOW WHAT LOYAL AMRICANS THINK OF TRATORS."

"The fagpole is an original touch," Quarrey said with a tired smile, and sipped his sherry.

There was a long silence. Thorne wanted it to end, but he couldn't think of the best words. He had been growing daily more ashamed since Nancy died—ashamed of not having understood before, in the guts where it counts, what suffering really meant. It was a tough job managing the vast sums that the guilty conscience of the Western world siphoned into Globe Relief, and no one denied that, including him; he was dealing with sums that exceeded the turnover of all but the largest European and American corporations. That alone, though, wasn't justification for the income he'd been drawing, even if it did average out to less than half a cent per person helped. So he'd taken refuge behind the additional defense that he had a wife to provide for and might well one day adopt a kid. (By a twenty-two-to-one chance he and Nancy had both been carrying the recessive gene for cystic fibrosis, and a child of their own would be mentally retarded.)

Without Nancy, it was as though cataracts had been

taken from his eyes. It had become suddenly clear: there are madmen in charge, and they must be stopped!

He had read feverishly, beginning with Austin Train's famous source-books that had taken one, two, even three years apiece to compile, soberly documenting the course of organochlorides in the biosphere, factory-smoke on the wind, pinning down some—not all, because often the information was denied to the public—of the places where dangerous substances had been dumped. Among the first things he'd come across was a description of the gas-disposal program in 1919. And on top of that radioactive waste, nerve gas, fluorine compounds, cyanide solutions . . .

It was as though you tore up the floorboards of an apartment you'd just bought and found a corpse grinning at you.

But even more educational were the things he couldn't find out. In the New York Public Library Train's works were on open shelves—there would have been riots if they hadn't been—but of the total of 1130 other books cited in the various bibliographies, 167 were withdrawn or restricted.

He'd asked why, and the answers came back pat—"Oh, there was a libel case over that. Something about General Motors, I believe." And—"Well, someone defaced our only copy, it says here, and it was out of print by then, I'm afraid."

One book in particular he remembered, a text on accidents with nuclear weapons, which was duly brought to him by a smiling librarian. But when he opened the front cover he found a hole had been carefully cut from first page to last.

"Do you know what's become of Austin Train?" Mrs. Quarrey said suddenly.

Thorne blinked. "As a matter of fact that was one of the questions I came to ask your husband. I understand the Trainites contacted you some while ago and asked for help in a nationwide survey they're doing on Puritan products—is that true?"

Quarrey nodded.

"And I've been hunting high and low in the hope of locating Train, but so far all my leads have taken me to one of these—these Doppelgängers of his." Thorne hesitated. "Do you think he's dead?"

"One does keep hearing rumors," Quarrey sighed. "He never had any direct connection with the Trainites, of course, but the latest story I've heard did come from a Trainite, for what that's worth. Claimed that he was burned to death in that slum apartment in San Diego."

"I've heard that too," Thorne agreed. "But I think it's another of these mistaken identity cases. Incidentally, do you know where that crazy fisherman got his napalm?"

"I don't think so."

"It was part of a consignment we supplied to the Mexicans to burn off marijuana fields."

"Well, that's the chickens coming home to roost with a vengeance," Quarrey said with a sour chuckle. "Why have you been hunting so hard for Train, by the way? More sherry?"

"Please, it's very good . . . Well, I guess because he seems to be about the only person who might lead us out of this mess. I mean so many people respect him and at least give lip-service to his principles. Do you agree?"

"In a way," the professor said thoughtfully. "We need something to break us out of this—this isolationism we've drifted into. I don't mean that in the standard sense; I mean more isolationism in *time*, as it were. We're divorced from reality, in the same way as the Romans went on thinking of themselves as invulnerable and unchallengeable long after it ceased to be true. The most awful warnings are staring us in the face—the stagnant Mediterranean above all, dead like the Great Lakes—yet we're so proud of being the richest, the most powerful, the whatever, that we won't face facts. We won't admit that we're short of water, we're short of timber, we're short of—"

"Food," Thorne said positively. "Or we shall be next winter. That's why they're so eager to resume production of Nutripon. I met a very interesting guy the other day, used to work for Angel City, an actuary called Tom Grey. He's based in New York now, and I met him through Moses Greenbriar, at the Bamberley Trust. He's been compiling masses of social data for years, for some obsessive project of his own, and Moses asked him to extrapolate the question of this year's crop failures. You know crops are bad everywhere."

"Bad? Disastrous!" Quarrey snorted. "Idaho, the Dakotas, Colorado, Wisconsin . . . Yes, you mentioned this survey the Trainites asked me to coordinate; frankly, I'm of two minds about going through with it."

"Not surprising!" his wife said with asperity. "He's had his life threatened, Mr. Thorne—no, dear, I will not keep quiet about that! It's disgraceful! We've had at least half a dozen anonymous phone calls threatening to kill Lucas if he carries on, and since as I said I'm sure the police are tapping the phone they must know we're telling the truth, but they won't do anything about it."

"But that's serious!" Thorne exclaimed. "They must know—everybody knows—Puritan is a Syndicate operation, and if you're trying to drive their prices down—"

"It's not quite like that," Quarrey cut in.

Thorne stared at him for a moment. Then he leaned back in his chair. "I'm sorry. I seem to have been jumping to conclusions. I assumed that you were looking for food being sold by Puritan which doesn't match their claims, so as to—uh—pressurize them into cutting their extravagant profit margins."

"There's no question of having to look for food which isn't up to their advertised standards," Quarrey said. "You stand about an even chance of finding it at random."

There was dead silence. Eventually Thorne shook his head. "I don't think I quite understand."

"It's very simple. It must have struck you that in spite of their exorbitant prices Puritan sells a colossal volume of food?"

"Yes, fantastic. It's an index of how frightened people really are. Especially parents of young children."

"Well, what some Trainite has discovered—I don't know who, this is all being conducted on an anonymous footing—what he's worked out is this. If you divide the amount of home-grown produce Puritan sells per year into the amount of ground you'd need to grow it on, there literally isn't enough uncontaminated land left in North America. Not after the watershed defoliation program of the sixties. And he's analyzed their stuff, and as I say about half of it is no better than you can get in a regular supermarket. I'm still checking out his calculations, but I'm fairly sure he's proved his point."

"I'm wondering," Mrs. Quarrey said, "whether it could be Austin Train himself."

Thorne glanced at her and back at her husband. "Well, I don't see why you don't publish straight away!" he exclaimed. "If you've been threatened, wouldn't publicity be the best protection?"

"I told him that," Mrs. Quarrey said firmly.

"And I was going to," the professor said. "Until the Trainites told me what's happening to those crops that are failing. Do you know what we've let into the country?"

"Well, some sort of insect pest, I gather. Or pests, at least, seeing they ruin so many different plants."

"It's the worm that caused the famine in Honduras, and indirectly led to the war."

"Oh, no!" Thorne's mouth was suddenly dry. "But *how*?"

"Imported under Federal license," Quarrey said with gloomy relish, as of a preacher at the graveside of an unreformed drunkard. "They were discovered at the Trainite wat in Colorado, and someone with Tupamaro contacts managed to identify them. Apparently one of the big insect importers sub-contracted his worm business to a guy who was supposed to supply Argentine worms, but he didn't give a hoot, cheated them right and left, palmed off thousands of gallons of these damned pests, and skipped to Australia with the proceeds."

"Incredible!" Thorne breathed. "But didn't they realize they weren't getting regular worms?

"Oh, they were mixed in with ordinary worms. And apart from being slightly bluish and a bit differently shaped, these *jigras*, as they call them, do look pretty much like real worms."

"But the experts at the importing company!" Thorne clenched his fists. "Or the customs! Didn't they worry about them being blue?"

"Of course not. He dyed them pink."

"Of course," Thorne said bitterly.

"The Trainites take it for granted that the customs officers and the firm's inspectors were bribed, but I find that hard to believe." Quarrey shrugged. "However it happened, though, the damage is done. And the damned things are resistant to just about every known insecticide, banned or legal."

"So you're afraid of the consequences if you frighten people off Puritan," Thorne said slowly.

"Yes, precisely. We're headed for a hungry winter. My Trainite contacts feel the same way, because even if half the Puritan food isn't as good as it's claimed to be, we're going to need every scrap that's even remotely edible."

"Half a loaf," Mrs. Quarrey said.

There was another silence. Eventually Thorne drained his glass. "I'd better be on my way," he muttered. "I'm dining with my lawyer. I guess he'll have another shot at making me drop my suit against the Defense Department. What the hell can you do when even your lawyer doesn't think you can get justice?"

"I understood you were enlisting the support of—well, other support," Quarrey put in.

"Angel City, you mean? Yes, I had high hopes of them. I mean, it's no secret I had a half-million dollar policy on Nancy's life. But they've paid up and kept their mouths shut. As for the nine cases of Lewisite in Florida—"

"Nine?"

"I'm morally certain, plus maybe one more. But everyone I've tackled so far has been well paid not to make a fuss." Thorne gave a bitter smile. "They can't reach me, though; I was rich already, and now Angel City has made me richer." He checked his watch.

"Might I have my umbrella, Mrs. Quarrey? And I think you took my mask as well."

But when she opened the apartment door to let him out, there were three men in dark clothes lounging against the opposite wall. His heart lurched into his shoes.

And stopped.

Like the professor's, and his wife's.

"Fish in a barrel," said one of the killers scornfully, and led his companions away.

BUILDUP OF FORCES Doug and Angela McNeil saw the troops encamped near the Towerhill road on their way to dinner at a favorite restaurant in the mountains. They had decided to go out on the spur of the moment. They could do that sort of thing because they had no kids. A lot of doctors nowadays didn't have kids.

All along the way they kept passing groups of the strange young people who had been drifting into Denver during the previous few days. By this time hundreds must have arrived. Most had come by bus, and a few among these had brought folding cycles that fitted in a bus's baggage compartment, but the majority were on foot. They obviously hailed from big cities. They had filter-masks around their necks, like the winter tourists who couldn't accept that Colorado air was safe.

"What are they all doing here?" Angela said as they passed one bunch of a dozen or so who had sat down to rest against a big billboard showing the monstrous silhouette of a worm, captioned: HAVE YOU SEEN ANY OF THESE INSECTS? IF YOU DO INFORM THE POLICE RIGHT AWAY!

"I thought at first they must be some kind of Trainite reunion, on their way to the wat. But they're not. Notice they're wearing synthetics? Trainites won't."

Angela nodded. Right: all the way from nylon shirts to plastic boots.

"So I guess they're just the mountain counterpart of beach bums." Unconsciously, Doug had slowed the car to look more closely at them; realizing they wouldn't take kindly to being stared at, he accelerated again. "They can hardly go to California this year, can they?"

"I guess not." Angela shuddered.

"And they can't or won't go to Florida because of the poison-gas scare. So that leaves the mountains. Probably the same is happening back east, in the Poconos for example."

"I can't see them being very warmly welcomed." Angela sounded troubled. "Can you?"

"Well, no. And the forces of lawnorder seem to agree." Doug pointed ahead. Two patrol cars were drawn up on the hard shoulder at a curve, and a group of stern-faced officers were photographing the kids with a Polaroid. Behind one of the cars others were searching a pale youth of about twenty. They had him down to undershorts. One of the police held his arms, though he was offering no resistance; another was feeling in his crotch with evident enjoyment; a third was searching the knapsack he'd been carrying.

A short distance further on was where they saw the troops: on a fairly level stretch of ground they'd erected tents like orange fungi. Five olive-green trucks were parked by the road.

Doug started. "Say, those are battle-lasers, aren't they?"

"What are?"

"Those trailer things! Christ, are they expecting a civil war? They can't mean to use them against those kids!"

"I should hope not," Angela agreed.

And then, around the next bend, a heavy iron gate was set in a concrete wall with spikes around the top. Alongside it was a big illuminated sign, which read: BAMBERLEY HYDROPONICS INC.—SERVING THE NEEDS OF THE NEEDY.

There was another sign hung on the gate itself which stated that parties of visitors were welcome daily at 1000 and 1500, but that was covered with a piece of sodden sacking.

CRITICAL

Well at least you could breathe up here. Even if you couldn't see the stars. Michael Advowson drew what consolation he could from that. Relishing freedom from the tyranny of a filtermask—though still irritated by a faint burning on the back of his tongue, which had haunted him since his arrival from Europe—he strolled uphill away from the hydroponics plant. It was good to go on grass, although it was dry and brittle, and brush between bushes, although their leaves were gray. Above all he was on his own, and that was a relief.

Christ. What wouldn't he give to be home right now?

What hurt him most of all, made him feel like a sick child aware of terrible wrongness and yet incapable of explaining it to anyone who might help, was that in spite of the evidence around them, in spite of what their eyes and ears reported—and sometimes their flesh, from bruises, stab wounds, racking coughs, weeping sores —these people believed their way of life was the best in the world, and were prepared to export it at the point of a gun.

Down in Honduras, for example. Heaven's name! Cromwell had done that sort of thing in Ireland—but that was centuries ago, another and more barbaric age!

He wore his uniform most of the time now. It indicated that he was more than just a foreigner, that he possessed rank in a hierarchy, and these people worshipped power. Recognizing his status, they behaved to him with frigid politeness. No. *Correctness.*

But that wasn't what he'd expected. He had kinfolk, going back to the brother of his great-grandfather, who had come here to escape the oppression of the British. He had expected somehow to be—well, greeted as a cousin. Not as a fellow-conspirator.

Loneliness in New York had driven him more and more into the company of the drunken girl who'd picked him up at that diplomatic cocktail party. Sylvia Young, that was her name. He had found something waif-like and wistful behind her façade of sophistication, as though she were in search of a dream from which she could recall only a mood, no details.

The latest meeting had been the night before last, and she was cured, she said, and wanted him to come to bed. But his subconscious was so disturbed he couldn't do anything, and when she snapped at him in frustration he snapped back, saying he'd never known a girl before who'd been infected, at which she gave a bitter laugh and swore she didn't know one who had not.

And the laughing dissolved into tears, and she fell against his shoulder and clung there like a frightened child, and from her moans emerged the shreds of that unspeakably pathetic dream: wanting to live somewhere clean, wanting to raise a son with a chance of being healthy.

"Everybody's kids I know have something wrong! Everybody has something wrong with one of their kids!"

As a doctor Michael knew that wasn't true; the incidence of congenital abnormality, even in the States, was still only three or four per cent. But everyone did insure against it as a matter of course, and talked as though the least fit of ill-temper, the least bout of any childish ailment, were the end of the world.

"There must be something that can be done! There must, there must!"

It had crossed his mind: I could offer you—well, not *entirely* a clean place to live, because near Balpenny, when the wind blows from the direction of the industrial estate around Shannon Airport, you go out for a deep first-thing-in-the-morning breath and find yourself choking. But they've promised to do something about that.

Also animals are sometimes born deformed. Still, you can kill animals with more or less a clear conscience.

But I could say: let me show you lakes that are not foul with the leavings of man. Let me reap you crops grown on animal dung and pure clean rain. Let me feed you apples from trees that were never sprayed with arsenic. Let me cut you bread from a cob loaf, that greets your hands with the affectionate warmth of the oven. Let me give you children that need fear nothing worse than a bottle dropped by a drunk, straight-limbed, smiling, clear of speech. And would you care if that speech were full of the echoes of a tongue that spoke civilization a thousand years ago?

But he hadn't said it, only thought it. And probably now he never would. After tomorrow's burning of the suspect food he intended to go straight home on an Aer Lingus flight from Chicago.

On the crest of a rise he paused and looked around. There was the hydroponics plant sprawling like a colossal caterpillar along the side of a hill. He could just make out by uncurtained lighted windows the home of the plant's manager, an agreeable man named Steinitz. More than one could say of his host, Jacob Bamberley . . . Staying in that great mansion, the enlarged ranch-house of the estate his grandfather had bought, was somehow *wrong,* even though it was surrounded by what were reputed to be marvelous botanical gardens. He had only glimpsed them; they appeared to be drab and ill-doing.

He must drive back there shortly. He had been engaged in a final review of preparations with the American officers in charge, Colonel Saddler, Captain Aarons and Lieutenant Wassermann, and the other UN observer, a Venezuelan called Captain Robles. Michael didn't like any of them, and following the meeting had needed to unwind. Which was why he was out here at midnight under the sky.

Not the stars. Apparently they hadn't been seen here this summer. Mr. Bamberley had said at dinner, "A bad year."

But would next year be any better?

He shivered despite the warmth of the light breeze, and an instant later had the fright of his life. A voice spoke to him from nowhere.

"Well, shit. Who's this nosy son of a bitch?"

He stared frantically around, and only then saw that a shadowy figure stood less than ten paces away: a black man in black clothes, very tall and lean. And in his right hand something lighter, a knife held in the easy fighting poise of someone who understood the proper way to use it, not stupidly raised to shoulder height but low where it could slash open the soft muscles of the belly.

"What the hell—? Who are you?" Michael demanded.

A moment of dead silence. During it other forms materialized from what had seemed bare empty ground.

"You're not American," the black man said. Man? Maybe boy; there was a lightness to his voice, all head tones and no chest.

"No, I'm not. I'm Irish!"

A flashlight speared him like a butterfly on a pin. How long before that image would be meaningless? He hadn't seen a butterfly in this country.

A new voice, a girl's, said, "Uniform!"

"Cool it," the black boy said. "He says he's Irish. So what are you doing here, Paddy?"

Michael felt sweat prickly on his skin. He said, "I'm a United Nations observer."

"And you're observing us, hm?" With irony.

"I didn't realize there was anyone here. I just came out for a walk."

"Hey, *man*. You surely are a foreigner." The black boy sheathed his knife and moved forward into the flashlight beam. "Thought you must be a pig. But they hunt in gangs."

"He's a skunk!" the girl snapped. Michael had heard the term; it meant soldier. He felt menaced.

"But he isn't wearing a gun," the black boy said.

The girl's voice changed suddenly. "Shit, that's right. Hey, Paddy, what kind of army is it where you don't carry a gun?"

"I'm a medical officer," Michael forced out of his dry throat. "Want to see my ID?"

The black boy moved closer, looking him over from head to toe. "Yes," he said after a while. "I guess we do."

Michael tugged it from his pocket. The boy studied it. "Well, hell. A major, yet. Welcome to this sick shit-pile we live in, Mike. How do you like it?"

"I'd give anything to get the hell out," Michael blurted. "And they won't let me."

"*They*"—heavily stressed—"won't let you do anything." He handed the ID back and stepped out of Michael's way. "I'm Fritz," he added. "That's Diana—Hal—Curt—Bernie. Come sit down."

There seemed to be no alternative. Michael moved forward. The group had camped here, he saw now: sleeping-bags hidden by a ring of bushes, a few dull embers on a hearth of flat rocks.

"Smoke?" Fritz said. "Chaw?"

"Fritz!"—from the girl Diana.

Fritz chuckled. "Ain't no skin off Mike's ass how we screw ourselves up. Right, Mike?"

The reference to a chaw had suddenly explained to Michael the light tone—close to shrillness—in Fritz's voice. He was high on khat, popular among the American blacks because it came from Africa: a stimulating leaf to be chewed or smoked or infused, exported from Kenya in enormous quantities by the Meru people who called it meru-ngi.

"No thanks," he said after a pause.

"Man, you don't know what you're missing." That was —Bernie? Yes, Bernie. He giggled. "One of the great natural medicines. You get the runs lately?"

"Yes, of course."

"No 'of course' about it. They said thirty-five million people caught them. We didn't. Where's the chaw?"

"Here." Curt, next in line, produced the sodden lump from his mouth and handed it on. Michael repressed a shudder. It was interesting, that point about escaping the universal diarrhea. Because of the constipating effect of the drug, no doubt.

He said, "What brings you here?"

"Tourists, us," Fritz answered with a high chuckle. "Just tourists. And you?"

"Oh, they're going to burn all this suspect food tomorrow. I'm here to see the job's properly carried out."

Dead pause. Suddenly the one called Hal said, "Well, you won't."

The girl Diana gave him a fearful sidelong glance. She was very fair, and pretty with it although plump. "Hal, you watch your mouth!"

"Fact, ain't it? Nobody going stop us!"

Michael said slowly, incredulously, "You're here to try and get your hands on that food?"

Hesitation. Then nods. Firm ones.

"But why?" He thought of all the young people he'd seen trudging up from Denver: hundreds! And Steinitz at the factory had said they'd been arriving for days on end.

"Why not?" That was Curt.

"Yeah, why not?" Hal again. "It'd be the first time, the very first time the government of this lousy country turned some of its *citizens* on." He made the word "citizens" sound obscene.

Diana licked her lips. She had broad full lips and a broad long tongue. There was a sound like "hlryup."

"Are you crazy?" Michael gasped before he could stop himself.

"Isn't crazy the only sane way to be in this fucked-up world?" Fritz retorted.

"But there's no drug in the food they have stored! I've seen the analyses."

"Sure, that's what they say." Shrugging. "But they said the same about that place in Africa, now they're saying it about Honduras . . . Stinking liars!"

"Oh, you don't know what you're talking about. I've *been* to Noshri! I've *seen!*"

Without warning it took possession of him: the memory of sights and sounds and smells, the clutch of mud underfoot, the sense of despair. He told about the children battered to death by their own parents. He told about the soldiers who fled weeping and screaming into the bush. He told about the women who would never again see such a common household object as a knife and not run away from it in terror. He told about the stench and the sickness and the starvation. He told it all, words flooding from him like water through a breached dam. And it wasn't until he had talked his throat sore that he realized he had been saying all the time, "The American food did this, did that . . . "

Lucy Ramage and her Uruguayan friend would have been pleased. But they were dead.

He broke off abruptly, and for the first time in long minutes looked at his listeners instead of the recollected horrors of Africa. They wore, all of them, identical wistful smiles.

"Ho, *man!*" Diana sighed at last. "To get that high!"

"Yeah!" Curt said. "Imagine a high that never stops!"

"They want to stop me getting a piece of that," Hal said, "they going to have to burn me before they burn the shit."

"But you can't want to go insane!" Michael exploded. He groped for the right phrase. "You can't want a—a bum trip that goes on for life!"

"Can't I, baby? Are you ever wrong!" Fritz, his voice cold, dead serious, *dead.* "Listen, Mike, because you don't understand and you ought to. Who's going to be sane in this country when you know every breath you draw, every glass you fill with water, every swim you take in the river, every meal you eat, is killing you? And you know why, and you know who's doing it to you, and you can't get back at the mothers."

He was on his feet without warning, towering over Michael, even when Michael also rose. He was more than six foot three, maybe six foot five. He looked like a medieval figure of death: merciless, gaunt, hungry.

"I don't want to die, baby. But I can't stand having to live. I want to tear those stinking buggers limb from limb. I want to gouge out their eyes. I want to stuff their mouths with their own shit. I want to pull their guts out their ass, inch by inch, and wind 'em around their throats until they choke. I want to be so crazy-mad I can think of the things they deserve to have done to them! *Now* maybe you understand!"

"Yeah," Diana said very softly, and spat the chaw of khat into the embers of their fire, where it hissed.

"Go 'way, Mike." Fritz sounded suddenly weary. "Far's you can. Like go home. Leave us take care of the mothers. One day maybe you could come back—or your grandchildren—and find a fit place for people to live, black or white."

"Or green," Diana said with a little hysterical giggle. "Irish, green."

He stared for a long moment into Fritz's eyes, and what he saw there made him turn and run.

Although the majority of the unskilled and semi-skilled workers from the plant had been sent to swell the crowds of unemployed in Denver, a handful of staff had been kept on standby, and with their assistance he and Robles spent the following morning poring over stock records and making sure that every single carton of the suspect Nutripon was removed from the interior of the factory. Troops with fork-lift trucks carried them out to an empty concrete parking lot and stacked them in a monstrous pile in front of the battle-lasers which had been lined up to calcine them into ash.

The records were good, and exact. The work went quickly. He kept hearing—he was meant to hear—comments from the soldiers: what the hell business have these lousy foreigners telling us what to do? One man in particular, a sergeant named Tatum, thin, gangling, tow-haired, seemed to be encouraging his squad to pass such remarks whenever Michael was around. But he bit back his bitter, angry responses. Soon, soon it would be over, and he could go home.

Every now and then he glanced up at the blank gray-green hillside behind the parking lot, expecting to see it alive with human figures: Fritz and his friends, and all the hundreds of others. But although he fancied he saw movement among the bushes, he never saw a face. Almost he could believe he had dreamed that terrible experience last night.

Wanting to go insane? Hardly more than children!

But finally the echoing dome of the warehouse was empty, and nothing else was left in the rest of the factory where new clean shiny air-purifiers dotted the roof and little certificates from the firm specializing in operating theaters had been pasted under ventilation grilles . . . and he agreed with Robles that they could safely go and inform Colonel Saddler. Robles had been chafing to do that for half an hour. Michael took a perverse delight in making him wait a while longer.

He had worked out, on the basis of what Fritz had

said, that among the reasons for his instant dislike of Robles was that the Venezuelan wore an automatic all the time.

"You took your time," Colonel Saddler rasped. "I thought we'd burn this lot before lunch!"

He'd said last night that he was hoping for a posting to Honduras.

Distant on the concrete, gray under the gray sky, reporters waited by their cars and camera trucks, ready to record the act of destruction as proof of good intentions toward the world.

"But now I guess wo might as well go to chow first," the colonel went on ill-temperedly. "Sergeant!"

It was Tatum, the tow-headed man who so resented Michael.

"Sergeant, tell 'em to break for chow, and make sure the fire-hose squad is back here ten minutes ahead of the— What the *hell*?"

They all swung around, and discovered that what Michael had been expecting all morning had occurred. They must have been watching from the hillside with the skill and patience of trained guerrillas. Now, realizing that the job of bringing out the food from the warehouse was over, they had risen into plain sight and were advancing on the chain-link fence that here defined the grounds of the factory. They looked like a medieval army. Two hundred of them? Three? With motorcycle crash-helmets, rock-climbing boots, and on their arms home-made shields that bore like a coat of arms the Trainite symbol of the crossed bones and grinning skull.

"Get those crazy fools out of here!" the colonel roared. "Bring me a bullhorn! Sergeant, don't let the men go for chow after all! Tell those idiots that if they're not gone in five minutes—"

"Colonel!" Michael exploded. "You can't"

"Can't what?" Saddler rounded on him. "Are you presuming to give me orders—*major*?"

Michael swallowed hard. "You can't risk firing the food when those kids are out there!"

"I wouldn't be risking anything," Saddler said. "They'd be no loss to this country. I bet half of them are dodgers and the rest lied to the draft board. But I'm going to leave it up to them. Thank you, sergeant"—as he was handed the bullhorn he'd requested. Raising it, he yelled, "You out there! In five minutes . . . " He strode towards the fence.

In the background, sensing the unexpected, the reporters were scrambling to their feet, cameras and microphones at the ready.

On the hillside, next to a fair-haired girl, a thin black figure, very tall. In his hand, something gleaming. Knife? No, wire-cutters!

Saddler completed the recital of his warning, and turned, checking his watch. "We'll play the fire hoses on them first, sergeant," he muttered. "Don't want that stinking mick—"

And realized that Michael had kept pace with him and stood in earshot. He flushed, and raised his voice. "I trust that meets with your approval?" he barked. "I bet most of them could do with a bath anyhow!"

"Maybe they don't come from homes where it's safe to take a bath," Michael said. He felt a little lightheaded. He had slept very badly after his encounter with the youngsters on the hill.

"What the hell do you mean by that?"

Michael glanced from the corner of his eye at the strange army descending the slope. All around sergeants were ranking their men to guard the perimeter fence. Hoses were being rolled out, that were here as a precaution in case the battle-lasers fired the dry grass and bushes. Over at the wellhead—the plant had its own wells, five of them, because the hydroponic process needed such vast amounts of water—engineers stood by their pumps, prepared to start up on the signal. With a dull roar, a helicopter rose into view from the far side of the factory, a man leaning out of its open door with a movie camera. The letters "ABS" were painted on its side.

"Let me go talk to these kids, colonel," Michael said. "I met some of them last night, I think I can handle this—"

Walking steadily, ignoring cries from the noncoms inside the fence, the first wave of young people had reached the wire. A cry from one of the nearest soldiers, nervously watching.

"Say, that bastard's got a gun!"

"Fix bayonets!" the colonel shouted through the bullhorn. "Don't let them get to the fence!"

Click-click-click. A line of spikes aimed at the bellies beyond the wire.

"Colonel!" Catching Saddler by the sleeve. "I have an idea!"

And a shout: "Colonel! Colonel Saddler! Over here!" Waving from a point near the reporters, it was Captain Wassermann.

"Oh, go to hell," Saddler snapped at Michael, and strode away.

All right, then . . . Michael took a deep breath and walked toward the fence, around the low edge of the irregular heap of food cartons. In the middle it was maybe twenty feet high by thirty each way, but around the sides it spread out untidily. Some of the cartons had burst.

"Hey, major!" It was the man who had called out about seeing a gun, a Pfc. "Don't go any closer—they'll kill you!"

"Shut up, soldier!" From Tatum; it was his squad guarding the wire closest to Fritz. "Let the major do as he likes. It's his funeral."

Michael walked on. He passed between the soldiers and confronted Fritz, who was standing a yard back, his mouth in a twisted smile, his wire-cutters dangling lax in his right hand.

"So that's what you look like by daylight, major," he said, and the girl Diana giggled at his side.

"You want to taste this food," Michael said.

"That's right. So?"

"Which carton?"

"What?"

"I said which carton." All around, eyes were turning to him. He raised his voice deliberately, wishing he had a bullhorn. "Last night I told you this food had been analyzed and given a clean bill. You don't believe it. None of you do. So pick a carton and I'll give you some of it. When nothing happens to you, go away."

There was a dead silence. Eventually Fritz gave a sketch for a nod. "Yeah, it figures. I can pick any carton I want?"

"Any one."

"It's a deal."

"Good. Soldier, your knife, please," Michael said, turning to the man at his right.

"Major!" Tatum again. "You can't do that!"

"Why not? They're here for the drug there's supposed to be in the food. When they find out there isn't any they'll go away. Right, Fritz?"

A hesitation. Then: "Sure."

"And you were going to chow anyhow, before burning the pile. Soldier, your knife!"

"Don't give it to him!" the sergeant rapped.

"Here's a knife!" Fritz called. "I'll take the carton it lands in!"

He produced his own and threw it, high in an arc over the fence. It struck one of the nearest cartons and sank home.

"Right," Michael muttered, and used it to rip a gash in the polyethylene-reinforced cardboard. By now dozens of the young people were converging on this point of the fence, and the news of what Michael was doing was spreading among them like wildfire. Some of them laughed and gave an ironical cheer, and those who were armed—mostly with pistols and knives, but Michael saw one shotgun—tucked their weapons in their belts or laid them down. Tatum, fuming, watched for a few moments, and then suddenly doubled away and could be heard shouting for Saddler, out of sight behind the pile of cartons.

Carrying a huge double handful of the Nutripon, Michael returned to the fence. Seeing him come, Fritz snip-snipped with his cutters, ignoring an order to stop from the Pfc, so that there was a gap a foot square to pass the food through. It was like feeding animals at the zoo, Michael thought detachedly, and watched the stuff melt into greedy hands and gaping mouths.

"More!" someone shouted who hadn't been lucky in sampling the first batch.

"Wait and see what it does for that lot," Michael answered. "It won't do anything, but telling you that doesn't seem to—"

"More!" It was a threatening growl. Yes, like feeding animals. Dangerous, savage animals . . .

He gave a shrug and turned away, and found Saddler confronting him, purple with fury.

"Major, what the hell are you doing?"

"Those kids believe this food is poisoned," Michael said. "They won't let you burn it until you prove it isn't."

"I'm damned if—"

"Or do you believe it is poisoned? Do you believe it was used to drive thousands of innocent people mad, in Africa, in Honduras?" Michael roared that at the top of his lungs.

A surprised cry from behind him—Fritz's high tones. "You tell him, Mike! You tell him! Great work, baby!"

For an instant Saddler didn't react. Then he flipped back the top of his holster and drew his pistol. "You're under arrest," he said curtly. "Sergeant, take this man into custody."

"Hey, no!" A girl's voice, Diana's maybe. Instantly echoed. A buzz of questions and answers moved away on the hillside, like the blurred complaint of insects, and reached a sudden unexpected climax in a single shrill voice, eerie, almost sexless.

"Kill the skunks!"

Later they listed Michael Advowson #1 of sixty-three. When they tried out the battle-lasers on the food, they worked fine.

JULY

GALLOPING CONSUMPTION

The fourteenth of October is a day to be remembered
forever
Because a scion of the Royal Family set in motion the new
power station by pulling a lever.
It was in the presence of many distinguished nobility and
gentry.
There was such a press of interested persons the re-
mainder had to be excluded by a sentry,
A tall and handsome private of the county regiment
Who from the barracks at Darlington had been sent
And stood guard with the rest of his military fellows,
Resplendent in scarlet, a much more attractive colour than
yellow's.
There was a memorable address from the Lord Lieuten-
ant of the county,
Who spoke in literary and poetical terms concerning this
new fruit of Nature's bounty.
From this day forward there can be power in every hum-
ble farm and cot,
Which will inevitably improve the standard of living
quite a lot.
When we enjoy the benefits of this let us hope everyone's
thoughts will centre
On Mr. Thomas Alva Edison, the celebrated American
inventor.

—"McGonigal Redivivus," 1936

FUSE

. . . now known to total fifty-nine in addition to the four US Army personnel previously reported. Commenting on the fate of these latter just prior to leaving for Gettysburg,

where he will mark Independence Day by delivering the Gettysburg Address in the character of Abe Lincoln before an audience predicted to exceed one hundred thousand, Prexy said, quote, Let it not be forgotten that they have hallowed American ground with their blood. End quote. Among the first items the inquiry will consider is the allegation that the riot was triggered off by Nutripon containing a hallucinogenic drug. It's known that some of the food was distributed, against the orders of the senior American officer present, by the ill-fated Irish observer from the UN, Major Advowson. Now Europe. The frontier between France and Italy has been closed since midnight to stem the horde of starving refugees from the south, and an outbreak of typhus . . .

THE CRUNCH

Since the terrible day of the—the *trouble* at the hydroponics factory, Maud had kept mostly to her room, refusing to speak to her husband and to do anything but the minimum for the boys. Mr. Bamberley had been compelled to hire the older sister of their maid Christy to help out. She needed the money becuse her husband was unable to work, having some form of palsy due to a chemical he'd once handled. She was vouched for as very capable.

Just as well that somebody was around here. She was effectively in charge of running the household right now. The sixty-three deaths right on his own land—even if they were at the plant instead of on the estate—had driven him nearly as far into a daze as Maud. He had forgone last month's trip to New York, his occasional visits to a nearby country club, even most of his involvement with his church. He sat every day for long hours staring out of the window of the room he invariably termed "the den"—not "my," "the"—which he had pre-empted when he inherited the house because of its splendid view.

This summer it wasn't what it should have been. For all the work his gardeners put in, the magnificent flower beds that stretched beyond the terrace eighteen feet below the sill were dusty and ill-doing. The grass was patchy and they'd had to returf several sections, at enormous cost. It wasn't due to lack of water. He'd been meaning to call in an expert soil analyst and find out whether it was lack of sunshine or some deficiency in the ground. But he hadn't got around to that yet.

Also the leaves on some of the most magnificent shrubs were marred by dull dry coin-sized blotches, and the flowers seemed to be dropping almost before they opened, and beyond, over the mountains, hung this permanent veil of pale gray haze.

So far this summer he hadn't seen blue sky except from an airplane.

He felt undermined. He felt battered. He felt exhausted. Until a week ago he had only been to the funerals of a handful of people in his whole long life: his grandmother, his parents, and of course most recently Nancy Thorne. Now all of a sudden sixty-three had been added to the total. That mass burial had been appalling!

But the worst part had been the parade the funeral cortège met at the cemetery gates. The police said later that more than two thousand people had joined it, mostly from Denver and the Air Force Academy. There they had stood at the side of the road and clamored their praise of Jacob Bamberley. They had brought flags with them, and banners that read TO HELL WITH THE UN and HANDS OFF AMERICA.

Later, someone had kindled a flaming cross on the mass grave.

Besides, officers from the Army's legal department, collecting evidence, and the FBI, and a smooth-tongued Republican lawyer acting as the governor's special representative, and the governor himself, whom he'd met at fund-raising dinners, and Senator Howell, who was barely less than a stranger, who'd sat in that chair there and said how glad he was that (obscenity, apology) Advowson had got what was coming to him and of course he must himself have put the drug in the food and probably the Tupas had paid him to do it . . .

All of them asked after Maud. All of them.

Now, though, most of the fuss had died down. It was bound to drag on for a while, as he'd explained to the boys when they put their diffident questions, but only so that justice might be done. There was a great tradition of justice in this country, he'd explained, founded on English common law that dated back a thousand years. If someone had been guilty of those deaths, he would be punished.

As for Maud . . .

It was the strain, of course. Dr. Halpern had said so. Accordingly he hadn't made an issue of her retirement to her room, her insistence on eating and sleeping alone, her refusal to greet him when they happened to encounter one another.

The time had come, though, to put an end to this farce. Today was after all a special day. There was a tradition about the Fourth of July in the Bamberley household, which he had inherited from his father and grandfather. He had risen at dawn to hoist the flag, and the boys—except Cornelius—had been roused to watch. Later, at breakfast, there had been presents: for the youngest, replicas of the Peacemaker Colt and the Bowie knife, for the others facsimiles on parchment of the Declaration of Independence, the Bill of Rights, the Gettysburg Address. Next there would be a formal luncheon, with a little homily such as his father used to deliver concerning the meaning of this anniversary, and in the afternoon they would watch the president on TV, all together, and finally before bedtime there would be fireworks. A firm of contractors from Denver had set up a fine display ready on the lawn; they tackled the job every year.

So, it being twelve-thirty, the—the ordeal.

Mr. Bamberley swallowed an extra capsule from the bottle of tranquilizers Dr. Halpern had given him, and headed for the dining-room.

Maud was already in her place: the first time for weeks. Beaming, he kissed her cheek—she barely flinched—and continued toward his own throne-like chair with a greeting for each of the boys. There was a hint of tension, but no doubt that would fade quickly enough.

Taking his stance, he checked that Christy was in position by the sideboard where bowls of salad were laid out—yes, fine—and bowed his head.

"O Lord—"

"No, Jacob," Maud interrupted.

Astonished, he found she was gazing fixedly at him.

"No, Jacob," she said again. It was the first time since before they were married that she had called him "Jacob" instead of "Jack" or "dear."

"You have blood on your hands. I will say grace."

"*What?*"

"You have killed hundreds of innocent people. Maybe thousands. It is not seemly that you should say grace for us."

A huge bursting pressure developed in Mr. Bamberley's head. He thundered, "Maud, have you taken leave of your senses?"

And remembered belatedly that servants must not witness a quarrel between their employers. He gestured for Christy to leave the room. But before she reached the door Maud spoke again.

"Wrong, Jacob. I have come to them. I know why you have never served the food made in your factory at your own table. I've been reading, shut away by myself. I've found out what you did to those poor black children in Africa, and in Honduras, too. And of course to the people who were buried last week. I've learned that Hugh was telling the truth about you."

Mr. Bamberley couldn't believe it. He stood with his mouth ajar like a new-hooked fish.

"So I will say our grace in future," Maud concluded. "My conscience is relatively clean. O Lord, Thou Who—"

"Silence!"

And that was the signal for Cornelius to keel over.

Maud made no move to go help him as he crashed to the floor. Over the sparkling silver and handsome porcelain she locked eyes with her husband.

"I'll call the doctor," Mr. Bamberley said at length. "Clearly you haven't recovered from your—uh—recent indisposition."

He turned to the door.

"After this incredible outburst I no longer have an appetite. If anyone wants me, I shall be in the den."

He was shaking from head to foot when he reached it and almost fell back against the door as it swung to.

Dear God! What had taken possession of the woman? Never in all their years of marriage had she uttered such—such foulness!

He groped on his desk—handsome, English, antique, roll-topped—for his bottle of tranquilizers, and took another dose: two capsules. Obviously the ones he'd taken already today weren't enough. He was after all a trifle heavier than average.

Facing the desk, a velvet chair. He lapsed into it, panting a little. To think of Maud saying that in front of the boys! What poison might she not have poured into their innocent ears? Even granting that she was—uh—disturbed, on this day of all days . . .!

Oh, it was all too much. He abandoned the struggle to think. And was thereupon reminded by his body that he'd told a white lie at the table. He did indeed have an appetite. His belly was growling.

What to do? One could hardly phone to the kitchen, since Christy had heard what he said about not being hungry, and in any case she was probably helping to attend to Cornelius—

Cornelius. Of course. That secret store of candy he'd confiscated from the boy, the stuff that had triggered his last attack. Well, a chocolate bar would at least stave off the worst pangs. Perhaps when Dr. Halpern had called, Maud would calm down or be confined to her room and they could eat lunch after all, pretending things were back to normal.

He bit savagely down on slightly stale chocolate.

Giddy?
Air!
Window!

Eighteen feet to the polished stone flags of the terrace.

"But he said he never ate candy," Dr. Halpern muttered, his mind full of visions of malpractice suits. "I warned him about cheese, but he said he never ate . . . Didn't he mention that?"

Knuckles locked around a tear-wet handkerchief, Maud whimpered, "Yes, he said you asked about that. He thought it was because he was—uh—overweight."

That was all right, then. Thank God. Dr. Halpern rose. "I guess we'd better carry him indoors. Is there someone?"

"Just the maids and the cook."

"They'll have to do."

BLOWBACK "We've duplicated it," the Cuban chemist said tiredly. It had been a terribly long job, and exhausting. But it was done. "Here. It's exact, down to the last side chain. There isn't much—we don't have facilities to manufacture nerve gas. So be sure you put it to good use."

"Thank you. We shall."

Fifteen minutes out of Mexico City for Tokyo a passenger aboard a 747 screamed that he was being eaten by red-hot ants, and managed to open the emergency door at 23,000 feet. He had been to the washroom and drunk from the faucet there before takeoff.

It was, after all, labeled DRINKING WATER.

"What the hell?" the ex-soldier said. "She's American, isn't she? And you know what those mothers did at Noshri!"

They found her by the washy light of dawn. According to the forensic experts she had been raped by at least three men and possibly as many as twelve. They couldn't say whether it was before or after she was strangled.

It had taken three days to locate her. Her dark skin was hard to spot among the underbrush.

A car pulled into a filling station in Tucson. Two black men got out and headed for the men's room. But when they reached its door they broke into a run.

The gas station burned for two hours.

Dynamite.

Also in Peoria, Milwaukee, Philadelphia, San Bernardino, Jacksonville, Albany, Evanston, Dallas and Baton Rouge.

The first day.

Under construction, a cloverleaf intersection near Huntsville, Alabama. The concrete was just starting to harden when it was hit. It turned out to be cheaper to scrap the lot than attempt repairs.

Also at eight other places where the roads happened to have arrived, not famous for anything in their own right.

At the big Georgia paper mill the saboteur was obviously a chemist. Some kind of catalyst was substituted for a drum of regular sizing solution and vast billowing waves of corrosive fumes ruined the plant. Anonymous calls to a local TV station claimed it had been done to preserve trees.

The same day, in northern California, signs were posted on a stand of redwoods that the governor had authorized for lumbering: about two hundred of the last six hundred in the state. The signs said: FOR EVERY TREE YOU KILL ONE OF YOU WILL DIE TOO.

The promise was carried out with Schmiesser machine-pistols. The actual score was eighteen people for seventeen trees.

Close enough.

In Little Rock Mrs. Mercy Cable, who had found a skull and crossbones painted on her car when she came out of the doctor's office with her sick son, died protesting that she had meant to wash it off.

Well, she was black anyway. The mob went home to lunch.

But the most ingenious single *coup* was later laid at the door of a Chicano working for the California State Board of Education. (Prudently he wasn't behind the door at the time; he'd emigrated via Mexico to Uruguay.) He'd used the computerized student records to organize a free mailing of literally thousands of identical envelopes, every one addressed to somebody receiving public education in the state. They never did find out exactly how many there had been, because although they were all postmarked July 1st the mails were so lousy nowadays they arrived over a period of a week, and by the end of that time parents alert to protect their kids from commie propaganda had been warned to destroy the envelopes before the intended recipients could open them. But they guessed that fifty thousand did get through.

On each envelope was printed: A FREE GIFT FOR YOU ON INDEPENDENCE DAY, COURTESY OF THE "BE A BETTER AMERICAN LEAGUE." Inside there was a handsome print, in copperplate engraving style, showing a tall man at a table with several companions handing pieces of cloth to a group of nearly naked Indians of both sexes.

Underneath was the caption: *First in a Series Commemorating Traditional American Values. The Governor of Massachusetts Distributes Smallpox-Infected Blankets to the Indians.*

OUT IN THE OPEN, SHUT UP

It was kind of a fraught scene around the Bay right now—there was this big drive on to catch dodgers. Anyone out on the street (though who'd want to be, when the wind was blowing off the miles-wide garbage pile that blocked the Bay?) who was young and male or a reasonable facsimile thereof, was apt to be dragged into a squad car and left to cool in a cell until he produced a discharge certificate or a valid excuse for not serving. Everyone went around sweating and wishing they'd made it to Canada, or to Mexico before that crazy spic mounted his fire-balloon raids on San Diego. Following that the border had become tighter than a khathead's asshole.

Must have something to do with Honduras, they figured, though there hadn't been much news from down there since the Tupas took Tegucigalpa and drove the legal government to San Pedro Sula. The Pentagon was doing the tar-baby bit.

It eased the problem when Hugh and Carl, together with their friends—or rather Kitty's—Chuck and Tab got in a fight one night with a pair of ex-Marines and acquired their discharge certificates after knocking them out. The man they were still calling Ossie even though they had long ago realized he wasn't the original Austin Train knew where he could get them copied and altered. So now they all had documents to prove they'd done their stint . . . at least to the local pigs. Trying them on at a state border post would have been dicey, which was why they hadn't headed inland.

Train-as-was hadn't mentioned his real name, but they had discussed the idea of his giving up the alias. He was disgusted with his former idol. Why in hell, he kept asking, didn't the mother come out of hiding and assume leadership of the revolutionary forces awaiting centralized command? It was a fair question. This summer the nation was aboil. People drifted in from out of state occasionally, and they all told the same story, though you wouldn't have known the truth from the regular news. You couldn't walk the streets of any major city without seeing the skull and crossbones. People had taken to painting signs on their own front doors; they were being marketed as skin decals like the one Ossie had been wearing when Hugh and Carl met him, and illuminated plastic models were offered to hang on gateposts. The whole agricultural section of the country was seething because of this pest that was killing crops, and that was new—normally the rural communities were blind-loyal. Moreover, the acts of sabotage tabulated in the underground papers came from literally every state, from sugar in a gas tank to caltraps on a freeway.

Also bombs—though they weren't in the Trainite tradition, strictly speaking.

But for Ossie's fair question Carl had a fair answer, and it sounded only too likely to be true.

"My guess is the guy's been liquidated. Making too much trouble for the bosses. Look at what happened to Lucas Quarrey and Gerry Thorne!"

Still, things weren't so bad you couldn't hold a party, and on the Fourth of July they decided to hold one. It was kind of swinging ahead of midnight. Eighteen people in the pad and lots of noise. All very high on pot or khat.

Also there was wine but hardly anyone touched it. They put things on the grapes and the pickers died. Kitty hadn't shown, but what the hell? There were other chicks here. So far Hugh had made it with two he hadn't met before, friends of Tab's, and he was reassured and felt great. Making it with Carl so much of the time led to worry, but Tab had scored for L-dopa, and it worked.

There was a phone. Owing to non-payment of a bill it was good for incoming calls only right now, and was going to be removed altogether some time soon. It rang and went on ringing until finally Hugh picked it up to say drop dead. But after he'd listened for a while he yelled for quiet.

"It's about Kitty," he explained.

Several friends of friends asked who Kitty was. He shut them up.

"Been to this fireworks party on the campus."

Someone turned down the tape-player until the group on it sounded as though they were on the phone themselves, long-distance.

"Well?"

"Busted. Not *just* busted. Beaten up."

"Ah, shit!" Carl frog-hopped toward him. "Her, or the whole bunch? And who's calling?"

"Chuck. He says the lot. Someone's uptight because they been bombing gas stations all over with like Roman candles."

"Shit, man, why din' we think of that?" Tab clapped his forehead with his open palm, smack.

"But why bust the campus?" demanded one of the girls Hugh had made it with earlier. Name of Cindy, Hugh believed. A student there. Black.

"Someone hoisted the skull and crossbones on that big flagpole near the dean's—"

"Oh, *fantastic!*" Cindy went sprawling backwards in a fit of laughter, flinging wide the shirt which was all she wore to show off her so to say negative tattoo: a skull whose eyes were her nipples, bared teeth across her midriff, crossed bones intersecting at her pubis, which she shaved. It was done by minor cosmetic surgery and could be reversed. She always assured people it could be reversed.

"Yeah," Hugh muttered. "But they got like clubbed and dragged in the wagon."

There was silence as he put down the phone. Ossie said suddenly, "We got to get back at them. We *got* to!"

"No use just hitting and running!" Carl snapped. "Got to hurt the man who gives the orders!"

"Well, who gives the orders?" Ossie rounded on him. "The rich! Shit, baby, who else?"

"Right. And we got a pipeline to the rich—you didn't notice? I've been thinking about this a lot. Hugh, how much is Roland Bamberley worth?"

Some of the listeners went back to what they'd been doing before, mainly screwing, but a few stayed to listen because they sensed this was strong.

"Christ, millions! Thirty? Fifty? *I* don't know!"

"You ever met him?" Ossie pressed.

"Well, just the one time. At Jack Bamberley's."

"And this son of his—what's his name?"

"Oh, Hector!" Hugh began to giggle. He was adrift on pot and khat both and maybe the L-dopa was having impact too; all three were fighting inside his head to keep him floating. "Shit, is that ever a ridiculous scene! He keeps that son of his like wrapped in Saran. Know he wasn't even allowed to eat with us? Special food checked out by this tame chemist. Travels everywhere with a bodyguard, night and day—armed, too. Hell, I swear I hardly saw his face. Made to keep his filtermask on all the time he's outdoors, even in Colorado!"

"And he's how old—fifteen?"

"I guess. Going on sixteen now, maybe." But Hugh was over his giggles and beginning to be puzzled. "What's this about?"

"One moment. One itty-bitty moment. You read how he got this franchise for the whole state with these Jap water-purifiers?"

"Yeah, they put one in where we go have breakfast sometimes. Make a thing of it on the wall. Posters."

"Well, don't you think Hector ought to be a little less protected, the rest of us a little more?" Ossie hunkered forward. "Like shouldn't we get next to him and—uh—invite him to see how the other half lives?" He waved at the smoky room and implied the entire filthy city beyond.

There was a confused silence. Carl said at length, "You mean like kidnap him? Hold him for ransom?"

"Ah, shit!" Hugh began, but Ossie cut him short.

"Not money, baby. Not a cash ransom. I'm thinking of"—he groped in the air as though seizing a number from a lucky dip—"like twenty thousand water-purifiers installed free of charge if he wants to see his boy again."

"Hey, that's music!" Tab exclaimed. He'd stayed to listen. "Yeah, that makes a lot of sense. Go 'way!"—to Cindy, who was fumbling in his crotch. At once the argument became general, ideas being thrown out a dozen a minute and most of them absurd.

But meantime Hugh was sitting back against the wall and thinking: Christ, it's crazy and it might work. It just, very just, *might.*

It was in the spirit of the whole national scene, too—would kick off a lot of support especially in the cities—and a hell of a sight closer to the original Trainite ideals than throwing bombs.

If it hadn't been for Ossie, of course, it would never have progressed from a pipe-dream to actual execution. Hugh wasn't sure quite how it developed—the moment he realized he was going to be the key to the scheme, he got high, and stayed high, and was still high the day they did it. But Ossie had spent fifteen years on the underground scene, getting busted now and then but never spending long inside because he had an instinct for self-preservation that was halfway to paranoia. Also he had contacts, and he used them.

Roland Bamberley had divorced Hector's mother years ago and kept a succession of respectable mistresses, unwilling to remarry because he wanted total control of his fortune. He and his son lived on a Stronghold Estate (where else?) near Point Reyes, built around an artificial lake with clean fresh water and lots of tall trees nearby to keep the air sweet. It was obviously no good tackling the job right there. Not with ex-Marine sharpshooters on patrol.

But Hector did emerge into the open now and then, even though he was invariably accompanied by his armed bodyguard. A friend of his from the same expensive prep school he attended lived on the hillside overlooking Sausalito, which had become a very sought-after location indeed during the past five years, because the greenery was still lush and some trick of micrometeorology made the air better than average. Ossie had an acquaintance who worked for a local TV station. Obligingly, the guy established that if he wasn't traveling during summer vacation Hector called on his friend once a week for a morning game of tennis (indoors, naturally), after which he stayed to lunch.

So they scouted the area while Ossie worked on a few of his other contacts, and figured out a route back to Berkeley from the north which avoided the main bridges, and did a couple of dry runs complete in every detail bar one: that for the actual operation they would steal a car and later abandon it.

And all of a sudden the day appointed was upon them.

It was just as well Hugh was living in a dream. If he'd believed what was happening was real, he'd have pissed in his pants with terror. As it was, he felt quite calm.

Just around the corner from the home of Hector's friend, which was screened from the road by dense trees and shrubs, there was a stop sign. At it the dark-blue air-conditioned Cadillac dutifully halted. Hugh stepped into plain view and grinned and waved and knocked on the car's window. He had put on his best—or rather, what had been until a day or two ago someone else's best—clothes, and shaved, and generally made himself presentable.

"Say, aren't you Hector? Hector Bamberley?" he shouted.

At the wheel, the bodyguard twisted around, one hand reaching under his jacket for his gun. Not wearing a mask inside the car, of course—Caddies had the best possible precipitators—Hector looked politely puzzled, a trifle startled.

"I'm Hugh! Hugh Pettingill! At your uncle Jack's!"

Recognition dawned. A word to the bodyguard, who gave a frown, and then also remembered their former meeting. He relaxed, then tensed again as Hector automatically touched the window switch.

"Hey, put your mask on if you're going to open that—"

But by then it was too late. Hugh had pitched the sleep-grenade into the car. It landed fair on the middle of the front seat. He spun and raced for the side of the road.

The grenade held the US Army's latest riot-control compound, PL. It had been mailed home from Honduras. Ossie knew someone who knew someone. And there was always a keen demand for weaponry.

They waited the requisite three minutes. The bodyguard's foot had slipped off the brake, of course, but the car had only rolled forward across the main road and gently bumped the bank opposite. They were prepared to take the risk of his remembering Hugh. In two cases out of three PL induced temporary amnesia, like a blow on the head. It was more likely than not that he'd wake up to find he couldn't recall a thing.

Then the others appeared from the scrawny underbrush, and Ossie drove up in the station wagon they'd stolen, and they piled Hector in the back under a blanket and split.

"He looks pretty green," Hugh muttered as they dumped him in the room—more, an oversize closet—they'd made ready at Kitty's. She hadn't been back since her bust at the Fourth of July party, and no one seemed to know where she'd gone, except it wasn't jail, but they were sure she'd have approved if she'd known what they were doing.

This was a gloryhole without windows, though very well ventilated—they'd made sure of that—with concrete walls, a good solid lockable door, and a sink in the corner whose tap worked fine. They'd fitted it up with a divan bed, a chamber-pot and a supply of paper, some books and magazines to help him pass the time. He'd hate it. But he wouldn't be getting much worse than some people had to live with all the time.

"He looks sick!" Hugh said, more loudly this time.

"Sure he is," Ossie grunted, pulling the boy's legs straight on the bed. "They always are when they wake up from PL. But we have the promise of the Pentagon that it isn't fatal." Grinning without humor.

"Me, I'll go mail the ransom note," he added, and turned to leave.

When Hector Bamberley struggled back from the depths of coma, he found Hugh squatting against the wall surrounded by roaches, some alive and some khat. You could chew it, infuse it, smoke it—come to that you could stick it up your ass, but Hugh hadn't tried that. Of the others, he'd decided he preferred smoking. Hastily he donned his filtermask.

Hector said, "What . . . ?" Tried to sit up. Fell back. Tried again. He was big for his age, as tall as Hugh, and in first-rate physical shape. So he ought to be, the way he'd been coddled all his life.

He nearly threw up—they'd left the chamber-pot handy in case—but managed not to. At the third attempt he reached a sitting position and focused his eyes. He was very pale, and there was a whimper in his voice when he said, "I . . . Do I know you? I think I saw . . ."

It tailed away.

"Where am I?" With a cry. "What am I doing here?"

Hugh kept on looking steadily at him.

"I do know you." Putting both hands to his temples and swaying. "You're . . . No, I don't know you after all."

There was a silence during which he recuperated from the worst effects and was able to drop his hands and regained a little color in his cheeks.

"Where am I?" he said again.

"Here."

"What are you going to do with me?"

"Take care of you," Hugh grunted. "Very good care. Expensive care. Look!" He reached under the bed, barely missing Hector's feet, and drew out a plastic tray on which they had arranged food: sausage, salad, bread, fruit, cheese, and a water-glass. There was no don't-drink notice in force at present, so they'd agreed to take the fact literally.

"This is all from Puritan. Got that?"

"I don't understand!"

"Simple enough," Hugh sighed. "You are not going to be starved, that's the first thing. You're not going to be beaten—nothing like that."

"But . . ." Hector took a firm grip on himself. Among the subjects they taught best at his expensive school was self-control. "All right, so I'm not here to be starved or beaten. What for, then?"

"Because your father inherited a fortune made by ruining the earth. Now he stands to make another out of his ancestors' shit. So we're going to keep you here, and feed you—all stuff from Puritan, the best kind—until your dad agrees to install twenty thousand of his new water-filters free of charge."

But Hector wasn't seriously listening. "I know who you are!" he said suddenly. "You had a quarrel with Uncle Jack and walked out!"

"Did you understand what I told you?" Hugh scrambled to his feet. So much for wearing a filtermask!

"Ah . . . Yes, I guess so." Hector looked nervous. Small wonder. "Say, I—uh—I need to go to the can."

Hugh pointed.

"What? You mean you're not even going to let me go to the bathroom?"

"No. You can wash down at the sink. You'll get a towel." Hugh curled his lip, not that it showed. "Don't know why you're so eager for the bathroom anyhow. We don't have one of your dad's water-purifiers here. We have to take the regular supply. Think about that. You'll have lots of time."

He reached with bunched knuckles to rap on the door, twice. Ossie had worked out a scheme: no one to go in the room without a mask, no one to go in without someone waiting outside behind the locked door, not to open until he heard the agreed number of knocks and that was to be changed every time.

Prompt, Tab opened to him, and Carl was seen in the background poised to block an escape. Both were masked.

Hugh stepped out and the door was slammed and locked.

"All cool?" Carl demanded.

"Shit, no. He recognized me." Hugh threw aside his mask in disgust. "Ah, I guess he was bound to. I mean, people wear them so much of the time, you go by the eyes and forehead. Should have known I had to take the risk. Well, never mind." Saying it made him feel bolder. He added, "Christ, khat makes me thirsty. Got a Coke or something?"

"Here." Chuck tossed one from a carton they had going in the corner. "Say, did he look at the books yet?"

"Hell, of course not. Why?"

Chuck grinned. "I put a stack of porn in with them. Might be handy for him while he's alone."

EARTHWAKE

"What the hell?"

Elbow in the ribs. Philip Mason swore at his wife. It was dark. Also hot. But the windows had to be shut because of the smoke from the river fires.

And then he realized: another stinking quake.

He sat up. "Bad one?" he muttered, driving sleep from his eyes with the palms of his hands.

"No, but Harold's crying." Denise was climbing out of bed, feet fumbling for slippers. There was another brief rumble and something rattled on her dressing-table: perfume bottles, maybe. A wail. No, a top-of-the-lungs yell.

"Okay, I'll come along, too," Philip sighed, and swung his legs to the floor.

THIS ISN'T THE END OF THE WORLD, IS IT?

Normally Moses Greenbriar distributed greetings like largesse as he waddled toward his office every morning. Today he distributed snarls. He was soaking with perspiration—the air outside was appallingly hot and wet—and he was more than an hour late. He stormed into his office and slammed the door.

"Dr. Grey has been waiting for you for over half an hour," his secretary said nervously via the intercom.

"Shut up! I know!"

He fumbled the lid off a small bottle of capsules, gulped one down, and in a few minutes felt somewhat better. But it was still horribly hot and humid in here. He buzzed the secretary.

"What the hell's wrong with the air conditioning?"

"Uh . . . It's overloaded, sir. It's on maximum already. They promised to send someone along and adjust it next week."

"Next week!"

"Yes, sir. They haven't caught up the backlog they accumulated during the enteritis epidemic."

"Ah, hell!" Greenbriar wiped his face and peeled off his jacket. Who cared if he showed a wet shirt? So would everybody on a day like this. "Okay, send Dr. Grey in."

And, by the time Grey appeared in the doorway, he'd composed himself with the help of the pill into something resembling his normal affability.

"Tom, do sit down. I'm sorry to have kept you hanging about—it was those dirty Trainites again."

"I hadn't heard there was another demonstration today," Grey said, crossing his legs. Greenbriar stared at him resentfully; the guy hardly showed a wrinkle, let alone a patch of sweat.

He said, "Not a demonstration. They seem to have given up such harmless stunts, don't they? I imagine you heard Hector Bamberley's been kidnapped?"

Grey nodded. "Was your trouble something to do with—?"

"Shit, no." Greenbriar seized a cigar and savagely bit off the end. "Though I can't say it hasn't caused plenty of trouble for us, that—what with Jack Bamberley dead, and Maud under sedation, we were expecting Roland to step into his shoes and help keep the organization on an even keel, stop this disastrous drop in our share price . . . But what happened to me, the police had a tip-off that some maniac was going to blow the Queens Midtown Tunnel by driving through it with a bomb in his car. And himself too, I guess. So they're stopping and searching everybody. Bet it's another stinking hoax!"

"Yes, threats are an excellent sabotage technique in themselves," Grey said with clinical interest. "Very much akin to the German V-1 flying bombs, you know. They carried warheads too small to do much damage, but everyone within earshot naturally took shelter, so they interfered remarkably efficiently with munitions production and public services."

Greenbriar blinked at him. After a pause, he said, "Well, maybe, but it's a stinking nuisance all the same . . . Say, I guess I should have started by saying I'm glad to see you better. You were indisposed, weren't you?"

"Nothing serious," Grey said. But he sounded, and was, aggrieved. Neither a drinker nor a smoker, celibate, and eating a balanced diet, he suffered from the subconscious assumption that disease germs would realize he was a hard nut to crack and keep their distance. Instead, he had gone down with brucellosis—he, Tom Grey, who *never* touched unpasteurized milk and invariably ate margarine instead of butter!

Now, naturally, he was cured; there were excellent and fast-acting specifics. But it irked him that he'd been deprived of three precious weeks he could have devoted to his project. At Angel City he had had a great deal of time to pursue what he regarded as the most important aspects of it. Here, by contrast, precisely because he had been engaged to work on it as a main job instead of a private venture, he had to subordinate his own preferences to the priorities of his employers.

"I believe it was because of Jacob's sad demise that you wanted to see me," he said.

Greenbriar studied the tip of his cigar with critical concentrated attention. He said, "Well—yes. It's no secret that this is the latest in a series of body-blows, as you might say. Even such an enormously wealthy organization as the Bamberley Trust has limits to the amount of punishment it can take. First the African business, then the Honduran affair, then the riot at the hydroponics plant, and now this—it's turned public opinion against us and practically wiped out confidence in our stock. So we're desperately in need of something, something dramatic, to improve our image. At our last Board meeting, I raised the matter of your—ah—precautionary program, and everyone felt that it had strong potential for this application. Is there any chance of putting the use of it on public offer in the immediate future?"

Grey hesitated. He had been half afraid of this. But . . .

"Well, actually, that brings to my mind a suggestion Anderson made the other week. That young programmer you assigned as my assistant, you know? I suspect he intended it as a pleasantry, but I've been pondering it during my confinement to bed. In effect he argued that we are less in need of extrapolatory analyses to prevent fresh mistakes being made, than of emergency solutions to problems already in existence. Not that he phrased it quite like that, of course."

"Then how did he phrase it?"

"What he in fact said," Grey replied, "was this." Not for the first time Greenbriar decided he totally lacked a sense of humor; the question had been put, he felt obligated to answer in detail. "He said, 'Doc, instead of looking for ways to avoid more and bigger messes, why not just look for ways out of the mess we're in right now? The way things are shaping, we may not be around long enough to make any more mistakes!' " Defensively he appended, "As I told you, I suspected him of being jocular."

"Joking or not, do you think he was right?"

"Well . . . You know, I have sometimes been accused of inhabiting an ivory tower, but I do keep up with the news even though my tastes incline toward the quiet life. I can't help believing that the public at large would welcome something similar to what Anderson proposed. I can't accept that our political leaders are correct in maintaining that concern about environmental deterioration was a fad, which now sounds stale if it's mentioned in a campaign speech and bores the listeners. My conclusion is rather that because the politicians appear to be bored with it the public are resorting to more extreme measures. You've noticed how many acts of sabotage have been committed lately?"

"Damn it, of course!" Greenbriar spoke curtly. Many of the Trust's major holdings had suffered, being concentrated in growth industrials.

"Well, there's one thing to be said in defense of the saboteurs, isn't there? They are striking at industries with high pollution ratings. Oil, plastics, glass, concrete, products generally which don't decay. And of course paper, which consumes irreplaceable trees."

"I had the impression you were on the side of progress," Greenbriar muttered. "This morning you sound like an apologist for the Trainites."

"Oh, hardly." A thin smile. "Of course I had to reread Train's work for incorporation in my program data, along with every other thinker who's had a major influence on the modern world—Lenin, Gandhi, Mao and the rest. But what I'm driving at is this. We've had centuries of unplanned progress, and the result can justly be called chaotic. Uninformed people, aware only that their lives may be revolutionized without warning, are naturally insecure. And they come to distrust their leaders, too, for reasons which might be exemplified by what happened at your hydroponics plant, when half a million dollars' worth of food, despite the government's insistence that it was perfectly edible, was destroyed against the background of starvation in Asia, Africa, even Europe. And, what is more"—he leaned forward intently—"against the depredations of these *jigras* throughout the agricultural states. A huge advertising campaign is being mounted, asking everyone to watch out for and report new outbreaks. But who's going to take it seriously when the government authorizes the burning of so much food purely to score a political point?"

Greenbriar nodded. Moreover, steaks in his favorite restaurant had gone up from $7.50 to $9.50 this summer.

"I suspect," Grey plowed on, "that young people in general want to believe in their leaders' good faith. After all, many of them are proud that the world's largest charitable organization is American. But instead of capitalizing on the fund of goodwill that exists, the government repeatedly tramples on it. Instead of exclaiming in horror at the fate of your friend's wife, Mrs. Thorne, they refuse to acknowledge any responsibility, they even try and deny the danger is a real one. And, reverting to the riot at your plant: wasn't it a terrible tactical error to use battle-lasers? There's been a considerable outcry over their employment in Honduras, and one must confess that the reports of their effect don't make for pleasant reading. One could imagine young people being deeply disturbed by descriptions of how a person standing at the fringe of the beam may instantly find that an arm or leg has been amputated and cauterized."

"You're beginning to remind me of Gerry Thorne," Greenbriar said slowly. Somewhere during that lengthy speech Grey had touched him on a raw nerve. "He put it more—more forcefully, of course. He said, 'There are madmen in charge and they've got to be stopped!' "

He looked at Grey, and the thin man gave a sober nod.

Yes, damned right. What would happen if someone didn't come up—and very soon—with a rational, scientific, practicable plan to cure this country's ills? You couldn't look to that straw dummy Prexy and his cabinet of mediocrities for anything more useful than pious platitudes. Their attitude seemed to be, "Well, it didn't work last time but it damned well should have done, so we'll do it again!" Meantime, what had been uncommitted support drifted steadily toward the extremist axis of the Trainites, or the radical right, or the Marxists. It was as though the public was taking the stand which came handiest, just so long as there was a stand to be taken that put an end to bumbling along from day to day.

He said, looking down at his fat hands on the desk and noticing that they glistened with perspiration, "Do you think your program can be adapted to offer—uh—real-world solutions?"

Grey pondered. He said finally, "I'll be frank. Right from the beginning of my project I've proceeded on the assumption that what's done is done, and the best we could hope for was to avoid compounding our mistakes. Obviously, though, the data that are already accumulated can be employed for other purposes, though certain necessary and perhaps time-consuming adjustments . . ."

"But you'd be willing to let us announce that Bamberley Trust is to finance a computerized study which may reveal some useful new ideas? I'll guarantee to keep it down to 'may.'" Greenbriar was sweating worse than ever. "To be honest, Tom, we're throwing ourselves on your mercy. We're in terrible trouble. And next year can only be worse if we don't hit on something which will make the public feel more favorably disposed toward us."

"I'd need extra funds, extra staff," Grey said.

"You'll get them. I'll see to that."

SCRATCHED

"Yes? . . . Oh, I'm very sorry to hear that. Please convey him our best wishes for a speedy recovery. But the president did ask me to pass this message informally as soon as possible; I may say he feels very strongly about the matter. Of course, not knowing if the rumor is well founded, we didn't want to handle it on an official level . . . Yes, I would be obliged if you could make sure the ambassador is told at the earliest opportunity. Tell him, please, that any attempt to nominate Austin Train for the Nobel Peace Prize would be regarded as a grave and—I quote the president's actual word—calculated affront to the United States.

PRIME TIME OVER TARGET

Petronella Page: . . . and welcome to our new Friday slot where we break our regular habit and cover the entire planet! Later we shall be going to Honduras for interviews right on the firing line, and by satellite to London for in-person opinions concerning the food riots among Britain's five million unemployed, and finally to Stockholm where we'll speak direct to the newly appointed secretary of the "Save the Baltic" Fund and find out how this latest attempt to rescue an endangered sea is getting on. But right now we have a very sad episode in focus, the kidnapping of fifteen-year-old Hector Bamberley. Over in our San Francisco studios—ah, I see the picture on the monitor now. Mr. Roland Bamberley! Hello!

Bamberley: Hello.

Page: Now everyone who follows the news is aware that your son vanished more than a week ago. We also know that a ransom demand of a very strange kind has been received. Are there any clues yet to the identity of the criminals?

Bamberley: Some things have been obvious from the start. To begin with this is clearly a politically motivated crime. During the kidnapping a sleep gas grenade was employed, and those aren't found on bushes, so it's plain that we have to deal with a well-equipped subversive group. And no ordinary kidnappers would have fixed on such a ridiculous ransom.

Page: Some people would argue that on the contrary such a grenade could have been obtained very easily, and that anybody annoyed with the notoriously poor quality of California water might have—

Bamberley: Bunkum.

Page: Is that your only comment?

Bamberley: Yes.

Page: It's been reported that a first delivery of forty thousand Mitsuyama water-filters destined for your company arrived yesterday. Are you intending to—?

Bamberley: No, I am not reserving any of them for this disgraceful so-called ransom! I am neither going to yield to blackmail, nor am I going to connive at the plans of traitors. I've told the police that this kidnapping is the work of a highly organized subversive movement intent on defaming the United States, and if they're any damned good at their job they ought already to have the culprits on record down to their—their taste in liquor! But I decline to collaborate with them in any way.

Page: How would ransoming your son amount to collaboration?
Bamberley: During the late sixties and early seventies there was a massive smear campaign against the United States. The world was told that this country was hell on earth. We've won back some of our proper pride in ourselves, and we dare not waste the ground we've regained. If I gave in, our enemies would pounce on the act as an admission that we supply our own citizens with unwholesome water. Think of the political capital they could make out of that!
Page: But you've already made that admission by arranging to import these purifiers.
Bamberley: Nonsense. I'm a businessman. When a demand exists I take steps to supply it. There's a demand for these purifiers.
Page: Wouldn't some people claim that the existence of the demand proves that the authorities aren't providing pure water? And that by ransoming your son you'd actually be improving the state of affairs?
Bamberley: Some people will say anything.
Page: With respect, that's no answer to my question.
Bamberley: Look, any reasonable person knows there are occasions when you need ultrapure water—to mix a baby formula, for instance. Usually you boil it. Using these filters I'm importing, you don't have to go to that trouble. That's all.
Page: But when it's your only son who— Hello! Mr. Bamberley! Hello, San Francisco! . . . Sorry, world, we seem temporarily to have lost— Just one moment, let's pause for —uh—station identification.
(Breach in transcript lasting appx. 38 sec.)

Ian Farley: Pet, you'll have to switch to the next subject. Someone's put out our Frisco transmitters. They think it may have been a mortar bomb.

BACK IN FOCUS There had been this endless—timeless—period of her life when everything looked flat, like a bad photograph. Nothing connected. Nothing meant anything.

She was aware of facts, like: name, Peg Mankiewicz; sex, female; nationality, American. Beyond that, a void. A terrible vacuum into which, the moment she let down her guard, uncontrolled emotions rushed such as fear and misery.

She looked at a window. It was possible to see a small patch of sky through it. The sky was as gray and flat as the entire world had been for—how long? She didn't know. But it was shedding rain. It must just have started. It was as though someone out of sight were flipping the bowl of a tiny spoon laden with thin mud. Plop on the pane: an irregular elliptical darkish splodge. And another, a bit bigger. And another smaller. And so on. Each dirty drop causing runnels in the dirt already accumulated on the outside of the glass.

She didn't much care for the idea of dirty rain. She looked at the foreground instead, and discovered that certain things had rounded out. There was a desk across which a black man of about forty was facing her. He reminded her of Decimus, but fatter. She said, "I ought to know who you are, oughtn't I?"

"I'm Dr. Prentiss. I've been treating you for a month."

"Oh. Of course." She frowned, and passed her hand across her forehead. There seemed to be too much of her hair. "I don't remember quite how I . . ."

Staring around the room, she sought for clues. Vaguely, she remembered this place, as though she'd seen it before on an old-fashioned TV set, in black and white. But the carpet was really green, and the walls were white, and there was a bookcase of natural pine in which there were blue and black and brown and red and multi-colored books, and behind this black desk sat—just a second—Dr. Prentiss in a gray suit. Good. It all fitted together.

"Yes, I do remember," she said. "In the hotel."

"Ah." Prentiss made the single non-word sound like an accolade. He leaned back, putting his long but chubby fingers together. "And—?"

It was like falling into a fairy tale: not the gentle Andersen kind, but the Grimm type, drawn from the cesspits of the communal subconscious. A magic poison, as it were. She didn't want to think about it, but she was thinking about it, and since she couldn't stop thinking about it, it was marginally more bearable to talk than to keep silence.

"Yes," she said wearily, "I remember it all now. They broke in, didn't they? Who were they—FBI?"

Prentiss hesitated. "Well . . . Yes, I guess you'd have worked that out anyway. They'd been following the people who called on you."

"Arriegas," Peg said. "And Lucy Ramage."

Poor babes in the wood. The jungle of New York was too much. Far away, mindless terror. She felt insulated from it now, as though she were trying to remember by proxy. Perhaps with Lucy Ramage's brain. Had she seen the front of her head after the bullet smashed it, or only invented the picture in her imagination? Either way it was repulsive. To distract herself she looked at the clothes she was wearing: shirt and pants of pale blue. Not her own. She detested blue.

"How do you feel now, Peg?" Prentiss inquired.

She almost bridled by reflex, having all her life hated men who presumed instant familiarity. And then realized: she had lost four weeks. Incredible. Time scissored out of her life like a tape being edited. She forced herself to take stock of her condition, and experienced a pang of surprise.

"Well—pretty good! Sort of weak, like when you get up from bed after being ill, but . . . Rested. Relaxed."

"That's the catharsis. You know the term?"

"Sure. A discharge of tension. Like lancing a boil."

"Yes, that's right."

"Was it the food they made me eat which—uh . . . ?"

"Landed you in this hospital?" Prentiss murmured. "Yes and no. You can't have had time to ingest a dangerous dose of the stuff they'd put in it, and of course when we worked out what had happened we pumped your stomach. But you must have been under strain for a considerable time. You were cocked like a hair trigger, ready to go bang at the least shock."

That made sense. Although he said something about "the stuff they put in it . . ." Surely it was there already? Still, she didn't feel inclined to argue.

She said, "You make it sound as though they did me a favor without meaning to."

"That's a very acute insight. I suspect they did. At any rate a lot of repressed material got purged out of your subconscious. That's why you feel pleasantly relaxed right now."

"What—kind of material?" With vague alarm, as though she'd suddenly discovered that a spyhole had been bored in her bathroom wall.

"I think you know," Prentiss murmured. "That's the benefit of this kind of experience, unpleasant though it may be at the time. You begin to admit all kinds of things you've always concealed from yourself."

"Yes." Peg looked at the window. The rain was heavy now, and the panes were almost opaque with dirty water. "Yes, it was the whole stinking world that had got on top of me, wasn't it? All the water filthy—like that." She pointed. "All the ground full of chemicals. The air thick with fumes. And not one friend anywhere that I could trust, who'd tell me how to stay alive."

There, it was out. And it must be the truth because

this dark quiet doctor was nodding. He said now, "But you did have one friend you trusted. You've been talking about him all the time. You probably know who I'm referring to."

With a start Peg said, "Oh! Decimus Jones?" He had seemed to be there, somewhere in the gray flatness of the other world.

"Yes."

"But he's dead."

"Even so, didn't he have friends? Aren't some of his friends your friends too?"

Peg gave a cautious nod. Now she felt so much more like her normal self, her guard was beginning to go up again. There was something fractionally too casual about this smooth black doctor's tone, as though he were leading up to something.

"You certainly talked about them a lot. Gave the impression you're very fond of them. You talked about Jones, as I said, but also about his sister, his wife, his adopted children, lots of other people who knew him and know you. You even mentioned Austin Train."

So that was it. Peg gathered herself and said in a cool level voice, "Did I? How strange. Yes, I used to know him, but only slightly, and many years ago. And of course I've run across some of these people who've adopted his name. Ridiculous, that—don't you think? As though it were some kind of protective magic!"

When she had been taken back to her quarters, the man who had been listening in the adjacent room entered, scowling.

"Well, you botched that!" he snapped.

"I did not!" Prentiss countered. "I did exactly as I was told. If you overlooked the fact that her references to Austin Train could just as well apply to someone who's adopted the name, that's your problem! And why are you so frantic to find the guy, anyhow?"

"Why do you think?" the other man exploded. "Isn't

this damned country falling to pieces around us? And aren't all these dirty saboteurs doing it in the name of Austin Train? Unless we find him and pillory him in public, make him look like the fool and traitor that he is, he can walk back into the spotlight any time he chooses and take command of an army a million strong!"

AUGUST

FOLLOWED BY THE EXPLOSIVE HARPOON

There she blows, bullies, yes, there she blows now!
There she blows, bullies, abaft of the prow!
Jump to it, bullies, come reef your topsails,
Take to the boats and go hunting for whales!

I'm a Newcastle whaler, I've money at home,
But my pleasure is on the Atlantic to roam,
To brave the rough ocean and add to my store—
I've killed fifty whales and I'll kill fifty more!
There she blows . . .

The holds are all full, there's an end to our toil,
We're going to be rich from the blubber and oil,
And when we're ashore and I walk down the street,
I'll march to the music of coin chinking sweet!
There she blows . . .

I'll go to the tavern and buy ale and beer,
And the girls will flock round me and call me my dear.
There's no king or emp'ror lives more gallantly
Than a Newcastle whaler just home from the sea!
There she blows . . .

—Broadside, about 1860, to the air of "An Honest Young Woman"

THE GRASS IS ALWAYS BROWNER

. . . described as quote disastrous unquote by airlines, travel agencies and tour operators. Hotel bookings are down by an average 40, in some cases 60, per cent. Commenting on the report just

prior to departing for Disneyland, where he is slated to deliver a major speech on education, Prexy said, quote, Well, you don't have to go abroad to know our way of life is the best in the world. End quote. A warning that food hoarding might be made a Federal offense was today issued by the Department of Agriculture, after another day of rioting in many major cities over sharp price increases. Hijacking of vegetable trucks . . .

WATERSHED

The phone on Philip Mason's desk rang yet again; it was about the tenth time in an hour. He picked it up and snapped, "Yes?"

"Well, that's a hell of a tone to use to your wife," Denise said.

"Oh." Philip leaned back and passed his hand across his face. "Sorry."

"Is something wrong?"

"Kind of. I've had eight or ten calls today demanding instant servicing. People saying their filters are choked." Philip tried not to let his voice convey too much gloom. "Teething troubles, I guess, but of course it means postponing new installations and reassigning the available men . . . Well, what can I do for you?"

"Angie McNeil just called. She and Doug can't make it to dinner tonight after all."

"Christ, again? That's the third time they've broken the date! What is it this time?"

Denise hesitated. She said after a pause, her voice strained, "So many emergency calls she says he'll be lucky to be through by midnight. Sounds as though just about everything is breaking loose at once. Brucellosis is the main one, but they have calls for infectious hepatitis, dysentery, measles, rubella, scarlet fever and something Doug suspects may be typhus."

"Typhus!" Philip almost dropped the phone.

"That's right," Denise confirmed soberly. "He says—or rather Angie says—it's because all these people have come up here for their vacations instead of going to the coast. The sanitation and water supply can't cope."

"You've told Harold and Josie not to help themselves to water?"

"Of course I have!" And she added, "Sorry, didn't mean to bite your head off."

"Well, this all sounds terrible, but what exactly do you want me to do?"

"Oh, I laid in food for six, of course, so I thought maybe you could ask Pete and Jeannie instead."

"Sure, good idea. Matter of fact I can see Pete right now, heading this way. Hang on." He covered the phone and shouted to Pete, who was visible through the office door, standing ajar because the conditioning couldn't cope with the heat. He was getting around fine now; he'd discarded his crutches and was using only a cane. Entering with a nod to Philip, he dumped something in a plastic sack on his desk.

"Can you and Jeannie come to dinner with us tonight?" Philip said before Pete could speak.

"Ah . . . Well, I guess we'd like to very much," Pete said, taken aback. "Is that Denise on the line? Would you ask her to call Jeannie at home and say if it's okay with her it's fine with me? Thanks very much."

He sat down as Philip relayed the message and cradled the phone, and reached to open the sack. Philip stared in disbelief at what it contained.

"What in hell's happened to that thing?" he exclaimed.

It was a filter cylinder from a Mitsuyama water-purifier. It was discolored; instead of being off-white, it was dark purulent yellow with patches of brown, and the close-packed plastic leaves it was composed of had been forced apart, as though very high-pressure air had been blasted through it from the tube down its center.

"That's what all the faulty ones look like," Pete said. "Mack's found three like that already today. Thought he'd better check with us before exchanging any more."

"Christ!" Philip touched it gingerly; it was slimy and loathsome. "Has Alan seen this?"

"By now I guess he must have. He went down to Doc McNeil's clinic. They have real trouble. Twelve units all blocked solid."

"Oh, *hell,*" Philip muttered. "And have these people who are calling in really used up all their spare filters?"

"Mack says the three he's spoken to have. They're getting through a pack of six in that many weeks. But I thought they were meant to last half a year."

"They are!"

"So what's going wrong?"

The phone rang. Philip snatched at it. "Yes?"

"Alan for you," Dorothy told him. "Alan, go ahead—"

"Phil!" Alan cut in. "We're in trouble!"

"I know. Pete just brought me a filter to look at. What in the world—?"

"Bacteria!"

"You have to be joking," Philip said after a pause.

"Like hell I am. I've run across this before, in big purifying plants. And you get 'em in domestic softeners, too. But those mothers at Mitsuyama swore blind their gear was proofed against the problem. Get a service engineer down here to the clinic right away, will you?"

Philip repeated the request to Pete, who shook his head. "Nobody here but Mack, and he has eight more—"

"I heard that!" From Alan. "Tell Mack everybody else can wait. He's to come here right away. Phil, put me back to Dorothy, would you? I want to book a call to Osaka!"

"Just little bugs," Pete said incredulously, turning the filter cylinder over and over. "Making a pile of shit like this!" He shuddered and let the disgusting object fall. "Scares the hell out of me," he added after a moment. "You know there's a new epidemic building up—brucellosis?"

"I did hear," Philip agreed.

"They say it brings on abortion," Pete said, eyes focused on nowhere. "Jeannie's getting nightmares. She's well along now, nearly two months . . . Ah, hell, it hasn't happened yet." He hoisted his stiff body off the chair. "I'll go see Mack on his way."

The phone rang. It was a man this time, for a change, but he had the same trouble: a six-pack of filters used up in six weeks, and now a mere trickle of water at his sink.

HAVE YOU SEEN ANY OF THESE INSECTS? *If you do inform the police immediately!*

LOW SUMMER Delegates from the five largest wats sat in conference with Zena and Ralph Henderson, in one of the bubble-shaped rooms leading off the big hall where the whole Denver community met for meals, like a side chapel from the nave of an ovoidal cathedral which had shrunk in the wash.

Hunched forward on clear blue cushions, Drew Henker from Phoenix said, "So we're agreed. We'll have to blast Puritan regardless."

There was a depressed silence. On the brown hills surrounding the wat there were few of the usual bright patches of summer color. Ever since its inception, the people living here had planted flowering shrubs round about to improve the view. But they'd been replaced by the tents and trailers of visitors who had picked the flowers, chopped down the smaller trees for firewood, created garbage dumps overnight and polluted their one clean stream with raw sewage. There had been a lot of trouble, too, with rowdy drunks who found it amusing to throw rocks at the wat's windows.

At least it was dark now so you couldn't see the mess.

Eventually Ralph said, "The idea scares the hell out of me, but I feel it simply has to be done." He rose and began to pace restlessly back and forth under the curved dome of the roof, having to stoop a fraction at the end of each pass as he turned. He was tall. "Those damned fools out there"—a wave at the blank black windows—"won't react to anything short of a real shock. They've been warned over and over, by Austin, by Nader, by Rattray Taylor, everybody. And do they take any notice? Not even when their own bodies fail them. Christ, we've practically had to turn our jeep into an ambulance!"

That was an exaggeration. But it was true that at least a dozen times since the influx of tourists began, strangers had come shouting to the wat for a doctor, or to have septic wounds bound up, or to ask advice for a sick kid.

"Bet they don't offer anything in return," Rose Shattock from Taos said morosely.

Once more, silence; it became too long. Zena said almost at random, "Oh, Ralph, I've been meaning to ask you. Rick's been pestering me to know what's causing the patches on all the broad-leaved plants this summer."

"Which patches? The brown are from lack of water, I guess. But if he means the yellow ones, that's SO_2."

"That's what I told him. I just wanted to make sure I'd given him the right answer."

"Wish the pollutants would kill the *jigras*," said Tony Whitefeather from Spokane. "But they're resistant to literally everything . . . Think there's any truth in this idea that they didn't get in by mistake, that the Tupas shipped them deliberately?"

"Why should they have to bother?" Ralph grunted. "Just let some stinking commercial concern lower its standards . . ."

"We bought from them before," Zena reminded him.

"Sure, but only because we had to. And anyway: importing earthworms, for God's sake! Bees! Ladybugs! Sometimes I think there's a mad scientist in Washington, controlling Prexy by posthypnotic suggestion, who wants us all to live in a nice sterile factory full of glass and stainless steel and eat little pink and blue pills so we don't have to shit."

"Then he's getting rid of a lot of us first," Tony Whitefeather said. "So when the factory's built it won't have to be too big."

"Like Lucas Quarrey and Gerry Thorne?" suggested Drew Henker.

"Oh, they didn't need to wipe them out," Ralph countered with a shrug. "The Syndicate attended to that chore for them. Still, they're due for a shock shortly. You're all staying over, aren't you? So we can discuss the initial news release in the morning."

Nods all around the circle. They started to rise.

"Any of you know anything about these new Mitsuyama water-purifiers?" Rose Shattock said. "We've been thinking of investing in some."

"Us too," Ralph nodded. "But the housekeeping committee agreed to postpone it. This will be the first year we haven't managed to grow enough food to last us through the winter, so our spare cash will have to go on provisions bought outside."

"It's not so much of a problem for you anyhow, is it?" Drew said. "Come snow-time you can always rely on natural purification."

"I'm not so sure," Ralph grunted. "With all this high-level haze, Christ knows what the snow's going to be like this year."

"Grimy," Zena said, and pulled a face.

At the same moment the distant drone of a light aircraft could be heard, growing louder, and they all glanced toward the window. Ralph exclaimed.

"Say! If those are the lights of that plane, he's low!"

"Sure is," Zena confirmed, peering past his shoulder. "Must be in trouble!"

"His engine's firing fine . . . Hey, what's he playing at? He's heading straight for the wat! Crazy joy-rider!"

"He's high, or drunk!" Drew decided. "The damned fool!"

"Let's get outside and warn him off with a flashlight," Zena proposed, and headed for the door.

Swinging around, Ralph shouted after her. "Hey, no! If

he is stoned, he'll think you're playing games with him and fly even lower!"

"But we can't just—"

It was as far as she got. The roar of the engine was almost loud enough to drown out speech, but that wasn't what cut off the rest of the sentence.

A sudden line of splintered holes, like the stabs of a sewing-machine needle, spiked the window, the roof, the floor, and Drew and Ralph.

On the second pass the plane dropped a stick of Molotov cocktails. Then it zoomed away into the night.

UNABLE NOW TO SEE THE MOUNTAINS

Surely from here on an August day you used to be able to see the mountains?

Pete looked around. They'd been detoured by police barriers from the route they'd intended to take—there was a house-to-house going on—and now here they were halted at the high point of Colfax, between Lincoln and Sherman, right next to the state capitol, while a group of young patrolmen went from car to car checking ID's and chaffing the pretty girls. On the mile-high step of the capitol frontage parties of tourists who'd been passed by the guards were taking each other's pictures, as usual. Usual Saturday morning crowds on the sidewalks, too.

But no mountains.

Funny. Made Denver feel kind of like a stage set. The arrow-straight line of Colfax pointing into blurred gray.

Almost one could believe that the world outside of what one could see was dissolving—that what the TV showed, the papers reported, was a fake.

On a notice-board hung to the fence enclosing the capitol grounds was a small version of the poster showing a *jigra* which had appeared throughout the Midwest and West in the past few weeks. Over it someone had scrawled the Trainite symbol in red: ☠.

The patrolmen reached their car, checked their ID's and looked into the trunk, and waved them on. He kept staring at that poster until he almost cricked his neck, which was sort of dangerous with his back condition. Another funny sensation: being a passenger all the time. He enjoyed driving. But it would be a long while before he could do that again.

Those stinking symbols were everywhere. They'd had three painted on the car, for instance, which Jeannie had had to clean off—trying not to damage the cellulose—wasting an hour or more on each occasion. If only, when it came to getting rid of one of the cars, they'd been able to keep the Stephenson . . . But it was so much smaller, so much harder for him to get in and out of, and of course the trade-in value of an electric was far higher than that of any gas-driven car nowadays, and since they had to find the money for their new refrigerator . . .

Damned silly not being able to get the old one repaired! But none of these kids nowadays would have anything to do with technical matters. Like it was black magic, and just touching it put you in the devil's power. They'd been expecting to recruit kids quitting school this year as trainee fitters at Prosser Enterprises. And hadn't hired half what they needed: maybe nine or ten, when they'd planned on thirty.

And now this trouble with the clogged filters. He was handing out two six-packs of the things as replacements under guarantee for every one sent to a new purchaser. Alan was talking about suing Mitsuyama, but that was talk and nothing more. You couldn't touch a billion-dollar corporation like that one, foreign or domestic. Best would be if the same problem hit, say, Bamberley in California or some other, bigger franchise holder who'd be prepared to make the suit a joint one.

Jeannie wasn't her usual talkative self today, but that was fine by him; he wasn't in a chatty mood himself. Anyway, she needed to concentrate. There was a lot of traffic. They were headed for Towerhill, to have lunch with her family, so they were on the road which led to many things not only tourists but local people out for a ride wanted to see: the site of the avalanche, the scene of the sixty-three deaths at the hydroponics plant, the burned-out remains of the Trainite wat . . .

Is it true the Syndicate was responsible, trying to kill these daily louder rumors about the quality of Puritan food? Have to be a real bastard of that kind to do what he did! It's one thing to object to Trainite demonstrations and sabotage and all, something else to kill children asleep in their beds.

"Say, honey, look!" Jeannie exclaimed. "There's a bird!"

But he was too slow, and missed it.

Half a mile out of the city she said, "Pete, what's doing it?"

"What?"

She pointed to the sere yellow hillside they were passing. The plants on it were dusty. Shabby. Like untended house-plants in an overheated room.

"Well, pollution, I guess," Pete said uncomfortably.

"Sure, I know. But what does that really mean?"

He forgot to answer. Around the next bend they came in sight of a highway patrol car drawn up on the hard shoulder. A couple of officers had got out and were walking up the slope to inspect something new, a monstrous skull and crossbones at least thirty feet overall, etched into the dry grass with some dark viscous liquid, maybe used lubricating oil. The driver still sitting in the car was an old acquaintance, so Pete called and waved, but the guy was yawning and didn't notice.

Further on Jeannie said suddenly, "Honey!"

"Yes?"

"I . . . Do you still think we ought to call him Franklin?"

That wasn't what she'd been going to say; he was sure of that. Still, he said, "I like it. Or Mandy for a girl."

"Yes, Mandy."

And then in the same breath, in a rush, "Pete, I feel so dirty inside!"

"Baby, how do you mean?"

"Like—like all my bones need to be taken out and washed!"

"Now that's foolish talk," Pete said gently.

"No, I mean it," she muttered. "I don't have too much to do all day now, while you're at work. Not having the garden any more, or a whole house to keep clean . . . I can't help thinking about it, honey, not when there's a baby growing inside me!"

"The baby's going to be okay," Pete declared. "You couldn't have a better guy than Doc McNeil to see you through."

"Oh, sure, and I always do just like he tells me. Eat the right kind of food, drink canned water, never touch milk or butter . . . But—Pete, what the hell kind of world are we going to bring the kid into?"

She snapped a harsh stare at him, lasting only a second, but long enough for him to recognize the real terror in her eyes.

"The doc says I probably won't be able to feed him myself. Says practically no mothers can. Too much DDT in their milk!"

"Baby, all that shit was banned years ago!"

"So how many times did you book someone peddling it?"

Pete had no answer for that. Even during one year of service in the police he had helped to arrest five or six people home-brewing illegal chemicals: not just insecticides, but defoliants, too.

"And proper food costs so much, too," Jeannie worried on, signaling right as she slowed for the Towerhill turn. "A dime here, a quarter there, without knowing it you're spending twice as much as you expected. And it's going to get worse. I was talking to Susie Chain the other day. Ran into her in Denver, shopping."

"Ah-hah?" She was referring to the wife of his former sergeant at Towerhill.

"She has cousins in Idaho, she said, and they've told her they're only going to bring in about a quarter of the potato crop this year. The rest's been spoiled by *jigras.*"

Pete whistled.

"They eat anything, she said. Corn, beets, squash . . . Say, you seen the Trainite wat?" She pointed across the valley. Blurred by the haze, but visible in enough detail to be gruesome, the hollow shell of the wat lay like a rotted lobster. Small parties of sightseers were wandering around it, poking at the wreckage in search of souvenirs.

The local fire chief had said on TV how many warnings he'd issued about building in Fiberglas and scrap plastic. Worse than timber. Something about the poisonous fumes given off.

"Is that the way our kid's going to go?" Jeannie said bitterly. "Burned alive like those three were?"

Pete reached over to pat her comfortingly on the knee. But she rushed on. "Think of all the things he'll never be able to do, Pete! Swim in a river, or even row a boat on it—pick fruit right off the tree and eat it—take off his shoes to walk in wet grass, all squelchy and thick!"

"Oh, honey, you sound like Carl," Pete chided.

"Why not?" She sniffed. "Carl's the bright one in our family, always was. Wish he'd write and let me know how he is . . . You know, I'd half like to catch this brucellosis that's going around, so there wouldn't have to be a baby."

"Shit, you mustn't say that!" Pete exclaimed in horror. "If we miss on this one, we may never—"

But at that point the road gave a shudder. It was as though every one of the hundreds of cars in sight simultaneously ran over a rock. He reached for the radio and switched it on, to find out whether the quake was going to be serious. It wasn't. And in another few minutes they were at Jeannie's mother's home and they had to try and pretend that everything was fine, just fine.

FED UP

. . . purchases of Nutripon to supplement welfare stocks, currently at their lowest level for years owing to the unforeseen impact of unemployment in resort areas deserted by tourists, where ordinarily casual jobs in hotels and restaurants absorb much surplus labor from June through September. Discounting fears expressed by black and poverty-group spokesmen, Secretary for Welfare Barney K. Deane pointed out that the Bamberley plant has been refitted to an extremely high standard, close to what you get in an operating theater, quote, unquote. Asked whether the plan would be extended later to relieve the impact of scarcity prices on underprivileged families, he said the question was actively under consideration but no decision had been reached. A call to ban exports of food to the United States was today issued by . . .

BACK

Not much changed. Garbage-cans fuller than ever and stinking. Buzzing flies. Kitty Walsh was pretty high. She stood for a while looking at the flies and wondering—not very seriously—where they'd come from. Imported, maybe? Last year, or the year before, or something, there hadn't been any at all.

But finally she picked her way among the cans and went indoors, trying to take off her filtermask as she went. It got kind of entangled with her hair. She'd let it grow while she was away.

The air inside was full of fumes, too, but that was pot. The windows were taped to keep the stench out. It was very hot.

"Christ, it's Kitty," Hugh said, and rolled away from Carl. They were both naked. And she was nearly: just a dress, slit up the front, and sandals.

"Where you been, baby?" Carl demanded.

"Places." She threw down the canvas airline bag which

was all she'd brought with her and reached for the joint they were sharing.

"Met this cat when I got busted at the fireworks party," she said after a while. "We went to Oregon. I didn't know it was so good up there. We had like three days of blue sky. Maybe four."

"No shit!" Carl said.

"No shit. Even found a lake we could swim in. And I got a tan, see?" She skinned her dress up under her armpits, and she was just a trifle brown.

After that there was silence for a while. It was the high. There was radio music coming soft from the back room, the gloryhole. She realized that finally and straightened her head, as far as she could. "Who's in back?" she inquired, glancing around. "And—say! You put a padlock on that door!"

Hugh and Carl exchanged glances. But it was after all her apartment.

"Hector Bamberley," Hugh said.

"What?"

"You didn't hear about that deal?"

"Christ, of course I did. You mean . . . " She almost rose to her feet, but fell back on the mattress-spread floor in a burst of helpless laughter.

"You mean right here? Like under the snouts of the pigs? Ah, shit! That's fantastic!"

Carl sat up, linking his hands around his knees, and chuckled. Hugh, though, said, "Not so funny. His stinking father won't play. And it's getting to be a grind, keeping watch all the time. Mustn't leave the pad empty, of course. *And* he's sick."

"Playing sick," Carl grunted. "It was one of the first ideas he hit on, trying to make us bring in a doctor he can talk to. Now he's back at the same game. It's getting me down to throw away so much expensive food."

"Huh?"

"All from Puritan. Ossie insisted. He's masterminding the deal."

Hugh exclaimed. "Say, isn't it about time we fed him again?"

"Could be," Carl nodded. "Kitty, any idea of the time?"

She shook her head. "Ossie?" she said. "You mean Austin? But you know he's not for real, don't you?"

"Oh, sure," Hugh sighed. "Been thinking of giving the name up, too. Says he's sick of waiting for the real one to come out of hiding and *do* something."

"If he did," Kitty said, "he'd raise the biggest army in history, just by snapping his fingers. Up in Oregon I saw—Hell, never mind. I'll take the food in. Always wanted to meet a millionaire's son. Where is it—in the icebox?"

"Sure, all ready on a tray. And when you come out, bang the door for us to unlock. One, one-two." Carl demonstrated. "So we'll know it's you and not him."

"Okay," Kitty said, and took one more drag on the joint before going to the kitchen.

Hector was lying asleep, his back to the door. She made a space for the food tray among a mess of books and magazines, mainly porn—German and Danish, good-quality stuff. Then she went around the bed and found that he had his fly open and his hand clasped around his prick. Half-hidden under the pillow was another porn magazine, a lesbian one. On the floor, a soiled tissue. Wet. She dropped it into the chamber pot.

Well, so that was what a millionaire's son looked like. Kind of ordinary.

But cute with it, she decided after a while. Handsome kid. Silly thin fuzz of beard showing on his cheeks. Hmm. Pussy cat.

Wake him?

Wait him out?

She sat down on the floor with her back to the wall and stared at him, not particularly thinking. She was adrift. She'd been floating already when she arrived, and that last extra charge from the joint Hugh and Carl were using had blown her way *way* up. Somehow it seemed like too much trouble to rouse him.

After a while, though, the sight of that open fly had its effect. She parted her legs and started fingering her crotch. It was good when she was as high as this, very slow, almost getting there and then not quite, but not getting lost either. Like climbing a snow-slope, slipping back a little at each step but never quite as far as where you'd been.

She almost failed to notice when his eyes opened and he realized she was in the room. She didn't stop what she was doing when she did notice.

"Who are you?" he demanded in a thin voice.

She looked at his prick. It was filling out. He realized, and dragged a corner of the sheet over it. The bedding was all tangled.

"Kitty," she said. "I guess it's kind of boring for you in here, huh?"

"What?" Shakily, he was trying to sit up.

"I mean like is that all you got to pass the time?" Pointing with her unoccupied hand at the magazine poking out under the pillow.

He blinked at her several times, rapidly. Then he flushed bright pink.

"You're cute," she said. "Kind of good-looking, too. Say, I made myself pretty horny by now. You too?"

"What the hell's keeping her?" Hugh said muzzily, a long while later.

"Probably screwing him," Carl said indifferently. "Ever know Kitty to miss the chance? But what the hell? The poor kid deserves it. I mean like he's been cooperative. It's only his stinking old man who's holding out."

CHECK AND BALANCE *Petronella Page:* Friday again, world, the night we break the regular rules and go clear around the planet. Later, we'll be talking to a senior officer from the famed

Special Branch at Scotland Yard, London, about the new British computerized system for control of subversion, widely praised as among the most modern in the world, and then we're going to Paris to talk about the weird weather they're having there, with snow in August, yet. Right now, though, we're going to tackle a subject closer to home. Waiting in the Chicago studios of ABS is a noted educational psychologist with strong views on a matter that concerns everyone with kids—or who's intending to have kids. He prefers to remain anonymous because his views are controversial, so we're going to bend our own standing orders and allow him to be called Dr. Doe. Are you there—?

Doe: Sure am, Miss Page.

Page: Fine. Well, let's start with your explanation for the present nationwide shortage of technicians, high incidence of college dropouts, and so on. Most people assume it's the result of distrust of industry and its effect on our lives, but you say it's not that simple.

Doe: Not too complicated, though, despite the fact that a lot of factors are interacting. The pattern is really pretty clear. It's not so much that kids today are more stupid than their parents. It's that they're more timid. More reluctant to take decisions, to commit themselves. They'd rather drift through life.

Page: Why?

Doe: Well, there have been a lot of studies—on rats, mainly—that demonstrate the crucial importance of prenatal environment. Litters born to harassed mothers, or poorly fed mothers, grow up to be easily frightened, afraid to leave an open cage, and what's more their life expectancy is reduced.

Page: Can experiments with rats prove anything about humans?

Doe: We know a lot nowadays about how to extrapolate from rats to people, but we don't only have to rely on that. In a sense we've made ourselves into experimental animals. There are too many of us, too crowded, in an environment we've poisoned with our own—uh—by-products. Now when this happens to a wild species, or to rats in a lab, the next generation turns out weaker and slower and more timid. This is a defense mechanism.

Page: I don't believe many people will follow that.

Doe: Well, the weaker ones fall victim to predators more easily. That reduces population. Competition is diminished. And the fouling of the environment, too, of course.

Page: But our population isn't diminishing. Are you saying we're having too many children?

Doe: It wouldn't be too many if we could guarantee adequate relaxation—freedom from anxiety—and plenty of nourishing food. We can't. Our water is fouled, our food is contaminated with artificial substances our bodies can't cope with, and all the time there's this feeling that we're in life-or-death competition with our fellow creatures.

Page: This strikes me as very sweeping. What evidence have you apart from rats and these wild creatures you haven't specified?

Doe: The school records, the employment roster, the panic the big corporations are in this year because there's close to a ninety per cent shortfall in graduate recruiting—isn't there?

Page: I didn't say anything. Go on.

Doe: Also, around the beginning of the year, a United Nations report was published which purported to show that intelligence was rising very markedly in the poor countries of the world, whereas by contrast in the wealthy countries—

Page: But that report was discredited. It was pointed out that you can't apply the same criteria to kids in—

Doe: Wrong. Sorry. I know all about that, and about the argument that owing to our superior medical facilities we're keeping alive sub-normal children who die in the underdeveloped countries instead of surviving to drag down the average. But that's not what I'm talking about. I'm referring specifically to apparently normal children, without obvious physical or mental defects. I'm convinced people are subconsciously aware of what's going on, and becoming alarmed by it. For example, there's an ingrained distrust in our society of highly intelligent, highly trained, highly competent persons. One need only look at the last presidential election for proof of that. The public obviously wanted a figurehead, who'd look good and make comforting noises—

Page: Dr. Doe, you're wandering from the point, aren't you?

Doe: If you say so. But I'd claim that this illustrates the fundamental anxiety which is now coloring our social attitudes. I'd say we've subconsciously noticed that our kids are less clever, more timid, and begun to worry that we may be less able than our parents were, and in consequence we're running away from anything that might tend to show that was true. When the politicians claim that the public isn't interested any longer in environmental conservation, they're half right. People are actually afraid to be interested, because they suspect—I think rightly—that we'll find if we dig deep enough that we've gone so far beyond the limits of what the planet will tolerate that only a major catastrophe which cuts back both our population and our ability to interfere with the natural biocycle would offer a chance of survival. And it can't be a war which does it, because that would screw up even more of our farmland.

Page: Thank you for talking to us, Dr. Doe, but I must say I feel most people will regard your theory as far fetched. Now after this break for station identification . . .

THE END OF A LONG DARK TUNNEL

Christ, Oakland had been bad. But New York was *awful.* Even indoors, even in the lobby of this hotel with its revolving door and the air-conditioning blasting so hard it almost shook the walls, Austin Train's eyes were smarting and the back of his throat hurt. He thought of losing his voice. Also of losing his mind. He had done that once and sometimes he suspected he'd been happier without it. Like those kids who'd testified before the inquiry into the riot at Bamberley Hydroponics, one after another stating in dull flat tones that they wanted most of all to be insane.

But he was here, anyway.

Many times on the journey he'd feared he might not reach his destination. Naturally, with a faked ID in the name of "Fred Smith," he dared not risk flying to New York, so it was a matter of taking a roundabout route on buses and by rail. Felice had offered him one of her cars, but that too was out of the question, because cars were the favorite means employed by saboteurs to deliver bombs, and they stole, or rented in a false name, so security was tight. Not that a car would have been much faster anyway, what with the police posts at state lines, the searches, the restricted zones not merely in cities—one expected that during August—but right out in the country, in agricultural areas. Because of hijackers after food trucks, of course.

Problems like that had been among the many reasons why he had postponed his decision to re-emerge into the open. All summer long he had prevaricated, half made up his mind, changed it again and gone back to toting garbage, driving a dumper truck, loading the endless succession of wagons that carted imperishable plastic up the mountains to be jammed into abandoned mine-shafts, baling kitchen refuse to be sold as compost for the desert-reclamation projects, tramping in huge tough sweat-saturated boots over mounds of glass and piles of squashed cans. In its way the job was fascinating. A thousand years from now these scraps that he was helping to bury might be seen on display in a museum.

If there were any museums.

It had been the attack on the Denver wat which settled the matter. When he learned that Zena had taken refuge at Felice's home, only a few miles from where he was staying, he had had to call up and talk to her. And from that it had just all followed logically. Like a flower opening.

And here she came, after he'd been waiting only an hour. It had started to rain during that time—not that rain in New York cleared the air any longer, merely moistened the dirt—and she pushed through the revolving door in a shapeless bundle: plastic coat, plastic one-piece brooties which combined boots and breeches and were on show in every other clothing-store window, and of course a filtermask. She didn't even glance in his direction, but went directly to the desk to collect her room-key.

He saw the clerk lean over to inform her in hushed tones that a Mr. Smith was waiting to see her.

She turned to survey the lobby, and the first time she looked his way failed to recognize him. That was hardly surprising. The infection which had turned his scalp to yellow scurf had killed most of his hair; now he was three-quarters bald and on the bare patches there were irregular smears of granular scar-tissue. It had spread to his eyebrows as well, and he'd lost the outer half of the right one. Since they had constituted his most recognizable feature, he'd shaved the other to match. And his eyes had grown weak, so he had arranged for Felice to take him and get glasses made. Altogether he looked very unlike the Austin Train who had been in the spotlight a few years ago.

Then, all of a sudden, she reacted. Came running to throw her arms around him. Christ, what's happened to Peg Mankiewicz, the Ice Princess?

She's crying!

Eventually she regained control of herself and drew back with a gasp.

"Oh, lord, I didn't mean to do that! I am sorry!"

"Do what?"

"Spoil your clothes. Look!" She raised her plastic-swathed arm and pointed here, here, here, to the big dirty wet marks she'd left all over his new suit.

"Oh, forget it," Austin said, in a tone that brooked no contradiction. Standing back, he looked her over, and added after a moment, "Peg, baby, I think something's changed."

"Yes." She smiled. It was a nice smile; it went deep into her dark eyes. "The world broke me into little bits. And when I was being put back together, I had a chance to decide which bit would go where this time around. I like myself better than I used to."

Hastily she peeled off her street gear, shaking it regardless of what might become of the carpet—it was shabby anyhow—then folded it over one arm and took Austin's with the other. A gesture that hadn't been in the repertoire of the old Peg.

"Christ, it's marvelous to see you! Let's go have a—"

And broke off in mid-sentence, her face clouding. "Shit, I forgot. This time of the afternoon the bar's probably shut. Half the staff has gone sick again. Mono, I think. Well, let's go look anyway; we might be lucky. We can't go up to my room—it's full of bugs."

"Which kind?"

"Both." She gave a wry grin. "Also I'm followed on the street pretty often. But they don't generally bother me in the hotel. They have the desk clerks in their pocket, paid to report my movements."

"Is this the same hotel where—?"

"Where they killed Arriegas and Lucy Ramage? Sure it is."

"But why did you come back to the same place?"

"Because I'm sick and tired of being cowed all the time, looking for a corner to hide in. I've decided to stand my ground, and the hell with them all."

"Is that going to get you very far? Think of the people who've tried before. Lucas Quarrey—Gerry Thorne—Decimus!"

"And what are they going to do to you?" Peg said, looking levelly into his eyes.

There was an absolute, dead, *terrifying* pause, during which his face was as impassive as a stone mask, all life drained except from his eyes. And they blazed. She felt her mouth open a little and a chill down her spine made her tremble. In his gaze she could read judgment.

When he spoke, it was like lightning striking.

"Crucify me."

Then they were installed at a dark table in a corner and a resentful man in a white jacket was bringing them drinks. The air was perfumed with something disgustingly artificial, but one had to endure that everywhere.

She was frightened. It was not until their order had been delivered that she was able to frame words again, and instead of asking about him—she sensed that she had learned too much too quickly a moment ago—she said, "How did you trace me?"

He explained, in a normal enough tone, seeming relaxed.

"I see. How did Zena take the loss of the kids?"

"Very hard—how else? But Felice is being very kind to her, and so's her husband."

"Have you spoken to anyone else from the wat? Are they going to make a fresh start somewhere else?"

"No, they're just scattering to the other wats," Austin sighed. "I phoned Ralph, and apparently everyone was already so tired, so frustrated . . . The attack was the last straw. Chances were they couldn't have got through the winter. The *jigras* ruined so many of their crops and what they did have in store was soaked with fire-fighting chemicals. And do you know what the worst blow of all was?"

She shook her head wordlessly.

"They'd just had a conference about their findings on Puritan. Drew Henker was there, Tony Whitefeather, Rose Shattock. And the only complete copy of the report was burned. Of course, they'll try and do it over, but . . ."

"Oh, Christ!" Peg clenched her fists. "So it was another Syndicate job, was it? Like Thorne and Quarrey? I'd been wondering."

Austin hesitated. "The grapevine says," he murmured at length, "that the plane was hired by a guy who works for Roland Bamberley."

Peg's mouth rounded into an O. "But it can't be true! He's not that crazy, is he? I mean, I know he's convinced his son was kidnapped by Trainites, but surely if he really believed his son was at the wat—"

"Oh, the grapevine carries a lot of garbage," Austin cut in. "It may very well not be true. If it is, he must have meant it as a warning, I guess."

"On the other hand . . ." Peg stirred her drink absently; the swizzle stick had a fleur-de-lys on the top. "Have you ever met that stinking mother? I did once. Interviewed him. I wouldn't be surprised if he'd rather lose his son than give in to the ransom demand. Afterwards he'd excuse it to himself by saying the boy died for the sake of his country."

"Meaning he'd rather have the profit on the water-purifiers than his son."

"That's right. He's proud of being a businessman, isn't he?" Peg gave a thin sour smile. "Still, there's nothing much we can do about that. Say, do you know who does have the kid?"

Austin spread his hands. "All kinds of crazy rumors in Oakland. I don't believe a one of them."

There was another pause. During it, she plucked up the courage to put a direct question about his own plans. By now, seeing him so much changed yet in some indefinable way so much more like himself than he had been for the past three years—perhaps because his confidence was back—she had almost convinced herself that that fearful instant by the door of the bar had been imaginary.

Still, her voice was unfirm as she said, "Why have you come here, Austin?"

"I guess I've come to the same decision as you. Or not so much come to it. Been driven to it. I have a mission, Peg. I don't want it. But who the hell else is there?"

"Nobody," Peg said instantly and positively. "And there are millions of people all over the country who'd agree."

He gave a brief bitter chuckle. "But that's the irony of it, Peg. Remember you once asked me whether it bothered me to have my name taken in vain? Well, it does. My God, it does! It was the thing I finally found I couldn't stand any longer. *I'm* not a Trainite!"

Peg waited for him to continue. She was trembling again, but this time from excitement. She'd hoped and prayed for this for so long. He was looking past her, into infinity.

"But then," he said, "Jesus wasn't a Christian, was he?"

She started.

"Think I'm crazy, Peg? I can read it on your face." He leaned forward earnestly. "So do I, much of the time. And yet . . . I can't be sure. I think perhaps I may really be very sane. If you want me to spell out what's happened to me, I'll have to disappoint you. It can't be described, and if it doesn't show it isn't true. It's just that—well, somewhere under this bald ugly dome of mine there's a sense of certainty. Knowledge. As though this sweaty summer shoveling garbage has taught me something no one else understands." He drew a deep breath.

"Peg, I think I may be able to save the world. Do you believe me?"

She stared at him for a long while. "I—" she tried to say, and found the next word wouldn't follow. She went on staring. Calm face. Level mouth. Those odd, unfamiliar halves of eyebrows. The glasses which—where had they been when she saw that lightning in his eyes? They had seemed to melt away, not be there at all, so she was looking direct into his soul.

Voicelessly, at last: "If anyone can, it must be you."

"Fine." He gave a grave smile and leaned back. "So where do I begin? I came to New York because it seemed logical. I thought maybe the Petronella Page show. If they'll have me."

"If they'll have you?" Peg almost upset her glass. "Lord, they'd throw out Prexy himself to make a slot for Austin Train! Give you the whole hour without commercials!"

"Do you think so?" He blinked at her with surprising shyness. "I've been away so long, and—"

She banged the table with her fist. "Austin, for heaven's sake! Don't you realize you're the most powerful man in the country right now? Whatever you think about the people who call themselves Trainites, they picked the name because *you exist*. Everyone's on your side who can't afford contract medical care for his kids—black, white, young, old! You've just crossed the States west to east. What do you see everywhere from Watts to Tomkins Square? The skull and crossbones, right? And the slogan, too—'Stop, you're killing me!' They're waiting for you, Austin! Waiting with their tongues hanging out!"

"I know!" His tone was almost a cry. "But I don't want that!"

"You've got it," she said ruthlessly. "What you do with it is up to you. I tell you this, though, and I mean it. I don't know about saving the world, but I'm damned certain if you don't speak up this country won't get through the winter without civil war."

There was a long cold silence. He punctuated it by uttering a single word: "Yes."

And then let it resume.

Eventually, however, he seemed to reassemble himself from many far-distant places, and said in a casual voice, "You know something odd? I can't remember the name of the guy who hit on that symbol."

"What, the skull and crossbones? I thought you did."

"No, it was the designer they assigned to my books at International Information. He had a little logo made of it and put it next to the number on every page. And I've forgotten his name. It isn't fair. He ought to have the credit for it."

"Maybe he'd rather not," Peg said.

"In that case I sympathize," Austin grunted, staring at the backs of his hands on the table. "I have this terrible feeling sometimes that I've stopped being myself. Do you understand that? I mean, I've been taken over—*made* over—into the patron saint of bombing, sabotage, arson, murder, God knows what. Maybe rape! If the skull and crossbones has a meaning, it's a warning. Like the international radiation sign. Instead of that, it's what everyone scrawls when they break a store-window in a fit of drunken rage, break into a bank vault, steal a car. It's an excuse for anything."

"So what's new about that? It happened to the Suffragettes in England. Any petty criminal would write 'Votes for Women' as he left the scene. And people did it deliberately, too, to discredit the movement. Women's Lib had a dose of the same medicine."

"I guess you're right." Absently he was sketching the stylized form of the symbol on the table, using the liquid from the wet rings their glasses had left. There were no coasters. Trainites had branded them a waste of paper, like disposable towels, and this was one case where they'd made their opinion felt.

"Yes," he went on, "but if something could be said to have driven me crazy, it's knowing I've been converted into a person who doesn't exist."

"But you do exist."

"I think so."

"Then get up and prove it." Peg checked her watch. "When do you want to be put on the Page show?"

"You really think you can fix it?"

"I keep telling you, honey! You're past the point at which you have to *fix* that kind of thing! You just ask."

"So let's ask." He drained his glass. "Where's a phone?"

DIRECT HIT *Target:* Grand Forks Missile Base, North Dakota.

Means: a psychotomimetic drug introduced into supposedly secure groceries delivered to the home of Major Eustace V. Barleyman, one of the officers responsible for the group of eleven Minutemen code-named "Five West Two." He ingested it in a portion of stewed prunes while breakfasting alone after his tour of duty.

Effect: he nearly killed his son Henry, aged six, and his daughter Patricia, aged four.

Suspect: any Tupa sympathizer with access to the food.

The implications were serious.

Martial law took off like a forest fire.

THE GENUINE ARTICLE "Christ, it's going to pull the biggest audience in television history! The Wednesday after Labor Day, when everyone's broke because of the holiday and staying home! We've got to lean on them!"

"Leaning on ABS is out of the question. Damn Prexy's loud mouth! First time we ever had a president with *all* the news media gunning for him!"

"Then we'll have to lean on Train. Ah—it is Train, is it? Not one of these stinking ringers?"

"Hell, yes, it all fits. We had a report from LA months ago that he was working on a garbage gang under the name of Smith, but he skipped and after that we got screwed up by the phonies. We had a check run on the prints he left on his beer-glass, though. He's Train."

"Any idea why he's chosen now to come out of hiding?"

"Must be big, that's all we know."

"What would he regard as big enough?"

"Maybe something that would lead to Prexy being impeached?"

"Well, in that case— Ah, shit. You're putting me on."

"I don't know if I am or not, I swear I don't. But it's definite that when ABS start their spot announcements, twenty or thirty million people will head for their TV sets at a run, wanting to be told what to do. Now I know what Germans must have felt like waiting to see how Hitler did in the elections."

"I guess so. Well, he'll just have to vanish, won't he? Get on to Special Operations and—"

"He thought of that."

"What?"

"He's given ABS a tape to be broadcast if he doesn't make the show. We can't get at it; it's in ABS's safety-deposit at Manufacturers Hanover. And if he isn't on the show, you can rely on Page to make maximum capital out of that."

"He's got us over a barrel, then."

"Yes."

INSUSCEPTIBLE OF RIGOROUS ANALYSIS

Justice: The inquiry established that there was no psychotomimetic drug in any sample of Nutripon held at the warehouse. It cannot have been this substance which caused the riot at the plant. That has been proven absolutely, even to the satisfaction of the UN.

Defense: On the other hand, analysis of the groceries at Major Barleyman's home shows that such a drug had been introduced into several items. The characteristics correspond

PORTION OF TRANSCRIPT OMITTED
ACCESSIBLE ONLY TO PERSONNEL WITH
TRIPLE-A-STAR SECURITY CLEARANCE

found to cause unpredictable mental disturbances and other unacceptable side effects. Consequently no studies of it have been conducted since 1963.

Intelligence: It's relevant here that several informants have advised us of an alleged synthesis of the substance which the Tupas claim to have found in relief food at

San Pablo, carried out in Havana on the basis of Duval's work in Paris.

Health: Putting that together with the now definitely established fact that the timing and location of the first outbreaks of that crippling enteritis coincide with a journey made by a foreign national during the preceding couple of weeks, ostensibly for legitimate business purposes . . .

Agriculture: And nobody can make me believe that these damned *jigras* acquired immunity to such a wide range of pesticides without help. Nor that a responsible and respected firm of importers could simply have overlooked the presence of the wrong kind of worm in so many of their consignments.

State: So it's obvious that we don't have to deal with the work of an isolated fanatic, like those fire-balloon raids on San Diego.

President: Yes, there's only one possible conclusion. I'd appreciate at your earliest convenience your views on whether or not to make the matter public, but there can't be any doubt any longer. The United States is under attack.

SEPTEMBER

MOTHER-RAPERS

. . . 'Mid fume and reek
That caused unmanly Tears to lave my cheek,
Black-vis'd as *Moors* from soil, and huge of thew,
The Founders led me ever onward through
Th' intolerable Mirk. The furnace Spire
They broach'd, and came a sudden gout of Fire
That leach'd the precious Water from my corse
And strain'd my Vision with such awful force
It seem'd I oped my eyes to tropic Sun
Or lightning riving Midnight's dismal dun,
Or stood amaz'd by mighty *Hekla's* pit.
I marvel'd how Man, by his GOD-sent wit,
Thus tam'd the salamander Element
And loos'd the Metal in the mountain pent
To make us Saws, and Shears, and useful Plows,
Swords for our hands, and Helmets for our brows,
The surgeon's Scalpel, vehicle of Health,
And all our humble Tools for gaining wealth . . .

—"*De Arte Munificente,*" Seventeenth century

STANDSTILL

. . . unanimously ascribed to fear of Trainite atrocities by traffic experts across the nation. In many places the car-per-hour count was the lowest for thirty years. Those who did venture out this Labor Day often did not meet with the welcome they expected. In Bar Harbor, Maine, townsfolk formed vigilante patrols to turn away drivers of steam and electric cars, persons carrying health foods, and other suspected Trainites. Two fatalities are reported following clashes between tourists and residents. Two more occurred

at Milford, Pennsylvania, when clients at a restaurant, angered at not obtaining items listed on the menu, fired it with gasoline bombs. The owner later claimed that supplies had been interrupted by food-truck hijackers. Commenting on the event by the shore of his private lake in Minnesota, Prexy said, quote, Any man has a right to his steak and potatoes, unquote. California: experts assessing mortar damage to the Bay Bridge . . .

FRAUGHT

"We can't go on," Hugh said doggedly. "The scene's too fraught. Christ, I been stopped and searched four times in two days."

"And your ID didn't stand up?" Ossie snapped.

"Shit, if it hadn't would I be here? But for how much longer? No, Ossie, we have to let the kid go."

"But his old man hasn't come across!"

"That stinking mother *never* going to come across!" Carl snapped. "He has the Abraham complex in a big way."

"And Hector is sick," Kitty said. She was unusually sober. "Hardly ate anything for a week. And his shit—ugh! All stinky and wet. And he sweats rivers."

The other two present were Chuck and Tab, the original co-conspirators. Ossie appealed to them.

"Hugh's right," Chuck said. He scratched his crotch absently; fleas and crabs were worse than ever around the Bay. Tab nodded agreement.

"We got to scatter if we turn him loose," Ossie said after a pause. He was frowning, but he sounded as though he'd been expecting this decision for a good while.

"No skin," Hugh said. "He's seen us, sure, but he doesn't know who any of us are. Except me, and that's my problem." Saying that made him feel heroic. He'd been rehearsing. "Ossie, he only knows you as 'Austin Train,' doesn't he?"

"Did you see ABS found Train?" Kitty put in.

"Sure!"—in chorus from them all, and Ossie continued.

"And I tell you one thing straight! If that bastard doesn't say what needs to be said, I'm going to walk clear to New York and tear him into little pieces. Unless someone beats me to it."

"Yeah," Hugh said, and reverted to the subject. "Well, the rest of us he knows by first names, but there are thousands of Hughs and Chucks and Tabs. And Kittys. Sorry about the pad, baby."

She shrugged. "Nothing here I specially want. I can pack all my gear in the one bag."

"But we can't just like take him down to the street and let him go," Tab said, worrying.

"When he's asleep, we simply drift," Hugh countered. "We leave the door unlocked. When he wants to, he walks out."

"If he's too sick?" Kitty said.

"Shit, he's not going to die in twenty-four hours. Give ourselves that much start, then call the pigs to come look for him if he hasn't made it on his own feet . . . Ossie, what're you doing?"

Ossie had taken a scratch-pad and a pen. Without looking up, he said, "Drafting the note we should leave behind. Got to make our point. Now we gave the kid the best food, like from Puritan, right? And regular water because there's no don't-drink notice in force. So if he fell sick it's because of the filthy mothers who are screwing up the world, right?"

Nods.

"All because his old man loves money more than his son, right? Wouldn't give water-purifiers to the poor."

"Maybe he did them a favor," Carl said.

"What?"

"Up in Colorado they're all getting blocked with bacteria. It's a scandal. Talking about suing the makers."

"Won't mention that," Ossie said.

Darkness. But starred with the brilliant horrible images of nightmare. He was sick at his stomach. He was wet with perspiration. His penis hurt, his anus hurt, his belly hurt. He screamed for someone to come to him.

No one answered.

He fell off the bed when he tried to stand up, bruised his hip and his left elbow. Staggering to the door to hammer on it, he knocked against the chamber pot and splashed urine and liquid excrement over his feet.

Banging the door opened it. He was too giddy to realize what had happened and was all set to beat on it again. His fists struck air. He fell forward, crying and moaning. Beyond, a room with soiled mattresses covering the floor. Some light from a street lamp. The sky was dark. It was the first time in eternities that he'd seen the sky.

He shouted again, hoarsely, and the world swam. He had fever, he was sure of that. And ached. And there was a foulness inside his pants, fore and aft. Hell. This was hell. The world ought to be clean, sweet, pure!

Weaker and weaker, he hobbled moaning toward the front door of the apartment and found that open, too, giving on to stairs, and he fell down those two or three at a time. At the foot a filthy hallway where children certainly, adults maybe, had relieved themselves. Like paddling in a sewer. But he made it to the street door. Clawed himself up to reach the catch on it. There was a step beyond. He fell down that also, sprawled on hard sidewalk, screaming.

"I'm Hector Bamberley! Help me! There's a reward! My father will give you a reward!"

But boys stoned or crazy were a common sight, and anyhow everyone knew that Roland Bamberley had downright refused to offer a reward for his son, for fear the kidnappers might receive it. It was more than an hour before any of the rare passers-by took him seriously, and by then he had lapsed into delirium.

Besides, the air had deprived him of his voice within a few minutes, and then it was hard to make out what he was trying to say through the bouts of coughing and vomiting.

"Well, doctor?" Leaner than his older brother Jacob, dedicated to exercise and what outdoor life was nowadays possible because he was proud of his stringy, tough, Western-pioneer good looks, Roland Bamberley addressed the masked man emerging from the hospital ward.

The doctor, removing his mask, passed his hand wearily across his forehead. He said, "Well . . . !"

"Tell me!" Stern, like a patriarch secure in the knowledge that God approved of him.

"It's a long list," the doctor said, and sat down, taking a notepad from the pocket of his white coat. "He's had a couple of lucid intervals, but much of the time he's been —uh—rambling. Let's see . . . Oh, yes. Says he's been well fed. Says the kidnappers gave him nothing but stuff from Puritan and kept complaining about how expensive it was. He's had regular breakfast, lunch and supper. But he had to drink tap-water. Straight tap-water."

"And?" No emotion discernible.

"He has hepatitis. Acute. He's running a high fever, about one-oh-one point eight. Also he has violent diarrhea, enteritis or dysentery I imagine, though I'll have to wait for a stool culture on that. Those are the most important things."

"What about the rest?"

It was an order. The doctor sighed and licked his lips. "Well . . . A skin complaint. Minor. Impetigo. It's endemic in the slums around here. One of his eyes is a bit inflamed, probably conjunctivitis. That's endemic, too. And his tongue is patched and swollen—looks like moniliasis. Fungus complaint. What they call thrush. And of course he had body-lice and fleas."

The mask of Roland Bamberley's self-possession cracked like a strained ice-floe. "*Lice?*" he rasped. "*Fleas?*"

The doctor looked at him with a sour twist of his mouth. "Sure. It'd have been a miracle if he'd escaped them. About thirty per cent of the buildings in the city center are infested. They're immune to insecticides, even the illegal ones. I imagine the enteritis and hepatitis will turn out to be resistant to antibiotics, too. They usually are nowadays."

Bamberley's cheeks were gray. "Anything else?" he said in the tight voice of a man looking for an excuse to pick a fight, wanting to be needled one more time so he can let go his charge of ill-temper.

The doctor hesitated.

"Come on, out with it!" Like a coarse file against hardwood.

"Very well. He also has gonorrhea, very advanced, and if he has that he's virtually bound to have NSU, and if he has those then he most likely has syphilis. Though that'll have to wait for the Wassermann."

There was a long silence. Finally Bamberley said, "But they must have been worse than animals. People can't live like that."

"They have to live like that," the doctor said. "They aren't given a choice."

"Liar! Fleas? Lice? Venereal disease? Of course they have a choice!" Bamberley barked.

The doctor shrugged. It wasn't politic to argue with a man as rich as this. Since his brother Jacob died he was almost unbelievably rich. He'd been next in line for the entailed portion of the fortune. Jacob's adopted children weren't eligible.

Nor was Maud.

"Can I see him?" Bamberley said after a while.

"No, sir. That's medical orders. I've put him to sleep, and he must be allowed to rest for at least twenty-four hours. The combination of drugs we've had to give him might—ah—disturb his reasoning powers anyway."

"But antibiotics—" Bamberley checked, like a hound-dog catching a new scent. He said suspiciously, "There was more. You didn't tell me everything."

"Oh, hell!" The doctor finally lost patience. He'd been on the job three hours without a break. "Yes, Mr. Bamberley! Of course there was more! You raised him in that practically gnotobiotic environment—he doesn't have the regular natural immunities! Inflamed tonsils! Pharyngitis! Allergies from the shit Puritan sell in their so-called 'pure' foods! Scatches that have gone septic, boils on his ass full of stinking pus! Exactly what *everybody* has who lives the way he's been living the past couple of months, only more so!"

"Everybody?" Steely; dangerous.

"Sure, everybody! I guess that was the point the kidnappers were intending to make."

The instant the words were out, he knew he'd gone too far. Bamberley jumped to his feet.

"You sympathize with those devils! Don't deny it!"

"I didn't say that—"

"But that's what you meant!" In a roar. "Well, you can take your filthy Trainite ideas somewhere else!"

The doctor debated only a moment whether to speak his mind and clear his conscience or keep his fee and multiply his income. He opted for the second choice, the sensible one. He was thinking of moving to New Zealand.

"I didn't mean to offend you," he said in a soothing tone. "Only to point out that your son isn't suffering from anything—well—extraordinary. He hasn't been beaten, or starved, or tortured. He'll recover."

Suspecting irony, Bamberley glared at him. He said, "Has he talked about the kidnappers at all?"

"Not really," the doctor sighed.

"You're holding something back. I'm used to dealing with people—I can tell."

"Well . . ." The doctor had to lick his lips. "Well, he's mentioned this girl Kitty, of course. He's not a virgin any more, obviously."

"Thanks to some whore who gave him the clap!"

"Well, sir, he must have cooperated. I mean, you can't rape a boy, can you?"

"Are you *sure* he wasn't raped?" Bamberley gritted.

"What? Oh!" For an instant the doctor thought he might not prevent himself from smiling. "No, you can rest assured he wasn't the victim of homosexual assault."

"Wouldn't have put it past the bastards!" Bamberley checked his watch. "What else has he been talking about since you brought him here? Come on! The police will be back as soon as they're through searching the place where he was locked up, and then you'll damned well have to talk, won't you?"

The doctor said reluctantly, "Well, one thing . . ."

"Out with it, damn you!"

"Well, he has been saying, over and over, that he was kidnapped by Austin Train." The doctor shook his head. "I don't get it. I'm sure it must be the delirium."

A SHIFT OF EMPHASIS Of course everyone knows what a marvelous aid Lenabix are to a slimmer's diet, with their balanced combination of essential nourishment, health-giving vitamins and specially selected tranquilizer. But has it occurred to you that they're also the perfect answer to the question which is facing more and more housewives without a weight problem? "What can I keep in the house for the rare occasions when our stocks run low, bearing in mind that I have a limited budget?" Yes, the answer has to be—Lenabix! They offer remarkable value for so much nourishment and so many vitamins, and what's more they can be relied on to calm that child who's woken up in the night asking for food. They'll send your kiddie back to refreshing, restful slumber. And have a Lenabix yourself while you're up, won't you? Lenabix!

MINE ENEMIES ARE DELIVERED INTO MY HAND Oh, marvelous! Wonderful, terrific, fantastic, great! Petronella Page kept running out of superlatives to fit the situation. And she'd come so close to missing the chance: a phone call she almost hadn't taken because she was so furious at having her apartment searched again—*another* house-to-house, the third in a month. Christ, you'd think they'd go look for Trainites where they hung out, in the slums!

And then she'd changed her mind because the name Peg Mankiewicz rang a faint bell, and *wow!* The real Austin Train! A man the nation—the world—had been crying out to hear from, who had hidden himself away for forty months and chosen *her* show to break his silence on. The research department had come up with that evocative figure, forty, and it was exact, and thanks to its Biblical associations it was pregnant but *pregnant* with overtones. Forty days the waters were upon the face of the earth, forty days in the wilderness tempted of Satan . . . "Anyone would think you had Jesus on the show!" Ian Farley had said crossly at one point during the frantic pre-broadcast hassles.

"Yes."

Which stopped him dead. Well, it was true that the crucifixion teams were ready and rehearsing, wasn't it? Not that she was going to let the guy be crucified the first time out. Ian had expected that she would, and it had taken two days to disabuse him and explain why to the Big Bosses in back of him. The crucifixion is for the *second* show—didn't you ever hear of the Right to Reply?

And are there ever going to be people who demand it!

Never in its history had ABS lavished this much attention on one single performer. Come to that, nor had Petronella. But it was essential that they actually put out the show. They'd asked their audience research unit two questions: how many people would watch the first show because they'd heard Train was on it, and how many would watch a second show because they'd seen the first or because they'd missed it?

The answer in both cases was an unbelievable sixty million.

Naturally, threats had started to flood in within minutes of the first spot announcement. They ranged from routine bomb scares to a warning that the studio would be occupied by armed volunteers and the show converted into a kangaroo court to try Austin Train for treason. So, against emergencies, they alerted every local studio they controlled within five hundred miles of New York, and set up extra landlines and line-of-sight links to their main transmitters, so that within half an hour of their deadline they would still have several options open. Then they scheduled the real show—Train had dismissed the idea of pre-recording—for a location they'd never used before, a derelict theater they'd bought for rehearsal space and were anyway intending to fit up before the fall season. Even the technicians installing mikes and cables didn't realize the place was going to be used for the crucial transmission. They only knew they were getting record wages.

But then there weren't many people in their trade nowadays.

"Sixty million, hm? I'm not surprised," Train said, and that wasn't vanity. He had reasonable grounds. Sitting with Petronella in the high-security penthouse where the Big Bosses had immediately insisted on putting him—at their expense—when they learned he was staying in the same shoddy hotel as Peg Mankiewicz. She was behind and to one side of him, in almost literally the same place she had occupied ever since Petronella first met them. Like a bodyguard. Not a mistress; ABS had verified through their bugs that she slept alone and so did he. Small wonder, Petronella had thought once or twice. She had been dismayed to find what the man looked like now, bald and with those hideous scars on his scalp. Moreover, she found his statue-like composure repellent. He barely moved even his hands when he was talking like this, and refused to touch tobacco, pot, khat, anything stronger than beer or wine and very little of those.

Peg was extremely attractive. But the ABS researchers said she was straight.

Too bad. Petronella returned her attention to what Train was saying.

"It would have been different a few years ago. That size of audience would only have been available for a major public event such as a moon landing or the funeral of a celebrity who'd been assassinated. But now, of course, people so seldom go out. In the cities, because it's dangerous; in the country, because—well, what is there to go out for? The puritan backlash has closed half the movie theaters and most of the drive-ins, particularly where they were a major social center, and thanks to the fear of shortage people don't make more than one shopping trip a week because they keep enough in the house to see them through a siege. Yes, for most people nowadays television is their only contact with the world beyond their daily work."

Ah. This could lead him on to lawnorder. Petronella baited her hook and cast it, and was rewarded.

"But the police encourage people to be afraid of them—in some cases, more afraid than they are of criminals. The intelligent ones among our young people catch the habit early and grow up with it. Recently, for example, I've seen a giant roundup of every man under thirty in a twenty-block area of Oakland. Most of them spent the night in a cell. No wonder there are twelve cities under martial law."

"But if they're looking for draft dodgers, who are by definition criminals—"

"More exactly revolutionaries, whether they know it or not. Our society fosters criminals, as the blood of a sheep nourishes the ticks on its back; indeed, they often find it more profitable past a certain point to conform rather than resist. The money made from bootlegging now finances Puritan, for instance, just as fortunes made from piracy ennobled many famous English families. But draft-dodgers have opted out of this system, which has proved that it both demeans the individual and degrades his environment."

Yum.

"Still, men who refuse to train in defense of their country—"

"No, that's not what an army trains men to do."

She let him interrupt. This was one guest who wasn't going through the stock interrogation; let him convict himself out of his own mouth. He was doing a better job than she'd ever dreamed of.

"It's natural for a man to defend what's dear to him: his own life, his home, his family. But in order to make him fight on behalf of his rulers, the rich and powerful who are too cunning to fight their own battles—in short to defend not himself but people whom he's never met and moreover would not care to be in the same room with him—you have to condition him into loving violence not for the benefits it bestows on him but for its own sake. Result: the society has to defend itself from its defenders, because what's admirable in wartime is termed psychopathic in peace. It's easier to wreck a man than to repair him. Ask any psychotherapist. And take a look at the crime figures among veterans."

Petronella was almost beside herself. So far, if this was a sample of what he planned to say during the actual show, he'd have managed to alienate both major political parties, the armed services, all the ex-service organizations except the bleeding heart Double-V, all big business interests, and the police along with everyone who still trusted them. (And possibly Puritan, one of her sponsors—but most of the Syndicate people she'd met were rather proud of their romantic gangster origins and didn't mind who knew about them.)

Oh, yes! This was going to be a *S*E*N*S*A*T*I*O*N*. She could almost see the big blue-and-red headlines which would appear the following day.

Memo to self: have extra phone lines rigged and hire extra operators to take the calls.

"So"—needling—"what have you done to the people who call themselves Trainites, who kill and blow things up and generally behave like your description of an army, a horde of madmen?"

"Nothing. I am no more responsible for the actions of the Trainites than Jesus for the behavior of the Christians on whom Paul of Tarsus projected his personal neuroses."

Add the churches to the list of people offended. Keep rolling, baby!

"So you don't approve of their sabotage and arson?"

"I don't approve of the situation that's driven people to such desperate measures. There is, however, such a thing as righteous anger."

"You think their anger is righteous, when all that we can foresee beyond it is anarchy, nihilism, a world where every man's hand is turned against his brother?"

"Not against his brother. The man who's being poisoned by the additives Universal Mills put in his food knows who his brother is—a stranger, starving in Africa because a foolish war has destroyed his field of mealies. The brother of the man who has to waste half his income on treatment for a child who was born deformed is the peasant in Laos whose wife died aborting an egg-bundle fetus. No, not against his brother. Against the enemies of his species. That they also happen to be human—well, that's regrettable. Is a cancer cell in your lung or liver any more welcome for being tissue spawned from your own body?"

That, unexpectedly, touched her. She was afraid of cancer. Among the reasons she had never married was that she thought of pregnancy as a kind of malignant growth, an uncontrollable independent organism in her belly. She spoke harshly to drive away such thoughts.

"Then you advocate violence as a surgical operation."

"The people who have brought it about have no more right to object to it than the long-time smoker has to object to cancer and bronchitis."

"I'd say they have as much right to object as someone who's been promised surgery and discovers the local butcher doing the job," Petronella retorted, quite pleased with the image. "Hacking off an arm, a leg, a breast"—better not say that on the show!—"and leaving the patient crippled . . . Unless someone can offer superior alternatives, he has no right to interfere."

"But there are superior alternatives," Austin Train said. Under those curious abridged brows sharp eyes fixed her. Suddenly thc room seemed to recede to a great distance.

She had of course seen him both in person—at a major academic conference where he had been a featured speaker—and repeatedly on television during his spell of previous notoriety. Despite his baldness, she had already been sure he wasn't a fake even before the ABS researchers surreptitiously contrived to check his fingerprints against his FBI dossier—in other words, managed to bribe the right person. She recalled him as a forceful and witty speaker with a ready repartee and a penetrating voice. He had once, for example, put down a spokesman for the pesticide industry with a remark that people still quoted at parties: "And I presume on the eighth day God called you and said, 'I changed my mind about insects!' "

Up to now, he had confirmed this long-standing impression. Thousands of people, though, could be both articulate and outrageous, and if it was going to turn out that she'd allotted an entire show to a man who was no more than that . . .

And then, all of a sudden, it was as though through those dark eyes an electrical circuit had been struck. She sat fascinated. Snake-and-bird fascinated. Afterwards she could not recall the details of what he had said. She remembered only that she had been absorbed, rapt, lost, for over ten minutes by the clock. She had perceived images conjured up from the dead past: a hand trailed in clear river water, deliciously cool, while the sun smiled and a shoal of tiny fishes darted between her fingers; the crisp flesh of a ripe apple straight from the tree, so juicy it ran down her chin; grass between her bare toes, the turf like springs so that she seemed not to bear the whole of her weight on her soles but to be floating, dreamlike, in slow motion, instantly transported to the moon; the western sky painted with vast heart-tearing slapdash streaks of red below the bright steel-blue of clouds, and stars coming snap-snap into view against the eastern dark; wind gentle in her hair and on her cheeks, bearing flower perfumes, dusting her with petals; snow cold to the palm as it was shaped into a ball; laughter echoing from a dark lane where only lovers walked, not thieves and muggers; butter like an ingot of soft gold; ocean spray sharp and clean as the edge of an axe; with the same sense of safe, provided rightly used; round pebbles polychrome beside a pool; rain to which a thirsty mouth could open, distilling the taste of a continent of air . . . And under, and through, and in, and around all this, a conviction: "Something can be done to get that back!"

She was crying. Small tears like ants had itched their paths down her cheeks. She said, when she realized he had fallen silent, "But I never knew that! None of it! I was born and raised right here in New York!"

"But don't you think you should have known it?" Austin Train inquired gently.

Petronella woke the morning of the show—or rather, afternoon, because her day was askew—with the muscles of her cheeks strained toward cramp; she had smiled so long and hard in her sleep.

Then it all stormed in on her: what they expected her to do tonight.

She sat up, afraid of drifting back to those tempting dreams, to that other impossible world where the ground was clean and the trees were green and the sun beamed down after the pure rain. She reached for a cigarette from the bedside shelf to distract herself, and instead of lighting it turned it over and over between her hands, frowning.

The present-day world was still here: the air on the Manhattan streets you breathed at your peril, the food in the Manhattan stores it was safer not to buy, the rain from the Manhattan sky that smirched a new dress in a moment and kept the dry-cleaners in business on wet days, the noise, the rush, and now and then a bang—an SST overshooting Kennedy, a saboteur taking revenge on a building, a policeman trying to stop a fleeing suspect.

Hell, she'd been conned. That *other* world could never have existed. It was simply a pipe-dream of paradise.

Though if Train's imagination could conjure up that kind of vision, it was small wonder he wouldn't touch drugs.

He didn't need them.

She reached finally for the phone and called Ian Farley, and said, "Ian baby! I've been thinking. The people we need for the second show, the crucifixion . . ."

Yet, in spite of everything, the vision haunted her. As the echo of her regular greeting died away— "Hi, world!" —and the star commercials of her sponsors went up on the monitor, she looked at them without her normal pride. Filtermasks? We evolved on this planet; why should we have to strain its air before we fill our lungs? Steam cars? Why cars at all? Ground is there to be walked on. A man, an athlete from England, had crossed North America on foot to show it could be done—and so, come to that, had relays of people protesting . . . something. (It had happened years ago and she had forgotten the reason. Likely something to do with a war that got aborted.)

And Puritan. She was worried about that account. Train had said in his simple dogmatic fashion that the Trainites were going to ruin them. It might be politic to dissociate from Puritan . . . though not until the current contract ran out. The Syndicate could be brutal.

She'd wanted to interview someone from the Denver

wat that got burned. Of course, with Puritan as a sponsor she hadn't been able to—

And she should have been able to! Suddenly, in the space of less than a minute, she reversed all her decisions about the handling of the show tonight. He had come to take his place beside her, soberly dressed in green—well, it had to be, didn't it? And she was in sky-blue and white. Overtones, baby. And the backdrop: a panorama of a snow-capped mountain range for the first set, then a vast long palm-fringed beach, then a forest, then a rolling wheat-field . . .

Right! The hell with the crucifixion team. Their turn can be later. Much later. I want to know if that charisma of his *will* go across.

Because I shall never get another chance to find out.

She felt instantly calm, absolutely in control, whereas moments ago she had been more nervous than the first time she was allotted her own show. She looked up, not at the prompter, but at the audience, wondering how they would respond. Heaven only knew how many distinguished guests they had here tonight: in every row she seemed to recognize a dozen faces, ABS's own stars and several senior executives of the network, the entire group Body English who were currently number one in the charts and Big Mama Prescott who was number three, a couple of academics, an author, a movie director, a fashion photographer, a psychoanalyst, an Olympic runner, the highest-paid call girl in New York . . .

She wanted to rub her hands as she thought of the admass out there, drawn to their TV sets by the twin compulsions of thirty spot announcements a day during the past week and the nationwide shortage of cash which always followed Labor Day.

A breath, not too deep, for the simple introduction she'd planned to consist of two words: "Austin Train!"

And—

Like a physical wound. Like a stab penetrating her back just below her left shoulder-blade and entering her heart. Something not right. Something happening in the studio in full view of *how* many millions? Guards! Where the hell are those guards? Why did they let these three men in, who are tramping down the aisle and attracting everyone's attention? One in black, one in gray, one in blue.

They separated, black turning to right, gray to left, the leader in blue marching stolidly toward her, holding a large sheet of white paper with writing on it.

And spoke, before she could.

"Austin Train?"

"What?" she whispered, dazed by the interruption, incapable even of using the mike in the back of her chair to call Ian Farley.

"I am an agent of the Federal Bureau of Investigation," the man said. He had a good voice; it carried right to the microphones in front of Petronella and Austin, which were live for the admass to hear them by.

"This is a warrant for your arrest on charges of complicity in the kidnapping of Hector Rufus Bamberley, a minor, and of conspiracy to deprive him of his civil rights, specifically his personal liberty and his good health, in that you connived at his infection with"—drawing himself up a little, conscious that some of the words he had to utter were not common fare on television—"hepatitis, syphilis, gonorrhea and other dangerous diseases. I apologize for interrupting your show, Miss Page, but I am required to execute this arrest. Miss Page . . . ?"

"I think Miss Page has fainted," Austin said, rising and offering his wrists for the handcuffs.

Later, when she had been brought round, Ian Farley said furiously, "Kidnapper! Torturer! Christ knows what else—murderer, maybe! And you were going to make a hero out of him! Don't deny it! I could see it in your eyes!"

TO NAME BUT A FEW *Opaque and pale as tissue paper the sky overlay America.*

Everywhere the voices of people saying in a doubtful tone, "But it didn't use to be like this, did it?"

And others saying with scorn, "Don't give me that shit about the Good Old Days!"

The mental censors rewriting history, not through rose-colored glasses, but gray ones.

Reading, as you might say, from the top down:

Dead satellites.
Discarded first and second stages of rockets, mainly second.
Fragments of vehicles which exploded in orbit.
Experimental material, e.g. reflective copper needles.

Combustion compounds from rocket exhausts.
Experimental substances intended to react with stratospheric ozone, e. g., sodium.
Very light radioactive fallout.

CO_2.

Aircraft exhaust.
Medium fallout.
Rainmaking compounds.

Smoke.
Sulphur dioxide.
Lead alkyls.
Mercaptans and other bad smells.

Car exhausts.
Locomotive exhausts.

More smoke.
Local fallout.
Products accidentally vented from underground nuclear tests.

Oceanic fluorine.
Nitric acid.
Sulphuric acid.

Sewage.
Industrial effluents.
Detergents.

Selenium and cadmium from mine tailings.
Fumes from garbage incinerators burning plastic.
Nitrates, phosphates, fungicidal mercuric compounds from "compacted soils."

Oil.
Oil-derived insecticides.
Defoliants and herbicides.
Radioactives from aquifers contaminated by underground explosions, chiefly tritium.

Lead, arsenic, oil-well sludge, fly ash, asbestos.
Polyethylene, polystyrene, polyurethane, glass, cans.
Nylon, dacron, rayon, terylene, stylene, orlon, other artificial fibers.

Scrap.
Garbage.
Concrete and cement.
A great deal of short-wave radiation.
Carcinogens, teratogens and mutagens.
Synergistic poisons.
Hormones, antibiotics, additives, medicaments.
Drugs.

Solanine, oxalic acid, caffeine, cyanide, myristicin, pressor amines, copper sulphate, dihydrochalcones, naringin, ergot.
Botulinus.

Mustard gas, chlorine, Lewisite, phosgene, prussic acid.
T, Q, GA, GB, GD, GE, GF, VE, VX, CA, CN, CS, DM, PL, BW, BZ.

CO.
—to name but a few.

CONSPECTUS Philip Mason in his office at Prosser Enterprises: burdened with work that had occupied him clear through the holiday weekend, just about getting on top of it, but bothered since a few days ago with this slight but recurrent ache in the joints, especially the knees and ankles. At the edge of his awareness a scrap of information gathered during his brush with the clap: among the minor symptoms are aches in the joints.

But Doug gave me a clean bill of health. Let it not, please not, be arthritis! At thirty-two? (Well, coming up to thirty-three . . .)

"Brothers and sisters, we are gathered together in the sight of the Lord and the presence of our friends to mourn the passing of Thich Van Quo, whom so many of you knew as Thad. Though, through no fault of his own, he was so grievously afflicted in body, he endeared himself to us all by his geniality, good nature and long-suffering spirit. We hoped that he might spend long among us, but it was not to be."

Ah, shit, another gate guard gone sick. Which of 'em this time, and complaining of what? (Not that it made much odds. Most likely a hangover, as usual.)

"You're Mrs. Laura Vincent? Sit down, please. Well, as you certainly know, there's an ordinance in the State of Nevada which requires that any person against whom a complaint has been recorded concerning the transmission of a social disease must be compulsorily hospitalized, and in your case I'm sorry to say we have five."

PRESCRIPTION

Mr./Mrs./Miss/child Felice Vaughan (patient)

.... (address)

R_x 30 caps. Salveomycin x 250 mg. 4 per diem

Squiggle (doctor)

HALKIN.—*In loving memory of Roger, Belinda and Teddy, victims of a cruel and unprovoked attack by a maniac on this our beloved country. RIP.*

In his office at the Bamberley Trust Building (it still had an unmended crack across the ceiling, but that wasn't relevant): Tom Grey, cursing. He was seldom a profane man. But there was a painful whitlow on his right forefinger, and it had just caused him—for the eighth or ninth time today—to mis-hit a crucial key on the computer reading he was using.

Dear Mr. Chalmers: Enclosed please find our check for $14,075.23 in respect of your claim against this company concerning the regretted demise of your son William. The delay in settlement is regretted but recurrent illness has handicapped our staff in recent months

"Angie? Denise here. Is Doug—? . . . Yes, of course, it must be awful for him right now. But if he's going to be in his office this afternoon? . . . Fine. Nothing serious, no. Just this headache, and nausea with it . . . Yes, but I never suffered from migraine in my life."

Rioting at New Fillmore East. Body English didn't show for their scheduled concert. Acute pharyngitis.

"Master Motor Mart, good morning . . . No, I'm afraid he's in the hospital. He got badly burned when the Trainites bombed us."

NANETTE'S BEAUTY CENTER: CLOSED UNTIL FURTHER NOTICE.

In the Prosser warehouse: Pete Goddard with acid indigestion. Doubtless due to worry. He hadn't felt it right to bother Doc McNeil what with the typhus outbreak. So he just kept gulping tablets from the box he'd bought at the drugstore. Anti . . . something.

"Ah, shit! Okay, here you are—*another* pack of filters!"

Thank you for your recent letter addressed to Mr. Stacy. Unfortunately Mr. Stacy died in 1974. No doubt our present managing director, Mr. Schwartz, will be pleased to deal with your inquiry directly he returns from Mexico. However, we have just learned he is indisposed and will not be well enough for the trip before the end of the month.

INTESTACY:—*Stanway, Brian Alderson, B.Med.* Any person having a claim against the estate of the above-named should at once contact . . .

In her sleazy hotel room: Peg Mankiewicz, boiling mad and saying so by way of her typewriter. Bare to the waist for the heat and resenting even the panties she had on because it was her period.

Bad this month. Funny. Mostly she got off lightly, but

this was the ninth day of bleeding. Some time soon she ought to see a gynecologist. Right now, though, pain-killers. She had urgent work.

They were holding Train incommunicado. Of course they denied it—said he himself was refusing to see or talk to anyone, even a lawyer. Dirty liars! (Though of course if the shock had caused a recurrence of his former trouble, a second and more severe breakdown . . .)

No. They were lying. She was convinced, and had to say so loudly to anyone who would listen. Half the country was already of that opinion anyway.

Now and then, when she broke off from the typewriter, she scratched the inflamed spot on her left wrist.

"Zena, honey! Zena! . . . Oh, God. How much longer before that stinking doctor gets here?"

IN MEMORIAM ISAIAH JAMES PRICE WILLIAMS, BORN 1924 IN CARDIGANSHIRE, WALES, FOULLY MURDERED IN GUANAGUA, HONDU (remainder deleted. By a mortar shell.)

. . . as well as can be expected, according to his personal medical attendants. Unofficially, the President is said to be suffering from . . .

Esteemed Señor: While we appreciate that the situation in your country is currently very difficult, we must now INSIST on an answer to our letters of May 2, June 3, July 19 and August 11. It was our son Leonard's special wish that he should be interred in our family vault if anything awful happens to him.

"These cramps are killing me! You've got to give me another shot or I can't make tonight's show."

"You won't make it if I do give you another shot, Miss Page. You might very well fall asleep on camera."

Three hundred and sixty thousand fans turned out in Nashville for the funeral of Big Mama Prescott, dead in New York of pneumonia aggravated by extreme obesity.

"Next! . . . Ah, hell, you again, Train! A'right, sit down and hit me with some more of your jawbreaking words. Me, I'm just a poor ignorant prison doctor! What's given you the collywobbles this time? Something else about jail your delicate constitution can't—? Hey! Get up! I said GET UP—that's an ORDER!

"Hey! Nurse! Quick!"

An American Hero: Jacob Bamberley 33
A Personal Account of his Last Days, by Gaylord T. Elliott
(Reprinted from *Colorado Patriot*)

In a Howard Johnson's which still bore the scars of a recent price riot: Hugh Pettingill. Even without his mask, which he wished he didn't have to take off to eat because the stench here was pretty bad, the plaster he wore to protect the weeping sores around his mouth disguised his features. Nonetheless he kept glancing anxiously around as he forced down the hotcakes which were the only item available from the menu today.

The coffee was awful. Probably wasn't coffee at all. Since the *jigras*, they said in lots of places it was burnt corn kernels or even acorns.

Another two or three mouthfuls and he'd be on his way. Not too soon. Christ, if only the car held out . . .

FOLLOWING THE REGRETTED DEMISE OF THE PRESIDENT OF THE ANGEL CITY INTERSTATE MUTUAL INSURANCE CORPORATION DEALINGS IN THE STOCK OF THE COMPANY ARE HEREBY SUSPENDED UNTIL TUESDAY NEXT.

Name: BURKHARDT Baird Tolliver
Address: 2202 S. Widburn

Grounds for claiming: DECEASED (heart failure)
**Person receiving benefit:* Widow

(*If not above-named)

Darling Lucy! It's so long since I heard from you! I know this isn't exactly the best place in the world for postal services, but it's among the few highlights of a two-year tour here when the mail plane comes skidding in. Do please write to me soon. I look forward every day to seeing you when I come back to Auckland, away from this eternal polar whiteness.

IN RE: Dependents of OBOU, Hippolyte (Major), *aet.* 24, *deceased* Noshri, *verdict* shot.
RULED: Unentitled to pension, death not having occurred on active service.

"What's your name? . . . Please, I'm trying to help you! Name! Who you? *Name!*"

"Maua! You want screw, soldier man? Twenty-five francs one time, hundred francs all night, baby!"

"Oh, God. She's off her rocker like the rest of them. Here, someone get—Hey, let go, you little bitch! *Hey!*"

THIS IS THE LAST WILL AND TESTAMENT OF ME BERTIL OLAV SVENSSON ordinarily resident at 45 Vasagatan, Malmö, who, being of sound mind and not having sampled or tasted or ingested poisoned food at Noshri (contrary to rumor) but having diagnosed in myself a strain of trachoma resistant to all known therapy which will inevitably make me blind, do purpose to terminate my life. I DEVISE AND BEQUEATH . . .

"Christ," he said. And repeated, "Christ! It's as if the world is just . . ."

"Crumbling?" she offered, and when he didn't disagree, gave a nod. She hadn't looked his way. She was watching the tanks and armored cars closing in on the food rioters. A stray rock had starred the window, but they'd fixed that with adhesive tape to keep out the street air.

"But I can't go to the House with a—a fucking *tube* stuck up me!" Howell barked.

"Yes, I know that," the doctor sighed. "But would you rather live to be governor or die in two weeks?"

"It's that bad?"

"Senator, you try going without a pee for a day or two, see if you prefer the catheter or not."

"What the hell is it due to, anyhow?"

"I don't know. Sorry. I'm waiting for the lab report, but they're taking anything up to ten days."

Command of the armed forces was today assumed by Colonel Joku Amnibadu, following the indisposition of General Kaika. It's understood that Brigadier Plitso, widely tipped as the heir apparent, is in Switzerland for a medical examination.

Washing the windshield of her—their—car: Jeannie Goddard. Taking Pete to work this morning the wipers hadn't coped with the greasy deposit left by the last rain. And she wanted to see her way clearly to the prenatal clinic. Find out whether this constant nausea was to be endured, or needed treatment.

But the size of the bill already . . .

Well, it was for the baby's sake, after all, not just her own.

"Oh, nothing to worry about, Mrs. Mason. A very common thing these days, this blepharitis, nothing at all to do with your little girl's strabismus. Why, I must have seen twenty or thirty similar cases in the past month. Now I'll give you a note for your own doctor—isn't it Dr. McNeil? —and . . ."

"The number you have reached is not a working number. Please hang up and—"

. . .

"The number you have reached is not—"

. . .

"The number you have—"

. . .

"Operator, can I help you? . . . Yes, sir, but you must appreciate we're very short of staff right now . . . Well, sir, what is the problem? I have lots of other— Can you spell that? . . . H-E-N-L . . . Henlowe. Yes, sir, just a moment. Ah, here it is. All calls to that number are being referred to— What was that? . . . Well, sir, on the memo I have here it says her sister is looking after their little girl until they come out of the hospital . . . I don't know, sir, but the memo is dated—I'm sorry? . . . You're welcome." You son of a bitch!

In his office at his handsome antique desk: Dr. Clayford. The phone rang.

"Hello? . . . No, I will not accept a call from my wife! Tell her to wait until I'm done with my morning appointments. She knows she mustn't bother me at work."

He slammed down the phone and looked toward the door, trying to discern who the next patient was. But the features blurred, and there was this discomfort at the corner of his right eye.

Funny.

Seems to be swimming.

And that damned noise. Got to complain to the police about—

"Doctor? Doctor!"

That hurt. Nose and cheekbone. Symptoms consistent with . . .

"Nurse, I think the doctor's passed out."

In his magnificent office, Roland Bamberley signing a letter to his lawyers concerning the faults so far found in the Mitsuyama water-purifiers and requesting advice on the possibility of a suit for breach of contract. He broke off after the Christian name because his arm had developed cramp all of a sudden. He shook it, and continued: Bam—

Again, without warning, the agonizing pain. He looked at his hand grasping the pen and saw with surprise how white the fingers were. Experimentally, he flexed them. The pen fell on the paper and left a long black streak; the letter would now have to be retyped.

But he couldn't feel his fingers, only the cramp.

He raised his left hand and began to massage his right one. A minute passed; so did the pain.

"Leave that ball alone! It's Rick's!"

"What? Ah, shit, I know it *was* Rick's, but like Zena said he's gone away and he won't be coming—"

"He is *so* coming back! Let go that ball—that's right! Now I'll put it back where you found it, so when Rick comes here he'll find all his things waiting nice and neat . . . I don't like you!"

Shouldn't have tried washing that foot in sea water, Tab thought. But when you tread on a nail sticking out of a piece of board that runs its rusty spike clear through your shoe, and you can't afford to go to a clinic . . .

He forced himself to forget about the pain and the swelling and the nasty wetness of the pus. Another passer-by was turning the corner. He hobbled forward.

"Say, friend, can you spare a—?"

"No!"

THINGS AROUND HERE JUST AREN'T THE SAME WITHOUT YOU. WE ACTUALLY GET SOME WORK DONE!

Only kidding! Best wishes to Mel for a quick recovery from the gang at the office.

Dear Sergeant Tatum:

I'm pleased to advise you that in view of your length

of service you are to be granted 48 per cent of your eventual pension. I honestly wish it could have been more, but naturally you'll appreciate there is a necessary distinction between injury in the line of duty which entails premature retirement, and the contraction of a disease, even one as severe as polio.

(On wall after wall after wall, from California to Nova Scotia, painted or scrawled or chalked or even carved, the same slogan accompanied by the same device: STOP, YOU'RE KILLING ME! ☧)

"In place of the advertised program, regrettably postponed owing to the indisposition of key staff members at our New York studios, we're giving you another chance to see . . ."

Terry Fenton? Septicemia. (Something got into a self-inflicted cut while he was razor-styling Petronella's hair. She quit going to Guido's the third time there was something awful in the water.)

Ian Farley? Bronchitis. (He'd left his filtermask at home, all the dispensers in the lobby of the ABS Building were empty, and it was a long time before he found a cab.)

Lola Crown? Earache and swollen parotid glands. (It won't yield to the standard therapy for mononucleosis, so maybe it isn't mono at all. They took her off antibiotics. Sulfa drugs might turn the trick, with luck.)

Marlon? Alternating between Terry's bedside and the can. (Convinced the doctor tending him is useless, because he makes such nasty remarks about his—uh—hemorrhoids. Oughtn't to be allowed to practice medicine if he won't help people in real pain. Wish he could feel that acid diarrhea going out!)

And others, from the Big Bosses right on down.

Same as everywhere.

"Mr. Greenbriar, look. Uh—would you have any objection to a *male* secretary? We've tried every agency in town, and— I'm sorry? . . .

"An out-of-work actor, sir. Stranded by the cutback in programs at ABS . . .

"Oh, highly recommended, sir . . . Yes, sir. Which ones are those—the blue pills, or the green ones?"

Name(s):	MURPHY Phelan Augustine MURPHY Bridget Ann née O'Toole
Address:	"West Farm," nr. Balpenny, Co. Waterford, Eire.
APPLICATION FOR ADMISSION TO UNITED KINGDOM: *REFUSED*	

The priest looked doubtfully at the vast bluish bruises on his forearms. Then he hauled up the skirts of his habit to inspect those on his legs. They were just as bad.

Why wouldn't these Satan-serving Tupas go ahead and hang him, as they'd hanged the American, Hannigan, and the major?

Oh, of course. The Tupas had gone away. He'd forgotten.

Since they left, many people in the prison-camp had talked about going home. Somehow they hadn't done anything about it. Several of them had simply lain down and not moved again. All with these dark marks under the skin, many with bleeding mouths, too.

Something to do with food. The Tupas had said something. But one would not take advice from servants of the devil.

Then he saw a mosquito and weakly made to swat it, and missed, and after that he couldn't quite recall what he'd been thinking about.

Entering his office after a call at the hospital, where they had trouble with blocked filters again: Alan Prosser.

"Dorothy! What in hell's happened to your eye? It's all swollen!"

"Just a sty," Dorothy said wryly. "My own fault. I

washed at the sink when my filter was out. Got something in the root of an eyelash. Come to that, you're not looking so good yourself."

"No, I'm a bit bilious. Can't seem to keep any food in my belly these past few days. I'll go see Doug this afternoon. Or maybe tomorrow. Christ, is that my mail? It's six inches high!"

"Dr. Farquhar? . . . Oh, morning, Alec. This is Angie McNeil. Look, Doug's laid up with a mild bout of"—cough—"so sorry!"—cough, cough, COUGH—"oh, *dear!* . . . No, no, nothing serious, Doug's given me something already, just the dust, I guess . . . But what I was calling about: Doug has all these patients in the hospital and . . . Oh, blast!" Cough cough cough, COUGH. "Sorry! . . . What? Mervyn got to you already? Damn. Well, do you know"—cough, cough, cough cough, COUGH—"Sorry! Do you know a good source of what-you-call-'ems around Denver—locums?" Cough. "Are you sure? No one at all? Doug thought maybe a medical officer at the Air Force Academy . . . They what? Are you putting me on? Mumps? Oh, Christ. How long is the quarantine going to last?"

(As though a bucket of sand had been thrown into a complex machine. This year, so many of the people who matter out of circulation, even if only for a week or two, and so many more—millions more—working far below their peak. On the Stock Exchange, dealings suspended in Angel City, Bamberley Trust Corporation, Plant Fertility, Puritan Health Supermarkets . . . and others.)

"Lady, I don't care if they're crawling up your cunt, you understand? I have thirty-five more calls to make before I get around to *your* rats!"

The use of the fine house had been assigned to Maud Bamberley during her lifetime, but Jacob had omitted to provide adequate funds to support it, her, and the remaining children. Querulous on the last morning before departure, she rang her bell for Christy. But it was Ethel the cook who answered, limping a little for the verrucae in her right heel. (She'd come to ask advice about them yesterday, but the sight was too disgusting; Maud had told her to wait for Dr. Halpern to call again, forgetting that they were compelled to move from here.)

"Christy's sick, ma'am," Ethel said. "It's her lungs, I guess. She wheezing all the time."

"Where is she?" Maud demanded. "In bed?"

"No, ma'am. She seeing to Mister Noel. He done wetted himself again."

Dear Jesus. Dear sweet kind loving Jesus. Maud gathered the silk sheets of her bed into a bundle on her left arm and began to croon to it.

Dr. Halpern had to come after all, despite his palpitations (since about two weeks ago), and the moving gang went away without anything; perhaps as well because they were eight men under their scheduled strength of fourteen. Cornelius went with the empty van—it was deemed advisable to hospitalize him what with his rash, his blocked sinuses and his non-stop trembling. Claude was pretty well okay. His broken wrist, three weeks old, was healing nicely considering his inability to metabolize calcium properly.

But Maud had to be given an injection, and when Ronald came to him all adult, as the oldest male in the houso and the father of Christy's baby (not yet known to Maud), demanding information, the doctor did not feel justified in offering a favorable prognosis.

Christy's child was about three months gone when she miscarried it from brucellosis. Just as well. Mongoloid. She was forty.

"Honestly, Mrs. Byrne, I don't know how Dr. Advowson coped—no, no, don't move your head, just hold still . . .

There! That'll do the trick, though it'll smart for a while. Very nasty, these furuncles, especially to someone like yourself—if you'll forgive my saying so—with a generous growth of facial hair. Put the ointment on night and morning."

Running water into the sink, reaching for the antiseptic soap.

"Sad about little Eileen, wasn't it? Tetanus is a terrible disease."

Cause of death:	Inhalation of vomitus (while intoxicated)
Name of deceased:	CLARK—

"Brian, do you spell that name with or without an E at the end?"

"Without. Was it the drink that did for him, then?"

"It was indeed. Trying to drown his sorrows and somebody taught them to swim."

Before the shrine of his honorable ancestors: Mr. Hideki Katsamura. In his right hand the necessary knife. About his body the correct silk—strictly, dacron—robe. No respectable alternative, following announcement of suit impending from California where Mr. R. Bamberley had so much difficulty with water-purifiers. Also in Colorado, Illinois, New York and Texas.

Place to aim for would be site of ulcer reputed doctor, friend of family, warned yesterday will perforate and cause marked physiological mishap within short time.

In company of ancestors conceivably not burdened with ulcerable intestines.

Arriegas! That name is one in our minds with those of Guevara, Uñil, and other great heroes of the continuing revolution, struck down by the foul agents of the imperialist conspiracy!

OWING TO THE INDISPOSITION OF PROFESSOR

DUVAL THE FOLLOWING CLASSES WILL NOT BE HELD, VIZ . . .

"Yes, this is Moses Greenbriar . . . Oh, how is she? . . . Cystitis? Is that serious?"

. . . ascribed to the continuing shortage of manpower. Many local police forces . . .

(The sound of creaking, as when a tree grows old and can no longer endure the thrashing of the gale.)

Of all the damned silly things, Carl thought, lying out on a hillside under bushes to wait for dark and his chance to elude the Colorado border patrols. Hiccoughs! And he couldn't stop them. They must have been going on for hours.

After being angry he had started to be afraid. They were making him so tired.

Name of patient:	YOUNG Sylvia June (Miss)
Address:	c/o UN
Ward:	B
Diagnosis:	Alcoholic poisoning

"Doug?"

"Yes, honey?"

"I don't want to worry you, but I've tried to get through to Millicent at least a dozen times, and there's no reply. Do you think I ought to run over there and see how she is?"

DURING THE INDISPOSITION OF MR. BOLLINGER THE FOLLOWING TEMPORARY RE-ALLOCATION OF RESPONSIBILITIES . . .

"This will clear it up in a few days, Mr. Cowper. It's a very effective vermifuge, this. I imagine it must have been badly-cured pork that caused the trouble. I've had a number of cases of trichinosomiasis lately."

Owing to the indisposition of the Reverend Horace Kirk, joint services will be held at . . .

"Where the hell is that black bastard? He should have been here two hours ago! I can't hang around all night!"

"He called in to say his wife's died."

"Oh, Christ. Who's going to let people in the building, then? I can't do his tour as well as my own!"

"Mom?" And then, louder: "Mom!"

The kid advanced slowly on the still dark form in the untidy bed. A fly was buzzing against the shut window, trying to get in, against its own interests because there was a fly-strip hanging right over the bed. Also on the seat of the chair that doubled for a bedside table, there were the usual sleeping pills.

The boy said again, "Mom!" This time the word peaked into a cry.

Who takes advice from a garbage-man?

"Sorry, Mr. President, Mr. Penwarren isn't in today. His doctor told him to take the rest of the week off . . . No, nothing serious, I understand. Something he ate disagreed with him."

FOR SALE: A substantial holding of 3241½ acres down to vegetables between Bockville and Candida, formerly operated by Mr. Lem Walbridge, together with the farmhouse (18 rooms, 2 baths, good structural condition), various outbuildings, all necessary plant and equipment including late-model tractors (6), cultivating and spraying machinery . . .

In a back room at a friend's pad: Ossie. He was making bombs. Now and then he paused to scratch his crotch. He had urticaria, and so did the friend, and so did everybody around here this month. It was the in disease. But those mothers mustn't be allowed to get away with arresting Austin Train on a false charge in plain sight of sixty million people.

NOTICE OF POSTING: Col. Rollo B. Saddler
From: Wickens Army Base, Col.
To: Active service in Honduras.
WITH IMMEDIATE EFFECT your unit is reassigned to . . .

Fritz and his friends were among the Sixty-Three. (One capitalizes the number now. Martyrs.)

"Mr. Steinitz? Sorry, he's not in the office. He's unwell. So's his deputy. We had this leak in the ventilating pipes, you know, and some of these here spores got loose and they breathed them in. Kind of nasty!"

To all patients of Dr. David Halpern:
Please note that until further notice your physician will be Dr. Monty B. Murray, at the Flowerwood Memorial Hospital.

Shivering and coughing, Cindy allowed them to undress her. When they found the skull and crossbones on her body they told her to get out of the clinic before she was thrown out.

"You'll be up and about in a day or two, Hector my boy! And then we'll fix that devil Austin Train for good and all."

Chuck in prison hospital; his forged ID let him down at last. The male nurses making a lot of jokes about his being yellow.

Jaundice.

Dear Mrs. Burleyman: It is my sad duty to inform you that your husband is unlikely to be well enough to return home in the foreseeable future.

"Kitty Walsh? Sit down. I have bad news, but I'm afraid it's your own fault. You should never have let it go on so long. You have acute salpingitis—that's inflammation of the Fallopian tubes, from the ovaries to the womb. You'll never be able to have a baby."

"What you mean, bad news? Who'd want to bring a baby into this filthy world?"

MEMORANDUM *From:* Dr. Elijah Prentiss
To: Hospital director

Owing to this damned fibrositis, I shall not be able to . . .

Drew Henker and Ralph Henderson, like the majority of Trainites, had willed their bodies for medical teaching purposes. But they turned out not to be required by any hospital in the state. All of them had as many gunshot wounds as they needed.

"Harold? Harold, where are you? . . . Oh, there." Painkillers had helped Denise's migraine, a little, and she'd dozed off. Waking in alarm she wondered what had become of the children. But it was okay; Josie was lying down, and Harold was sitting in the corner of his bedroom, quite quiet, his bad leg tucked under him as usual.

"Harold darling, it's about time you . . . Harold?"

He just sat there, staring at nothing.

He was the first.

THE IMAGE is of a house: large, old, once very beautiful, built by someone whose imagination matched his skills. But he squandered his substance and fell on evil times. Sublet and then again sublet, the house became infested as though by vermin with occupants who felt no sense of attachment to its fabric, and were prepared to complain forever without themselves accepting responsibility for its upkeep.

Thus from a distance it may be seen that the roof is swaybacked like a standard whale. Certain of the slates were cracked in a long-ago hurricane and not repaired; under them wood has warped and split. A footstep, be it never so light—as of a toddling child—will cause the boards anywhere on any floor to shift on their joists, uttering creaks.

Also the basement is noisome. It has been flooded more than once. The foundations have settled. A stench permeates the air, testimony to generations of drunks who pissed where the need overtook them. There is much woodworm. Closets and cupboards have been shut for years because inside there are the fruiting bodies of the dry-rot fungus, and they stink. The grand staircase is missing a tread about halfway to the noble gallery encircling the entrance hall. One or two of the ancestral portraits remain, but not many; the majority have been sold off, along with the marble statues that once graced the front steps. The coach-house is dank and affords crowded lodging for a family of mentally sub-normal children, orphaned, half-clad, filthy and incestuous. There are fleas.

The lawn is covered with wind-blown rubbish. The goldfish that used to dart among the lily-pads in the ornamental pond were seen to float, belly-up and bloated, one spring following a winter of hard frosts; now they are gone. The graveled driveway is obscured with dandelions and docks. The gates at the end of it have been adrift from their hinges for far longer than anyone can remember, half rusted through. So too the doors within the house, if they haven't been chopped into firewood.

More than half the windows have been broken, and hardly any have been made good. The rest are blocked with rags, or have had bits of cardboard tacked over them.

In the least damaged wing the owner, in an alcoholic haze, conducts delightful conversations with imaginary ambassadors and dukes. Meantime, those of the other inhabitants who know how to write pen endless letters to the government, demanding that someone come and fix the drains.

SPASM

Later, they mapped the earliest cases on the western side of Denver, around Arvada, Wheatridge, Lakewood and other districts which had exploded during the past few years. To meet an almost doubled demand for water, which Denver was already sucking from a vast area of thousands of square miles by a piping system as complex and random-seeming as the taproots of a tree, the lakes and reservoirs were no longer adequate: Ralston, Gross, Granby, Carter, Lonetree, Horsetooth . . .

So they had drilled, and sunk pipes to deep porous strata, and moreover carved great gashes into the rock of the mountains to expose the edges of those strata. The principle was this: when the snow melts, vast quantities of water run off and go to waste. If we draw on the water-table under the mountains, thus making room for more, we must arrange that every spring melting snow will soak into the porous rock and replenish the supply.

It had been new last year. It had worked fairly well, bar the teething troubles which occurred when one of the newly-tapped aquifers proved to be contaminated with sewage. That led to the issuing of don't-drink notices now and then. There had been a few complaints, too, that Boulder Creek and the Thompson and Bear Creek had been even lower this summer than they should have been —but those came only from people with long memories, not from the wealthy new arrivals who had abandoned the old boom state of California for the new boom state of Colorado.

Now, today . . .

Black Hawk: Giddy, the owner of a newly-built house with a magnificent view fumbled out a cigarette, felt for his lighter, couldn't find it, used a match instead. It fell from his shaking hand onto the day's newspaper. He watched the flame take to the edge of the paper, fascinated. It spread—beautiful, how beautiful! All yellow and gold and orange, centered with black, like a moving flower!

He started to laugh. It was so lovely. He picked up the paper and threw it at a rug to see if that would burn too, and it did, and so, not long afterwards, did he.

Towerhill: "Mom," the little boy said in a serious tone, "I hate you."

And pushed the butcher-knife he'd brought into her belly.

US 72: "The more we are together, together, together!" sang the driver of the Thunderbird howling at ninety toward Denver, to the air of *Ach Du Lieber Augustin,* "the more we are together the happier we'll be! For your friends are my friends and—"

Caught sight of a pretty girl in the next car ahead and jammed on the brakes as he drew alongside and crowded her off the road so he could say hello and kiss her and share his ecstatic happiness.

There was a culvert. Concrete. Crash.

Golden: Luxuriating in the deep warm bath, she sipped and sipped at the tall julep she'd brought with her, the ice-cubes making a melodious jingle as they melted. She was there about an hour and a half, listening to the radio, humming, and at one point masturbating because she had a very special date this afternoon. Eventually, when the glass was empty, she lay back and let the water close over her face.

Wheatridge: He struggled and struggled with the

faulty TV, and still the picture wouldn't come right. It was all wavy and the colors bled into one another.

As time passed, though, he realized that in fact this was much prettier than regular TV. He sat down before the set and stared at it, sometimes chuckling when one of the faces turned green or bright blue. Unthinking, he put his hand to his mouth, meaning childlike to suck his thumb. He happened to be holding a test lead connected to the power.

Sss . . .

Thump.

Arvada: Time to start dinner, damn it, or my stinking husband will—and the kid bawling again, and . . .

Absently, her mind on the TV she'd spent the afternoon watching, she bundled up the baby and put him in the oven and set the thermostat, and went back to her chair cradling the chicken.

That stopped his racket. Sure did!

Westminster: "You stinking white bastard," the black man said, and swung his wrench at the man behind the counter. After that, he sat down and began to stuff his mouth with odds and ends: candy, aspirin, chocolate bars, indigestion tablets. Sometimes he dipped them in the blood from the clerk's head, to improve the color.

Lakewood: Hey, man, wowowow! I never had pot like this before. This is a high—I mean *H*I*I*I*G*H*!!! Ho-ho! I feel light, like I could fly, I mean like I am flying I mean like I'm not even on the floor already just bobbing around in the draught from that fan there WOW! But these four lousy walls in the way—get in the open, enjoy it more, they keep coming and banging up against me, where's the door? Door. Window closer. Open it. Fall out on the wind and just blow away across the mountains, wow.

Four stories from the street, which was hard.

Denver . . .

FIT

"Alan-n-n-n!"

It was Pete's voice, from the warehouse. Philip broke off in mid-sentence and looked at Alan and Dorothy. They were having a kind of council of war to review the firm's financial situation. It wasn't good. Replacements under guarantee had wiped out about a third of their expected income and screwed up most of the regular plumbing business they were still carrying on. The only good news was bad: Bamberley in California had hit the same trouble and they expected to mount a joint suit against Mitsuyama. Outcome, in about eighteen months with luck . . .

It was another close, clammy, hot day with dense overcast, so the door was open for what breeze might be around and they'd heard shouts and banging noises from the warehouse, but paid no attention. People's tempers always frayed in weather like this.

"That sounds bad!" Alan snapped, and headed for the door. The others followed. Down the corridor separating the administrative section from the—

"It's Mack!" Pete shouted. "He's gone crazy!"

They stopped, crowded into the doorway of the warehouse: strutted shelves full of cartoned parts, mostly the filters in green and red boxes with Japanese characters on the end. At the door of his cubbyhole office, wood and glass about ten feet on a side, Pete, his face agonized, clinging to the jamb for support because his cane was out of reach. Lying on the floor a yard away. Philip grabbed it, gave it back, steadied him and felt him shaking. From out of sight behind a barrier of shelving came noises: things being dragged down and flung aside.

"What happened?" Alan rasped.

"He—he came in a few minutes ago without his helper," Pete forced out, panting so violently he could hardly spare the breath for speech. "Yelled something to me about black mothers thinking they own this place, and went storming down there and started smashing things!"

"Anybody else around?" Philip demanded.

"Nobody! It's four o'clock, so the fitters are still out, and I sent Gladys home. She's sick—tonsilitis."

"Dorothy, call the pigs," Philip said. She nodded and ran back along the passage.

"But we can't just let him go on!" Alan snapped. "Where is he?"

"Here I am!" Mack shouted. "Peek-a-boo!"

He forced apart the two top cartons of a pile about six feet tall, at the end of an aisle between the shelving, and leered at them. He was a big man with broad shoulders. His face gleamed with perspiration.

"And jigaboo, too!" he added. "You get that filthy nigger out of my hair or I'll wreck everything in the place!"

"Mack—!"

Alan took a step forward, but in the same instant Mack pitched the cartons to the floor, crash-crash, and there were little crunching noises as the brittle plastic shells of a dozen purifiers broke. Then he started to stamp on the pile. He weighed a good hundred and sixty, maybe eighty.

"You bastard, stop that!" Alan roared.

Mack curled his lip and seized something from the nearest shelf and threw it. Alan ducked. It smashed the glass of Pete's office. Mack giggled like a three-year-old child and went on pounding the cartons to pulp. After a moment or two he started to sing in rhythm.

"I'm—the king—o' the castle! Go wipe—y'r fucking—asshole!"

"He's really crazy," Philip whispered, feeling as though all the blood had drained from his head to his legs, making his brain sluggish and his feet lead-heavy.

"Yes." Alan wiped his face. "Go get my gun. Know where I keep it?"

"Yes."

But as Philip turned, he almost bumped into Dorothy running back.

"Phil, the line's dead! And I've seen fires—all over the place! Half the downtown section is ablaze!"

The three of them froze: Pete, Philip, Alan. They recalled suddenly things heard during the past half hour—fire sirens, police sirens, shots. But one was always hearing those, all day, in any big city!

Mack, meantime, went on happily trampling those cartons flat. Now and then he dragged more down to add to the pile.

"Are we at war?" Alan said slowly. It was the thought in all their minds.

"I got a radio in there," Pete said, pointing into his office now bright with shards of glass.

Philip rushed to it, spun the dial, hunting for a station broadcasting something other than music. In a moment, a man saying, "Hey, Morris baby, you piss in this cah-fee or sump'n? Say, I hate that last disc. Gonna break it. Heh-heh! An' fuck Body English, they're a bunch of creeps and queers!"

The station went off the air as though a switch had been turned, and that was the moment Mack chose to get bored with his game and shatter another of the office's windows. They all ducked, except Pete because of his back brace.

"Dorothy, bring my gun," Alan whispered. "Pete, could you stand him off with it? I guess they taught you to use a gun when you were a pig, huh?"

"Taught me!" Pete snorted. "My whole training lasted like six weeks! But yeah, I can shoot pretty well."

"Dorothy—"

She was already gone.

"What the hell can have happened to him?" Philip muttered to Alan, crouching.

"Come on, everybody!" Mack yelled, jumping up and down. "This is fun! Whyncha join in?"

"That DJ didn't sound as though he had his head too

straight," Pete said equally softly, keeping a wary eye on Mack. "And what about these fires?"

"Rioting!" Alan snapped. "Don't worry about that right now, we got problems of our own—ah, thanks!" To Dorothy as she handed him the .32 he kept in his office against intruders. "Pete, take this, and Phil and I will try and get in back of him, see? If we can jump him we can maybe knock him out. Phil, come on—"

Which was the point at which Mack noticed the gun, not quite hidden as Alan held it toward Pete. His face instantly deformed into a mask of blind fury.

"You son of a bitch!" he bellowed, and charged them. Philip cried out and drew back, thinking to protect Dorothy, and Alan fired.

"You mother!" Mack looked down at his chest, bare in the opening of his shirt, and saw the round hole beside his breastbone. His expression altered to complete astonishment. "Why, you . . ."

A dark patch spread down his pants leg. "Hell," he said mildly. "I wet myself."

And slowly collapsed on his knees and laid his face on the floor.

Dorothy started to sob.

There was a long silence. Blood began to mingle with the urine.

"Now we got to contact the pigs somehow," Alan said at length. "Phone dead or not dead. But . . ." He looked from one to another of his companions, beseechingly. "I did have to do it, didn't I?"

"Yeah." Pete licked his lips. "If ever I saw murder in a man's eyes . . . Christ, what could have done that to him? He never even joshed me about being black, like some of the men do. And then all of a sudden—this!"

"Dorothy," Alan said, not tearing his eyes from the corpse, "could you drive down to—?"

"No," Dorothy interrupted. She was pressing her hands together to stop them trembling. "You haven't seen what it's like out there. I can't drive anywhere by myself right now. Wouldn't dare."

Philip and Alan exchanged glances.

"I guess we better see what she means," Philip said, and led the way back to his own office—not Alan's where they had been conferring earlier, from which the view was of a high black wall the other side of the road. The instant he thrust open the door, he exclaimed in horrified amazement.

In the distance, smoke was rising in vast billowing clouds to join the eternal gray overcast. Opening the window let in the stench of burning: rubber, plastic, wood, heaven knew what else. It was infinitely worse than any river fire.

A moment, and a highway patrol car came screaming past and made a frantic left toward the downtown area, siren blasting. They caught a glimpse of a man next to the driver, perfectly white, barking into a microphone.

After that, rumbling, Army trucks, at least eight or nine, each crammed with masked men carrying guns.

"Run out and ask what's happening!" Dorothy cried, and Philip jolted into action. But before he made it to the road they'd driven past. He came back wiping his eyes and coughing.

"Too late!" he forced out. "But there must be some way to find out what's going on! Do we have another radio?"

"Yes, mine," Dorothy said, and hurried to fetch it.

Set to the Conelrad band, it uttered a little girl's voice, chanting. Or was it a little girl? "Castor was bigger than Pollux! So when they were both at their frolics, Pollux offered his ass to Give pleasure to Castor, Who had a huge prick and three bollocks."

The voice dropped an octave and a half and added in normal businesslike tones, "Stand by. Keep your sets tuned to this wavelength for further information."

Philip, growing frantic, wound the dial again. Pasty-pale, Dorothy tried the phone and confirmed that it was totally useless, not even a hum on the line.

"Wowee, man!" the radio said, and gave a neighing laugh. "This is a great high, surely is. This is a *fantastic*— Hey, you stinking mother, leave that switch alone! This is *my* show! You cut me off and I'll cut you off." The sound of a bottle being smashed. "Get away from there or I'll carve you good, hear?"

Another station was playing the Ode to Joy from Beethoven's Ninth at 45 instead of 33, and someone was finding that so funny he was laughing louder than the music.

There was nothing else on the dial at all, not even on the police band, but that meant nothing. The lie of the land here was bad for short wave, and this set wasn't a very good one.

Alan reached past Philip and switched the set off.

"Phil, you got a wife and kids down there. Get along home."

"But—"

"You heard me!" Gruffly. "I'll lock up with Dorothy, then drive her home. I got my gun, I'll be all right. You tell the police about Mack on the way, okay?"

Philip nodded, heart hammering. "I'll ride Pete home too, then. He can't drive." He hesitated. "Thanks."

THE DESCENT INTO HELL It was hard for Pete to get into Philip's car. Some impulse —a pang of conscience, maybe—had led him to switch to the next size smaller in the range he patronized when he bought the year's new one back in June. Having made sure Pete was settled okay, he felt in the glove compartment. Filtermasks.

"Here!" he said, offering the one Denise generally used—the kids' would be far too small. Pete took it with a mutter of thanks. Even with the precipitator on the ventilator, this stench would be hard to endure. Already the air was full of greasy black smuts.

"Think it is an attack?" he said, muffled. "Or just rioting?"

"God knows," Philip answered, bringing something else

out of the glove compartment: Denise's .22. "Take this as well."

"Right." Pete set it on his lap, dark hand loosely around the butt.

"So let's go. Your place first."

Philip gunned the engine and headed for the exit from the parking lot—and had to stand on the brake as he reached it. Coming from the city center like a bat out of hell, a madman with wide staring eyes at the wheel of a Maserati.

VROOM!

"What the—?"

And behind him a Mustang, and a Camaro, and a big Lincoln, and . . .

There was a gap. Philip grabbed it. And heading into the city: nothing. Not a car for ten blocks, twelve, fifteen! But coming the other way so many cars they were cramming the whole of their half of the road, overflowing into the other half, ignoring red lights, cutting in on each other, scraping though not in fact colliding . . .

"I seen that before," Pete said. "Panic."

"Yeah."

Ahead, an Econoline jumped a red from their right and cut across their bows to try and join the out-from-town traffic. It locked fenders with a Cadillac and both stalled.

"Oh-oh," Philip murmured, and dodged around the Econoline's tail before the light turned red against him. He felt extraordinarily calm. It was as though he had been subconsciously awaiting this day, the day when the heavens would fall, and had used up his whole reservoir of fear and anxiety. He would get home, and either find Denise and the kids, or not find them. Then he'd either find them later somewhere else, or never find them because they were dead. It was all fixed, all outside his control.

He glanced at Pete. "Is Jeannie home?" he demanded.

"Likely," Pete grunted. His hands tensed suddenly on the gun. "Look out ahead!"

A block in front of them: a gas station afire, huge yellow licking tongues of flame. Someone vainly struggling to rig a hose. Passers-by, delighted, yelling and trying to prevent him by throwing cans and bottles. Philip made a fast right and dodged through some side streets he hadn't known about, which brought them out eventually in the right place. Miraculous. People obeying a red light. He got on to the parallel avenue and rolled.

All the time the scream of sirens.

Now and then the crisp snap of guns.

"Try the radio again," Pete said, and pressed the on button. Music. Everything quite normal. Roaring Mortimer's crazy version of *Summertime* with the high-speed double talk like an old King Pleasure number.

"Summertime boys and girls and those intermediate and the killing is wheezy laze an' gemmun an' it's a GAS a GAS a KNOCK SEE JIM! Heddle-ah-boh!"

At which point: silence. Pete, surprised, turned the set off and on again, but now there was nothing anywhere.

Here, the windows of five or six stores broken. But so far none of the other regular symptoms of a riot day like barriers closing streets and patrol cars and detour signs and . . . Wonder what became of the Army trucks and the men in them? And everyone on the sidewalks kind of cheerful. Slowing as traffic became more dense in the road ahead, Philip stared from side to side. They were still nowhere near the main area of the fire which was making the air so dirty. It might be somewhere around 18th and Stout, he guessed, maybe at the big post office. He saw a boy grab a middle-aged woman by the skirt and smack her bottom, and she jumped away and left the skirt in his hand, and she wore no panties and walked on quite unconcerned.

"Everybody's going crazy!" Pete whispered. "Like Mack!"

"I don't believe it," Philip snapped. "Look, there's a squad car ahead. We can ask them . . ."

Surrounded by a grinning group of young people. Hell!

Very slowly, Philip crept past the squad car, drawn up by the curb, and saw incredulously why the crowd had gathered. The driver and the man beside him were locked in each other's arms, kissing passionately.

A girl was drawing a skull and crossbones on the car's trunk with a lipstick. It was a good one, artistic, with the right number of teeth and everything.

But at that point someone shot at them, and there was a sudden hole in the rear left corner of the car's roof and the back window shattered and starred.

Philip was so startled, he almost ran off the road, but recovered before he hit any of the pedestrians. And then there was a proper police barrier. Being familiar, it was a reassurance as well as a stinking nuisance.

"Hell, I know that cat!" Pete said as a black patrolman waved them to a stop. He wound down his window and peeled off his mask, risking a fit of coughing.

"Chappie! Chappie Rice!" he called.

"Who the—? Ah, shit, it's Pete Goddard! Didn't see you in months, man!" The patrolman glanced up to make sure no more cars were approaching, and bent to Pete's window.

"Chappie, meet Phil Mason that I work for now. Say, what the hell is going *on*?"

"Man, I just got here! Didn't ought to be on duty, but they recalled everyone they could reach. All I know is the city's like bent its brain. Back in Arvada and Wheatridge they put the Army in, two hundred fifty men from Wickens. Like three or four hundred houses afire, gangs of crazy kids out on the street bare-ass naked, singing this wild song and breaking everything up. Over by the post office they's like four big buildings afire, stores and office blocks, and gas stations being blown up all over, and now right here we got a sniper— Say, you see that hole in your roof?"

"We saw it!" Philip snapped. "Officer, I'm trying to ride Pete home. What's the likeliest way? He lives at—oh, shit! What's the number?"

Pete gave it. Chappie Rice looked grave.

"Like they say, man, if I wanted to get there I wouldn't start from here! But if you back up to that last intersection and go three blocks south and . . ."

And they made it.

The area was dead. Everything disturbing the city seemed to be very far away, though in fact it was no more than five blocks distant at its closest. The street Pete lived on had closed up tight like a scared clam. There was literally no one in sight as Philip drew up in front of his apartment building, except that curtains were fluttering at windows.

"Wait," Philip advised. "Snipers?"

Thirty tense seconds. Nothing happened. Pete said, "Oh God. Thank God. I see Jeannie!"

Philip glanced toward the window of their home. There she was, waving wildly.

"Thanks for the mask—and the gun!" Pete said, opened the door, awkwardly struggled to get his legs out of it. Philip set the parking brake, hastened around the car to help him, but here came Jeannie at a run.

"Oh, Pete baby! I been trying to call you, and all the phones are out!" She flung her arms around him and nearly knocked him off balance. "Are you okay, honey?"

"We—uh—we had a bit of trouble at the warehouse," Pete said. Philip recalled with a pang of dismay that he'd said nothing to the patrolman about Mack's death; against the scale of what was happening to the city it had seemed negligible.

"But are *you* okay?"

"Yeah, fine, thanks to Phil."

Jeannie rounded on Philip and hugged him and kissed him and left his cheek a trace wet: tears. "I don't know how to thank you!" she exclaimed. "If anything bad happened to Pete, I'd go crazy."

Like everybody else . . . "That's all right," Philip said

gruffly. "I—uh—I better be getting home myself. Can you make it indoors, Pete?"

"Oh, from here it's easy. I do it all the time. Uh—thanks again."

Philip turned to get back in the car. Crossing the sidewalk, Pete called out.

"See you tomorrow, if they sort all this out!"

"Yeah!"

In his own home street: a car burning lazily, its nose against a mailbox. On the opposite sidewalk, a dog squatting on its haunches howling. The sound made Philip's spine crawl. Nobody was visible around here, either.

Across the entrance to the underground garage beneath his apartment block, the steel anti-thief grille. He stopped inches from it and blasted his horn.

No one came to let him in.

Somewhere he had a key they'd given him, but he'd never used it because . . .

He rustled in the glove-compartment, hoping it might be there, and while he was stirring up the contents—used tissues smeared with Denise's lipstick, broken sunglasses belonging to Josie, BankAmericard receipts, a spare spark plug, incredible junk—the car, and the ground, shook, and a monstrous thump hurt his ears. He jumped and stared wildly over his shoulder. Soaring into the air not more than a half a block away, a cloud of smoke shot through with dazzling sparks, like a magnesium flare.

The hell with the car!

He leapt out, not slamming the door, not even shutting off the engine, and ran for the street-level entrance. For this grille he did have a key; he'd demanded one because the guards kept falling sick. He didn't shut it behind him, but raced for the elevators—

And couldn't wait for one to arrive, so made for the stairs.

Panting, he reached his own floor, and the door of the apartment was locked against him, and he hammered and banged and pounded on it and there was another explosion outside that shook down dust from a crack in the ceiling he didn't recall seeing before.

Inside the apartment, the sound of movement. He shouted.

Locks being unfastened. The clink of the security chain.

And there was Denise weeping.

"Oh, honey!" He swept her into his arms, frantic, and felt her shake and shake. "Honey, it's all right now! I'm here, and . . ."

And I left my gun in the car, and I left the car door open and the engine running. Christ, am I crazy too? Has the whole fucking world taken leave of its senses in an hour?

"It's not all right," Denise said. Her tears had ceased, and her voice had the chill of marble. She shut the door and turned to face him. "I can't contact the police."

"Honey—"

"It's not all right. It's Josie."

There was an instant of utter silence. Nothing happened. Inside, outside the building—anywhere, to the ends of the universe.

"I thought she was just asleep. But Harold killed her."

THE REFERRED PAIN *. . . burning out of control. As darkness falls, Denver from the air looks like the pit of a volcano. Gas stations, stores and private homes are going up in smoke. All the time, mingled with the roar of flames, one hears the crackle of shots. Sometimes that's the police fighting a desperate rearguard action against the populace of a city which seems to have turned against them in the blink of an eye. Sometimes it's the Army and National Guard reinforcements which are trying to restore order in the surrounding suburbs. Already two thousand men destined for Honduras have been reassigned and parachuted into the area with full battle equipment. For this is no ordinary riot.*

And the lava of this volcano—well, it's people. Tens

of thousands of them, old and young, black and white, overflowing into the surrounding country. All major highways serving the city are blocked by colossal jams, involving an estimated eighteen thousand cars. Some collided, some broke down, the drivers of others were killed by snipers . . . but the reasons don't matter, only the outcome. Abandoning their cars, often within a block or two of home, the population is on the move, carrying what they can, leaving what they can't to the flames. Observers are comparing this to the aftermath of war to give an idea of the scale of it, but that doesn't tell you much. The catastrophe has struck from nowhere, and no one knows what the hell is going on . . .

OUT OF HAND

President: But we need those men! The Tupas are within mortar range of San Pedro Sula!
State: Let the spics do their own dirty work for a change. This isn't just a riot—this is civil war.
Defense: I'm afraid that's broadly true, Mr. President. This is not a subversive uprising, though. It's more like what you'd expect if someone were to

PORTION OF TRANSCRIPT OMITTED AVAILABLE ONLY TO PERSONNEL WITH TRIPLE-A-STAR SECURITY CLEARANCE

so of course the antidote was never stockpiled. We must try and obtain supplies from a pharmaceutical company at once. In the meantime—well.
Intelligence: In the meantime, there's only one thing to do. Put the area under martial law, the whole state if need be, and cordon it with troops under orders to shoot to kill if anyone refuses to obey them.
Justice: Yes, there's no alternative, sir. This country is simply not equipped to cope with four hundred thousand lunatics.

OCTOBER

THE TICK-TOCK MEN

FERNANDO: . . . Why, he does,
Nor will contented rest until the world,
The whole great globe and orb by land and sea,
Ticks to his pleasure like a parish clock.
You are a cogwheel, Juan, as am I:
He's shaped us round, and prettied us with jags,
And gilded us with gold—

JUAN: Add: gelded us!

FERNANDO: Aye, so he has, my brother. And 'tis all
Part of his clockwork. See you, he's the weight;
We follow from him in an engined train;
Ducats are oil to make our axles turn
Without a squeak.

JUAN: I'll squeak, i'faith! I'll rant
And call down hurricanoes on his head,
I'll conjure earthquakes to beset his path!

FERNANDO: You've no escapement, Juan. You're enchained.
At your vain wrath he will politely nod
And say you have come forth to strike the hour,
He's 'bliged to you . . .

—"The Tragedy of Ercole," 1625

STATEMENT OF EMERGENCY

"Thank you. Friends and fellow Americans, no president of the United States has ever had a more melancholy task than I have at this moment.

It is my sad duty to inform you that our country is in a state of war. A war that is none of our choosing. And, moreover, not a war with bombs and tanks and missiles, not a war that is fought by soldiers gallant on the field of battle, sailors daring the hostile sea, airmen streaking valiant through the skies—but a war that must be fought by you, the people of the United States.

"We have been attacked with the most cowardly, the most monstrous, the most evil weapons ever devised by wicked men. We are the victims of a combined chemical and biological attack. You are all aware that our crops have failed disastrously last summer. We, the members of my cabinet and I, delayed announcing the truth behind that story in the vain hope that we might contain the threat of the *jigras*. We can no longer do so. It is known that they were deliberately introduced into this country. They are the same pest which ruined the entire agriculture of Central America and led to the sad and unwished-for conflict in Honduras.

"That by itself we could endure. We are resilient, brave, long-suffering people, we Americans. What is necessary, we will do. But alas there are some among us who bear the name 'American' and are traitors, determined to overthrow the legitimate government, freely elected, to make the work of the police impossible, to denigrate and decry the country we love. Some of them adhere to alien creeds, the communism of Marx and Mao; some, detestably, adhere to a creed equally alien yet spawned within our own borders—that of the Trainites, whose leader, thank God, is safely in jail awaiting his just punishment for kidnapping an innocent boy and imprisoning him and infecting him with foul diseases that endangered his life.

"We are fighting an enemy already in our midst. He must be recognized by his words as well as his deeds. One of the great cities of our nation today writhes in agony because the water supply, the precious diamond stream that nourishes our lives, has been poisoned. You may say: how can we resist an enemy whose weapon is the very faucet at the sink, the very water-cooler we go to for relief in the factory or the office? And I will say this! It is you, the people of our great land, who must provide the answer!

"It is not going to be easy. It is going to be very hard. Our enemies have succeeded in reducing our stocks of food to the point where we must share and share alike. Following my speech, you will be informed of the emergency arrangements we are putting in hand for equal and fair distribution of the food we have. You will be informed, too, of the plans we have for silencing known traitors and subversives. But the remainder is up to you. You know who the enemy is—you met him at work, you heard him talking treason at a party, you heard about his attendance at a commie-front meeting, you saw the anti-American books in his library, you refused to laugh at his so-called jokes that dragged the name of the United States in the mud, you shut your ears to his anti-American propaganda, you told your kids to keep away from his kids who are being taught to follow in his traitor's footsteps, you saw him at a Trainite demonstration, you know how he lied and slandered the loyal Americans who have built our country up until it is the richest and most powerful nation in history.

"My friends, you elected me to lead you into the third century of our country's existence. I know you can be trusted to do what is right. You know who the enemy is. Go get him before he gets you!"

THAT'S TELLING 'EM! "Did you hear what that son of a bitch said about Train?"

"I sure did! And he hasn't even been put on trial yet!"

GETTING STRAIGHT Knock.

Grimy, unshaven, in clothes he had worn for more than a week, Philip snatched for his gun even before opening his eyes. It was still nearly dark in the living-room of the apartment, which they had decided on as a home base. There had been no power since the start of the emergency. Nor had there been water. Before the battery of their one transistor radio ran down, they had learned it had been the water supply which drove the city mad . . . and Harold.

He sat there in the corner, soiled, uncaring, sucking his thumb and staring at infinity. He had not spoken since the moment he killed his sister. He might as well have been autistic.

Josie was in the deep freeze with the lid shut. She was starting to stink. But that was nothing to the reek from the toilet.

Denise, as dirty as himself, without her wig, her ringworm scars like brands across her scalp, sat up and whispered, "Who can that be?"

"How the shit should I know?" Philip snapped, steadying himself on the corner of a table and rubbing sleep from his eyes with the knuckles of his gun hand. He was feeling very sick this morning, worse than yesterday, but they'd broken their one thermometer when trying to take Harold's temperature, and on his only two expeditions out-of-doors so far he hadn't made it to a drugstore. The first had reclaimed his gun; the second had yielded nothing except the information that all the nearby food stores had been looted. They were living off deep-frozen hamburger and orange juice.

Detour on the way to the spyhole, around their improvised hearth. It was no fun living in a modern apartment with all the utilities out. Gas had been cut off around the same time as the power. They'd been lucky to find a sheet of asbestos on which they could rig cook-stove bars.

He peered cautiously out, and tensed.

"Army!" he said under his breath, and at the same time became aware of noises from the apartment next door, which had been dead silent for two days.

"Are you sure?" Denise on her knees, trembling. "It could be someone pretending—"

But there was something convincing about the man outside the door: a top sergeant, face half-hidden by an issue filtermask, holding a clipboard and a pen, making some kind of register, maybe. Then, behind him, another man came into view, a private with medical corps collar badges. He carried a box of phials and a jar of white pills.

"It's okay," he muttered, and slipped the locks, although he retained the security chain and made sure his gun was poised where it could be seen.

And—

"Drop the gun or I'll drop you!" As though by magic, the sergeant had a carbine leveled; it must have been slung at his back, muzzle down, where a flick of his arm sufficed to bring it into firing position.

"But I'm not going to do anything," Philip said weakly. "I live here. It's my home!"

Filthy. Stinking. Grimy. Foul. Mine.

"Drop the gun!"

He shrugged and tossed it on to a nearby cushion.

"That's better," the sergeant said. "Are you Philip A. Mason?"

"Y-yes."

"ID!"

Philip fumbled in his hip pocket for his billfold and offered his driver's license. Taking it, the sergeant added, "And open this stinking door, will you?"

"I—uh, sure!" He released the chain. The private entered and glanced around, wrinkling his nose. He'd dropped his filtermask below his chin and looked as though he wished he hadn't. But the air in here was no worse than you got by opening a window; some of the fires in the downtown area had burned five days, and the wind was still bringing in smoke from the suburbs.

"And you're Mrs. Mason?" the sergeant said, handing the license back. "And you got two kids?"

The sound of authority in the sergeant's voice, Philip found, was curiously reassuring. Since Josie's death he had been able to imagine that no one any longer anywhere in the world knew what he was about. He himself had spent hours on end, sometimes half the day, staring out of the window at the wreaths of smoke, incapable of reacting, let alone of making plans.

Denise struggled to her feet, clutching a blanket to her bosom. Since she was fully dressed—neither she nor Philip had had their clothes off in the past week—it made no particular odds.

Now a third man entered the apartment, another private, carrying a gunny sack with something heavy in the bottom. On spotting Philip's gun he snatched at it, stripped the remaining shells out, and dropped it in the bag.

"Hey, that's mine!" Philip objected weakly.

"Ban on firearms in this city," the sergeant grunted. "We had like twenty thousand people shot to death so far. That your son?" Pointing at Harold, who was not even following the intruders with his eyes.

"Uh—yes."

"And the other kid, the girl?"

"Well . . ."

"She's dead." Clearly, from Denise.

The sergeant made a check mark, not in the least surprised. "Uh-huh. How?"

"Harold killed her. Want to see her body?"

That penetrated the sergeant's matter-of-fact pose. Lowering the clipboard, he stared at her.

"He killed her. I thought she was just asleep, but he'd cut her up and covered her with her favorite blanket." Denise's voice was quite level, drained of all emotion. It had been a week of hell; there was nothing left.

The sergeant and the medical private exchanged glances.

"I guess I'd better get the doc to check this one out," the private said after a moment. "It's beyond me, sarge."

"Yeah." The sergeant licked his lips. "Go see if he's through with the bodies next door."

"Bodies?" Philip took half a pace forward. They'd never been very friendly with the Friedrichs in the adjacent apartment, but they had been on nodding terms, and the day the crisis broke, when he was still thinking of joining forces and resources, he'd gone to try and talk to them—but they'd refused to open the door.

"Sure, bodies," the sergeant said curtly. "We didn't find anyone but you alive in this building yet. You done your military service?" Pen poised to make the next check mark on his form.

"I . . ." Philip swallowed hard. "Yeah, here's my discharge certificate." Out with the billfold again. One had had to carry that all the time since about the time the Honduran operation turned sour; they were very fierce on dodgers.

"Mm-hm? Manila? I was there too," the sergeant said, busily writing. "Why in hell didn't you report like you should have done?"

"I don't understand," Philip said slowly.

"You were supposed to report to Wickens if you weren't either sick or crazy. Or to the Arsenal. Three days ago." The sergeant handed the certificate back. "You gon' be in trouble, Mr. Mason."

Philip shook his head. "Was it on the radio or something?" he said faintly. "Because our radio's been out for more than three days—we kept it on all the time at the beginning because we were trying to find out what was going on—and the phone's out, and last time I went down to the street I got shot at."

The sergeant looked at him thoughtfully. "Well, I guess they won't be hard on you. We need everyone we can find who's neither sick nor crazy."

"I am kind of sick," Philip said. "Fever, I guess."

"Ah, that's easy. It's this rabbit thing that's giving us headaches—what's it called, Rocco?"

The medical private said, "Tularemia. But the typhus is worse, and I keep hearing they got smallpox, too."

Philip looked at Denise and found she was so overcome she was simply gaping. He felt that way himself.

"Got a bag for the kid?" the sergeant went on, turning to the other private, the one collecting guns. The man nodded and produced a thing like a fat black cigar; shaken, it unrolled into a plastic bag about six feet by eighteen inches.

"Coffins," the sergeant said with a wry grin. "Best we can—"

"My God, it's Phil Mason!" A shout from the door, and Doug McNeil thrust his way in. "And Denise! Thank God you're alive, at least!"

He was haggard, newly bearded, and dressed in khaki fatigues a size too big, but from the way he moved he was well. Philip wondered whether he dared fall on his neck and cry.

But before he could react in any such ridiculous fashion, Doug had caught sight of Harold. A single glance, and he rounded on Denise.

"He got at the water!"

Denise gave a dull nod. They'd been over that a hundred times, reconstructing the way in which, while his mother was dozing after taking that massive dose of painkillers for her migraine, he must have drunk from the deadly supply, then taken a knife to his sister's belly.

"Josie?"

"Here," Philip said, and led Doug to the kitchen.

He was silent for a long time, then turned away, shaking his head.

"Disposal detail!" he snapped at the man with the plastic bag, and added, "Sorry, Phil. But we have to get all the bodies out of the city and burned, quick as we can. There'll be a mass cremation, with a service. We're holding three a day. Denise can attend if she likes."

"But not me?"

Doug hesitated. Then, with rapid professional deftness, he checked Philip's pulse, rolled back one of his eyelids, and asked him to put out his tongue.

"No, not you. You're lucky. You have no idea *at all* how lucky you've been. Rocco, you have treated them, have you?"

"Not yet, sir," the medical private said awkwardly.

"Hell, get on with it!" Moving out of the way of the man trying to get Josie into the plastic bag. Denise had made no move to help. Presumably she couldn't. And continuing to Philip: "I'm told we had about one and a half guns to every two people. Those that haven't been shot went insane, those that aren't insane mostly have one of the three or four killer diseases that are rife . . . We're still picking up the bits."

Rocco was offering a pill and a phial. Numb, Philip took them.

"The pill is a broad-spectrum antibiotic," Doug said. "One of the tailored penicillins, all we could get in sufficient quantity right away. It's better than nothing, I guess, though it does provoke allergy reactions in some people. Which is why it hasn't already been sown broadcast to the point where the bugs don't give a fart about it. And the liquid is a specific antidote to the nerve gas."

"Nerve gas!" A cry from Denise, accepting her own allotment from Rocco.

"Well, that's what we're calling it for convenience. It's actually a military psychotomimetic. God knows how they got it into the water. Must have been literally a ton of it to do this much damage! I don't know all the details, but experts from the Defense Department came rushing in the day before yesterday with supplies of the antidote." He sighed. "Trouble is, in most cases it's too late. People who weren't warned in time did the logical thing, like filled the bathtub and every container they had, and went right on drinking the poisoned water. Forty-eight hours, and they were beyond hope."

"But who did it?" Philip whispered. "And is it the whole country, or just us?"

"It's just Denver and the environs," Doug said with a shrug. "But it might as well have been the whole country. They've put us under martial law, they've instituted rationing, and it's going on until the government change their minds."

"Doctor, you watch your tongue!" the sergeant snapped.

"Oh, shut up!" Doug retorted. "I'm not under military discipline—I'm a civilian volunteer. And what's more, I seem to be one of only about a dozen doctors fit for work in the whole of the city and its suburbs. And all I'm saying is that my job would be a sight easier if they told us the whole truth. I'm working in the dark half the time—and so are you, aren't you?"

The sergeant hesitated. "Well, doc, when it's a case of thousands of lunatics all of a sudden . . ." He spread his hands.

"Yes," Doug said ironically. "All of a sudden!" Looking past Philip's shoulder to where Rocco and Denise were trying to persuade Harold to take the pill and the antibiotic—with no success; he let himself be handled like a dead rabbit, but would not cooperate.

"Phil." Dropping his voice suddenly. "You've got to report for duty now—everyone who was ever in the armed forces has been recalled from the reserve, and you're fitter than most of the serving soldiers I've seen around here. That means it's going to be tough on Denise."

"How do you mean?" Philip's mind had been full of fog for days. It was obstinately refusing to clear.

"Well . . . Well, Harold's never going to be any different, you know. We're certain about that, when it comes to kids that young. And if you're going to be whipped away, and—I didn't tell you!"

He had been half turned away; now he swung back to confront Philip directly.

"Alan! He was killed!"

"Oh, my God. How?"

"Burned to death in his warehouse. Along with Dorothy. I was on the detail that checked out the ruins." Doug licked his lips. "We think someone who'd had trouble with his filters must have put two and two together when the warning went out about poisoned water. Decided it was the Mitsuyama purifiers that had caused it. He and Dorothy went back to the office the day after the crisis, and someone threw gas bombs in. Burned a cop, too. Hadn't someone been shot?"

"Mack," Philip said slowly. "Who told you?"

"Pete Goddard. He's okay—and Jeannie. They're helping with casualty admin."

So a few people at least were likely to survive. Philip said, "About Harold?"

"Oh. Oh, yes. He's going to be a—a burden for Denise."

"I guess so." That damned mental fog wouldn't lift; it was like trying to think between the anesthetic and the coma. "But they'll get help, won't they? And I mean we do have some money, and—"

"Oh, shit, *Phil!*" So agitated, he had to grasp Philip's arm to halt his words. Still in a low tone, privately: "The banks are shut, everything's closed down here, and there's no transport out of the city, nothing, *nothing!* And Harold in his condition . . ." He waved his hand.

"But I've seen worse than him. Being tended like by Earth Community Chest." So far back in the past, a boy with a shrunken leg hobbling across the entrance to Angel City's parking lot in LA. "Or being helped by Double-V. I mean, he's a sick kid."

"They've been proscribed," Doug said.

"What?"

"Earth Community Chest and Double-V. They were both on the list of subversive organizations to be closed down when the country went on to a war footing. Along with all the civil rights groups, all the left-wing publishers . . ." Doug shook his head. "And they won't tell us who we're fighting."

"Them!" the sergeant said. Philip hadn't realized he was listening. "This is the filthiest attack in history! Kids like yours driven crazy! Women! Everyone! Not even killed clean!"

Philip gave a slow nod.

"Okay, I won't make my offer after all," Doug said, and turned away as Rocco offered him a pad of printed forms. "By the way, what was Josie's full name and date of birth? I have to clip this to her bag."

Philip supplied the data dully. And went on, "What—what offer?"

"A bag like this one," Doug said, not looking around. "It's that, or starve to death, or be killed in an accident, or die of typhus . . . Well, you've made it clear you'd refuse."

"You're *killing kids?*" Philip burst out.

"No. Saving them the trouble of dying by themselves." Doug turned and faced him again. There was something in his eyes which might have been pity, but Philip wasn't receptive to pity any more.

His voice softened. "Look, I'll do you another favor. Right now you can't think straight. You may even have had a sub-clinical dose of the nerve gas—the hallucinogen. I'll give you a note to say you won't be well enough to report for duty until tomorrow. Think about Harold and Denise while you have the chance. It's the only one you'll get."

Philip gazed at him without comprehension.

"One more thing," the sergeant said. "You got any food? Because we got to take away anything more than you need for tomorrow. They promised ration wagons the day after, with like soup and bread."

And that was too much. Philip turned away to the kitchen with a gesture and went to lean his forehead on a wall. It was covered with a film of greasy dirt, but it was at least cool. In the background he heard Denise saying, "What about Angie? And Millicent?"

"My mother's dead," Doug answered. "But Angie's okay. She was a nurse. She's with another detail like this one."

When the door had closed Philip said, "If I could get my hands on the bastards responsible for this, I'd—I'd . . ."

And couldn't think of anything bad enough.

THE ROUGH DRAFT

. . . include prima facie but not ipso facto *the following: (a) Homosexuality or gross indecency with another male person; (b) Possession of or trading in an illegal narcotic or other drug; (c) Living upon the earnings of prostitution; (d) Membership in the Communist Party or one of its front organizations (see schedule attached); (e) "Trainism"; (f) Advocating the violent overthrow of the government; (g) Slandering the President of the United States; (h) . . .*

ACID TRIP

Hugh was very sick. Sometimes he thought it must be blood-poisoning because he had these like sores on his face, right up to his mouth so when he licked around he tasted the foul sweetness of pus. Sometimes he thought it was something else he could have caught, a separate fever altogether. But most of the time he thought it was a trip he was taking, only he'd forgotten when he dropped the cap of acid. The world was all rubbery, especially his own limbs.

But he knew where he was going, and he'd got there, despite dodging pigs and skunks and there not being any cars on the road to hitch a ride with. His own had quit on him, or he'd driven it into something, or something. He wasn't thinking too good, what with the fever and the lack of food—he hadn't eaten in days, though he'd found plenty of water.

Water?

A drop of rain on his hand. Shit. But at least he was in sight of home. These were the botanical gardens around the Bamberley house—weren't they? He looked, bewildered, the darkness gathering. Real evening.

Those trees. Too bare for this early in the fall and some of them not the kind to drop their leaves anyhow. Blight of some kind? He touched a trunk, found the bark come away at the brush of his hand.

Shit. Never mind trees. The house in that direction. More rain. It reminded him he was thirsty again, and he tilted his head to let the drops run on his tongue. His sense of taste was poor. Some sort of thick whitish mass had covered the inside of his mouth. Kitty had had it in her cunt, he remembered. Fungus. Thrush, they called it. Fucking stupid name. Everybody knew there were no more birds.

The rain was sour. He stopped dead, not believing what his senses reported. Sour? Must be the stinking thrush or something. Rain isn't sour. Only—

"Christ," he said aloud, and a shaft of terror went down his spine like an icicle. Battery acid! There was no doubt about it; he'd owned an electric car long enough to be certain.

Raining acid!

He screamed and ran headlong for the house, and under the next tree but two a sentry challenged him with a carbine. He stopped and looked at the man blankly.

"Acid rain," he said. "It's impossible."

"Shut up," the sentry said. "Who are you?"

"I live here," Hugh said. "It's my home."

"Your name Bamberley?" The sentry cocked his head.

"No—uh—no. I'm Hugh Pettingill." There were papers in his pocket . . . somewhere. He found something that felt right, handed it over.

"You were in the Marines!" the sentry said. "Ah-hah!

You're going to be useful when you're cleaned up." He scrutinized Hugh's face in the gathering dusk. "Bad sores on your face. You been laid up sick?"

"Y-yeah." When was I in the Marines?

"But you're reporting now?"

"Yeah."

"Fine. Go straight on in and ask for Captain Aarons." The sentry handed back the discharge certificate.

"Where are the—the family? Maud and the rest?"

"Huh? Oh, Mrs. Bamberley? Went crazy, I hear. A bit before the rest of them." A sour grin. "So since the place was empty, and big, they put us in. Handy to Denver."

"What are you doing here?"

The man shrugged. "Work gangs. Clearing the wreckage in the city. Dodgers, Trainites, people like that. Pacifists. Walk 'em into the city every morning, bring 'em back at night. Get some honest work out of 'em. You better carry on to the house and report. See you later, maybe."

"Yeah," Hugh said dully, thinking: acid rain? Hell!

One of the work gangs was being returned for the night as he reached the house. They were in chains.

"This certificate's a forgery," Captain Aarons said curtly. "He was never in the Marines. Where is he right now?"

Startled, the sergeant said, "I think he's seeing the doctor, sir. Got like sores on his face."

"Get him out of there and put him on a work gang," Aarons said. "Unless the doc says he's not even fit to dig rubble."

WORK IN PROGRESS "Tom, this is Moses. Do you still not have anything we can use?"

"No, damn it, I don't! When the power went out the other night it was like—like hitting a man on the head with a blackjack! Sorting out the data after that isn't being made any easier, either, by the way you keep pestering me! *Goodbye!*"

HOMECOMING Gradually, this sense of adjustment to the strange new way of the world . . . They had cleared this area now and officially declared it safe for habitation, but it was so—so *empty!*

Even though it hadn't been home for long, though, it was great to put her key in her own door, Jeannie thought. And they'd got off so lucky! The fires hadn't come within a quarter-mile of here; the building hadn't been shot up, or bombed, or anything.

Though of course the Army had put them into a motel out of the city for the time being, and they'd worked at what they could, she tending the sick in spite of being not so well herself and Pete dealing with casualty registration forms and death certificates, the kind of thing he'd learned already in the police, easy.

But it was so weird, so *weird!* Knowing the apartments upstairs were vacant, a whole building with like thirty homes in . . . and the street, with the cars just standing there, no traffic, not even audible in the distance, except the rumble of Army trucks . . . and the state of the country! Every fit man drafted, no excuses: loyal, to serve under military command, or disloyal, to serve in some other way like clearing ruins and carrying corpses to be buried. They were still unearthing corpses all the time.

Home, though. Just to check whether she could bring Pete here tonight. They didn't have gasoline for the car, but the Army was mounting regular patrols and so were the police, and Chappie Rice, this old friend of Pete's, would fix it so they could ride to and from work every day. Until the crisis was over. Would it ever be over?

She was thinking so hard about that she didn't see him.

"Don't move. Put your hands— Christ, it's Jeannie!"

She cried out and spun around, and there he was looking at her over the back of their long chesterfield: Carl.

But Carl changed, nearly out of recognition. He was so much older. His thin face was drawn into the lines of premature maturity; he wore a dirty black sweater with a bandolier crossing the shoulder, and held a sporting rifle leveled at her.

He looked at her, then at the gun, and abruptly lost the extra years he'd acquired. Leaping to his feet, he dropped the gun and rushed to embrace her.

"Oh, Carl! Carl, baby!" She was almost crying; she'd been sure her favorite brother must be dead. "What are you doing here?"

"Hiding," he said, and laughed cynically. "You? Is Pete with you?"

"No—uh—we been put in this motel, see, but tomorrow . . ." She explained rapidly.

"All empty upstairs? Groovy. Then I can move into one of the other apartments."

"No, they're going to use them to rehouse people whose homes got burnt."

"Ah, shit." His face fell. "Am I ever a stupid *bastard!*"

"What?"

"See . . ." His age returned to him; he moved away to sit down beside the rifle, his thin fingers caressing its stock. "See, I got to hide out, Jeannie. This killed a state border guard."

"Oh, Carl!" She pressed her hands tight together.

"Had to. Him or me. I wanted to get by. And I don't have this love of skunks anyhow . . . See, I was out in Berkeley, but I had to split from where I was. And when I heard about this big thing here in Denver, I thought Christ, it's the revolution and not before time and I'm damned if I miss out. See what I mean about being a stupid bastard?"

She nodded, her face drawn.

"So when I found out what the real scene was, I could've kicked myself back to Berkeley. I tried to find you, then. You wrote me, I got the letter, said you'd moved, and I knew the street though I forgot the number, so I just worked along till I found Goddard on the plate. Wasn't hard; so few buildings left standing here."

He stared at nothing.

"I did think it was the revolution. Really did. Guess I was out of touch."

"But what are you going to do now?" Jeannie cried.

"God knows." Suddenly weary. "I'm a dodger, in possession of a forged ID, killed a border guard . . . I did have to, Jeannie. He called me a black motherfucker and put up his gun. Would've shot me. Only I got him. I guess I'll have to lie low at least until they lift the martial law here, then try and sneak into Canada or something. They got an underground railway going over the border."

He hesitated. "That is, unless Pete gives me away first."

"He wouldn't do that!"

"No? He joined the pigs, didn't he? Matter of fact, I think I may be crazy talking to you this way—you married him. Only I been so long without anyone to talk to."

"I—I know!" Inspiration. "Pete's working in casualty administration. Got all kinds of official forms. I'll sneak one, say you were hit with the nerve gas, still kind of on a trip, antidote hasn't worked properly yet! We got dozens like that every day, people like found wandering."

"Ah-hah?" Interest woke in Carl's eyes. "And—?"

"And you pretend to be kind of woozy. Not all there. Act dumb, act stupid. You'll have to get in on some kind of like work gang, but . . . And hide the gun!"

"I heard. They put a ban on private guns, didn't they? Found a car with a radio that was still working, caught one of the official broadcasts." He rose and came to embrace her again.

"Jeannie, honey, if you weren't my sister I'd kiss the hell out of you. Ten minutes ago I was thinking I should shoot myself."

All of a sudden the lights came on. They stared in sheer amazement for long seconds. Then Carl let go a yell of pure joy and did kiss her.

She let him. It seemed only fair. Besides, he did it very well.

MAKING A GOOD RECOVERY

"The bastard's faking it to evade retribution!"

"No, Mr. Bamberley, I assure you. He's genuinely ill. Suffered a massive kidney collapse. But he's responding well to treatment and we should be able to set the trial for the first week of next month. I'm making the arrangements right now. Such as they are. He won't cooperate, won't nominate a lawyer, nothing. Still, that's his lookout. How's your son?"

"Him? Raring to go. Wants to settle with that bastard—what do you think? By the way!"

"Yes?"

"Don't call me 'mister.' It's Colonel Bamberley, even if I am only in the reserves. And come to that, why aren't you in uniform?"

EVEN KEEL

. . . restored this evening, and some areas of the city are due for resettlement tomorrow, though others where the fires were fiercest will have to be razed. Commenting on the speed of this return to more-or-less normal circumstances in Denver, the President said, quote, It will be a source of dismay to our enemies to see how rapidly we can get the ship of state back on an even keel. End quote. Pockets of Trainite and black militant resistance in city centers up and down the nation are collapsing as hunger and cold take their toll, and the illnesses which are everywhere rife. New smallpox warnings have been issued in Little Rock and Charleston, Virginia. Pressure to put Austin Train on trial continues to grow, as the long delay has encouraged his supporters who eluded the mass roundup of subversives to resume their sabotage attacks and propaganda. Jigra *infestation has been reported in Canada and Mexico today. Now the weather. Over much of the West*

and Midwest acid rain has been falling, the result of atmospheric action on smoke containing sulphur, and . . .

THE LATE NEWS

"Thanks," Peg said to the driver of the truck. She'd ridden the last part of the way with one of the teams checking out the purity of the local water, making sure the last trace of poison had been flushed away before the pipes were reconnected. The man didn't answer, but sneezed instead.

She showed her authorization to the gate guards and was passed through toward the former Bamberley mansion. They were allowing a lot of privileges to the press; foreign propagandists were making hay of the use of chained prisoners in and around Denver, and she was supposed to write an objective piece about the situation. It was the usual technique, the same they'd used for Train when he was appearing regularly on TV and advising government committees, the same they'd meant to use in the case of Lucas Quarrey.

But she'd taken the assignment purely for the sake of having a travel permit. After this stopover she was determined to get to California, legally or illegally. They'd taken Austin there, because Bamberley refused to bring his son to New York.

In any case, that was where he had been held captive.

A gang of prisoners was being marched the opposite way along the drive as she approached the house, and to her astonishment she recognized the last man in the line. Hugh. Hugh Pettingill. Horribly changed—his cheeks and lips covered in scabs, his expression slack as an imbecile's. But it was Hugh all right.

She exclaimed, and he turned, and the light of recognition dawned in his eyes. He stopped, and that pulled the chain taut, and the man ahead cursed, and the guard in charge swung around and for a moment Peg thought in horror Hugh was going to say, "Didn't I meet you at the wat?"

For the guard to know she had ever remotely sympathized with the Trainites would be fatal. Why she was still at large at all, she hadn't known until a few days ago, and she still hardly credited the reason.

It was thanks to Petronella Page.

That hard-boiled bitch who had pilloried hundreds of better men and women on her show had been touched by Austin's teaching; perhaps she was his only genuine convert up to now, perhaps she would remain unique. But she was using the leverage her show gave her to do Peg favors.

She had called up and asked Peg to visit her office; reluctantly, Peg had complied, and there she had been shown a photostat copy of a detention order in the name of Margaret Mankiewicz.

"I had it suspended," Petronella said.

"How?" (Peg remembered the way her nails had bitten into her palms as she asked.)

"Who do you think has the tape Austin made in case he was prevented from appearing on my show?"

"*What?*"

A slight smile. "Yes, that's a point you'd probably overlooked. Before anyone else thought of claiming it from the safety deposit, I got my hands on it." Turning them over to inspect the neglected state they were in, some nails cracked, all the lacquer growing away from the half-moons. Also she was wearing a sweater and old jeans, but that was instant fashion—we're at war, so put on shabby clothes to prove you care.

"It's terrifying," she said. "I've played it a dozen times. Made copies, too. At home. I have a good electronics setup. They're in the proper hands. If anything happens to me, they'll be used. The Trainites aren't beaten, just held in check for the moment. Stunned."

Peg was almost beside herself. "But why haven't you released the tapes? Had them broadcast? Published the text?"

"Because Austin is still with us, isn't he? And I guess

he has a reason for what he's doing, though I can't for the life of me imagine what it is. Still . . ." She hesitated. "I trust that man. The way you do, I guess."

When Peg didn't answer, she raised her head sharply. "Don't you?" she demanded.

"He—he had a breakdown once. I wish he'd let me talk to him! I'm so afraid they could drive him insane! Permanently!"

"You know, after the inquiry into the riot at the Bamberley hydroponics plant, I had some of the kids who gave evidence on the show. All of them said crazy was the only way to be. Maybe they were right."

But she was loose, at least, and freedom was too precious to be gambled with. By a miracle, Hugh realized. He let his face slump back to sullenness.

"Stubbed my toe," he told the guard, who drove the gang onward.

". . . So, you see," Peg concluded her explanation to the reluctant Colonel Saddler, who had already mentioned three times how furious he was to be back in the States when he'd been beating the pants off those Tupas in Honduras, "I thought if I could talk to a few of these—uh—workers . . . ?"

"Pick any you like," the colonel grunted, and sneezed, and apologized, and went on. A lot of people were sneezing around here today. Peg hoped she wasn't due for another bout of sinusitis. "You'll find them blatant—blatant! Doesn't matter which you hit on; I'll guarantee you'll find he's a subversive, or a traitor, or pro-Tupa, or a draft-dodger. It is an absolute *lie* that we've arrested innocent civilians. They are people who in time of need have failed to answer their country's call."

Which was how Peg found herself talking to Hugh in relative safety that evening.

"Sorry," Hugh said in a low voice. "I nearly gave you

away. My head's kind of funny now and then. I drank some water on the way here and it must have had the stuff in it." He hesitated. "It is you, isn't it? I mean, I'm not mixing you up with someone else? It's so hard to keep track!" Almost in a whine. "You were the friend of that guy—uh—Decimus!"

Peg nodded. There was a great ache in her heart. When she'd known Hugh before she hadn't liked him. But he hadn't been in this pitiable condition, trembling, talking as though to prevent himself from thinking.

"I know someone else who was a friend of his," Hugh said. His eyes were glazing. "Carl. You met him. Worked at Bamberley Hydroponics. He knew Decimus. Liked him. Maybe I would have, if I'd met him. Carl gave him a present once, he said. Gave him food. Took some from the plant. He worked at packing it or loading it or something."

"Did you say he gave Decimus food from the plant?" Peg said slowly.

"You're not listening! I just told you, didn't I? A Christmas present, he said. You remember Carl, huh? Seen him lately? Wish I knew where he was. I love Carl. I hope he's okay . . ."

He started drumming on his knee with his fingertips as his voice tailed away.

"Your friend Carl," Peg said, her throat as tight as though a noose had been drawn around it, "gave Decimus some of the food from the plant, as a Christmas present?"

"Christ, if you don't listen to what I'm saying I might as well shut up," Hugh said, and walked away.

"Oh, my God," Peg whispered. "Oh, my God."

NOVEMBER

WHEREWITHAL SHALL IT BE SALTED?

A chemist in an old-established corporation
succeeded after many decades of research
in isolating the active principle from oceans

Hopes were high for its immediate appeal
as a safe additive for preserving food
and miraculous enhancer of natural flavor

Regrettably however it was discovered
that in a solution as weak as three per cent
it caused dehydration and delirium and death

—"Our Father Which Art in Washington," 1978

ALIAS

He had used the name for so long he had even come to think of himself as "Ossie," but he didn't want the credit for what he was doing now to go to that mother who had tamely let himself be arrested—and worse yet was now meekly going to stand trial!—by the lackeys of the establishment he'd had it in his power to overthrow.

So he had put in his pocket a piece of paper which said, "I am Bennett Crowther." With his photo.

He didn't expect to last much longer. He'd hoped to go down fighting. Now he could barely walk, barely see, barely breathe. They said it was a new kind of influenza; it was killing people in China and Japan and just getting a foothold here on the West Coast. Still, the news from Honduras was good: the Tupas had taken San Pedro Sula and were spreading north, and their first edict as *de facto* rulers had been to make all industries generating noxious effluent or fumes subject to immediate nationalization. Take a while for it to be implemented, what with the famine, but . . .

He placed the last of his bombs and coughed and spluttered and wheezed. His temperature was a hundred and three but a revolutionary can't go to the hospital, a revolutionary is solitary, self-reliant, dies alone if need be like a wounded wolf. His fingers shook so much he had trouble setting the timer. Also he could scarcely read the dial.

But it would blow some time tomorrow morning and right now that would have to do.

He left the toilet, left the building, went home and never came out.

THERE IS HOPE YET Armed guards at the courthouse. Some incredibly foolhardy Trainite had waved a skull-and-crossbones flag earlier, had been arrested and dragged away, but the crowd had mostly been quiet. There were two hundred National Guardsmen in the street and fifty armed police in the corridors and the courtroom. The quietness might be illusory. The sabotage wasn't showing any sign of letting up. Every city in the nation over about two thousand population had had some kind of incident by now, and people were frightened. Hungry, too. The first prosecutions were pending for food-hoarding and evasion of ration laws.

But the Trainites generally—or people who had thought of themselves as such, which meant most of the more intelligent young people and some of their elders—were puzzled and dismayed and didn't know what to do. After that incredible gaffe in the president's state-of-war announcement, they'd expected an instant request for the charges to be dropped, on the grounds that they could now never be tried by an unbiased jury. Like a shout of jubilation another wave of demonstrations and riots had broken out . . . and been suppressed. Without a clue from Train himself, all these people who'd imagined they had found a leader began to wonder whether he might indeed have been involved in the Bamberley kidnapping. The most optimistic started to murmur that he must be dead, or being starved and brainwashed into confessing regardless of his guilt. Only the most sophisticated looked at the sky, which was overcast as usual, and watched the rain eat into clothing, brickwork, concrete—and despaired.

There were TV lights in the courtroom. They would be transmitting the case live, all over the country. The precedent had been set years ago in Denver, but the Watkins case was recorded and edited for broadcasting. This was being covered like the Army-McCarthy hearings, only more so. It was going to have a colossal audience despite its daytime slot. It didn't seem right for the networks to be putting on old movies and repeats of comedy shows when the nation was on a war footing. (One said carefully: "war footing." Because there was no enemy yet to throw the big bombs at.)

Moreover, the networks were glad of the chance to economize. Some of the wealthiest sponsors had had to withdraw support. Who was buying cars at the moment? Who was selling insurance?

The country, so to speak, was idling. Industries were closed down all over, either through sabotage or because they were intrinsically non-productive, like advertising. Men, if fit, had been drafted. But millions upon millions of women were at home, not out shopping or visiting friends, because of rationing and the economy drive. There was gasoline only on a permit. There was a policeman or National Guardsman on the corner with a gun, ready to check the permit. There was TV, though, and "in the national interest" the major networks were today going to pool their facilities.

So the number of viewers would be fantastic.

Great, Roland Bamberley thought as he steered his son in the wake of the armed guards clearing a way through the pressmen before the courthouse. We'll pillory the bastard the way he deserves. Even the president, we know, will be watching.

He sneezed and apologized to Hector, hoping his mask had trapped the germs.

Great, Peg thought, taking her place among the reporters, rubbing her arm where she had received an obligatory injection. Against the new flu, the medic on the door had said, but not to put too much faith in it because it had been rushed into production.

She'd managed to see Austin. Just for a few minutes. And she wasn't worried any more about him being crazy.

She wasn't sure even yet what bombshell he had up his sleeve. She was convinced, though, that his purpose in refusing to cooperate, to apply for bail, to engage a lawyer, must be a valid one. He had dropped one clue; when she told him what she'd just learned about Decimus's fate, he gave a faint smile and commented that at least in jail he wasn't exposed to that kind of risk. And that was that. But it was enough.

It hadn't occurred to her before, but it had now crossed her mind that maybe things were going the way he wanted, the right way. And that being so he was safer in prison than out.

She'd know soon, anyhow, and so would the world. If only Zena could be here! And Felice! But Felice was too sick and Zena was in jail. Widow of a famous Trainite.

That would be put right when they tore down the jails.

The judge took his place, trying not to scowl at the TV lights because he knew he was the star of the show. He looked out over the court: prosecuting attorney (nod), lawyer appointed by the state to defend Train who hated his client anyway and had learned to detest him even more owing to his obstinate non-cooperation, press, TV commentator murmuring into his mike, prospective jurors . . .

"Is everything in order?" he asked the clerk. "Then let the prisoner be brought in."

Meekly into the box, amid a rustle and buzz as people half rose to stare at him.

"Who's that?" Hector Bamberley asked his father.

"What do you mean, 'who's that?' "

The prosecuting attorney twisted in his seat. "What did Hector say? I didn't quite catch it."

The judge, poised to launch the proceedings, noticed the conversation and frowned his disapproval. TV cameras were closing on Hector and his father, while another remained fixed on Austin. The judge coughed to attract attention back to him, which was foolish; it was a good thirty seconds before he was in a state to talk clearly again, and by then Austin had said in a clear voice, well carried by the microphones, "Your honor, if that's Hector Bamberley over there, perhaps you'd ask if he's ever seen me before. My name, of course, is Austin Train."

Someone booed from the back of the court. Gasping, the judge said, "Be quiet! I must make one thing clear from the very outset—I will not tolerate any disturbances during this trial!"

"But that's not Austin Train!" Hector shouted. He looked as though he was about to cry. "I never saw him in my life!"

There was a moment of astonished silence. Then Peg, deliberately, gave a giggle. A nice loud one. It was echoed.

"Quiet!" the judge snapped. She received glares from all sides and one of the armed ushers moved menacingly toward her. She subsided.

"Now, young man," the judge said in an avuncular tone, "I realize this trial is a great strain for you after all you've been through, but I assure you your chance to speak—"

"I *won't* shut up!" Not to the judge; to his father who was trying to keep him in his seat. Forcing himself to his feet, he went on, "Sir, that isn't in the least like the man who locked me up. That one was fatter, with lots of hair, brown teeth, no glasses, always dirty—"

"But you said you were kidnapped by Austin Train!" his father roared.

"That's not him!" Hector cried.

It looked as though the judge might be going to faint; a camera zoomed in on him as he briefly shut his eyes. Recovering, to the accompaniment of a hubbub of comment in the court as well as the coughs and snuffles which were so continual now in any public place it would have seemed uncanny for them to stop, he said, "Am I to understand that this boy has never been confronted with the accused?"

A hasty consultation. Then: "Your honor, a recess please!"

"Denied!" the judge said without hesitation. "This is the most extraordinary, I may say the most ridiculous case of confusion I have ever encountered in nearly twenty years. I'm waiting for an answer to my question!"

Everyone looked toward the Bamberleys. Eventually Roland rose, very stiffly, like an old man.

"Well, your honor, in view of the strain on my son—and he's barely recovered even now from all the disgusting diseases he was given . . ."

"I see," the judge said. "*I* see. Who is responsible for this incredible piece of incompetence?"

"Well, your honor," the prosecuting attorney said, looking dazed as though the sky had just fallen on him, "he did positively identify pictures of Train—"

"I said yes to make you stop badgering me!" Hector flared. "You were worse than the people who kidnapped me, the way you kept on and on!"

By this time the court was in uproar; the boy's voice could scarcely be heard. Peg was jigging up and down in her seat with sheer delight. Oh, shame to have suspected Austin of being crazy! They built the pillory and here they're in it themselves!

"Order!" the judge shouted, rapping with his gavel, and

the noise died away little by little. Obviously everyone present wanted some sort of explanation as much as he did.

"Now!" he continued when he had the chance. "Am I to understand that you, Hector, identified this man from photographs?"

"Oh, they kept on showing me photographs all right," was the sullen answer. "They said he could have been wearing a wig, couldn't he? They said he worked as a garbage-man—wouldn't that make him dirty? So in the end I said, yes, yes, yes, just to make them leave me alone!"

He sat down suddenly and buried his face in his hands. At his side his father stood, frozen and pale as a marble statue.

"Your honor!" Austin said suddenly. The judge turned as though so bewildered he would accept help from any quarter.

"What is it?"

Peg clenched her fists because if she didn't keep control she feared she might scream like a teenager at a Body English concert. There had been a—a *ring* to those last two words. Something of the timbre which had been in his voice when he converted Petronella Page. Was he going to get a chance now to speak to all the millions watching?

"Your honor, I gather you'd welcome an explanation of the way this laughable situation has arisen."

"I do indeed want an explanation!" the judge rasped. "And certainly it ought to come from you! You've sat in jail with your mouth shut when a single word could have saved us this—this farce!" And he added, "But be brief!"

"I'll try, your honor. Briefly, then, it's because even though my prosecutors knew there are some two hundred people who've adopted my name, they were so eager to crucify me they ignored the fact and so stupid they didn't bother to show me to Hector."

"Train!" The judge was on the verge of explosion. "Silence! This is a court of law, not a forum for your treasonable mouthings!"

"I have kept quiet in face of even a prejudgment by the president!" Austin barked. "I'll leave it to the American public to decide what justice I'd have received from a judge who accuses me of treason—which I'm not on trial for!"

"Made it!" Peg whooped, discovering to her surprise that she was out of her seat and waving despite the orders of an armed man to sit down. She obeyed, contentedly enough. Now he was over the watershed; if they cut him off at this point, literally millions and millions of people would be demanding why, and prepared to do something about it.

And the judge knew it. His face had gone paper-white, and his mouth was working as though he was about to throw up. Suddenly, without warning, he left his chair and stormed out of the court. There was commotion in his wake.

Austin waited, his hands on the bar of the box. At length he murmured to the microphone nearest him, "I think most people would like to hear what I have to say, even if the judge is afraid to."

"Oh, I love you! I love you!" Peg whispered. She felt tears coursing down her cheeks. It was the most spectacular theatrical gesture she had ever seen: Petronella Page's treatment of the studio audience amplified to the tenth power. She tried to shout, "Yes, go on!" But her voice was lost somewhere in the depths of her throat.

It didn't matter. There were fifty other shouts to compensate.

"Thank you, my sick friends," Austin said as the cameras closed on him. "Poisoned, diseased, and now about to be starved as well . . . No, I'm not joking; I wish I were.

And above all, I wasn't joking when I spoke of the people who have put me on trial as being stupid.

"That is the worst thing they have done to you: damaged your intelligence. And it's small consolation that now they are doing it to themselves.

"Those charges that the intelligence of people in this country is being undermined by pollution are all true—if they weren't, do you think I'd be here, the wrong man, the man who didn't kidnap Hector Bamberley? Who could have been so *silly*?"

There was laughter. Nervous, drive-away-the-ghosts laughter.

"And because of that"—he drew himself up straight—"at all costs, to me, to anyone, *at all costs* if the human race is to survive, the forcible exportation of the way of life invented by these stupid men must . . . be . . . *stopped.*"

His voice suddenly rose to a roar.

"The planet Earth can't afford it!"

He's got them, Peg thought. I never believed he'd do it. But he's got them. Christ, that cameraman: he's shaking, shaking from head to foot! In a moment he's going to weep like Petronella did!

"Our way of life," Austin said, resuming a conversational tone. "Yes . . . You're aware that we're under martial law? It's been claimed that we're at war, that at Denver we suffered a sneak chemical attack. As a matter of fact, the stuff that caused the Denver Madness is a military psychotomimetic based on the ergot that infects rye, known by the US Army code 'BW,' manufactured on an experimental basis at Fort Detrick, Maryland, from 1959 to 1963, stored at the Rocky Mountain Arsenal until the latter year, and then disposed of in steel drums in an abandoned silver mine. Are you interested in hearing what happened to it?"

He grinned suddenly; it made his newly bald head

resemble the skull of one of the Trainite symbols they had —for a very short time—marketed for people to hang on their gates, three-dimensional in sterile plastic.

"Well, shortly before Christmas last year, one of the now frequent earthquakes in that area ruptured the first of the drums. Its contents leaked into the water-table serving the wells at the Bamberley Hydroponics Plant. As far as I've been able to discover, only one American citizen died from that contamination, my late friend Decimus Jones. Hearing he was about to make a trip to California, an acquaintance of his made him a present of some Nutripon filched from the factory. Part of the same batch that went to Noshri and San Pablo! He went insane, and he died.

"You now know who started the war in Honduras, by the way."

Quite distinctly, Peg heard several people say, "So that's what happened!"

"Later there was another earthquake. It must have broken open not one but scores of the drums containing BW. So now you know about Denver and the Madness, too. You know why you're eating scant rations, why you're forbidden to travel freely, why you're at risk of being stopped and searched by any soldier who dislikes your face. The other thing you should know concerns the *jigras*. They weren't made deliberately resistant for use as a weapon against us! They simply learned the technique of biological adaptation. Any of you had trouble lately with fleas? Lice? Roaches? Mosquitoes?"

Roland Bamberley was sitting silent, Peg realized suddenly, when he should by rights have been on his feet screaming. Why? She glanced at him, and saw that his face was perfectly rigid, his eyes were shut, and he was clutching his right arm.

But no one was making any move to help him, though he was obviously in such pain he had almost fainted. What could be wrong?

And then she forgot about that. Austin was talking again.

"I could have said most of this months ago, all in fact except the story of Decimus Jones. Indeed, I was going to. On the Page show, as you'll recall. But then, when I realized what was going to happen to me, I decided I was better advised to wait. One more thing remained to be done.

"When did you last bask in the sun, friends? When did you last dare drink from a creek? When did you last risk picking fruit and eating it straight from the tree? What were your doctor's bills last year? Which of you live in cities where you don't wear a filtermask? Which of you spent this year's vacation in the mountains because the sea is fringed with garbage? Which of you right now is not suffering from a nagging minor complaint—bowel upset, headache, catarrh, or like Mr. Bamberley there"—he pointed—"acute claudication of a major artery? Someone should attend to him, please. He needs an immediate dose of a good vasodilator."

Astonished, the medic by the courtroom door who had administered shots to the press selected the right hypodermic from his kit and ran to obey. There was a spontaneous burst of clapping which Austin waved down.

"He'll recover, though I'm afraid he can't expect to live very long. None of us can. I don't mean because we're going to be gunned down, though that's likely, but because our life expectancy is slipping. Ten years ago it was thirty-second in the world—strange, that: tho world's richest country having only the thirty-second-best life expectancy—but now it's down to thirty-seventh and still falling . . . Still, there's hope for man!"

Let there be, Peg said under her breath. Oh, let there be! She remembered: "I think I can save the world!"

She'd been right about the cameraman. His cheeks were wet.

"In Europe, as you know, they've killed the Mediterranean, just as we killed the Great Lakes. They're in a fair way to killing the Baltic, with help from the Russians who have already killed the Caspian. Well, this living organism we call Mother Earth can't stand that treatment for long—her bowels tormented, her arteries clogged, her lungs choked . . . But what's happened inevitably as a result? Such a social upheaval that all thoughts of spreading this—this *cancer* of ours have had to be forgotten! Yes, there's hope! When starving refugees are besieging frontiers, armies can't be spared to propagate the cancer any further. They have to be called home—like ours!"

Again his voice rose to that pitch that commanded total attention.

"Keep it here! For God's sake if you believe in Him, but in any case for Man's sake, keep it here! Although it's already too late for us, it may not be too late for the rest of the planet! We owe it to those who come after that there never be another Mekong Desert! There must never be another Oklahoma dustbowl! There must never be another dead sea! I beg you, I plead with you to take a solemn oath: though your children will be twisted, and dull-witted, and slow of speech, there will remain somewhere, for long enough, a place where children grow up healthy, bright and sane! Vow it! Swear it! Pledge it for the species we have so nearly— Yes?"

Blinking at the cameraman with tear-wet cheeks, who now sniveled, "I'm sorry, Mr. Train, but it's no good!" He tapped the earphones he was wearing. "The president has ordered you to be cut off!"

There was total silence. It was as though Austin were an inflated dummy and someone had just located the valve to let the gas out. He seemed inches shorter as he turned aside, and scarcely anyone heard him mutter, "Well, I did try."

"But you mustn't stop!" Peg heard herself scream, leaping to her feet. "You—"

The wall behind him buckled and the ceiling leaned on

his head with the full weight of a concrete beam. Then the roof began to cascade down on everybody in a stream of rubble.

Ossie's last bomb had worked well.

ARMED "There, baby—how does that grab you?" Pete said proudly.

Jeannie clapped her hands and gasped. "Oh, honey! I always wanted one of them! A microwave cooker!" She rounded on him. "But how did you get hold of it?"

He knew why she was asking. Goods of all kinds had become scarce in the past weeks. Partly it was due to lack of transportation; trucks were being reserved to essentials, mainly food, and convoyed from city to city under Army guard. But also it was because people were dropping out of their jobs, emigrating from cities like a new wave of Okies. One had seen what happened in Denver. If the same fate overtook New York, or Los Angeles, or Chicago . . .

There were reports of farmers standing off would-be squatters with a gun. Not, of course, in the papers or on TV.

"It was liberated," Pete said with a grin.

"You mean you stole it?" Carl, from the doorway. "Tush, tush. And you an ex-pig. Who shall guard the guardians?"

"I did not steal it!" Pete snapped. He found his brother-in-law almost impossible to tolerate. Even after that crazy speech on TV he still seemed to think that Austin Train was God. And the hell of it was, so did far too many other people. It was making Pete nervous. The station house in Towerhill where he'd worked most of last year had been bombed and Sergeant Chain, his former chief, was dead. There had been a rattle of gunfire only a few blocks distant as he came home tonight, most likely a suspected curfew-breaker being stopped from running. The whole city felt like a factory whose owners had gone bankrupt without warning: a shell, emptied of its workers, who now stood at its gate seething with fury.

"Then how did you get it?" Carl pressed. Aware he was being needled, Pete drew a deep breath.

"It came from that big discount warehouse over in Arvada. The owner got killed. His widow's just been telling people to help themselves."

"Looting with permission, huh?"

"No! The Army's supervising it all, and I got a certificate—"

"Oh, quit wrangling, you two!" Jeannie ordered. "Don't spoil my treat. This is something I've wanted for ages, Carl. I don't care how we got it, so there."

Carl sighed and turned away. After a moment Pete said awkwardly, "Like a beer, Carl? I managed to locate a six-pack. In the icebox."

"Ah . . . Yeah, I guess I would; thanks. I'll bring you one in the living-room, shall I?"

It was so hard all the time pretending to be dull from the aftermath of the BW, when at long long last the revolution had arrived! Well—maybe not quite THE REVOLUTION, in capitals, but certainly the chance to make a revolution work. There had never before been so many people so absolutely angry with the system, and striking back against it.

He was stuck here, though, until the opportunity arose to slip through the cordon around the city and go underground. Because of the massive forces which had been poured into Denver to clear up after the Madness, this was almost certainly the most completely controlled city in the nation. What a place to be stranded! He distrusted Pete because he had been in the police, and he was even afraid of Jeannie because he'd confessed to her the killing of that state border guard.

Hell, how could these two be so wilfully *blind?* They

conceded that the Madness had been caused by poison gas, but because it was Train who had given chapter and verse about it, they were ready to argue that "it wasn't the government's fault!" They wanted the clock turned back to where it was before, they wanted the government to regain control even though it had lied to and cheated and even killed its people!

If they were capable of that degree of stupidity and docility, they might all too easily sell him out . . .

"You picked the right day to have it delivered, too," Jeannie was saying as she patted the cooker's shining side. "Mom got me a chicken. Don't hang around too long with your beer, will you? Dinner's only going to be a minute with this beauty."

Carl curled his lip in disgust as he collected the beer cans and headed for the adjacent room in Pete's wake. Sitting down, he said, "Seen the sun lately, have you?"

"Oh, stop it!" Pete snapped. "I've heard it all before! But things are getting back to normal, aren't they? We got water on again, morning and evening. We got power though we don't have gas. Yeah, back to normal."

"You're damned right," Carl said with earnestness. "This is going to be 'normal' from now on. The situation we're in now, I mean. Martial law. Travel restrictions. Protest banned. Half the country rocking with dynamite explosions. This *is* the future, unless we prevent it. And what sort of a life is it going to be for my nephew?"

"The kid's going to be okay," Pete insisted. "Doc McNeil says he's coming on fine, we got special rations for Jeannie because she's pregnant—"

"And you're happy with that?" Carl exploded. "You're happy that he's never going to be able to move from one city to another because he wants to, without applying for police permission? That's the kind of freedom we're going to lose for good unless we seize it back for ourselves!"

"I thought you were the one who objected to freedom," Pete sighed. "At least the freedom to make what you want, where you want. Where would you let someone build a factory?"

"Any place it wouldn't spoil other people's lives," Carl retorted. "But why have so many factories, anyway? Why can't you like have a car that lasts half your lifetime? Why—?"

"Now then, you two!" Jeannie shouted from the kitchen, interrupting the cheerful tune she'd been humming. "I want this to be a nice happy evening, hear?"

"Okay," Carl called back, and went on in a lower tone. "But what bugs me is this—and I'm not the only one, thank God. *They're still there.* The people who covered up the sun, the people who jailed Train on a count he wasn't guilty of, the people who made that poison gas: they're still there, and they'll be there until the stink gets so bad they move to New Zealand. They'll be able to afford to. You and I can't. That's what we've got to put right!"

"Even if it's true about the gas," Pete grunted, "Train himself said it was an accident. An earthquake."

"What's accidental about an earthquake in Denver? Mom told me: there weren't any around here when I was a baby. All that poisoned waste they poured down old mine-shafts made the rocks slip under the mountains. Nothing accidental there, man!"

It was the same argument. Tenth time through? Twelfth?

"Here goes nothing!" Jeannie sang out merrily from the kitchen. "Sharpen your appetites!"

"Know one of the reasons I got that cooker?" Pete said under his breath. "To cut short the time I have to listen to your talk before we go to the table." He chuckled and sipped his beer.

And there was a thump from the kitchen and the sound of a dish breaking, and Carl ran to the door and stared in, and said, "Oh, Christ. What happened? She get a—a shock, maybe?"

Hobbling frantically in his wake, clutching at tables and chair-backs because his cane was out of reach, Pete stared in horror at Jeannie prostrate on the floor. Carl dived for the socket and unplugged the cooker.

"But it's brand-new!" Pete said foolishly. "Jeannie! Jeannie!"

There was an hour to wait in the lobby of the hospital, where the breeze drifted in through broken windows and brought with it the scent of smoke. They had passed the fire on the way, and the police escort who was riding with them to vouch for their right to traverse the street-corner checkpoints after curfew—it was Pete's old friend, Chappie Rice—said it was the third he'd heard about tonight, all due to arson.

Carl paced up and down, staring at the flames and wishing they might engulf the country. Pete, confined to a chair by his weak back, spent the time in quiet cursing.

At long long last Doug McNeil came down the passage and Carl rushed to meet him.

"Is she—?"

"Jeannie's going to live," Doug muttered. "Just. Pete, what make is that cooker of yours? Is it an Instanter?"

"Why . . ." Staring, Pete gave a nod. "How did you know?"

Doug didn't look at him. He said, "I thought it might be. We've had trouble with that brand before. I've seen —oh, four cases. Don't know what the hell stopped them from closing down the company."

He drew a deep breath.

"It leaked, Pete. Leaked some of its radiation. Bad shielding. And it literally cooked Jeannie's baby in her womb."

At two in the morning Carl was roused by the sound of movement in the living-room, and padded barefoot to see what was happening. He found Pete turning the pages of a book and making notes on a memo-pad.

"What are you doing?" he demanded.

Pete didn't raise his head. He said, "I'm learning how to build a bomb."

THE SHOCK OF RECOGNITION

Still not used to being in uniform again after ten years in civilian clothes . . . Philip Mason wriggled his shoulders inside his shirt. The cloth was rough. But discomfort was among the penalties people were going to have to pay to buy back the good life of the past, and it didn't really amount to much, in his view.

There must be a hell of a lot of people refusing to part with even that token, though. He glanced up uneasily as a vast noise came from the sky, and saw a flight of helicopter gunships just disappearing into the overcast, no doubt to mount another strike against the insurrection in Cheyenne. It was incredible how the cities were going off like a string of firecrackers, one after another . . .

He wondered whether the guy he'd taken over this demolition gang from was up there in one of those gun ships. He'd been pulled out, like the majority of the career soldiers originally assigned to reconstruction duty, as the situation worsened. They said that in Harlem and the Bronx the Army was committing tanks . . .

But best not to worry about other people's problems. Best to concentrate on the way things were coming right for himself, little by little, just as these ruins here were being cleared. It was going to take months to make Denver presentable again; it was already showing signs of the firm central control it enjoyed, though, and there were even a few stores open around noon each day for three hours. For himself life had been fairly easy since he was promoted acting sergeant: a gas ration, use of his car, permission to sleep and eat at home with Dennie except when it was his turn as duty noncom.

And with Harold. But he tried not to think about Harold any more than Harold apparently thought about him.

"Hey!"

He turned to see who was calling. From across the street where another gang was clearing a house which had been burned to a shell like the one his own men were pulling down, a National Guard sergeant. He looked vaguely familiar. Hunting in memory, Philip placed him. One of the fitters he and Alan (poor Alan!) had hired to install the Mitsuyama purifiers.

If only they'd been installed all over the city! If only they hadn't clogged with those filthy bacteria!

But it was no use wishing.

He told his Pfc to keep the gang working and strolled over to say hello. He couldn't quite remember the man's name. Chicano, though. Gomez? Perez? Something like that.

"You're Mason, aren't you?" the man said. "Thought I recognized you. You're the mother that put in those foreign filters and poisoned the water. What the hell are you doing running around loose—and in one of our uniforms, too? Well, if no one else has taken care of you, I will."

He unslung his rifle and shot Philip at pointblank range.

THE RATIONAL PROPOSAL *Page:* Well, I'm sorry about the gunfire on that last segment, which I hope didn't spoil your viewing and listening pleasure, but as you heard the fire in Chicago Old Town is now officially "under control" and the rioters are being contained. Before we go on to our next guest, I've been asked to say that the guerrilla strikes against Jacksonville, Omaha and San Bernardino, which our on-the-spot reporter mentioned while speculating about the cause of the Chicago fire, are unconfirmed, repeat not confirmed. So! Let me just reassure our audience here in the studio that even if something similar to what we were just hearing about took place in New York, we'd be in no danger—this building was designed in conjunction with Civil Defense experts. Are we ready for . . . ? Yes, fine, I see we are. Well, world, everyone knows by this time that an astonishingly large proportion of our population accepted the precepts of the late Austin Train and still clings to them, despite what the president has said about their being based on an appeal to emotion and a rejection of rationality. Just where that's led us, you all know. One man, however, while all this has been going on, has been quietly and persistently pursuing another path. As you've almost certainly heard, the famous Dr. Thomas Grey of the Bamberley Trust has been trying for years to work out, with the aid of computers and all possible modern methods, a solution to the desperate problems facing us. I'm delighted that he's chosen this show to take the wraps off his findings. Tom Grey! (*Audience applause.*)

Grey: Thank you, Miss Page.

Page: Speaking of wraps, I notice you have your arm in a sling, Tom. I hope—Oh, excuse me just a second . . . I'm sorry, world, but we've been asked to yield a minute of air time for a public service announcement. We'll be back with you in a moment. Go ahead.

Naval commander: This is an emergency announcement from the Department of Defense, Navy. Hear this, hear this, all personnel currently on shore leave in the following states: New York, New Jersey, Pennsylvania, Florida, Texas, California. Report at once to the nearest Army or Air Force base or National Guard headquarters and place yourselves at the disposal of the commanding officer. Your assistance is required in quelling civil disorder. That is all.

Page: I see we have someone right here in the studio who's off to answer that call. We'll just stand by for a moment while he's leaving. (*Audience applause.*) That's okay, then. Tom, I was wondering about your arm.

Grey: It's nothing serious, I'm glad to say. I—uh—I got caught on the fringes of one of those civil disorders they were just talking about. (*Audience laughter.*) But I got off with just a wrenched shoulder.

Page: Fighting back? *(Audience laughter.)*

Grey: No, my car ran over a caltrap and hit a lamppost. (*Audience laughter.*)

Page: Well, I hope you're better soon. Now about this idea of yours— Just a second, is something wrong?

Voice from audience: Smoke! I'm sure I can smell smoke!

Page: I'll check with my producer. Ian? . . . You're right, friend, but it's nothing to worry about. It's blowing up from Newark, apparently. You know there's a big fire there. Count yourself lucky to be in here—I'm told it's far worse out-of-doors! (*Audience laughter.*) Tom, this undertaking of yours must have been incredibly complex. You've had to analyze literally every major factor affecting our predicament, right?

Grey: Yes, every one.

Page: And you're now in a position to reveal the chief conclusion— Sorry! Hold on. Yes, Ian, what is it this time? . . . Oh. Yes, of course; that sounds urgent. I'll tell them . . . Another announcement for you, world—sorry to keep interrupting like this, but of course we can't ignore what's going on. And this is an important and very tragic piece of news. It seems the Niagara Falls Bridge is out—either blown or collapsed, no one yet knows which, but because there are so many people trying to get over the Canadian border there, all TV and radio networks are being asked to tell people to avoid the area so that essential help can get through—the highways are kind of crowded up that way, I'm told . . . Tom, as I was saying: you can unveil your conclusions now, right?

Grey: Yes, and they're crucially important. Of course, I've been able to take into account only such items as natural resources, oxygen level, food stocks, water reserves, and so on, and—ah—it's curiously ironical in a way because one might say—

Page: Tom, I'm sorry, but the producer is buzzing me again. Yes? . . . I see. Will do. Tom, they're going to pre-empt us in about two minutes. The president is winding up to a new pitch. Can you keep your main point short, please?

Grey: Well, as I was about to say, it's sort of ironical, because we're already engaged, in a sense, in the course of action my findings dictate.

Page: Don't keep the world on tenterhooks, Tom! Out with it! What's the best thing we can do to ensure a long, happy, healthy future for mankind?

Grey: We can just about restore the balance of the ecology, the biosphere, and so on—in other words we can live within our means instead of on an unrepayable overdraft, as we've been doing for the past half century—if we exterminate the two hundred million most extravagant and wasteful of our species.

Page: Follow that if you can, Mr. President. It's your reward for pre-convicting Austin Train. World, what about lighting him a funeral pyre? Doesn't he deserve—?

(Transcript ends.)

THE SMOKE OF THAT GREAT BURNING

Opening the door to the visiting doctor, all set to apologize for the flour on her hands—she had been baking—Mrs. Byrne sniffed. Smoke!

And if she could smell it with her heavy head cold, it must be a tremendous fire!

"We ought to call the brigade!" she exclaimed. "Is it a hayrick?"

"The brigade would have a long way to go," the doctor told her curtly. "It's from America. The wind's blowing that way."

NEXT YEAR

The hungry sheep look up, and are not fed,
But swoln with wind, and the rank mist they draw,
Rot inwardly, and foul contagion spread.

—Milton: "Lycidas"

BY ARTHUR C. CLARKE IN BALLANTINE BOOKS EDITIONS

EXPEDITION TO EARTH
A highly successful first collection of Clarke's stories, which will grip you and haunt you for a long time to come.

REACH FOR TOMORROW
A second collection; "A dozen stories, all written with the sense of style one has come to expect from Clarke, all literate and all, in the best sense, entertaining." *The New York Times*

EARTHLIGHT
A most timely novel about what life would be like on the moon. "I had the eerie feeling that I had just returned from an actual stay on the moon . . . a tale of supersonically high-keyed suspense."
J. Francis McComas

CHILDHOOD'S END
A towering novel—the classic of science fiction. "A real staggerer by a man who is both a poetic dreamer and a competent scientist."
Gilbert Highet

To order by mail, send $1.25 per book plus 25¢ per order for handling to Ballantine Cash Sales, P.O. Box 505, Westminster, Maryland 21157. Please allow three weeks for delivery.

THE WORLD OF STAR TREK

David Gerrold

Here are the worlds of *STAR TREK*:

GENE RODDENBERRY's brilliant conception—the first viable science fiction world designed for a TV series

---

THE SHOW ITSELF and the people who created it—the writers, the stars, the technicians

---

THE FANS—the world the show created—and how they kept *Star Trek* alive in the face of network opposition

---

With sixty-four pages of pictures from the episodes themselves and with original photos by Stan Burns

The book on how to write for TV!

THE MAKING OF STAR TREK

Stephen E. Whitfield • Gene Roddenberry

The complete story on how the ***U.S.S. Enterprise*** was designed, her weaponry, equipment and power sources, the original concept behind the show, backgrounds of the characters, biographies of the stars, and photos, diagrams and illustrations—the whole authentic history.

". . . for would-be TV writers, directors and producers, this will be an education in itself, a polished but nonvarnished look at how TV really works."
—*Publishers Weekly*